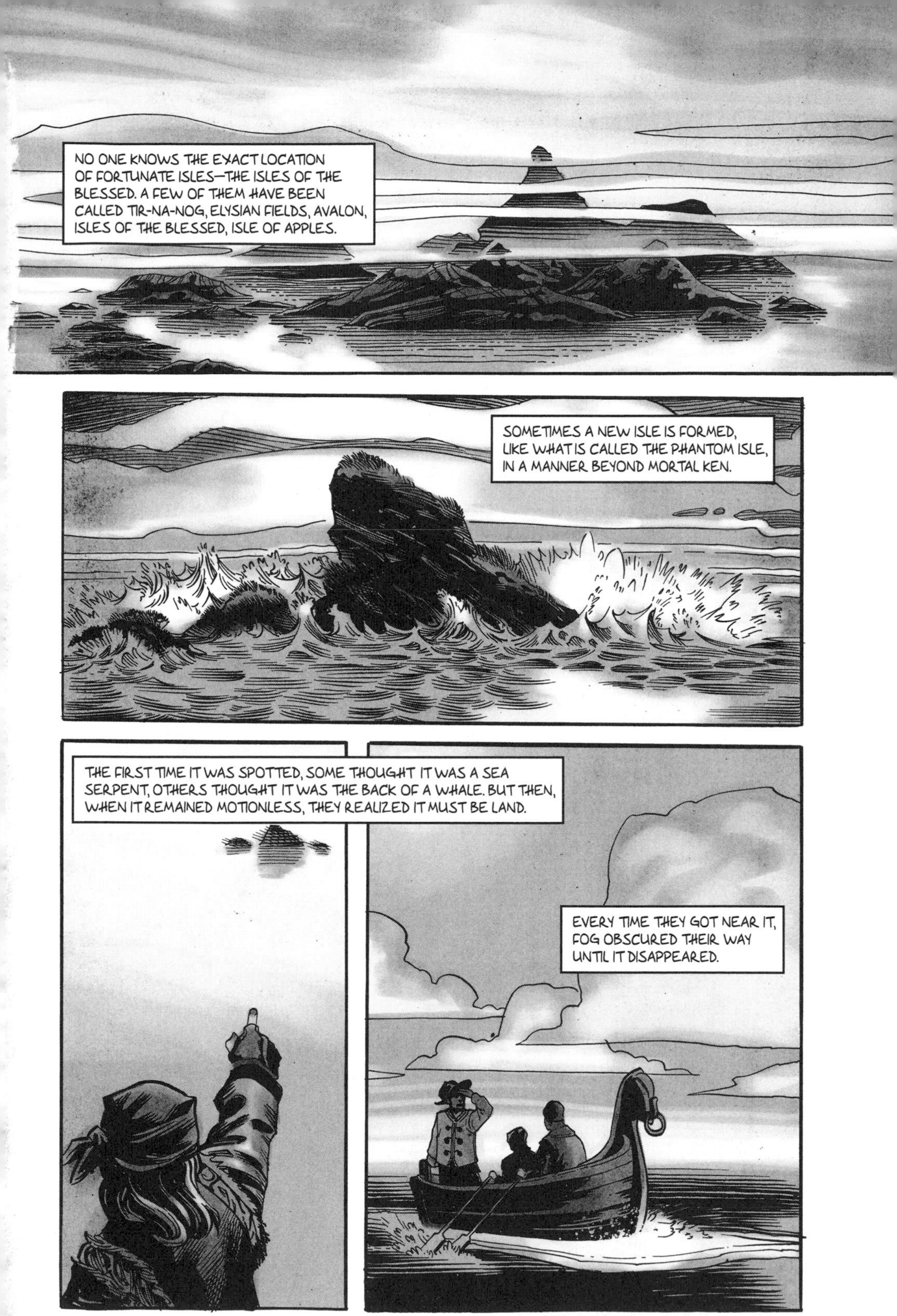
NO ONE KNOWS THE EXACT LOCATION OF FORTUNATE ISLES—THE ISLES OF THE BLESSED. A FEW OF THEM HAVE BEEN CALLED TIR-NA-NOG, ELYSIAN FIELDS, AVALON, ISLES OF THE BLESSED, ISLE OF APPLES.
SOMETIMES A NEW ISLE IS FORMED, LIKE WHAT IS CALLED THE PHANTOM ISLE, IN A MANNER BEYOND MORTAL KEN.
THE FIRST TIME IT WAS SPOTTED, SOME THOUGHT IT WAS A SEA SERPENT, OTHERS THOUGHT IT WAS THE BACK OF A WHALE. BUT THEN, WHEN IT REMAINED MOTIONLESS, THEY REALIZED IT MUST BE LAND.
EVERY TIME THEY GOT NEAR IT, FOG OBSCURED THEIR WAY UNTIL IT DISAPPEARED.

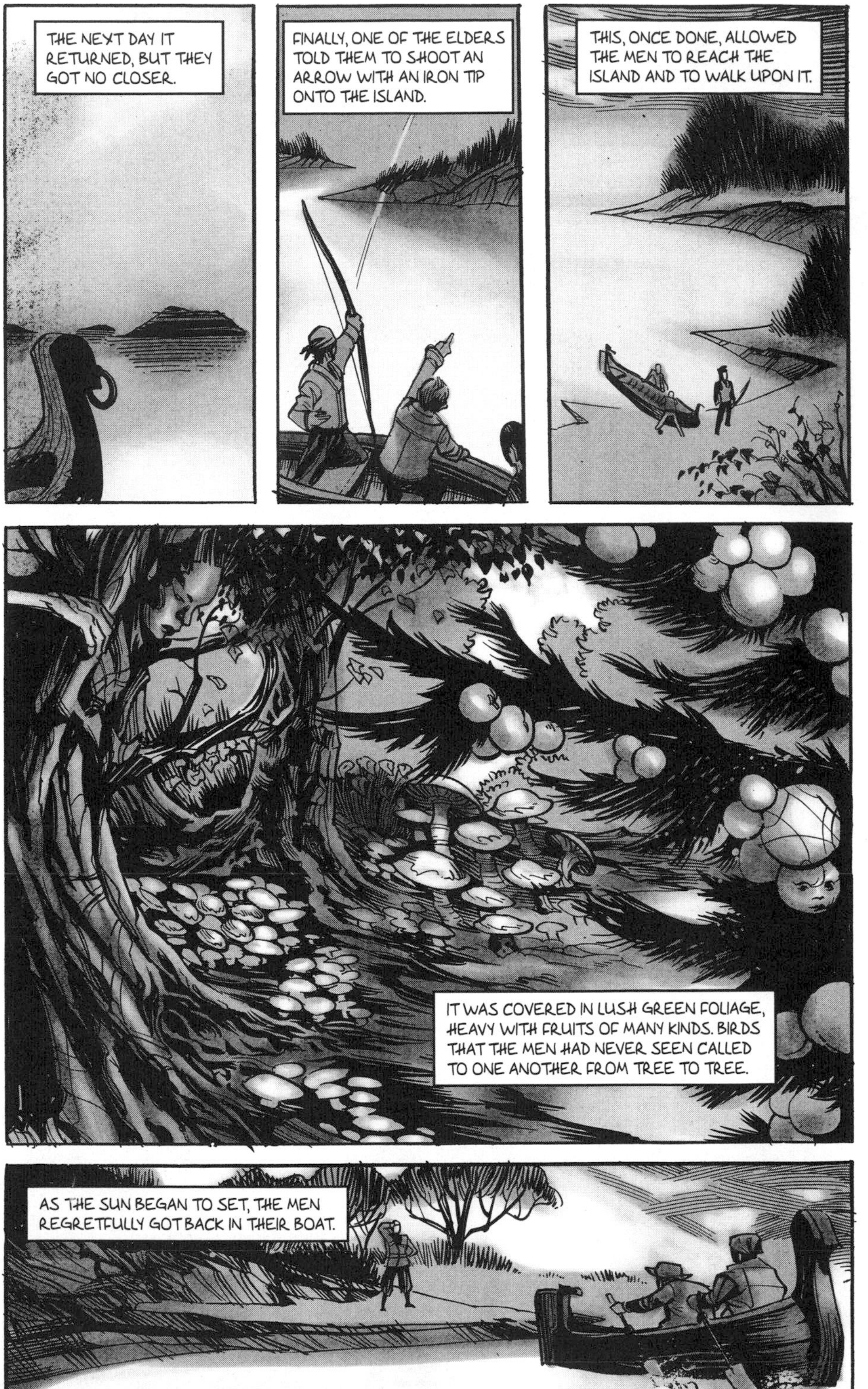
THE NEXT DAY IT RETURNED, BUT THEY GOT NO CLOSER.
FINALLY, ONE OF THE ELDERS TOLD THEM TO SHOOT AN ARROW WITH AN IRON TIP ONTO THE ISLAND.
THIS, ONCE DONE, ALLOWED THE MEN TO REACH THE ISLAND AND TO WALK UPON IT.
IT WAS COVERED IN LUSH GREEN FOLIAGE, HEAVY WITH FRUITS OF MANY KINDS. BIRDS THAT THE MEN HAD NEVER SEEN CALLED TO ONE ANOTHER FROM TREE TO TREE.
AS THE SUN BEGAN TO SET, THE MEN REGRETFULLY GOT BACK IN THEIR BOAT.

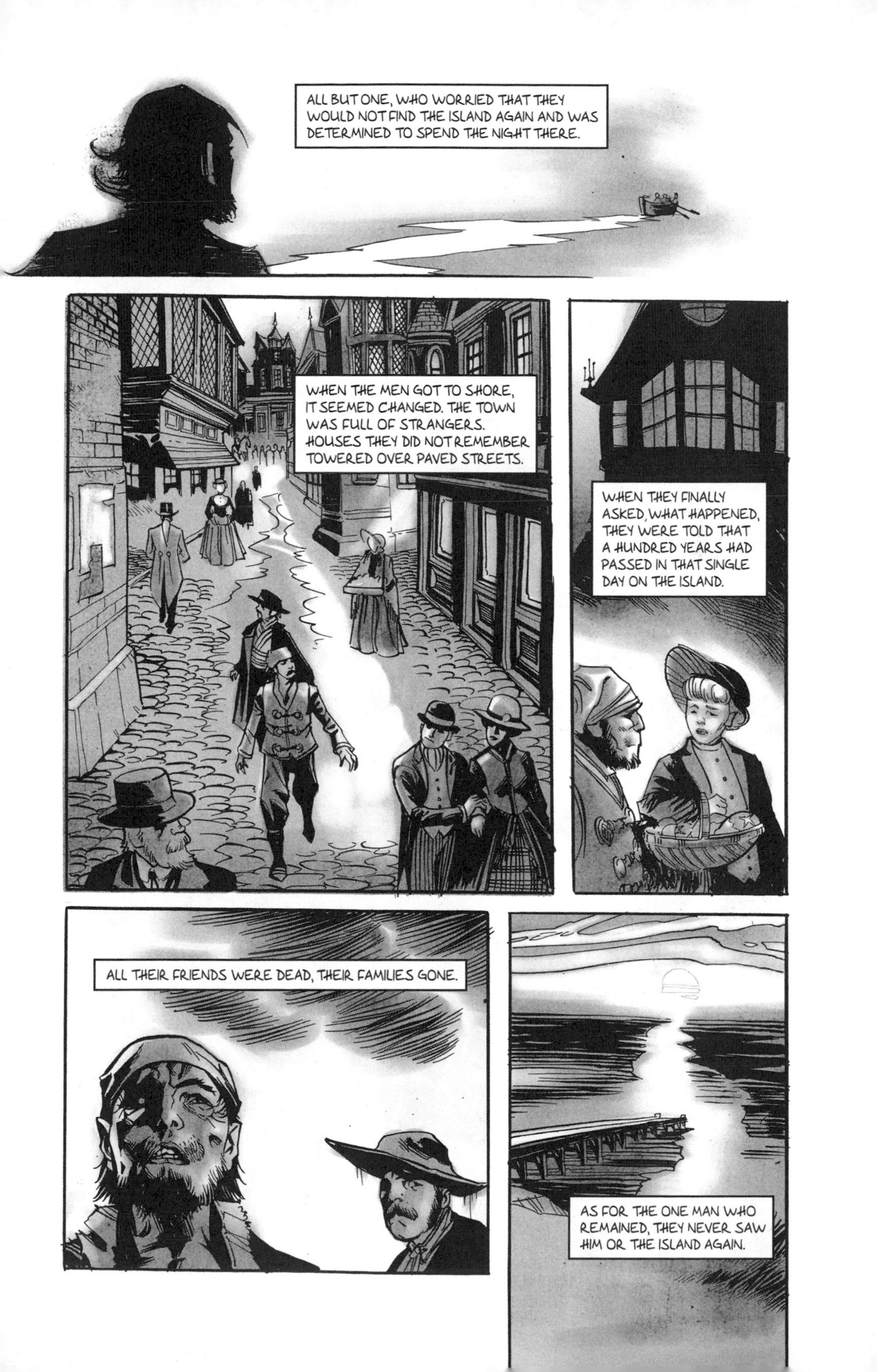
ALL BUT ONE, WHO WORRIED THAT THEY WOULD NOT FIND THE ISLAND AGAIN AND WAS DETERMINED TO SPEND THE NIGHT THERE.
WHEN THE MEN GOT TO SHORE, IT SEEMED CHANGED. THE TOWN WAS FULL OF STRANGERS. HOUSES THEY DID NOT REMEMBER TOWERED OVER PAVED STREETS.
WHEN THEY FINALLY ASKED, WHAT HAPPENED, THEY WERE TOLD THAT A HUNDRED YEARS HAD PASSED IN THAT SINGLE DAY ON THE ISLAND.
ALL THEIR FRIENDS WERE DEAD, THEIR FAMILIES GONE.
AS FOR THE ONE MAN WHO REMAINED, THEY NEVER SAW HIM OR THE ISLAND AGAIN.

the Good Neighbors

Text copyright © 2010 by Holly Black
Art copyright © 2010 by Ted Naifeh

Library of Congress Cataloging-in-Publication Data Available

ISBN 978-0-439-85564-8

10 9 8 7 6 5 4 3 2 1   10 11 12 13 14

First edition, November 2010
"Good Neighbors" title lettering by Jessica Hische
Lettering by John Green
Edited by David Levithan
Book design by Phil Falco
Creative Director: David Saylor
Printed in the U.S.A.   23

the Good Neighbors

By

HOLLY BLACK
& TED NAIFEH

book three
KIND

graphix

New York   Toronto   London   Auckland   Sydney   Mexico City   New Delhi   Hong Kong

WHAT DO YOU DO AFTER
THE END OF THE WORLD?

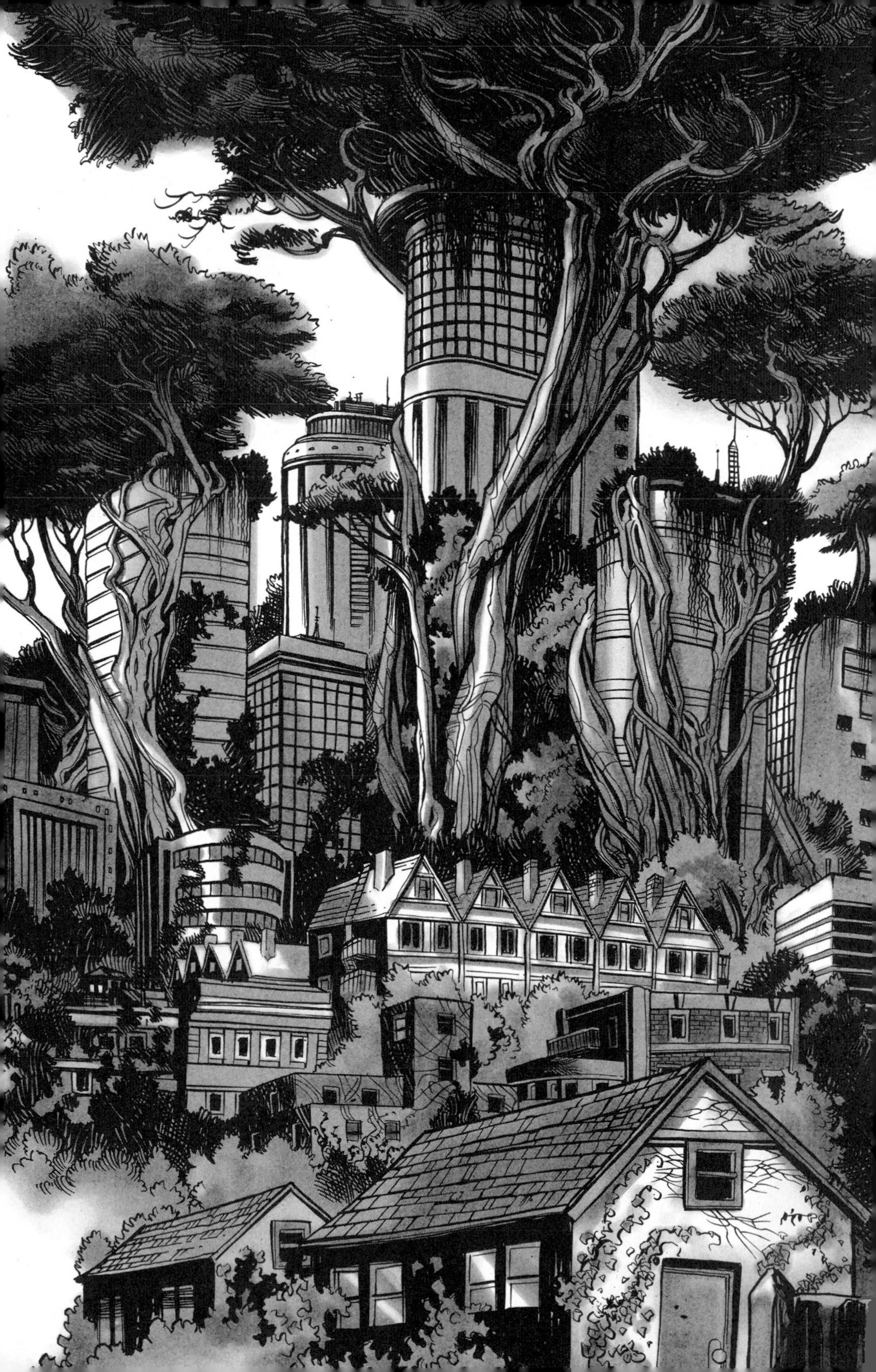

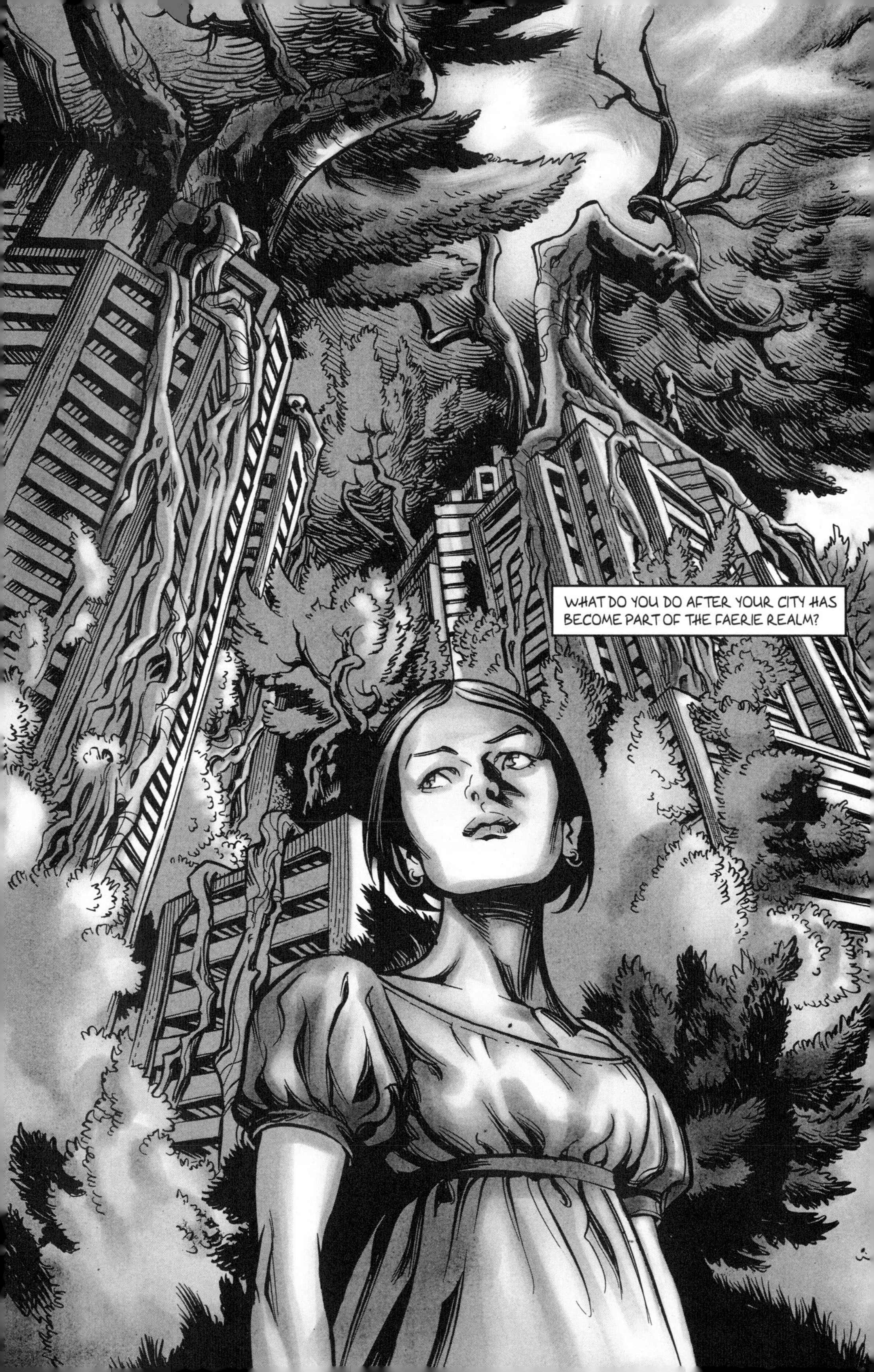
WHAT DO YOU DO AFTER YOUR CITY HAS BECOME PART OF THE FAERIE REALM?

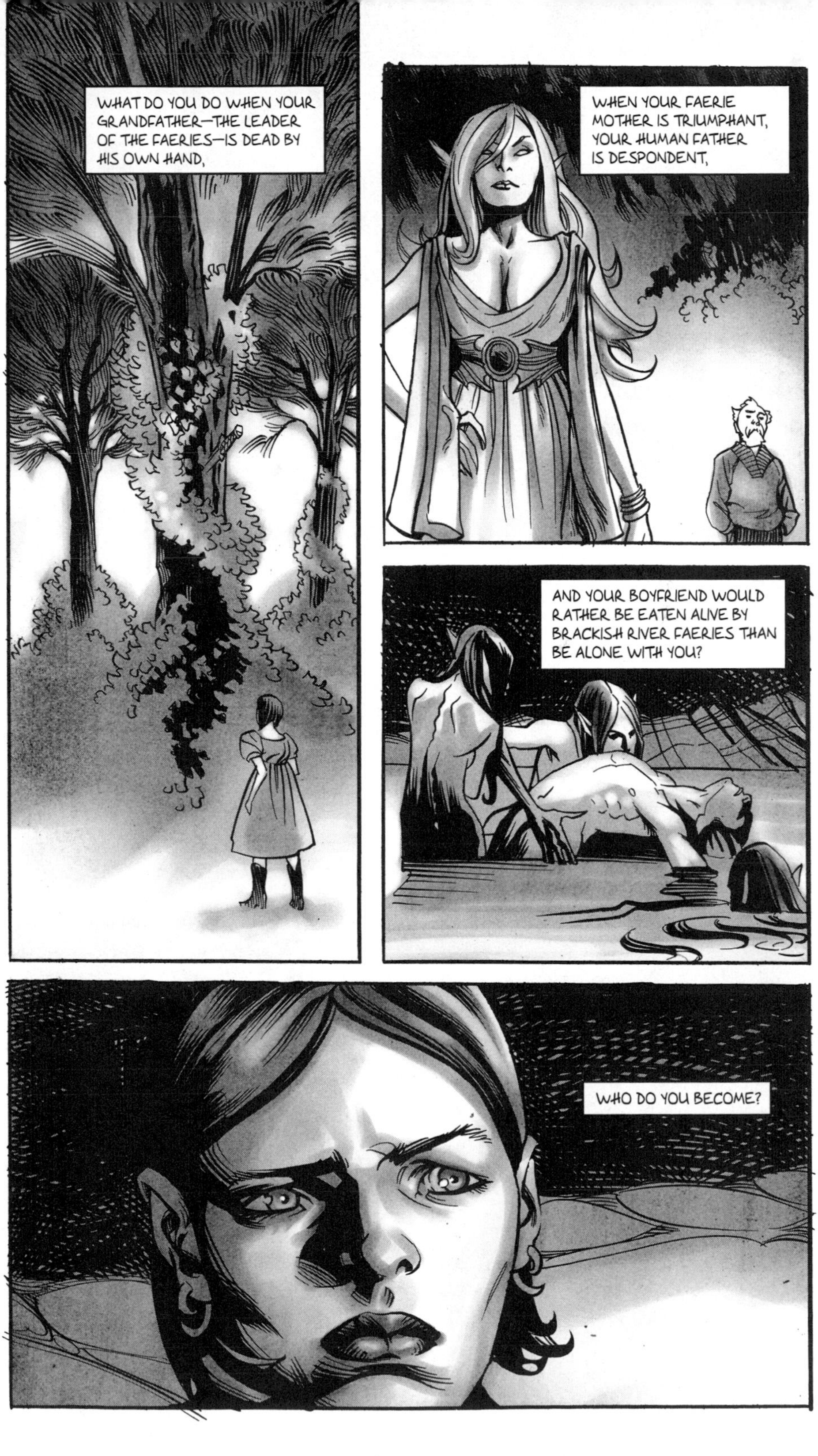
WHAT DO YOU DO WHEN YOUR GRANDFATHER—THE LEADER OF THE FAERIES—IS DEAD BY HIS OWN HAND,
WHEN YOUR FAERIE MOTHER IS TRIUMPHANT, YOUR HUMAN FATHER IS DESPONDENT,
AND YOUR BOYFRIEND WOULD RATHER BE EATEN ALIVE BY BRACKISH RIVER FAERIES THAN BE ALONE WITH YOU?
WHO DO YOU BECOME?

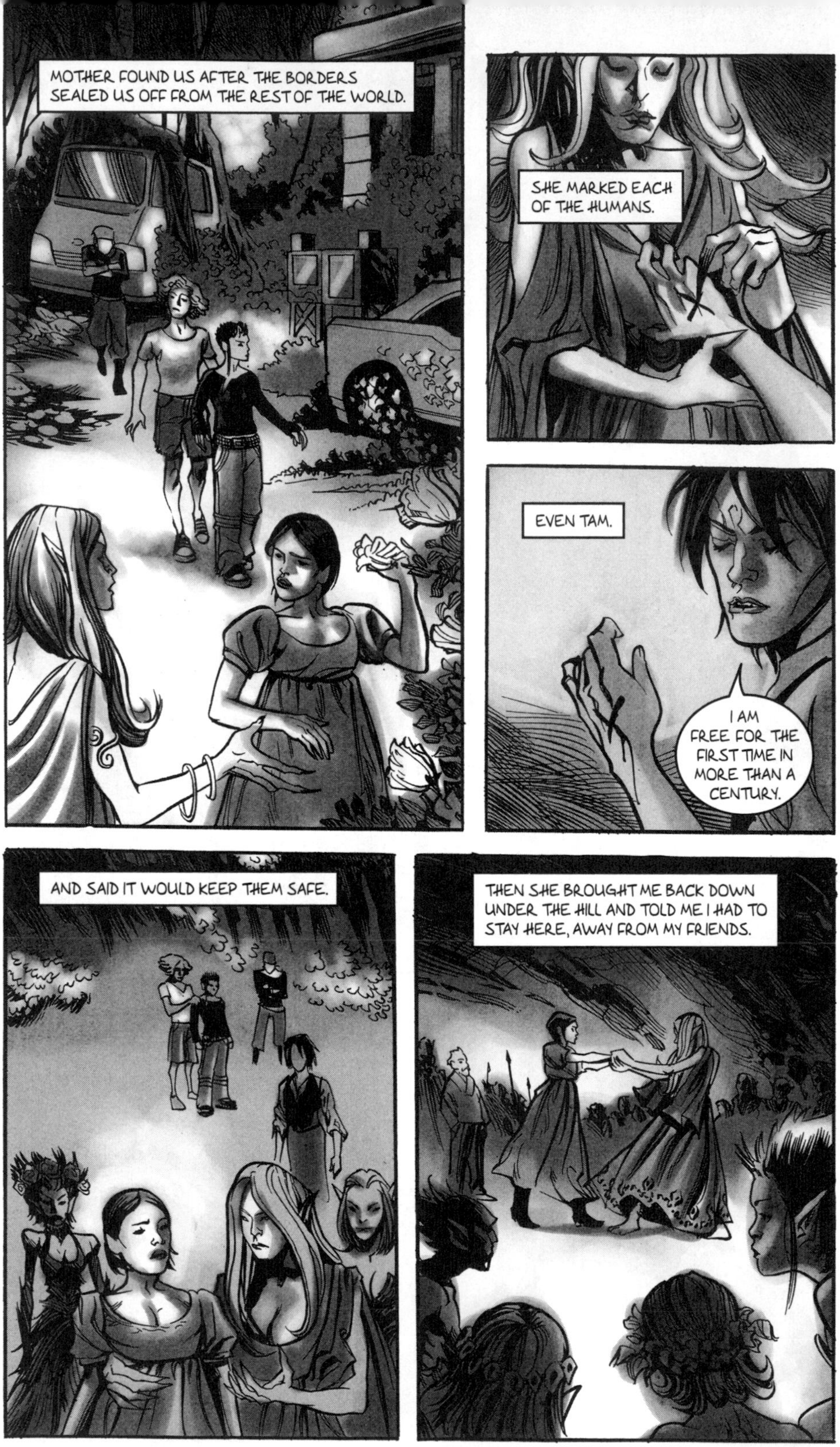
MOTHER FOUND US AFTER THE BORDERS SEALED US OFF FROM THE REST OF THE WORLD.
SHE MARKED EACH OF THE HUMANS.
EVEN TAM.
I AM FREE FOR THE FIRST TIME IN MORE THAN A CENTURY.
AND SAID IT WOULD KEEP THEM SAFE.
THEN SHE BROUGHT ME BACK DOWN UNDER THE HILL AND TOLD ME I HAD TO STAY HERE, AWAY FROM MY FRIENDS.

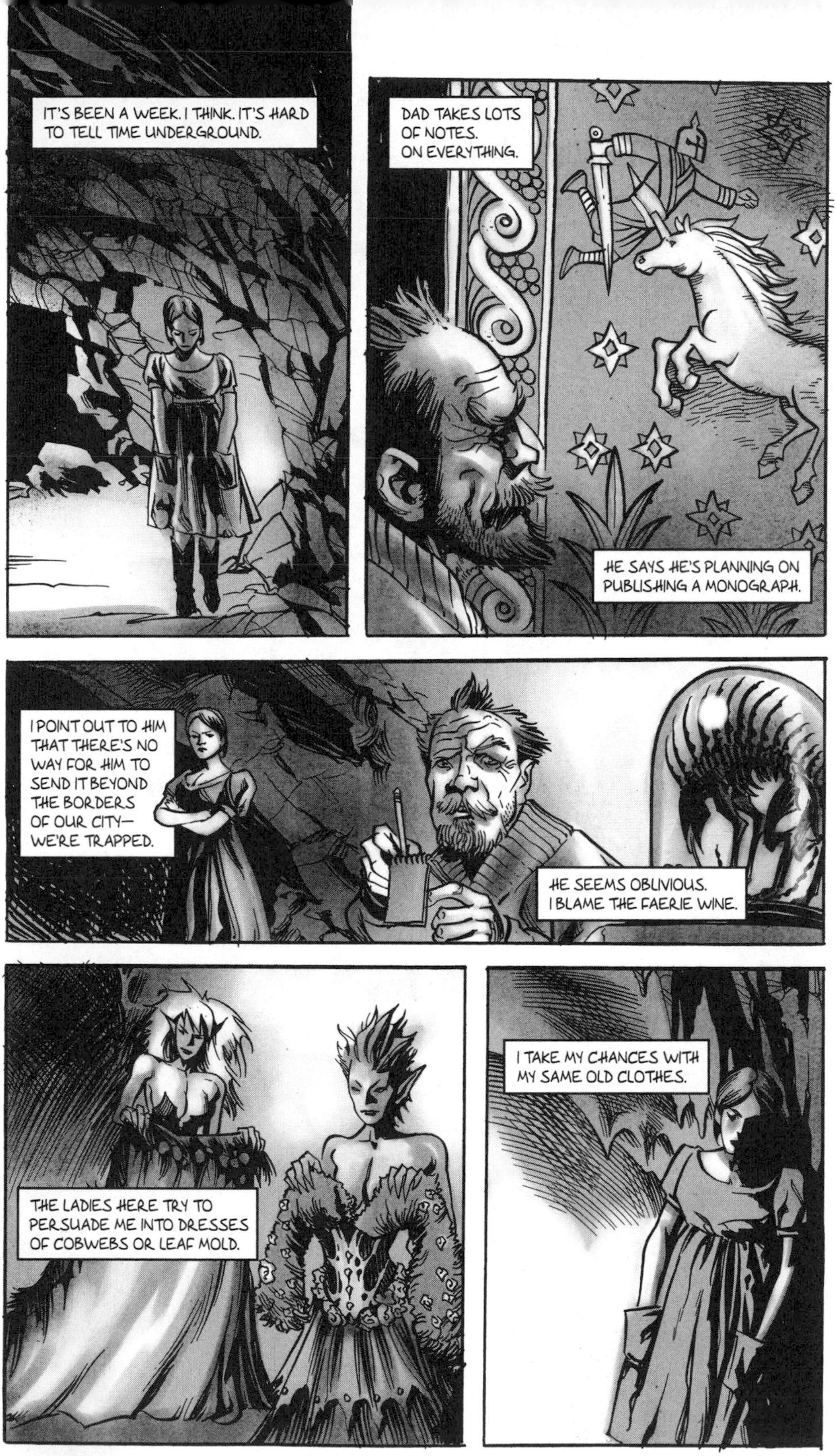
IT'S BEEN A WEEK. I THINK. IT'S HARD TO TELL TIME UNDERGROUND.
DAD TAKES LOTS OF NOTES. ON EVERYTHING.
HE SAYS HE'S PLANNING ON PUBLISHING A MONOGRAPH.
I POINT OUT TO HIM THAT THERE'S NO WAY FOR HIM TO SEND IT BEYOND THE BORDERS OF OUR CITY— WE'RE TRAPPED.
HE SEEMS OBLIVIOUS. I BLAME THE FAERIE WINE.
THE LADIES HERE TRY TO PERSUADE ME INTO DRESSES OF COBWEBS OR LEAF MOLD.
I TAKE MY CHANCES WITH MY SAME OLD CLOTHES.

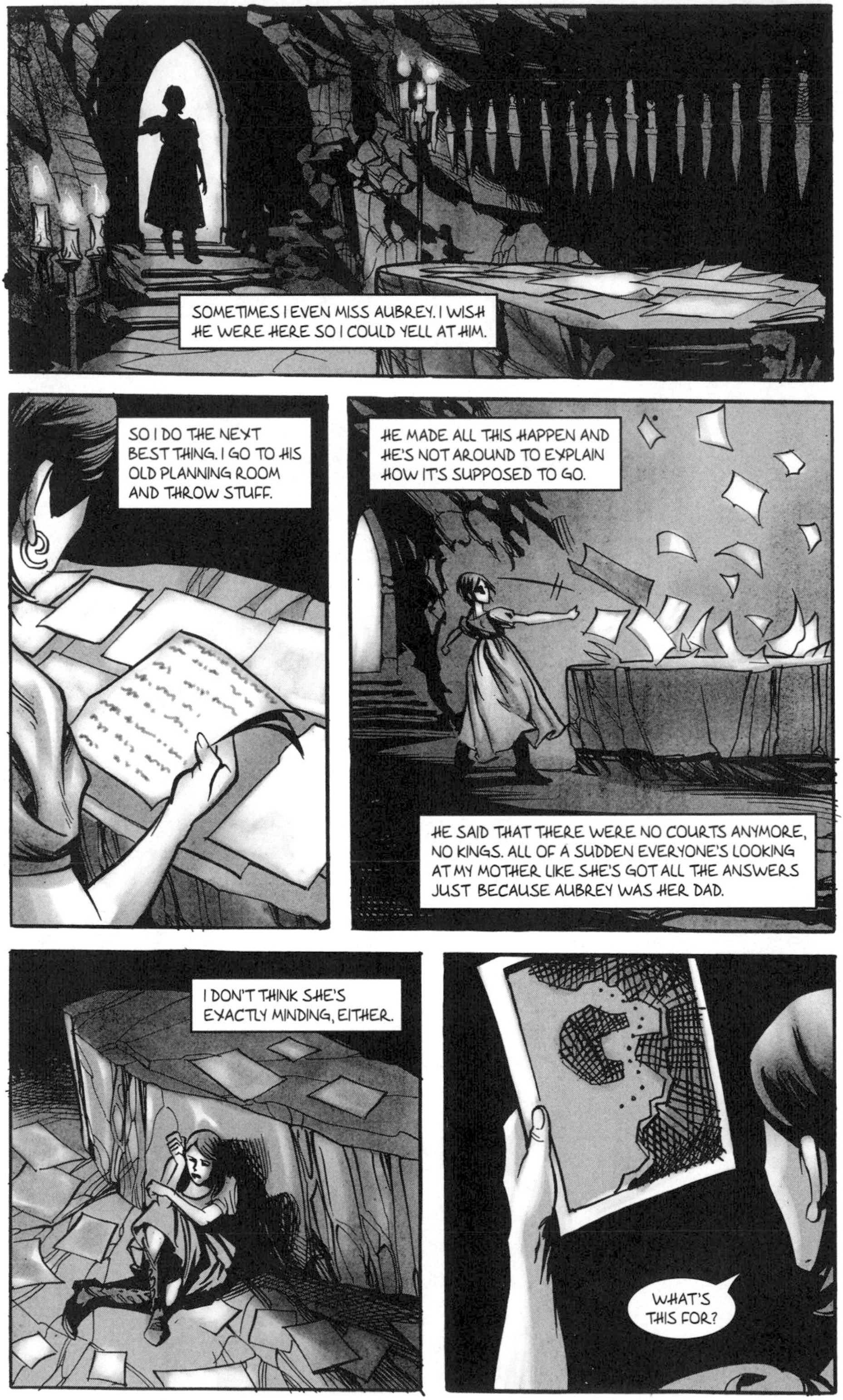
SOMETIMES I EVEN MISS AUBREY. I WISH HE WERE HERE SO I COULD YELL AT HIM.
SO I DO THE NEXT BEST THING. I GO TO HIS OLD PLANNING ROOM AND THROW STUFF.
HE MADE ALL THIS HAPPEN AND HE'S NOT AROUND TO EXPLAIN HOW IT'S SUPPOSED TO GO.
HE SAID THAT THERE WERE NO COURTS ANYMORE, NO KINGS. ALL OF A SUDDEN EVERYONE'S LOOKING AT MY MOTHER LIKE SHE'S GOT ALL THE ANSWERS JUST BECAUSE AUBREY WAS HER DAD.
I DON'T THINK SHE'S EXACTLY MINDING, EITHER.
WHAT'S THIS FOR?

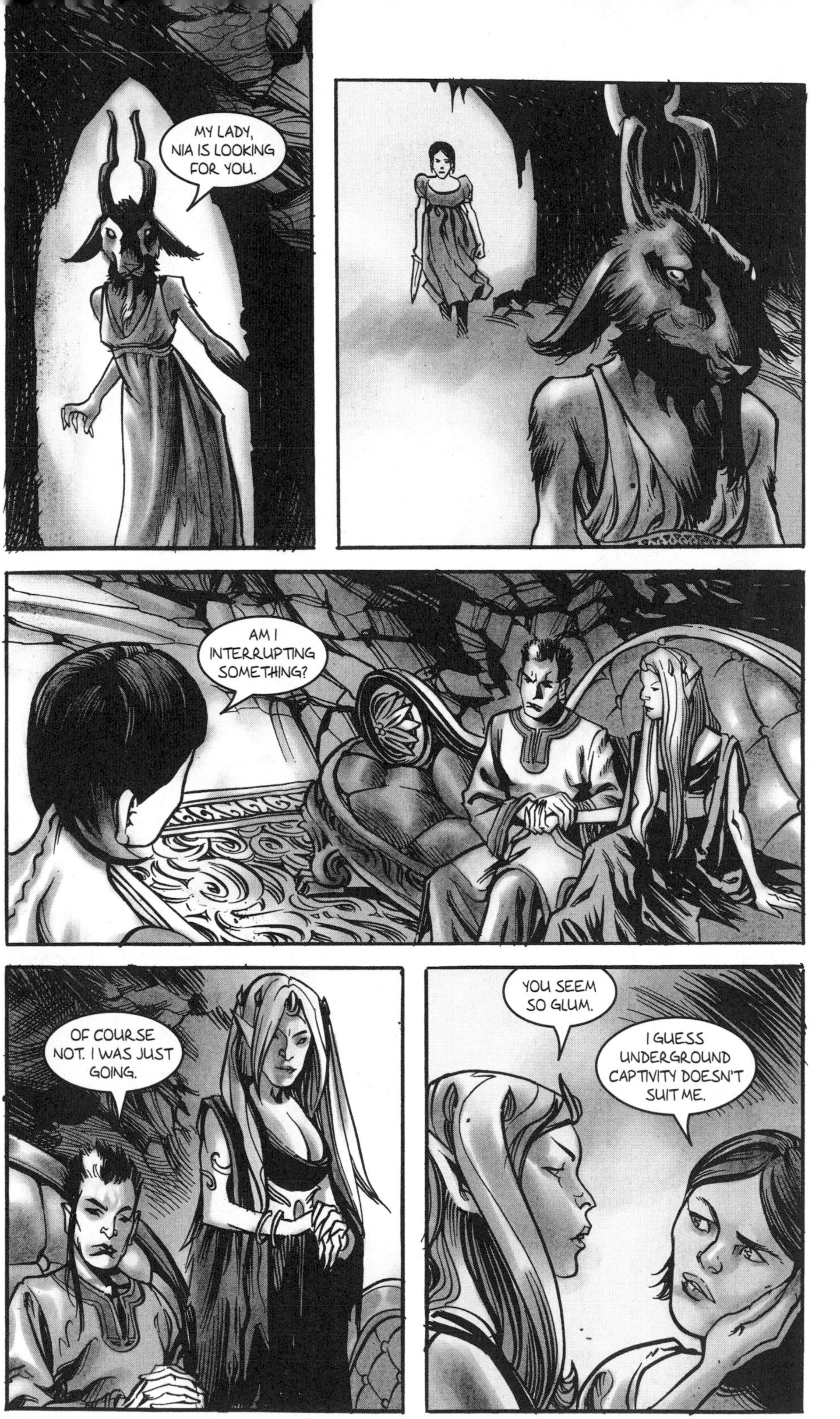
MY LADY, NIA IS LOOKING FOR YOU.
AM I INTERRUPTING SOMETHING?
OF COURSE NOT. I WAS JUST GOING.
YOU SEEM SO GLUM.
I GUESS UNDERGROUND CAPTIVITY DOESN'T SUIT ME.

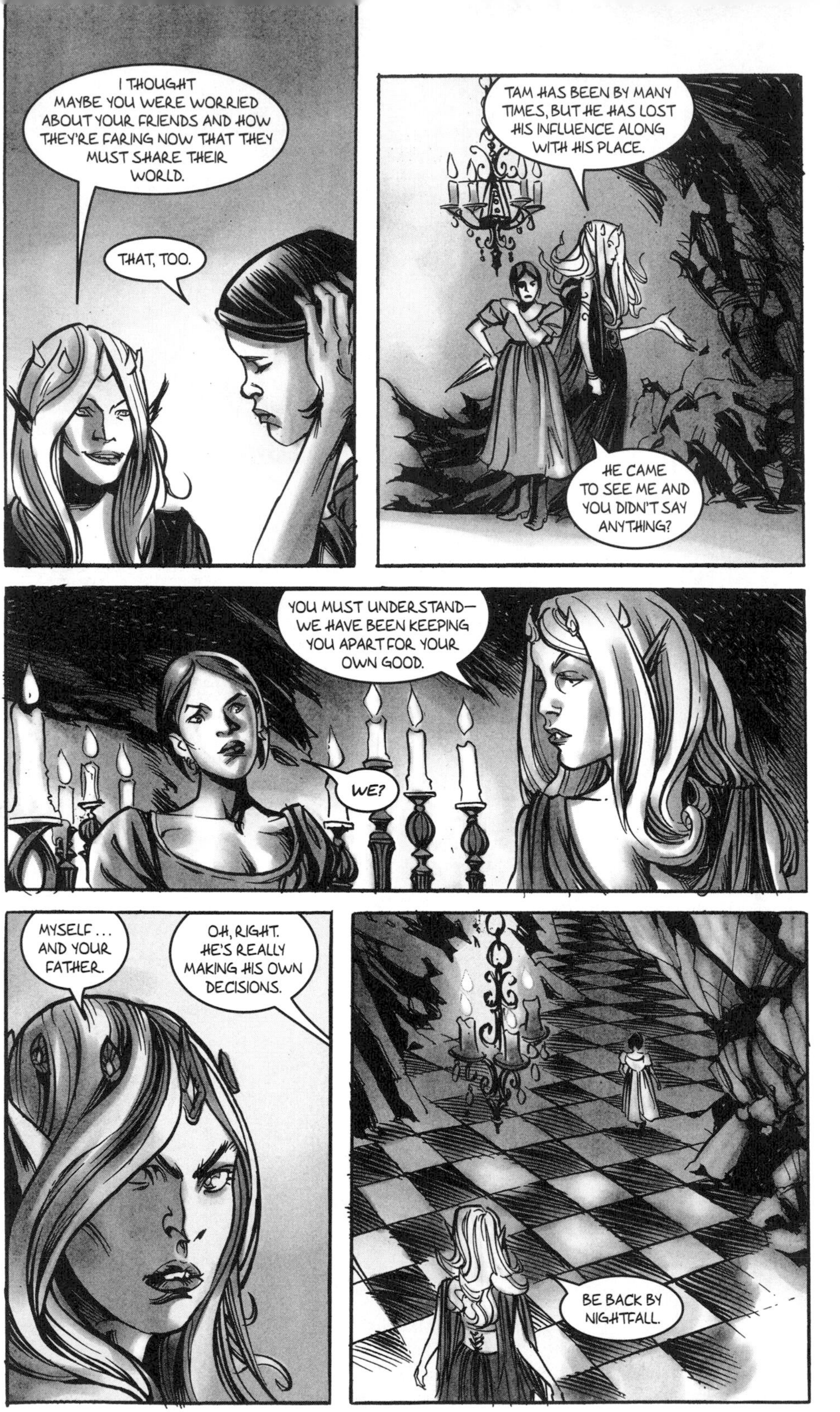
I THOUGHT MAYBE YOU WERE WORRIED ABOUT YOUR FRIENDS AND HOW THEY'RE FARING NOW THAT THEY MUST SHARE THEIR WORLD.
THAT, TOO.
TAM HAS BEEN BY MANY TIMES, BUT HE HAS LOST HIS INFLUENCE ALONG WITH HIS PLACE.
HE CAME TO SEE ME AND YOU DIDN'T SAY ANYTHING?
YOU MUST UNDERSTAND— WE HAVE BEEN KEEPING YOU APART FOR YOUR OWN GOOD.
WE?
MYSELF . . . AND YOUR FATHER.
OH, RIGHT. HE'S REALLY MAKING HIS OWN DECISIONS.
BE BACK BY NIGHTFALL.

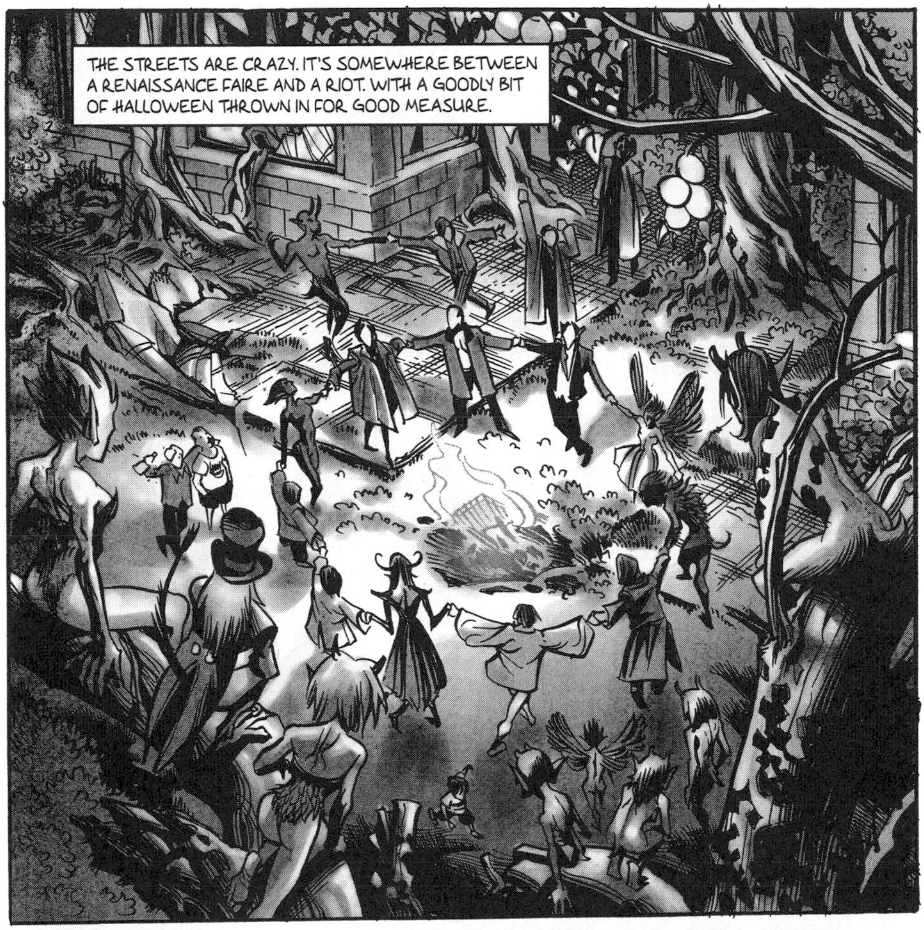
THE STREETS ARE CRAZY. IT'S SOMEWHERE BETWEEN A RENAISSANCE FAIRE AND A RIOT. WITH A GOODLY BIT OF HALLOWEEN THROWN IN FOR GOOD MEASURE.

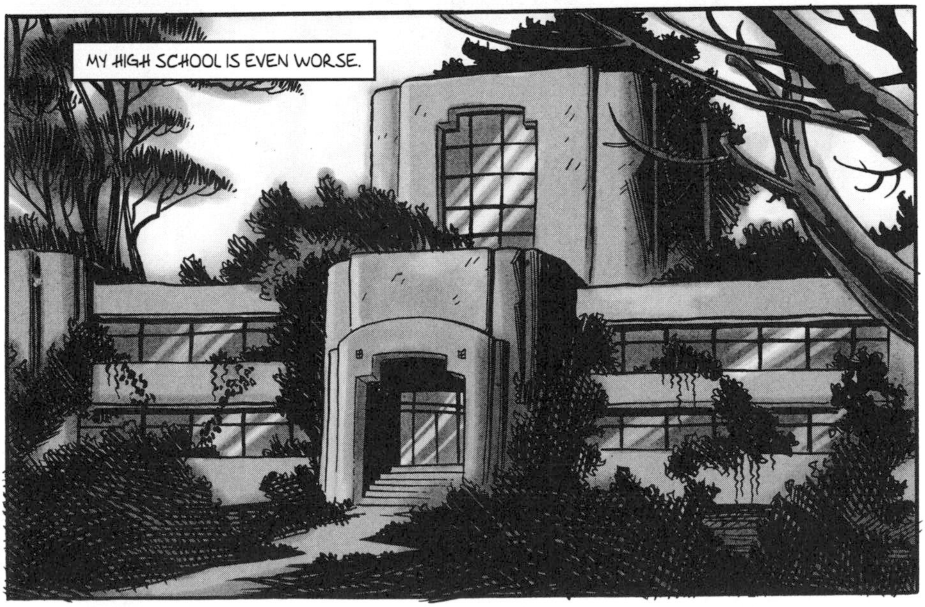
MY HIGH SCHOOL IS EVEN WORSE.

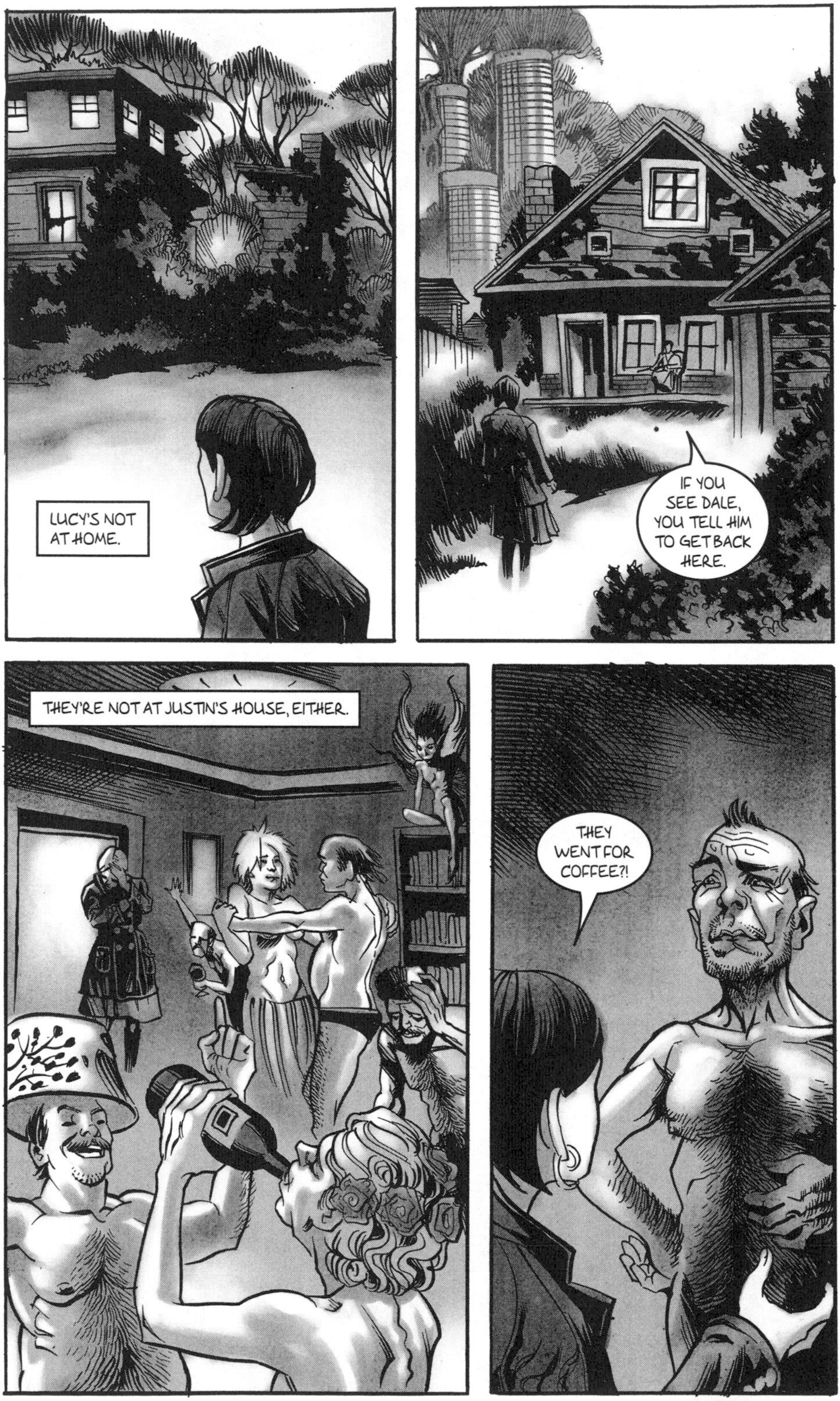
LUCY'S NOT AT HOME.
IF YOU SEE DALE, YOU TELL HIM TO GET BACK HERE.
THEY'RE NOT AT JUSTIN'S HOUSE, EITHER.
THEY WENT FOR COFFEE?!

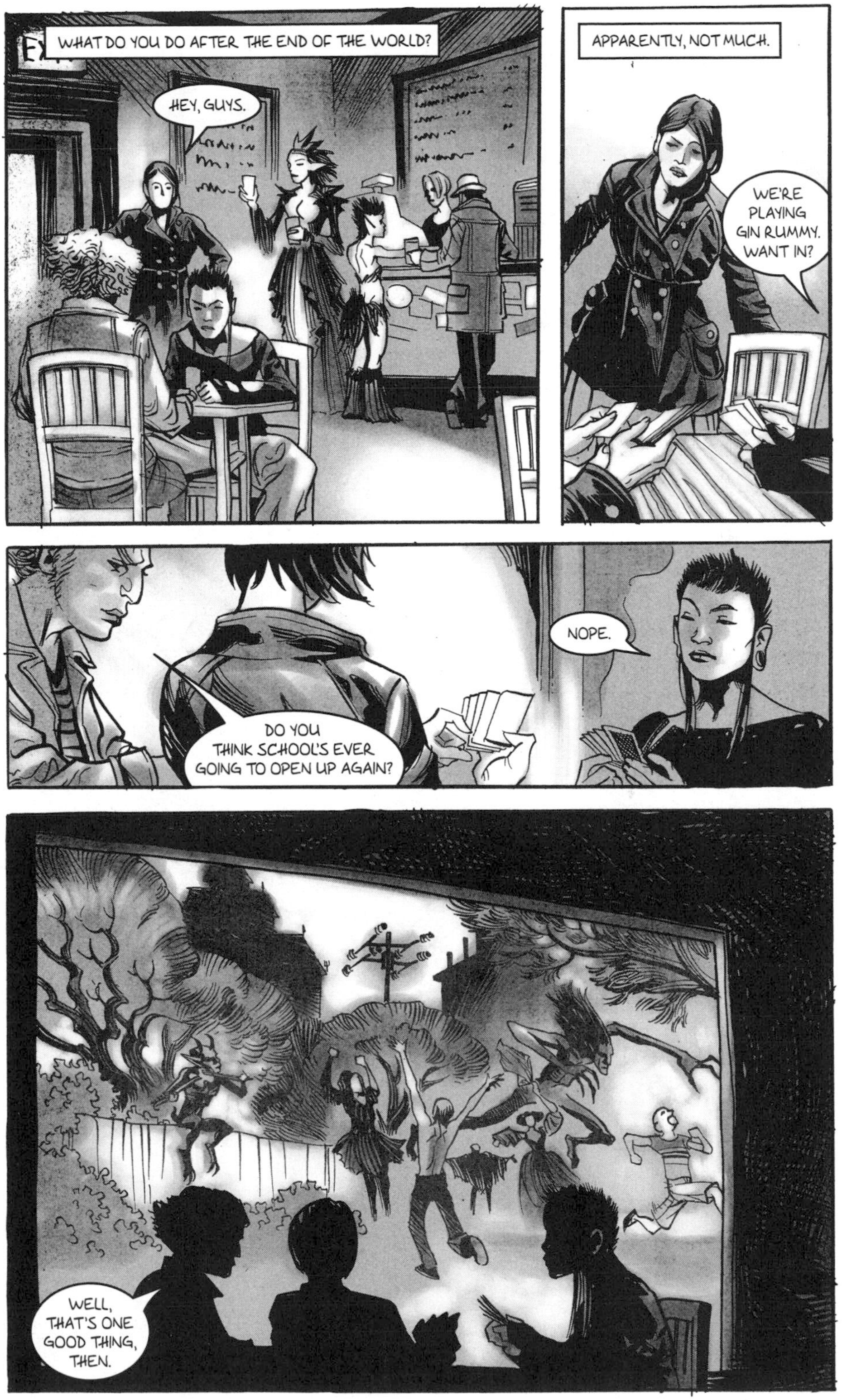
WHAT DO YOU DO AFTER THE END OF THE WORLD?
HEY, GUYS.
APPARENTLY, NOT MUCH.
WE'RE PLAYING GIN RUMMY. WANT IN?
NOPE.
DO YOU THINK SCHOOL'S EVER GOING TO OPEN UP AGAIN?
WELL, THAT'S ONE GOOD THING, THEN.

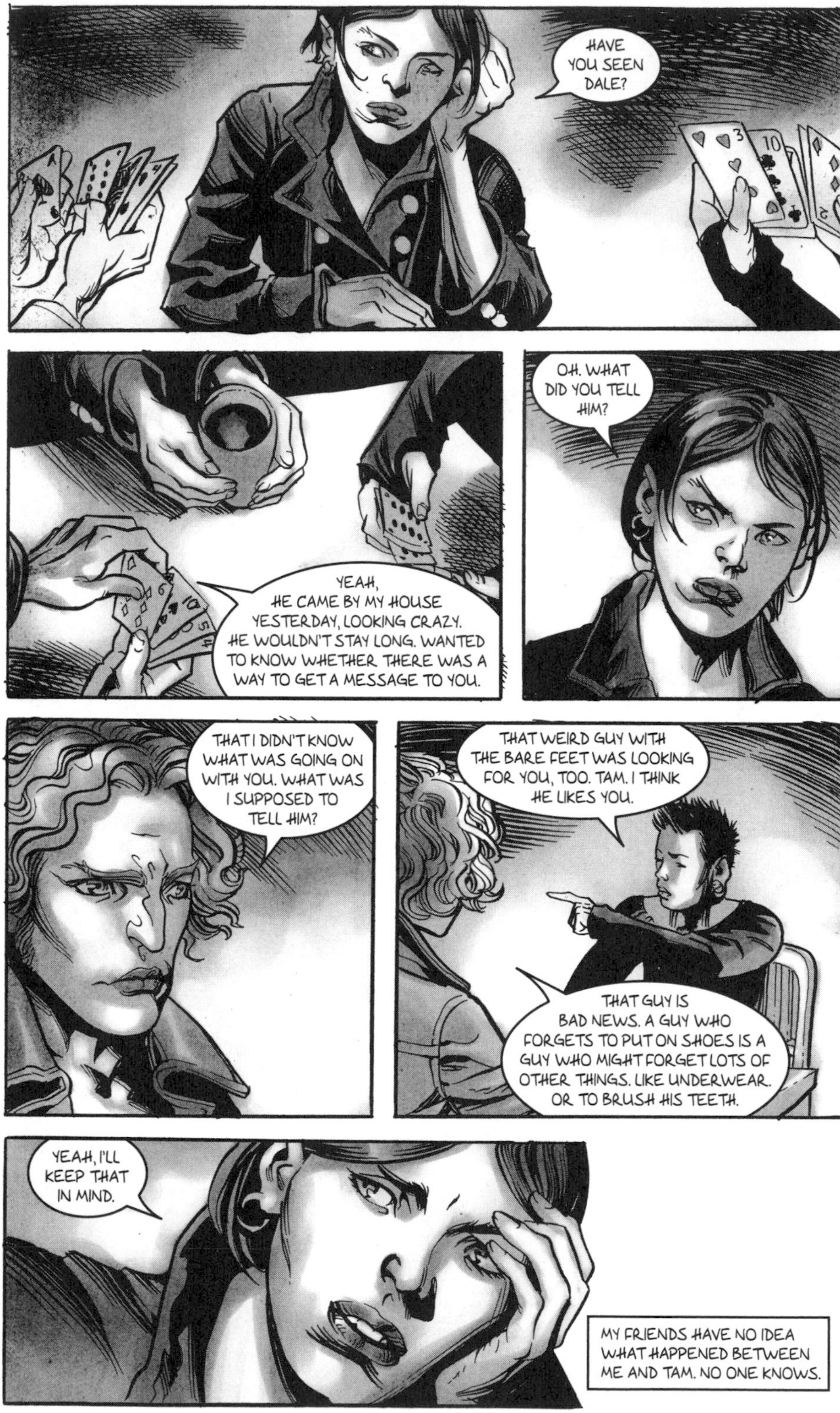
HAVE YOU SEEN DALE?
OH. WHAT DID YOU TELL HIM?
YEAH, HE CAME BY MY HOUSE YESTERDAY, LOOKING CRAZY. HE WOULDN'T STAY LONG. WANTED TO KNOW WHETHER THERE WAS A WAY TO GET A MESSAGE TO YOU.
THAT I DIDN'T KNOW WHAT WAS GOING ON WITH YOU. WHAT WAS I SUPPOSED TO TELL HIM?
THAT WEIRD GUY WITH THE BARE FEET WAS LOOKING FOR YOU, TOO. TAM. I THINK HE LIKES YOU.
THAT GUY IS BAD NEWS. A GUY WHO FORGETS TO PUT ON SHOES IS A GUY WHO MIGHT FORGET LOTS OF OTHER THINGS. LIKE UNDERWEAR. OR TO BRUSH HIS TEETH.
YEAH, I'LL KEEP THAT IN MIND.
MY FRIENDS HAVE NO IDEA WHAT HAPPENED BETWEEN ME AND TAM. NO ONE KNOWS.

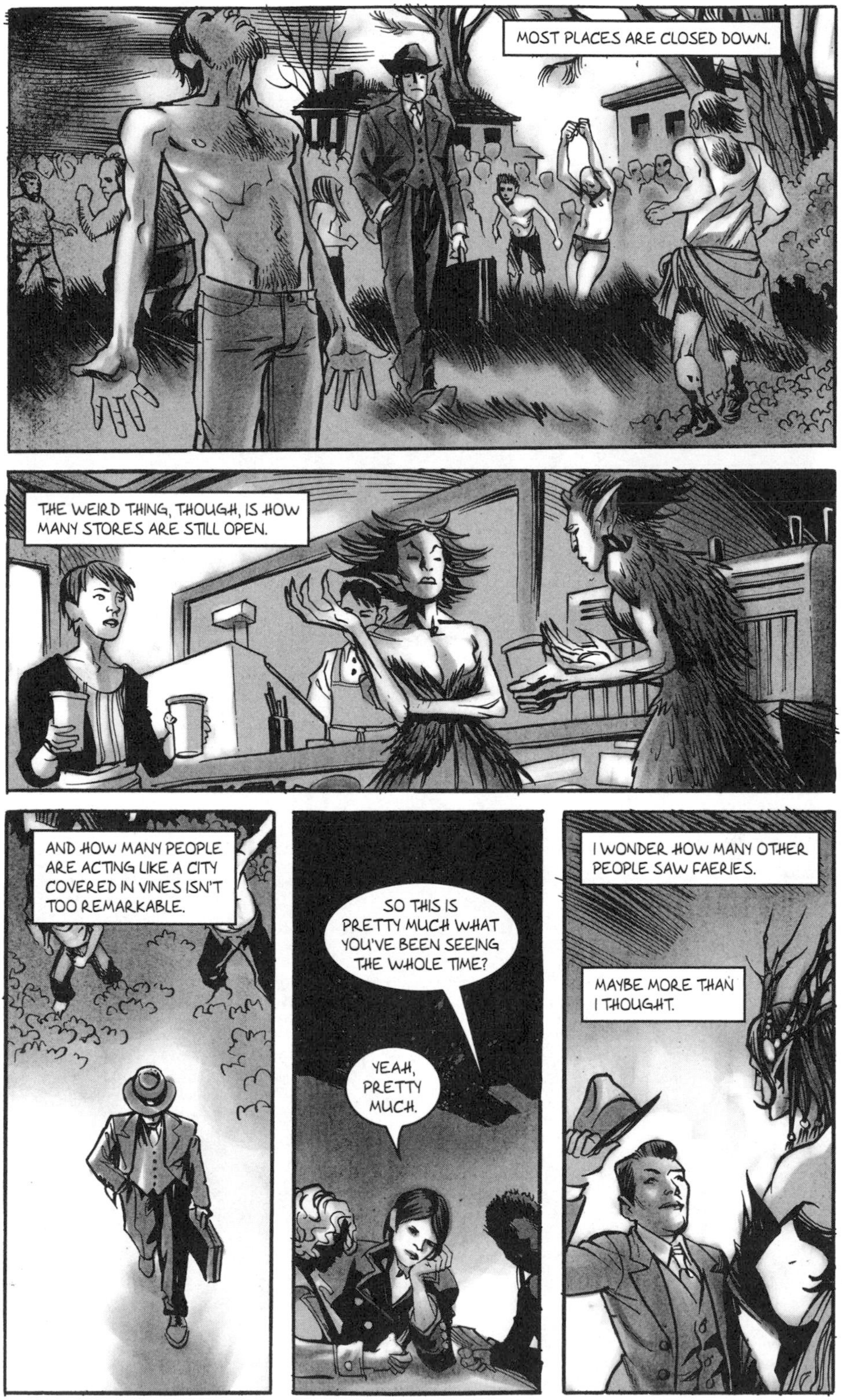
MOST PLACES ARE CLOSED DOWN.
THE WEIRD THING, THOUGH, IS HOW MANY STORES ARE STILL OPEN.
AND HOW MANY PEOPLE ARE ACTING LIKE A CITY COVERED IN VINES ISN'T TOO REMARKABLE.
SO THIS IS PRETTY MUCH WHAT YOU'VE BEEN SEEING THE WHOLE TIME?
YEAH, PRETTY MUCH.
I WONDER HOW MANY OTHER PEOPLE SAW FAERIES.
MAYBE MORE THAN I THOUGHT.

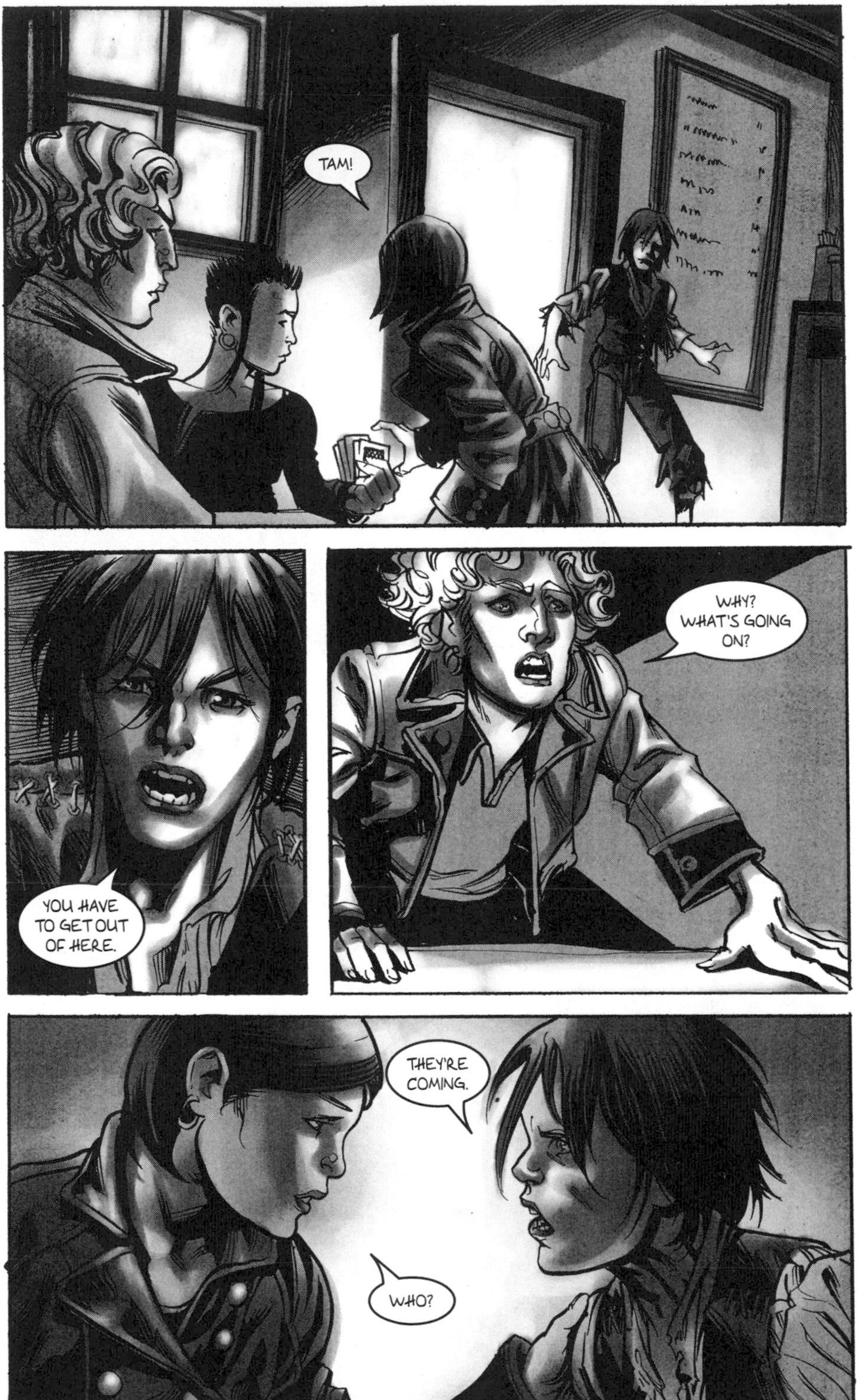
TAM!
YOU HAVE TO GET OUT OF HERE.
WHY? WHAT'S GOING ON?
THEY'RE COMING.
WHO?

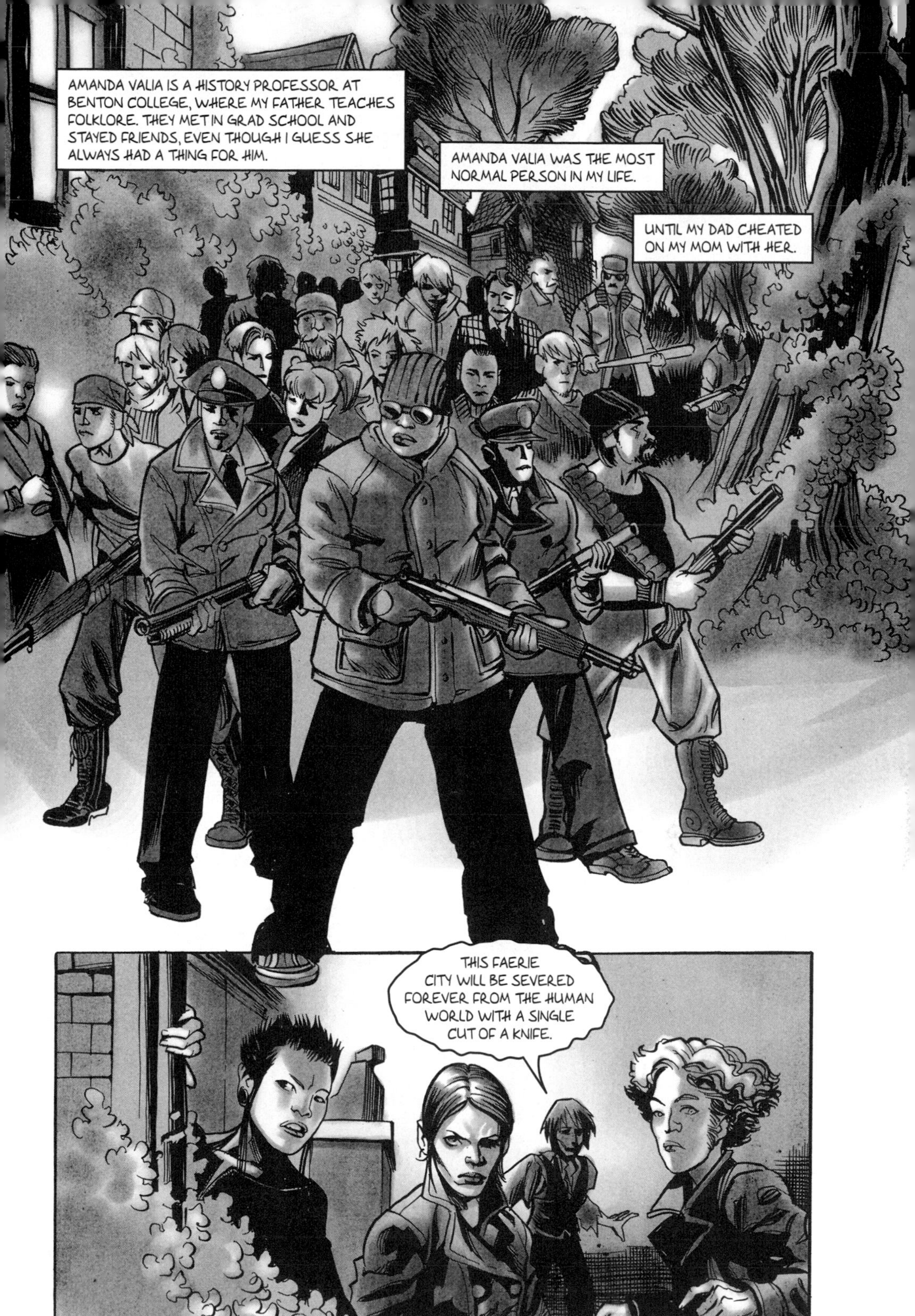
AMANDA VALIA IS A HISTORY PROFESSOR AT BENTON COLLEGE, WHERE MY FATHER TEACHES FOLKLORE. THEY MET IN GRAD SCHOOL AND STAYED FRIENDS, EVEN THOUGH I GUESS SHE ALWAYS HAD A THING FOR HIM.
AMANDA VALIA WAS THE MOST NORMAL PERSON IN MY LIFE.
UNTIL MY DAD CHEATED ON MY MOM WITH HER.
THIS FAERIE CITY WILL BE SEVERED FOREVER FROM THE HUMAN WORLD WITH A SINGLE CUT OF A KNIFE.

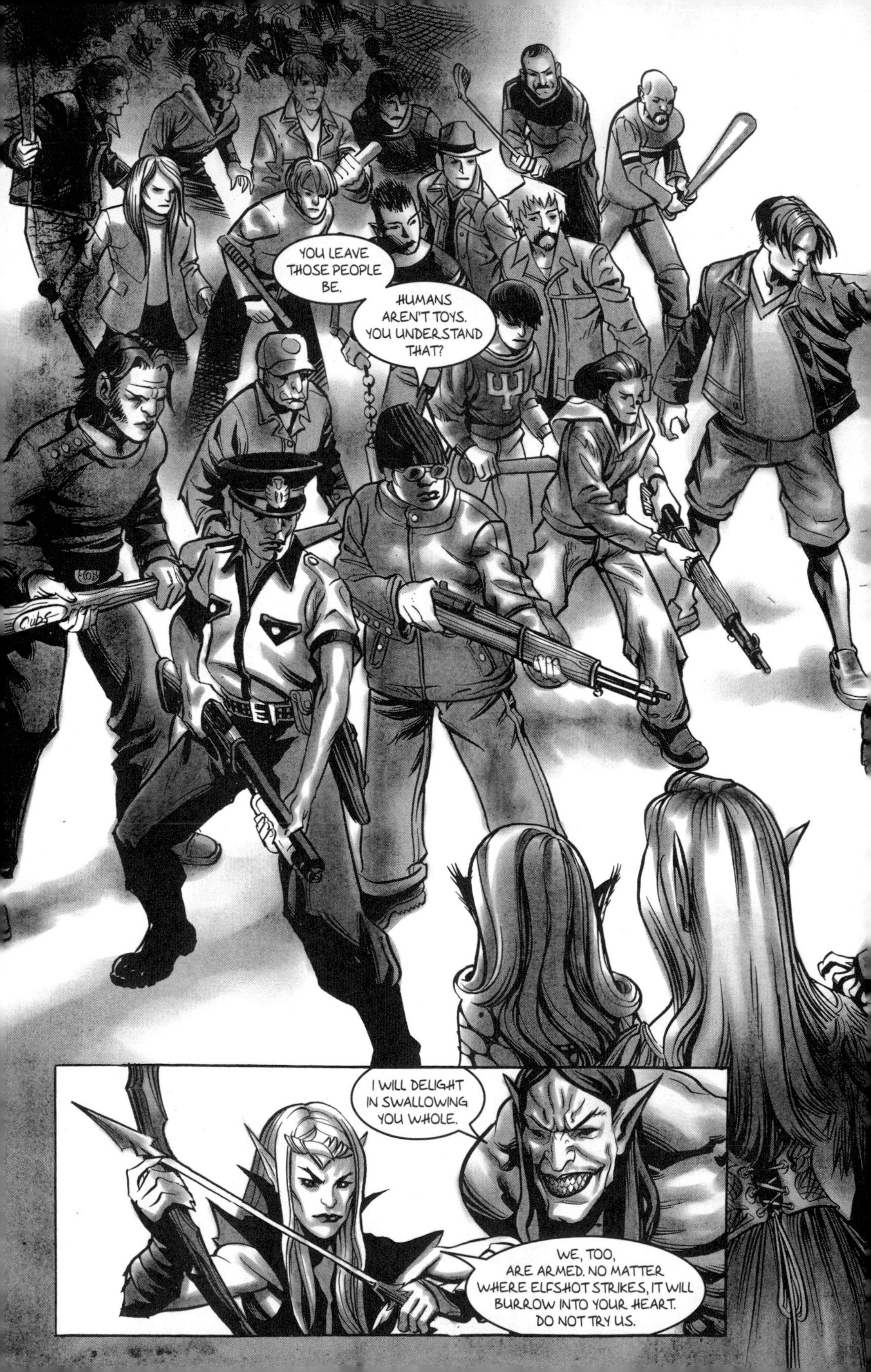
YOU LEAVE THOSE PEOPLE BE.
HUMANS AREN'T TOYS. YOU UNDERSTAND THAT?
Cubs
I WILL DELIGHT IN SWALLOWING YOU WHOLE.
WE, TOO, ARE ARMED. NO MATTER WHERE ELFSHOT STRIKES, IT WILL BURROW INTO YOUR HEART. DO NOT TRY US.

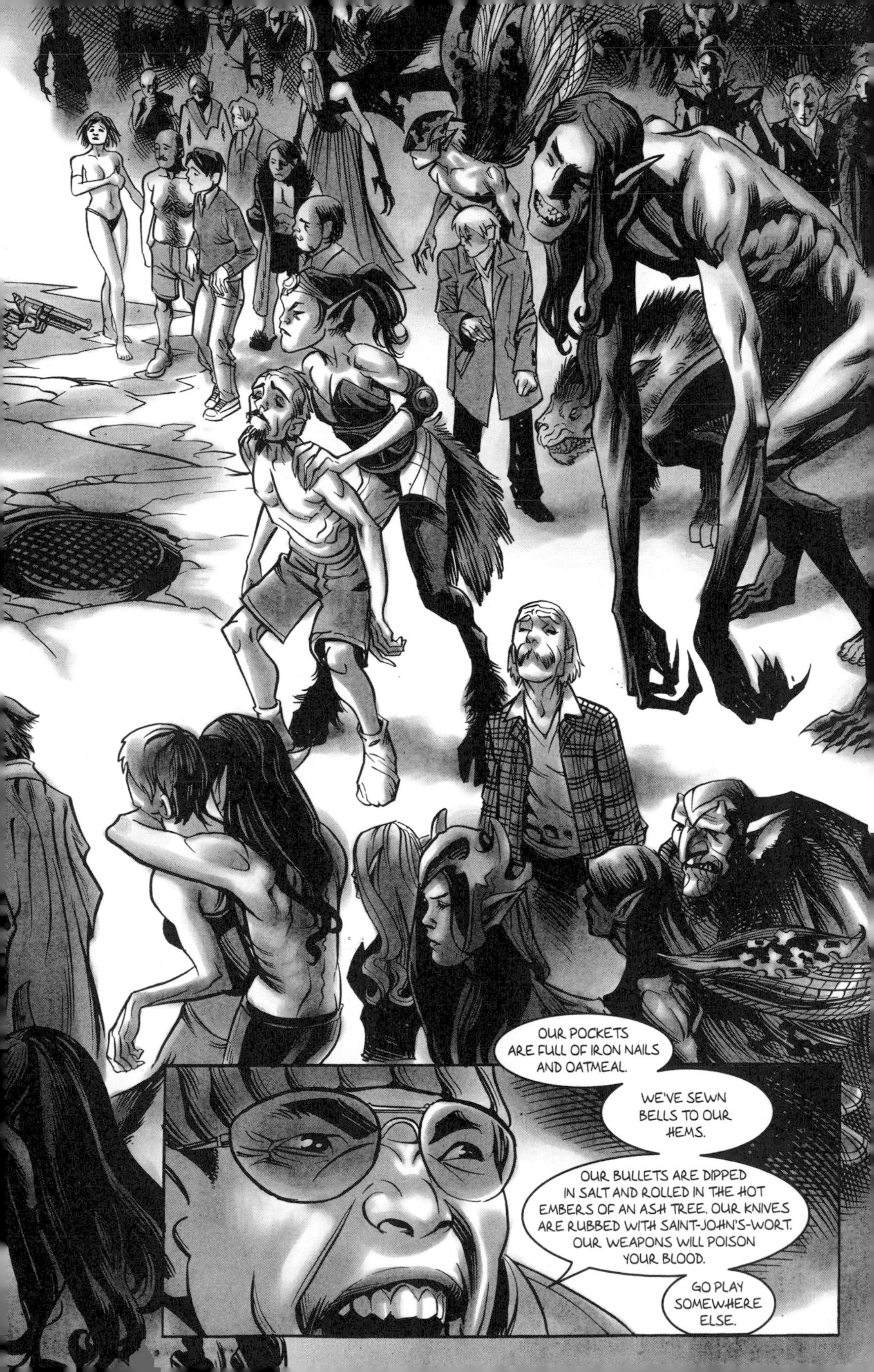
OUR POCKETS ARE FULL OF IRON NAILS AND OATMEAL.
WE'VE SEWN BELLS TO OUR HEMS.
OUR BULLETS ARE DIPPED IN SALT AND ROLLED IN THE HOT EMBERS OF AN ASH TREE. OUR KNIVES ARE RUBBED WITH SAINT-JOHN'S-WORT. OUR WEAPONS WILL POISON YOUR BLOOD.
GO PLAY SOMEWHERE ELSE.

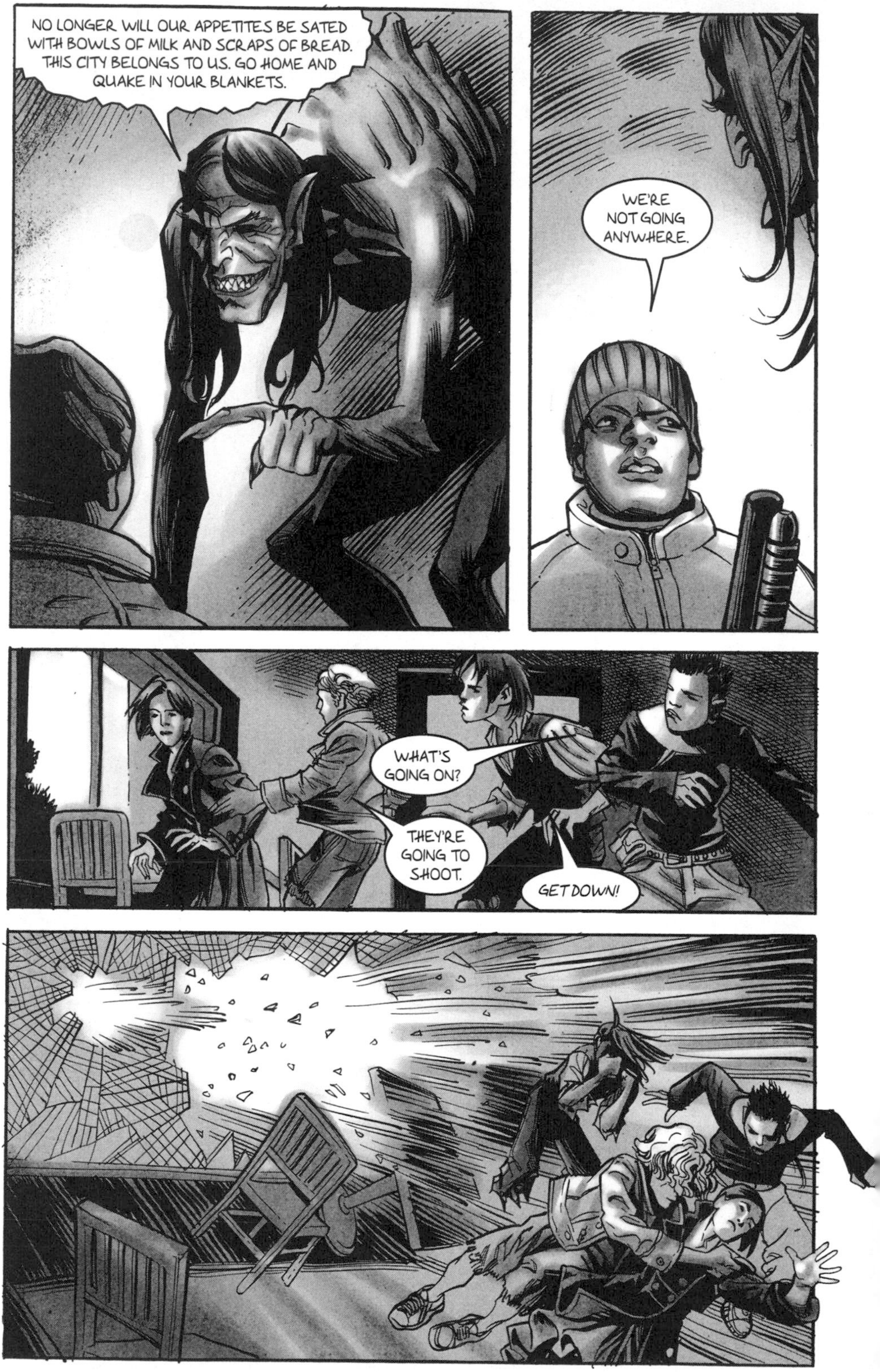
NO LONGER WILL OUR APPETITES BE SATED WITH BOWLS OF MILK AND SCRAPS OF BREAD. THIS CITY BELONGS TO US. GO HOME AND QUAKE IN YOUR BLANKETS.
WE'RE NOT GOING ANYWHERE.
WHAT'S GOING ON?
THEY'RE GOING TO SHOOT.
GET DOWN!

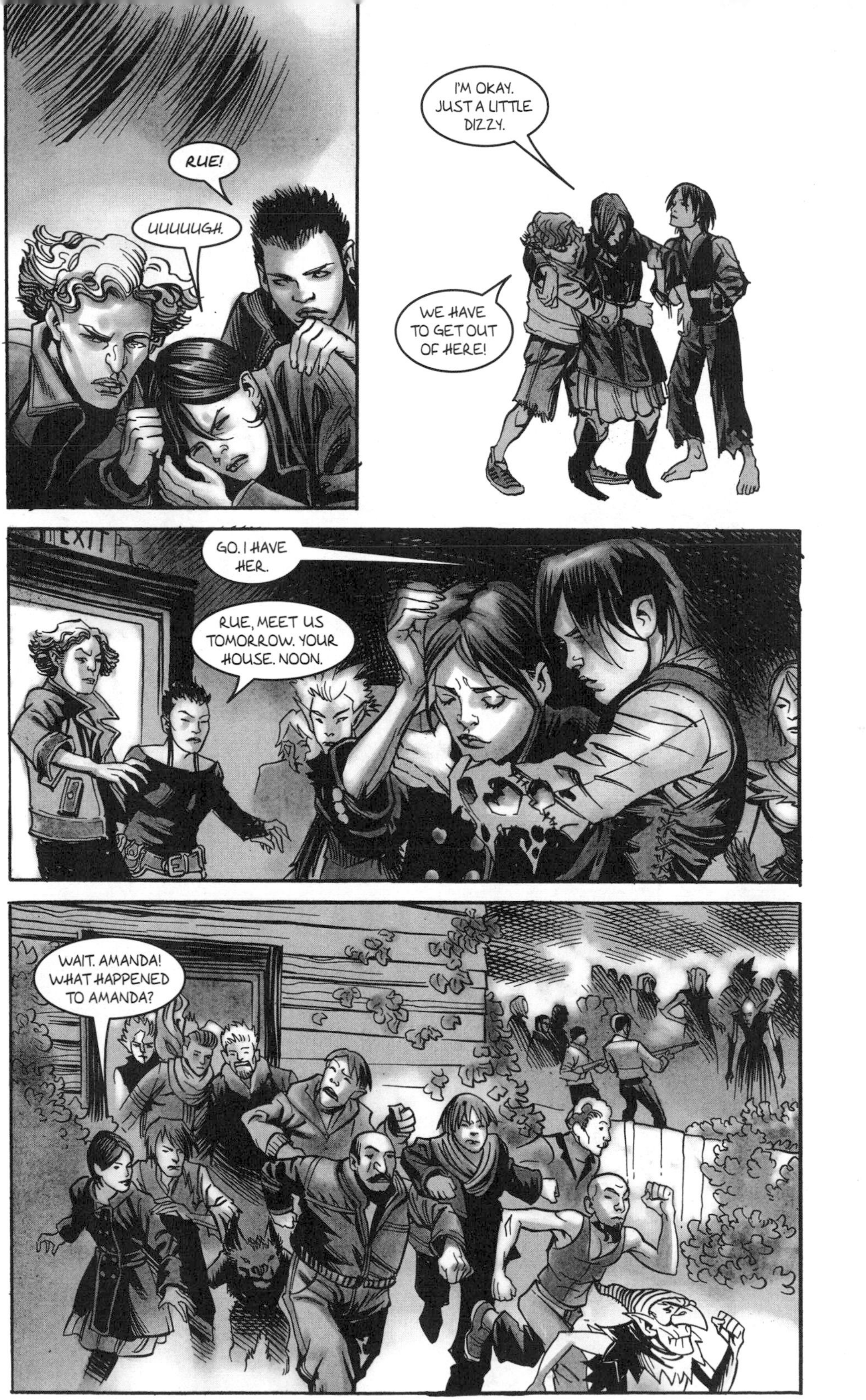
RUE!
UUUUUGH.
I'M OKAY. JUST A LITTLE DIZZY.
WE HAVE TO GET OUT OF HERE!
EXIT
GO. I HAVE HER.
RUE, MEET US TOMORROW. YOUR HOUSE. NOON.
WAIT. AMANDA! WHAT HAPPENED TO AMANDA?

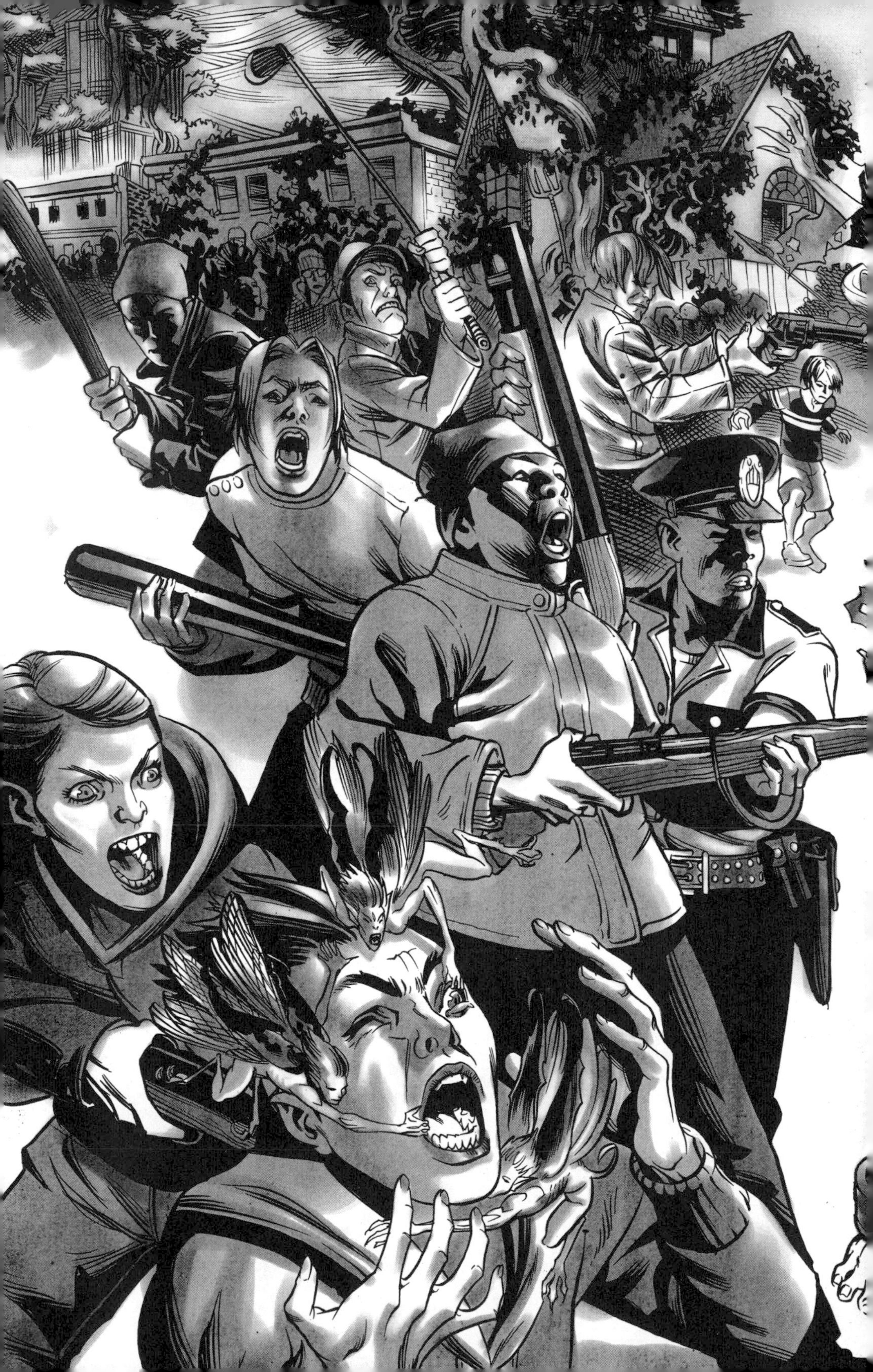

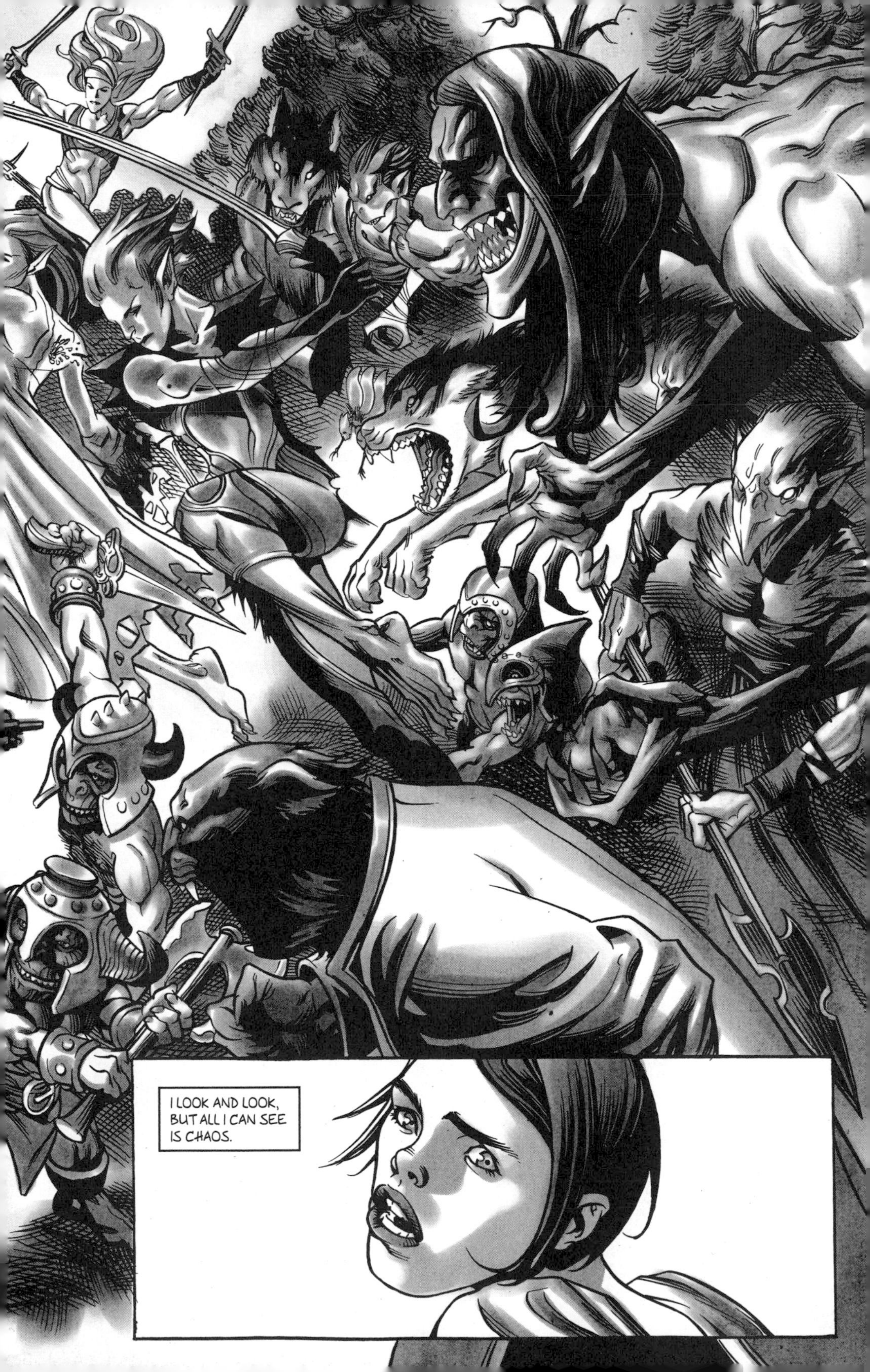
I LOOK AND LOOK, BUT ALL I CAN SEE IS CHAOS.

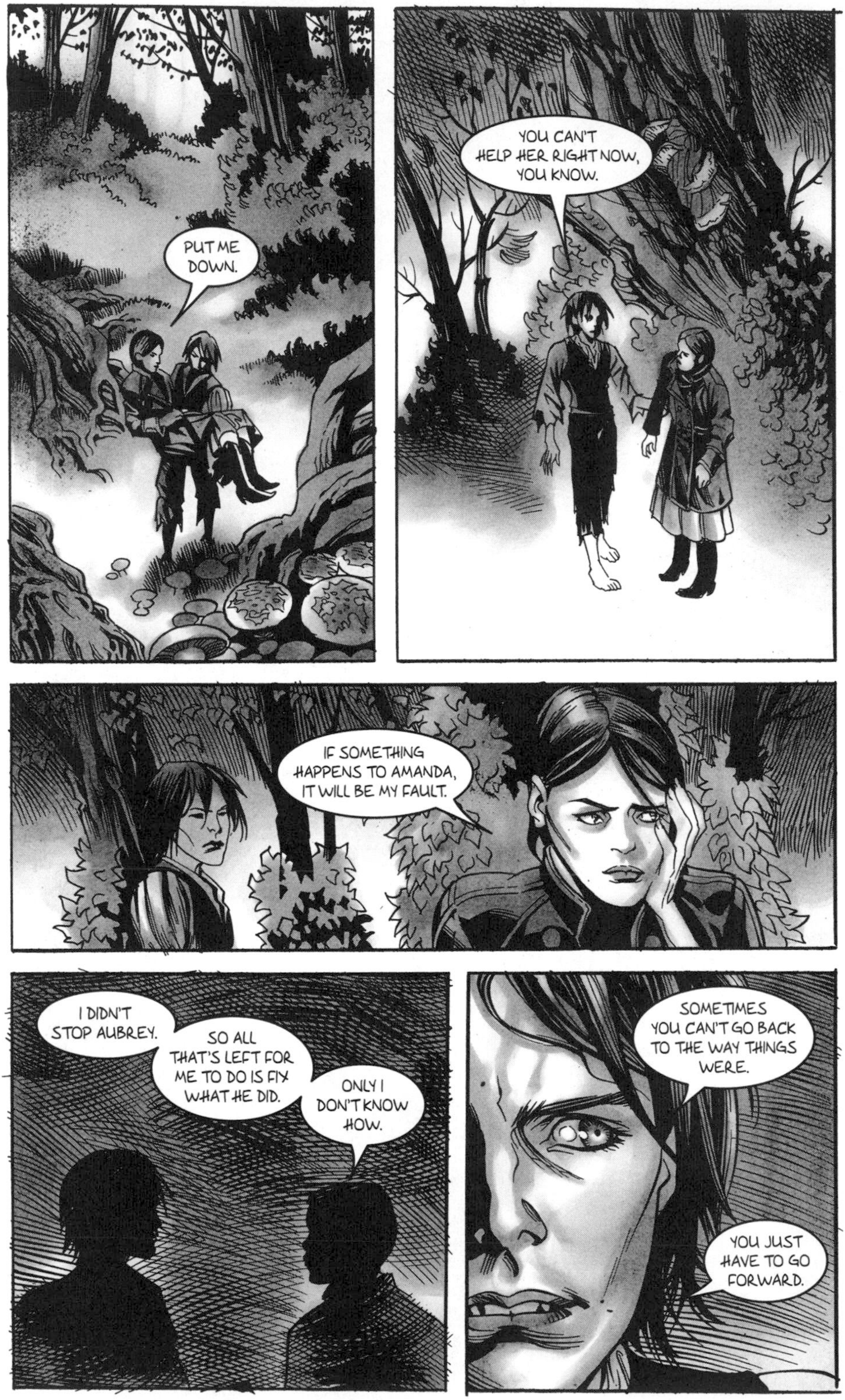
PUT ME DOWN.
YOU CAN'T HELP HER RIGHT NOW, YOU KNOW.
IF SOMETHING HAPPENS TO AMANDA, IT WILL BE MY FAULT.
I DIDN'T STOP AUBREY.
SO ALL THAT'S LEFT FOR ME TO DO IS FIX WHAT HE DID.
ONLY I DON'T KNOW HOW.
SOMETIMES YOU CAN'T GO BACK TO THE WAY THINGS WERE.
YOU JUST HAVE TO GO FORWARD.

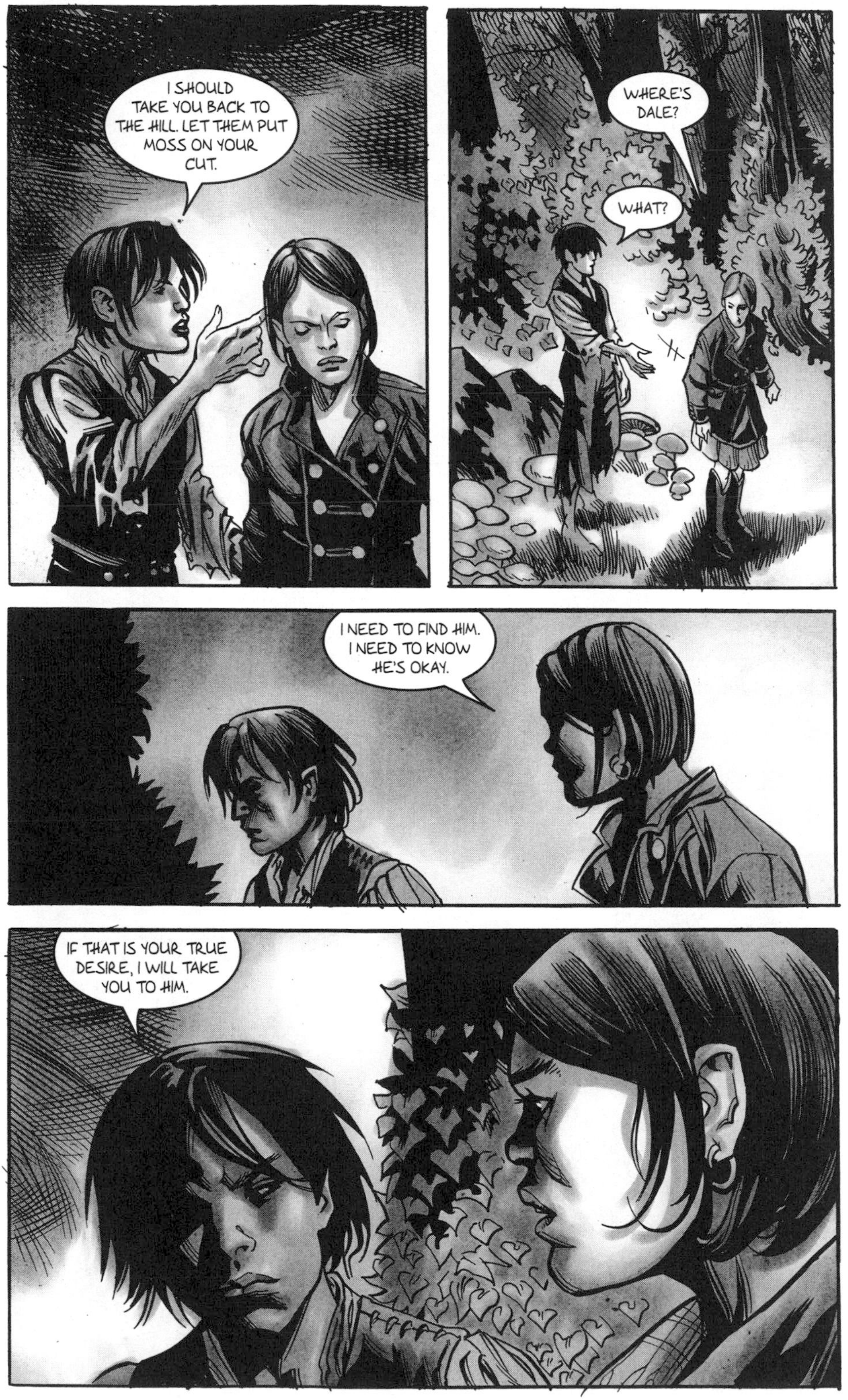
I SHOULD TAKE YOU BACK TO THE HILL. LET THEM PUT MOSS ON YOUR CUT.
WHERE'S DALE?
WHAT?
I NEED TO FIND HIM. I NEED TO KNOW HE'S OKAY.
IF THAT IS YOUR TRUE DESIRE, I WILL TAKE YOU TO HIM.

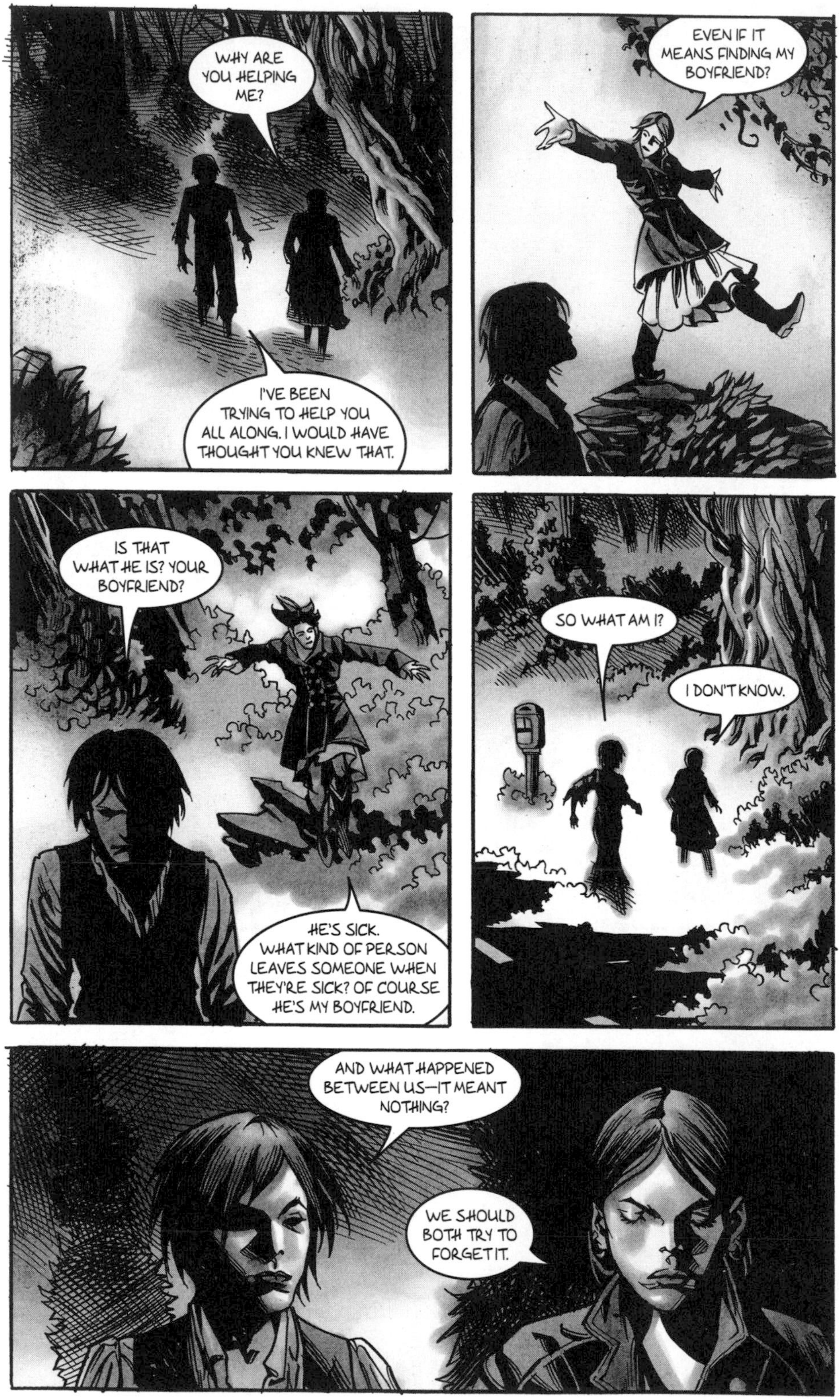
WHY ARE YOU HELPING ME?
I'VE BEEN TRYING TO HELP YOU ALL ALONG. I WOULD HAVE THOUGHT YOU KNEW THAT.
EVEN IF IT MEANS FINDING MY BOYFRIEND?
IS THAT WHAT HE IS? YOUR BOYFRIEND?
HE'S SICK. WHAT KIND OF PERSON LEAVES SOMEONE WHEN THEY'RE SICK? OF COURSE HE'S MY BOYFRIEND.
SO WHAT AM I?
I DON'T KNOW.
AND WHAT HAPPENED BETWEEN US—IT MEANT NOTHING?
WE SHOULD BOTH TRY TO FORGET IT.

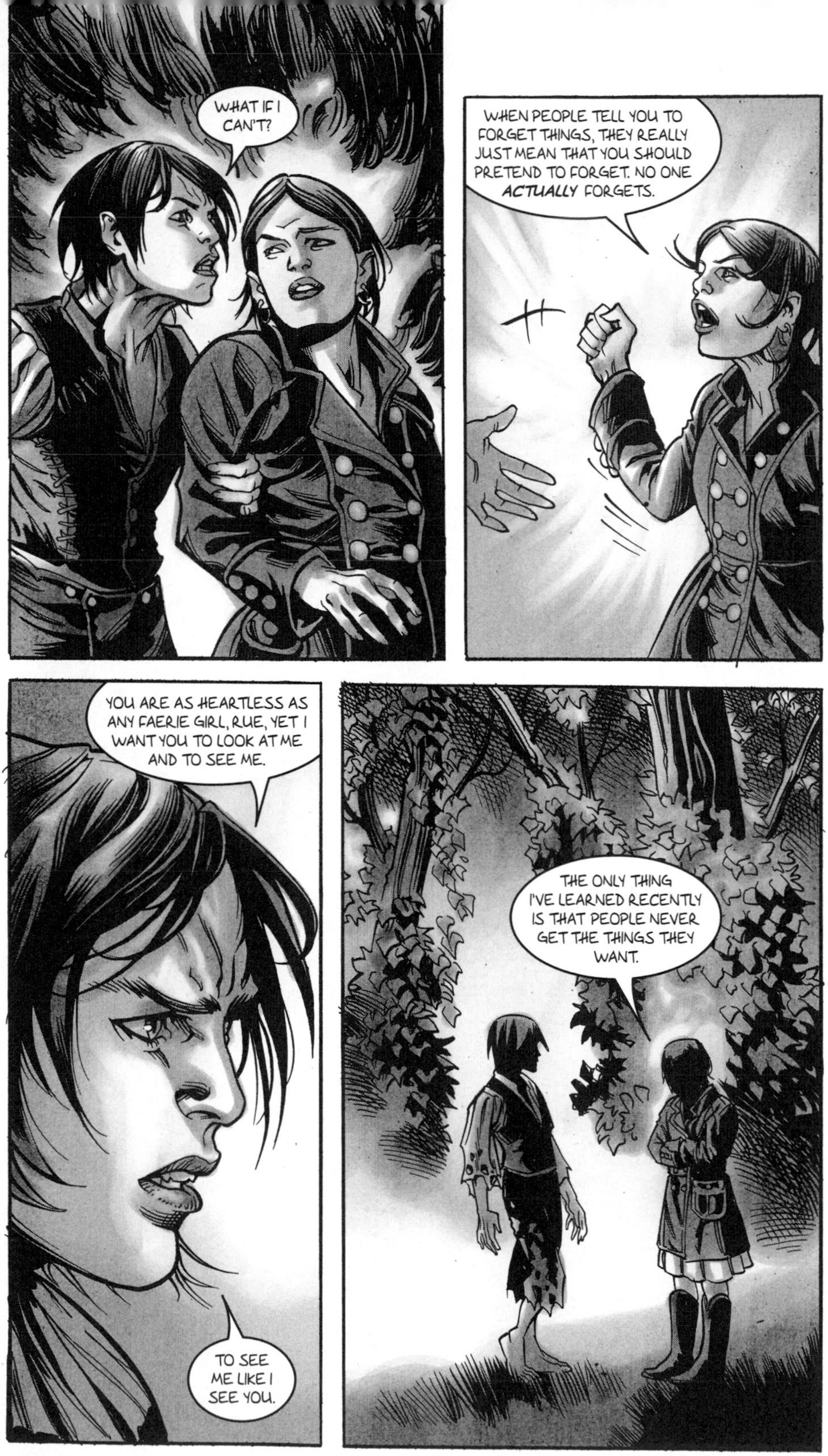

WHAT IF I CAN'T?
WHEN PEOPLE TELL YOU TO FORGET THINGS, THEY REALLY JUST MEAN THAT YOU SHOULD PRETEND TO FORGET. NO ONE ACTUALLY FORGETS.
YOU ARE AS HEARTLESS AS ANY FAERIE GIRL, RUE, YET I WANT YOU TO LOOK AT ME AND TO SEE ME.
TO SEE ME LIKE I SEE YOU.
THE ONLY THING I'VE LEARNED RECENTLY IS THAT PEOPLE NEVER GET THE THINGS THEY WANT.

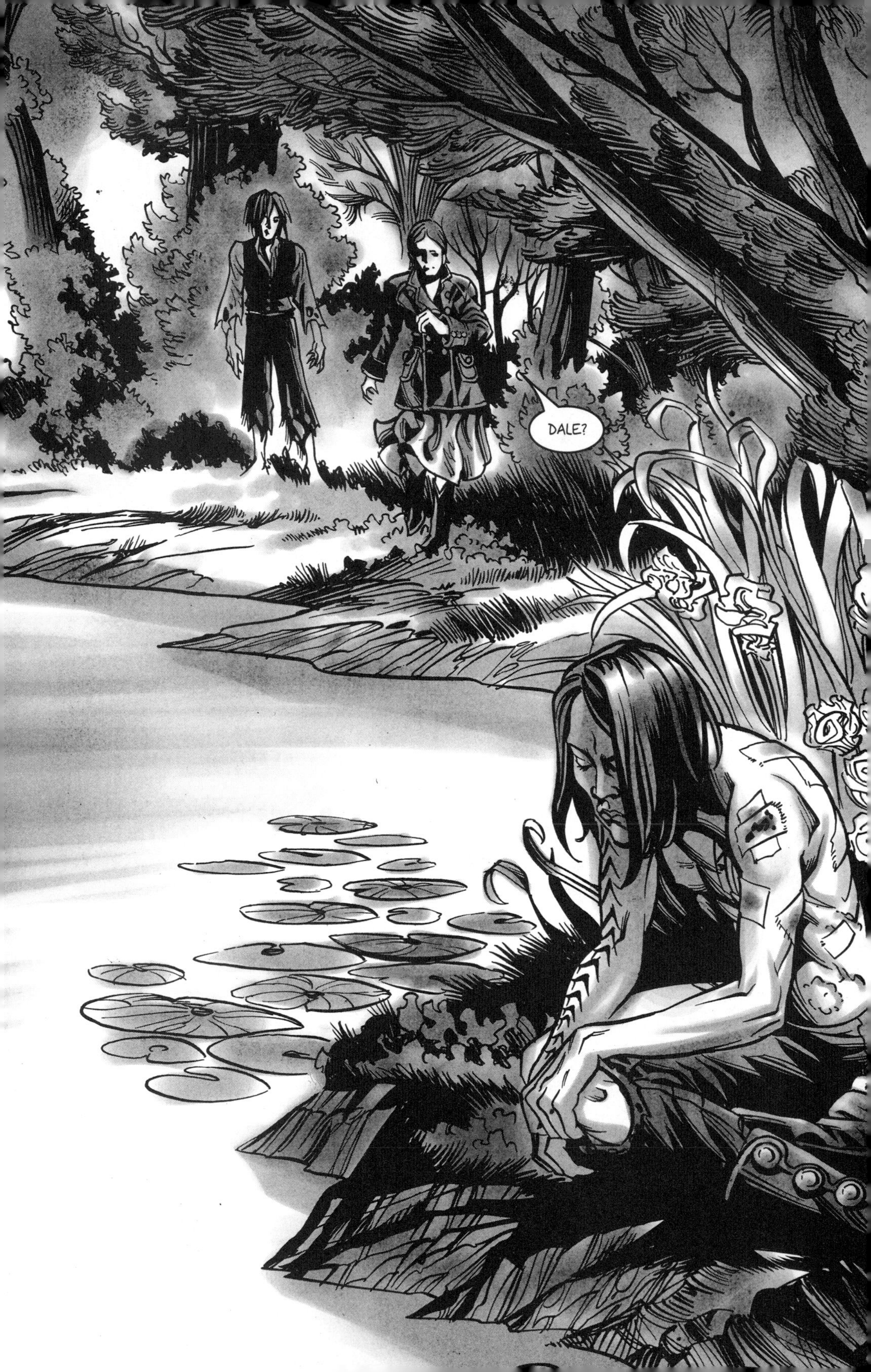
DALE?

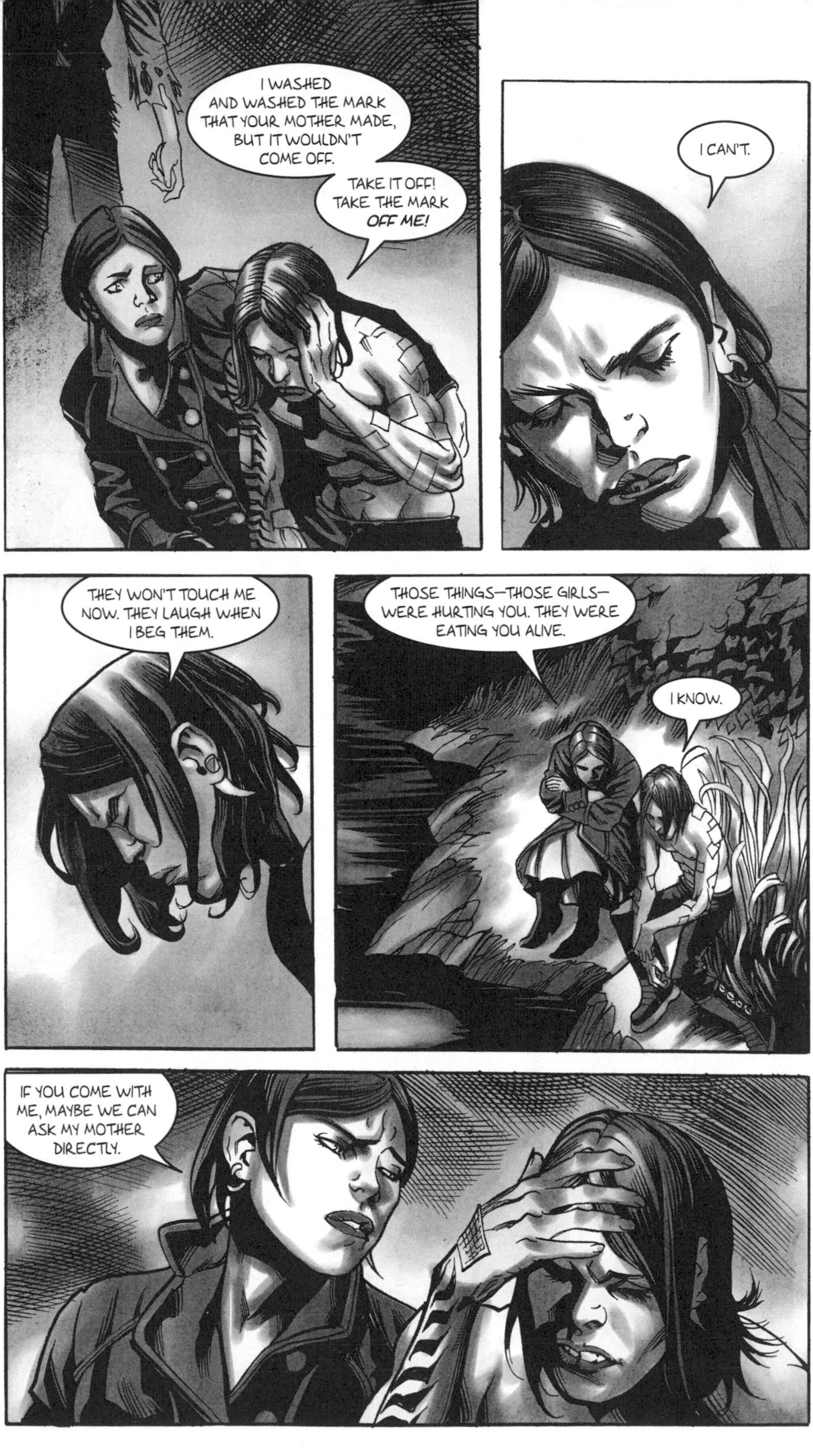
I WASHED AND WASHED THE MARK THAT YOUR MOTHER MADE, BUT IT WOULDN'T COME OFF.
TAKE IT OFF! TAKE THE MARK *OFF ME!*
I CAN'T.
THEY WON'T TOUCH ME NOW. THEY LAUGH WHEN I BEG THEM.
THOSE THINGS—THOSE GIRLS—WERE HURTING YOU. THEY WERE EATING YOU ALIVE.
I KNOW.
IF YOU COME WITH ME, MAYBE WE CAN ASK MY MOTHER DIRECTLY.

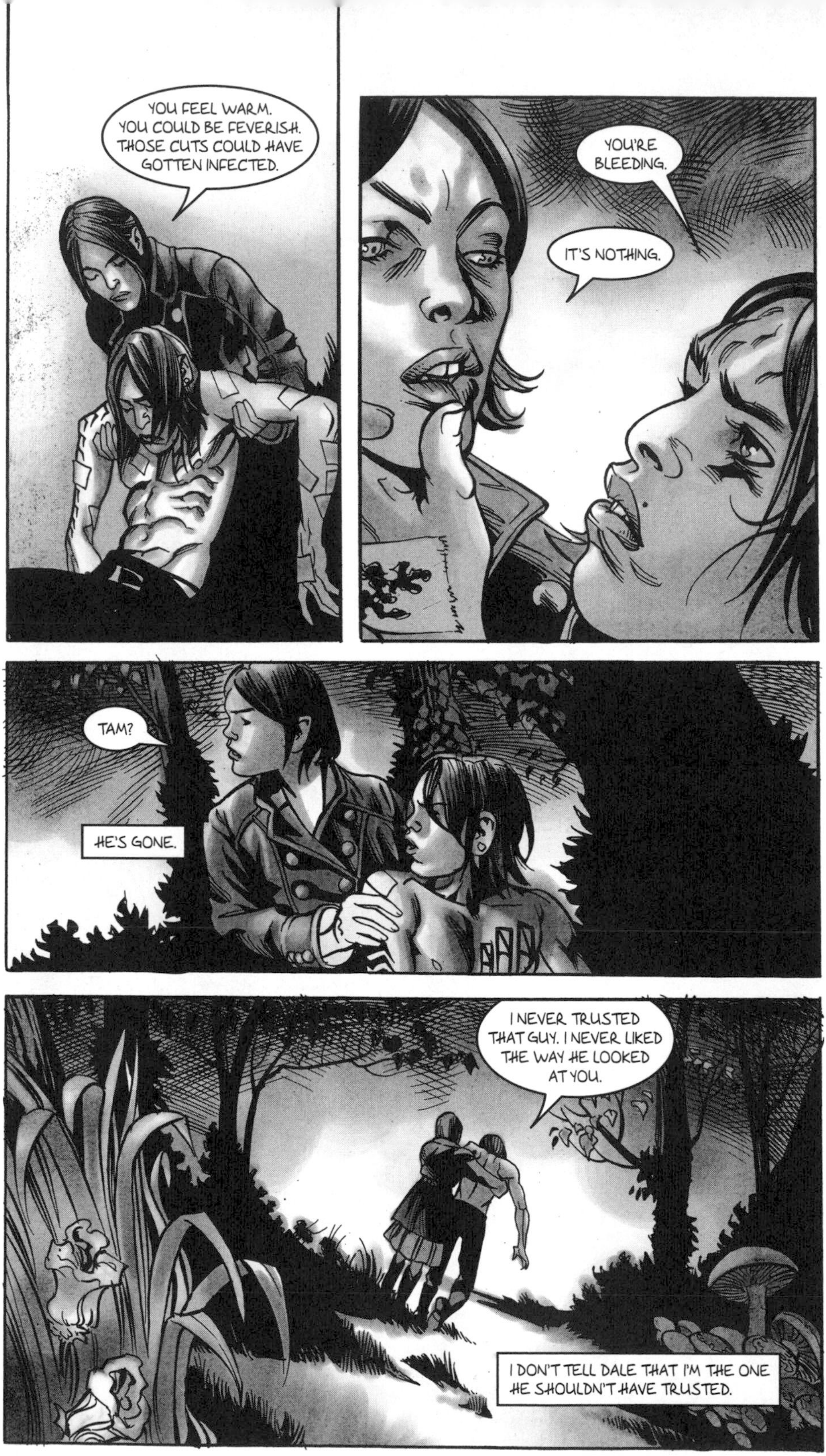
YOU FEEL WARM. YOU COULD BE FEVERISH. THOSE CUTS COULD HAVE GOTTEN INFECTED.
YOU'RE BLEEDING.
IT'S NOTHING.
TAM?
HE'S GONE.
I NEVER TRUSTED THAT GUY. I NEVER LIKED THE WAY HE LOOKED AT YOU.
I DON'T TELL DALE THAT I'M THE ONE HE SHOULDN'T HAVE TRUSTED.

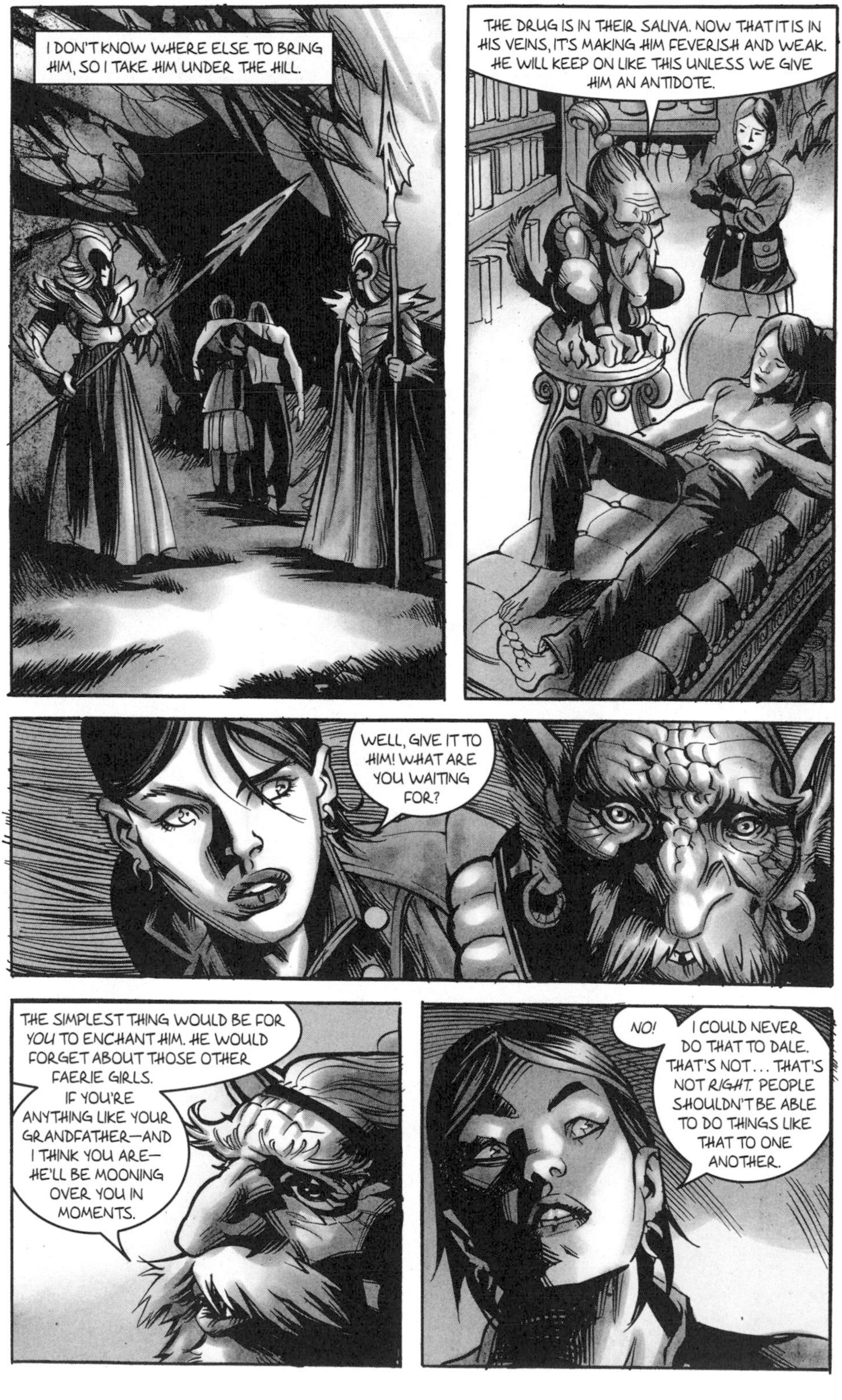

I DON'T KNOW WHERE ELSE TO BRING HIM, SO I TAKE HIM UNDER THE HILL.
THE DRUG IS IN THEIR SALIVA. NOW THAT IT IS IN HIS VEINS, IT'S MAKING HIM FEVERISH AND WEAK. HE WILL KEEP ON LIKE THIS UNLESS WE GIVE HIM AN ANTIDOTE.
WELL, GIVE IT TO HIM! WHAT ARE YOU WAITING FOR?
THE SIMPLEST THING WOULD BE FOR YOU TO ENCHANT HIM. HE WOULD FORGET ABOUT THOSE OTHER FAERIE GIRLS.
IF YOU'RE ANYTHING LIKE YOUR GRANDFATHER—AND I THINK YOU ARE—HE'LL BE MOONING OVER YOU IN MOMENTS.
NO!
I COULD NEVER DO THAT TO DALE. THAT'S NOT... THAT'S NOT *RIGHT.* PEOPLE SHOULDN'T BE ABLE TO DO THINGS LIKE THAT TO ONE ANOTHER.

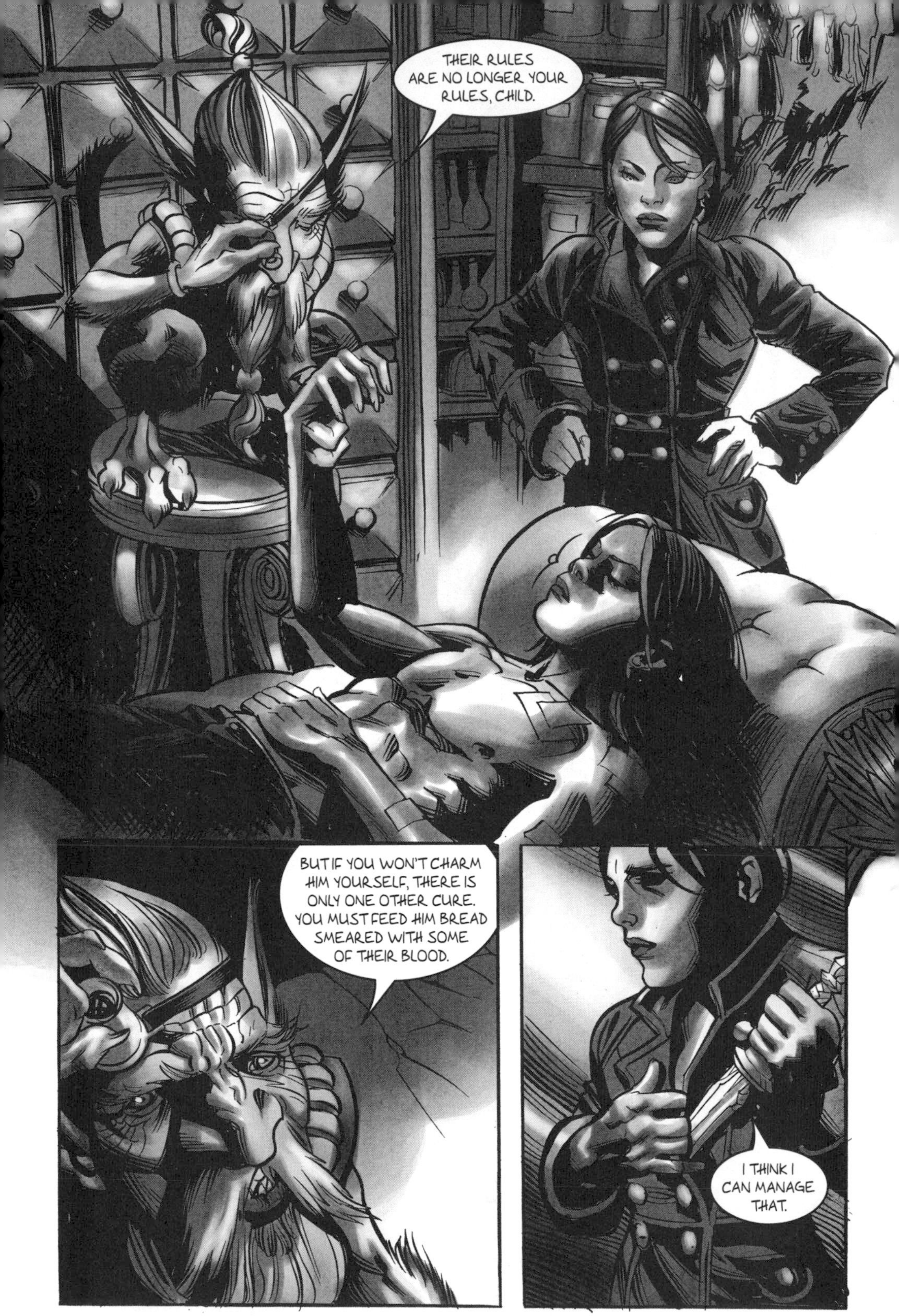
THEIR RULES ARE NO LONGER YOUR RULES, CHILD.
BUT IF YOU WON'T CHARM HIM YOURSELF, THERE IS ONLY ONE OTHER CURE. YOU MUST FEED HIM BREAD SMEARED WITH SOME OF THEIR BLOOD.
I THINK I CAN MANAGE THAT.

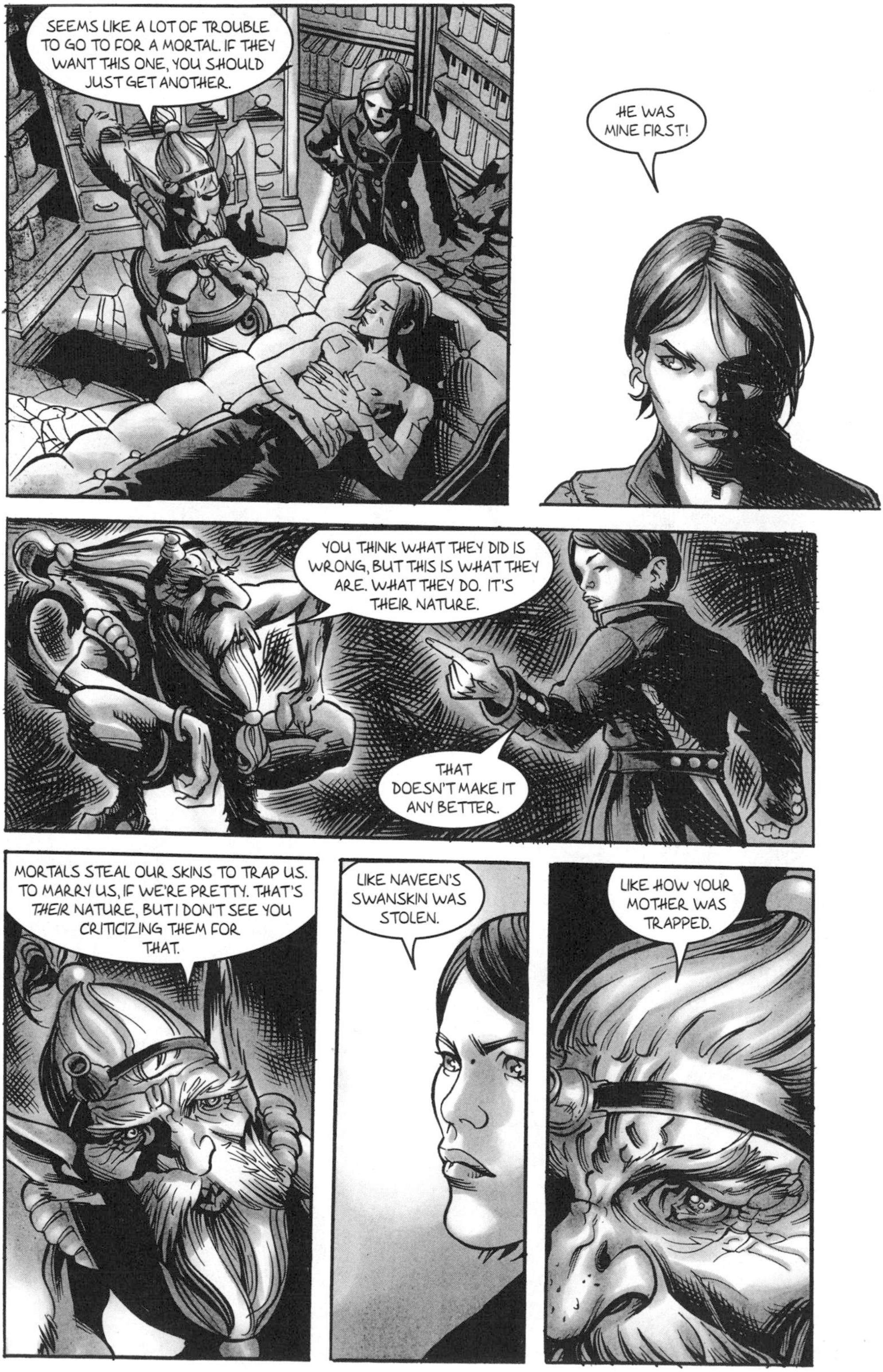
SEEMS LIKE A LOT OF TROUBLE TO GO TO FOR A MORTAL. IF THEY WANT THIS ONE, YOU SHOULD JUST GET ANOTHER.
HE WAS MINE FIRST!
YOU THINK WHAT THEY DID IS WRONG, BUT THIS IS WHAT THEY ARE. WHAT THEY DO. IT'S THEIR NATURE.
THAT DOESN'T MAKE IT ANY BETTER.
MORTALS STEAL OUR SKINS TO TRAP US. TO MARRY US, IF WE'RE PRETTY. THAT'S *THEIR* NATURE, BUT I DON'T SEE YOU CRITICIZING THEM FOR THAT.
LIKE NAVEEN'S SWANSKIN WAS STOLEN.
LIKE HOW YOUR MOTHER WAS TRAPPED.

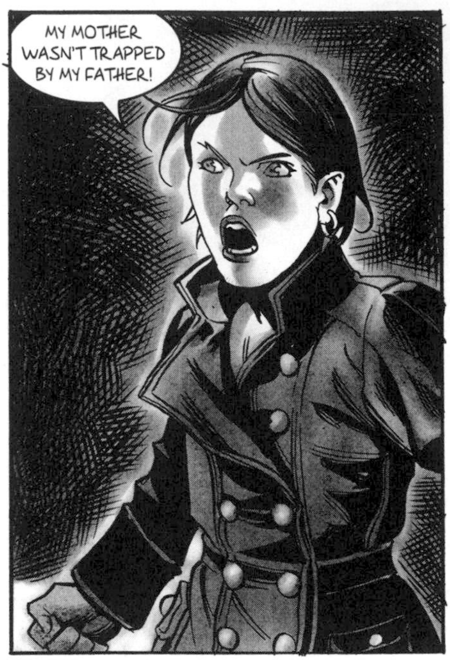
MY MOTHER WASN'T TRAPPED BY MY FATHER!

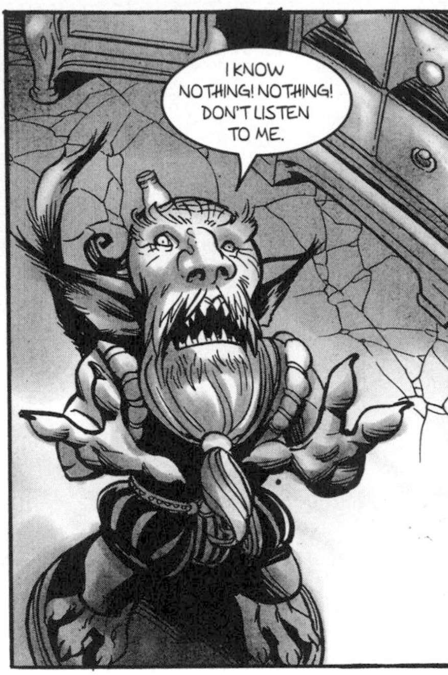
I KNOW NOTHING! NOTHING! DON'T LISTEN TO ME.

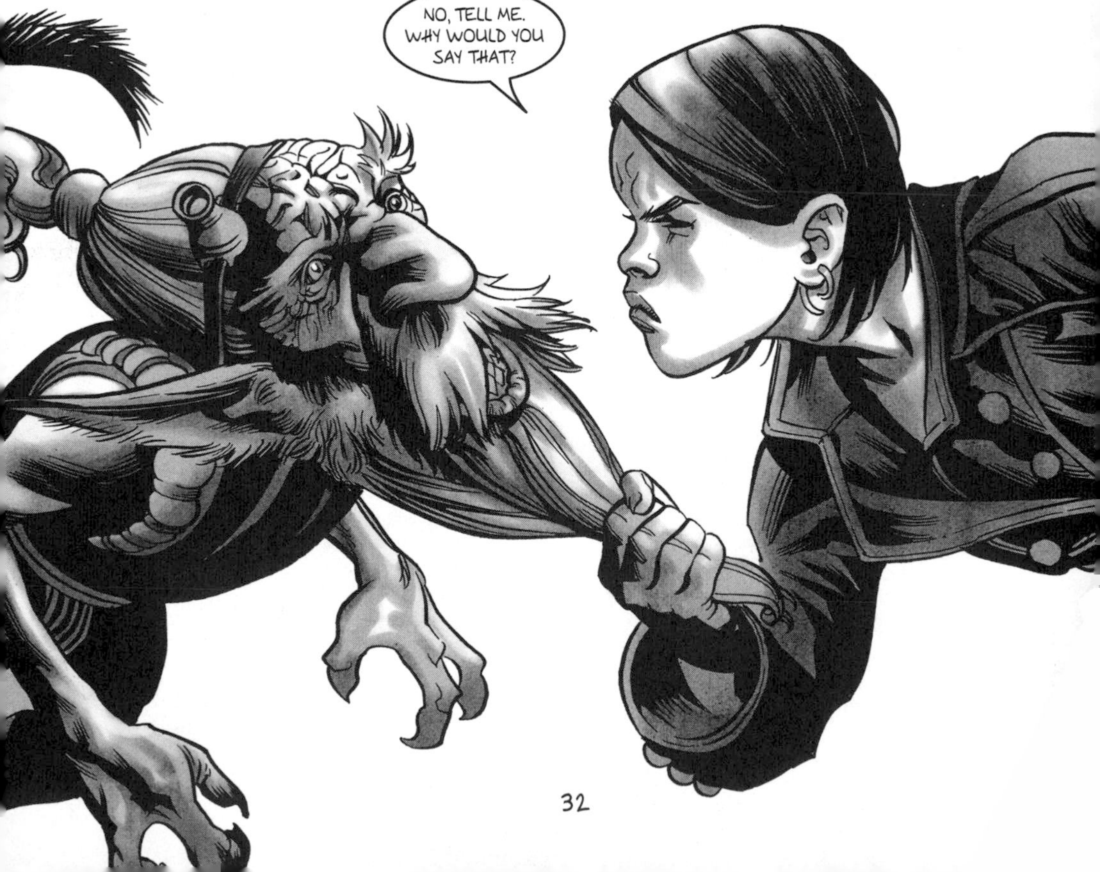
NO, TELL ME. WHY WOULD YOU SAY THAT?

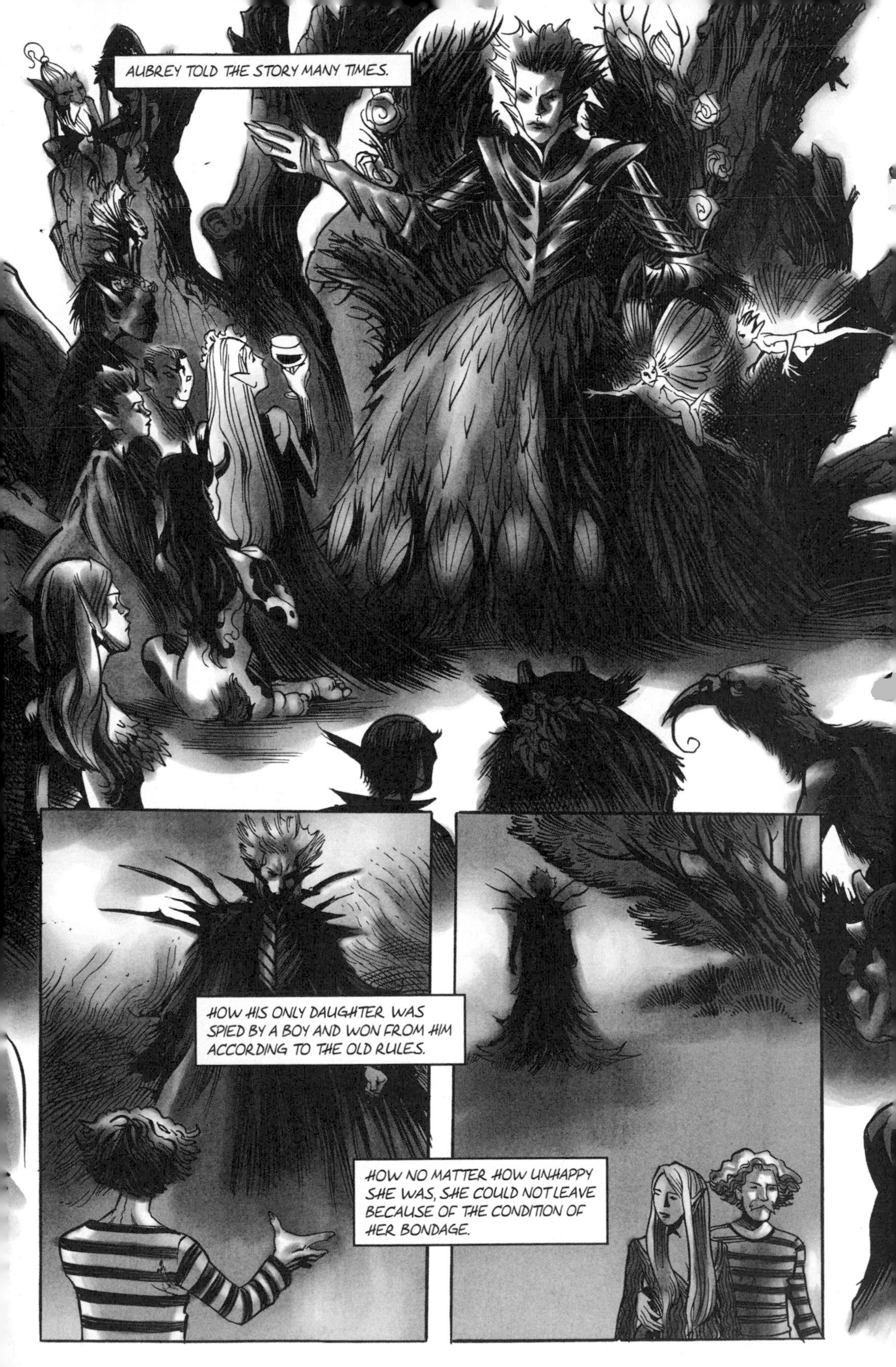
AUBREY TOLD THE STORY MANY TIMES.
HOW HIS ONLY DAUGHTER WAS SPIED BY A BOY AND WON FROM HIM ACCORDING TO THE OLD RULES.
HOW NO MATTER HOW UNHAPPY SHE WAS, SHE COULD NOT LEAVE BECAUSE OF THE CONDITION OF HER BONDAGE.

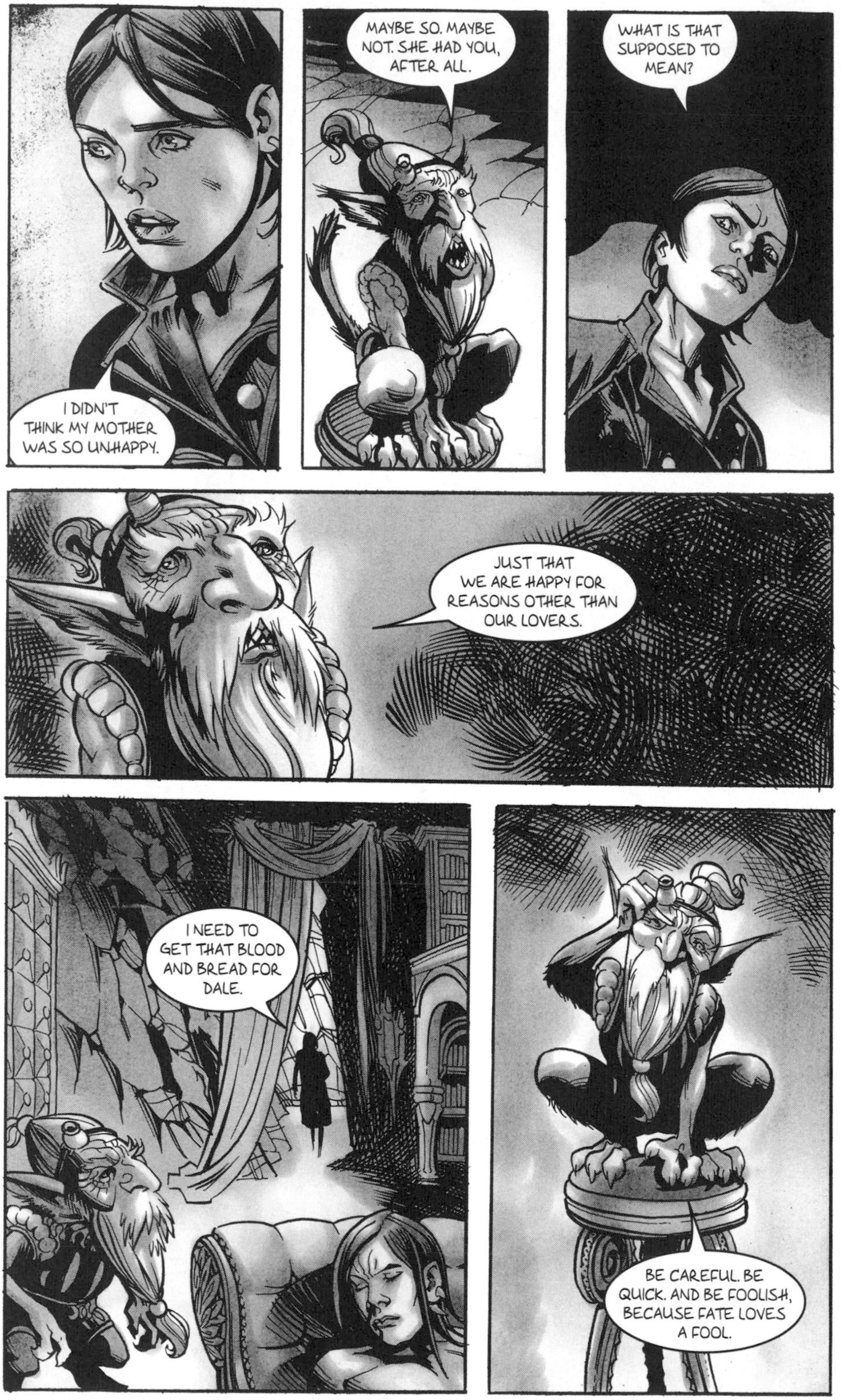
I DIDN'T THINK MY MOTHER WAS SO UNHAPPY.
MAYBE SO. MAYBE NOT. SHE HAD YOU, AFTER ALL.
WHAT IS THAT SUPPOSED TO MEAN?
JUST THAT WE ARE HAPPY FOR REASONS OTHER THAN OUR LOVERS.
I NEED TO GET THAT BLOOD AND BREAD FOR DALE.
BE CAREFUL. BE QUICK. AND BE FOOLISH, BECAUSE FATE LOVES A FOOL.

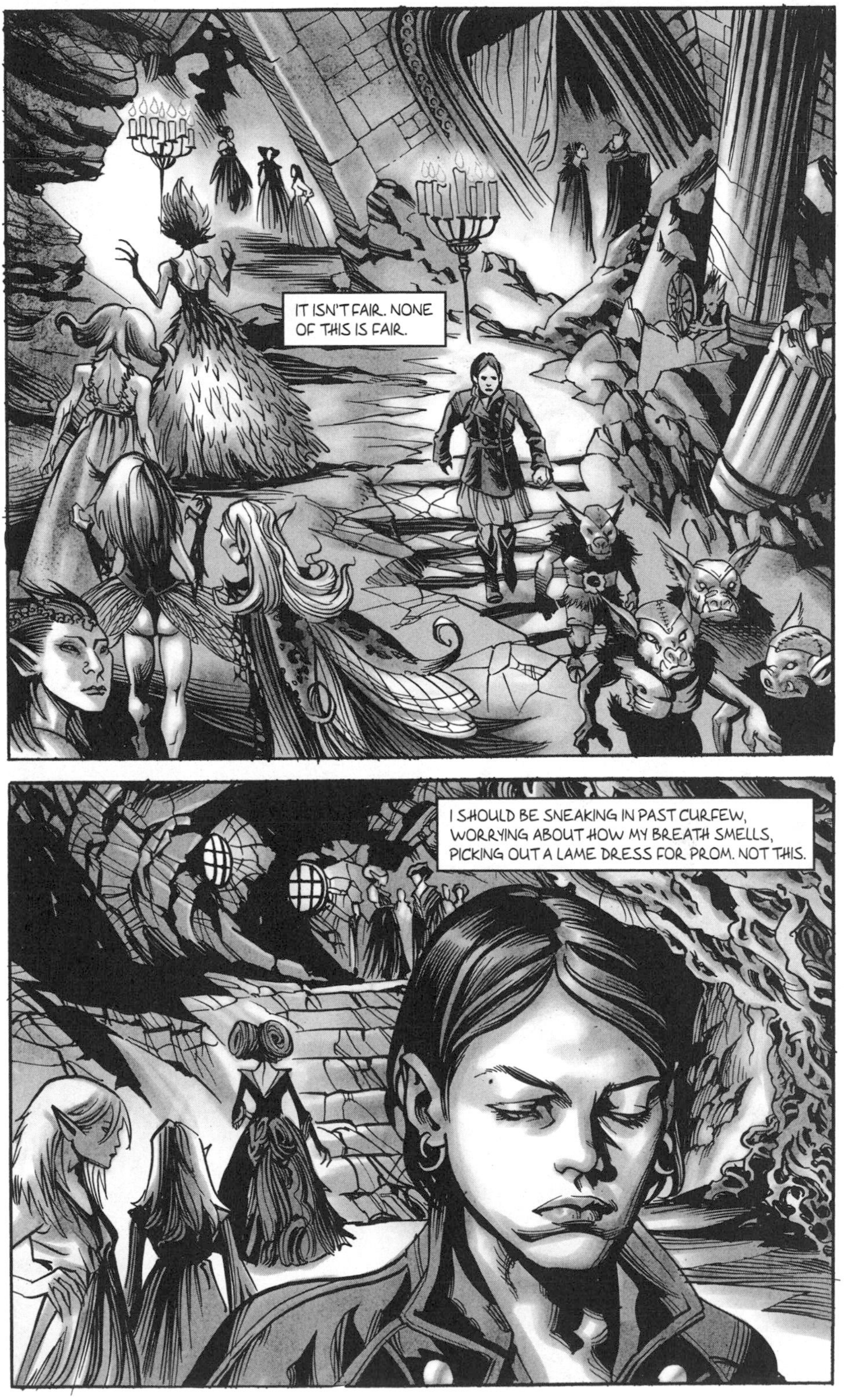
IT ISN'T FAIR. NONE OF THIS IS FAIR.
I SHOULD BE SNEAKING IN PAST CURFEW, WORRYING ABOUT HOW MY BREATH SMELLS, PICKING OUT A LAME DRESS FOR PROM. NOT THIS.

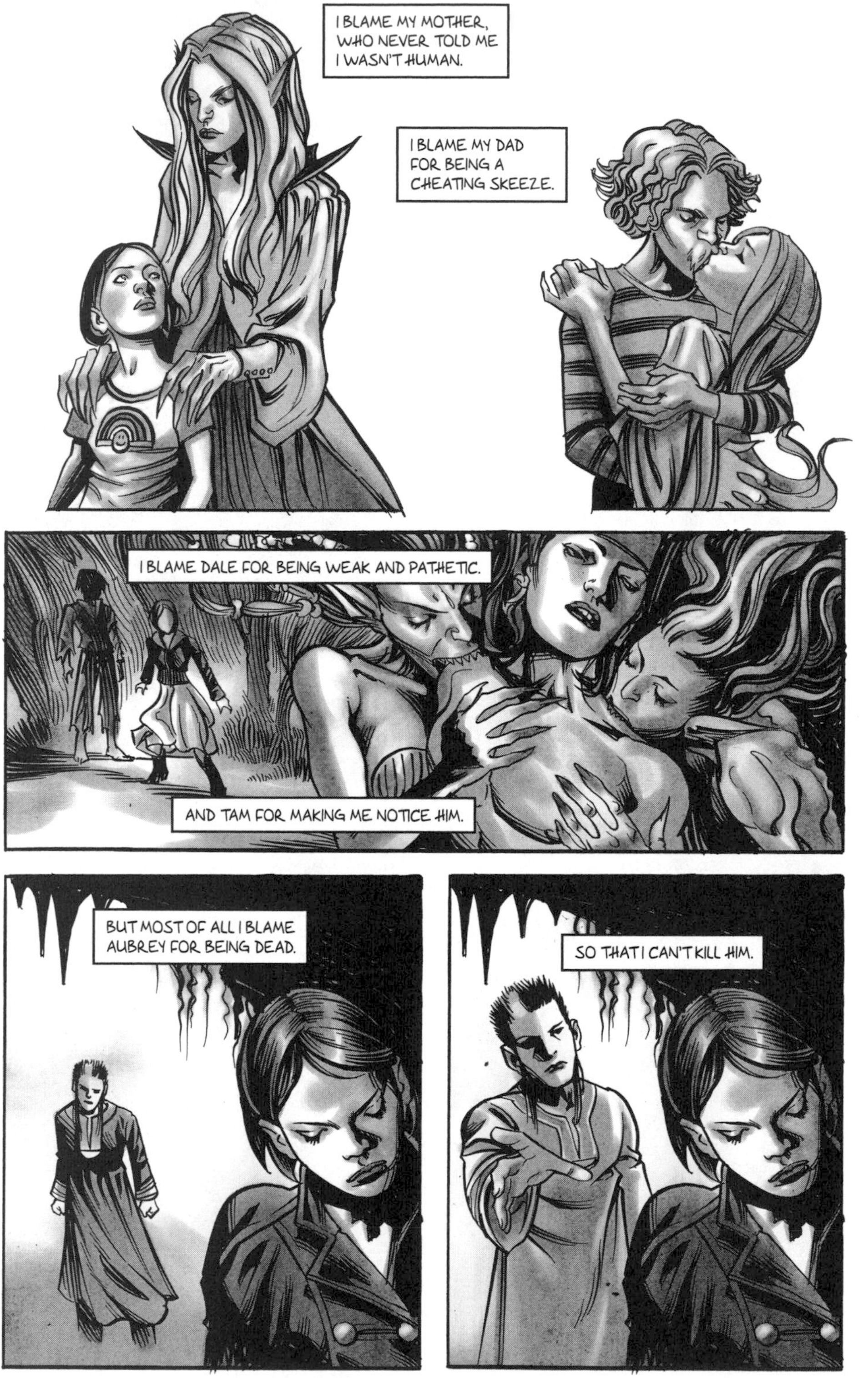
I BLAME MY MOTHER, WHO NEVER TOLD ME I WASN'T HUMAN.
I BLAME MY DAD FOR BEING A CHEATING SKEEZE.
I BLAME DALE FOR BEING WEAK AND PATHETIC.
AND TAM FOR MAKING ME NOTICE HIM.
BUT MOST OF ALL I BLAME AUBREY FOR BEING DEAD.
SO THAT I CAN'T KILL HIM.

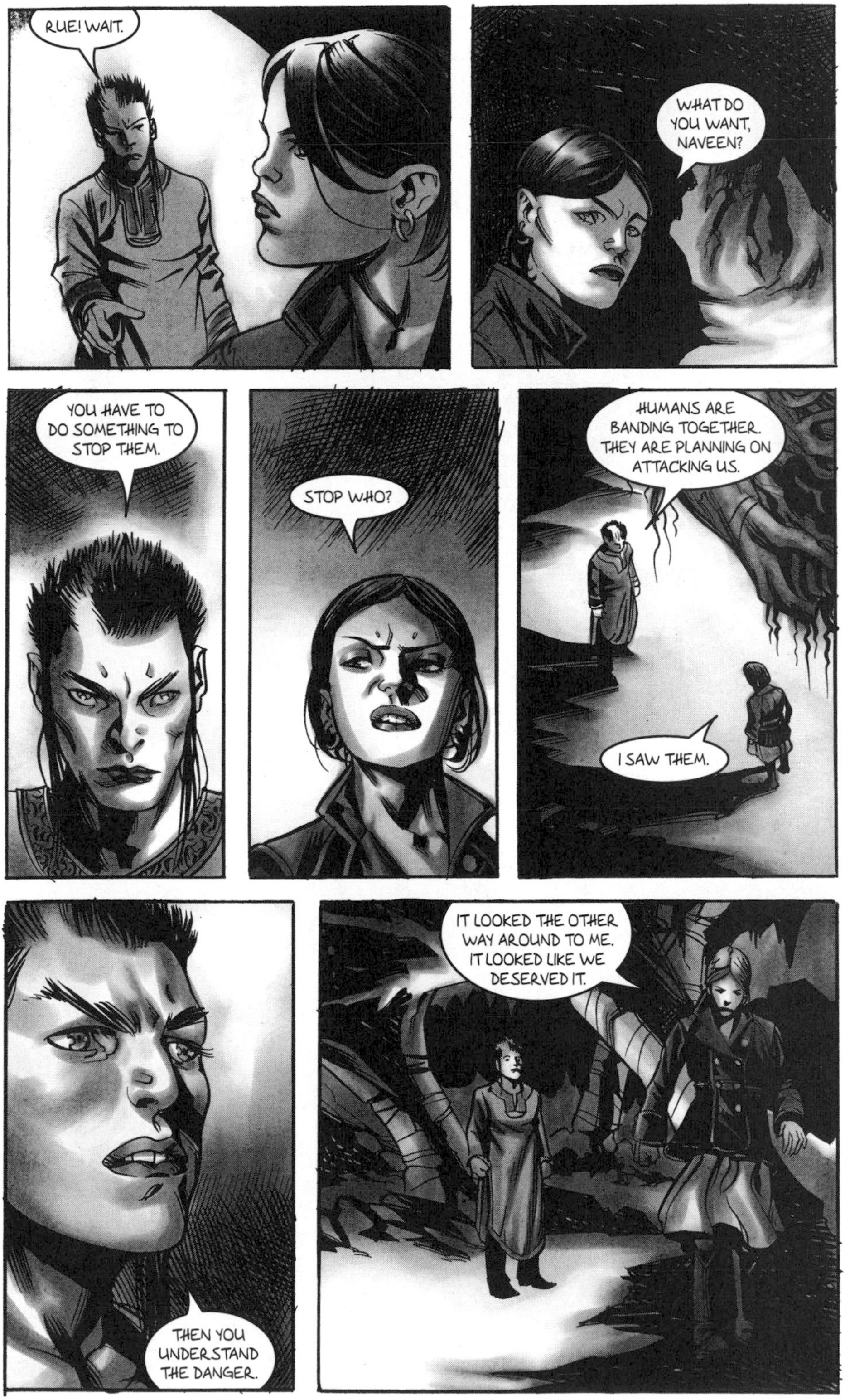
RUE! WAIT.
WHAT DO YOU WANT, NAVEEN?
YOU HAVE TO DO SOMETHING TO STOP THEM.
STOP WHO?
HUMANS ARE BANDING TOGETHER. THEY ARE PLANNING ON ATTACKING US.
I SAW THEM.
THEN YOU UNDERSTAND THE DANGER.
IT LOOKED THE OTHER WAY AROUND TO ME. IT LOOKED LIKE WE DESERVED IT.

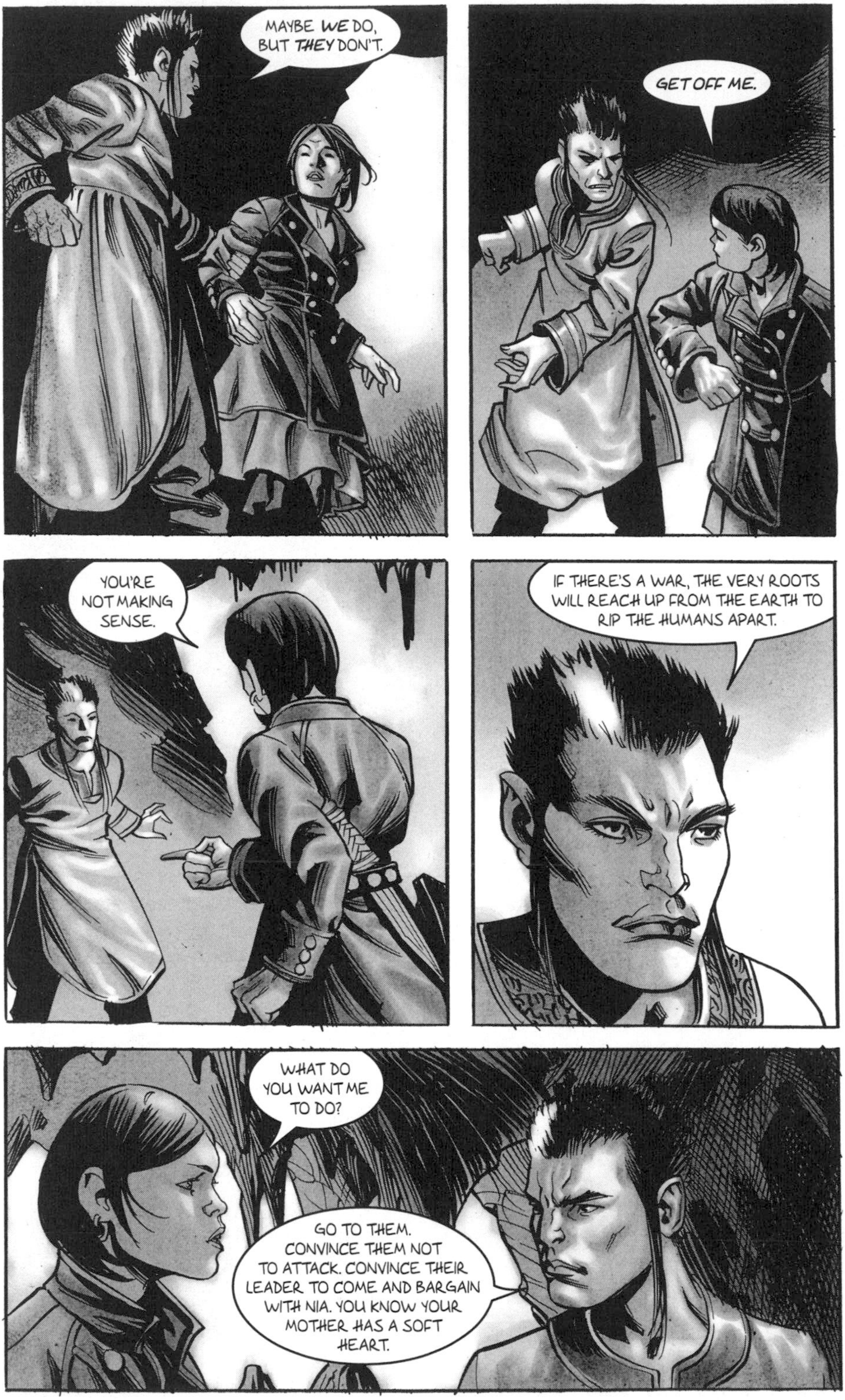
MAYBE WE DO, BUT THEY DON'T.
GET OFF ME.
YOU'RE NOT MAKING SENSE.
IF THERE'S A WAR, THE VERY ROOTS WILL REACH UP FROM THE EARTH TO RIP THE HUMANS APART.
WHAT DO YOU WANT ME TO DO?
GO TO THEM. CONVINCE THEM NOT TO ATTACK. CONVINCE THEIR LEADER TO COME AND BARGAIN WITH NIA. YOU KNOW YOUR MOTHER HAS A SOFT HEART.

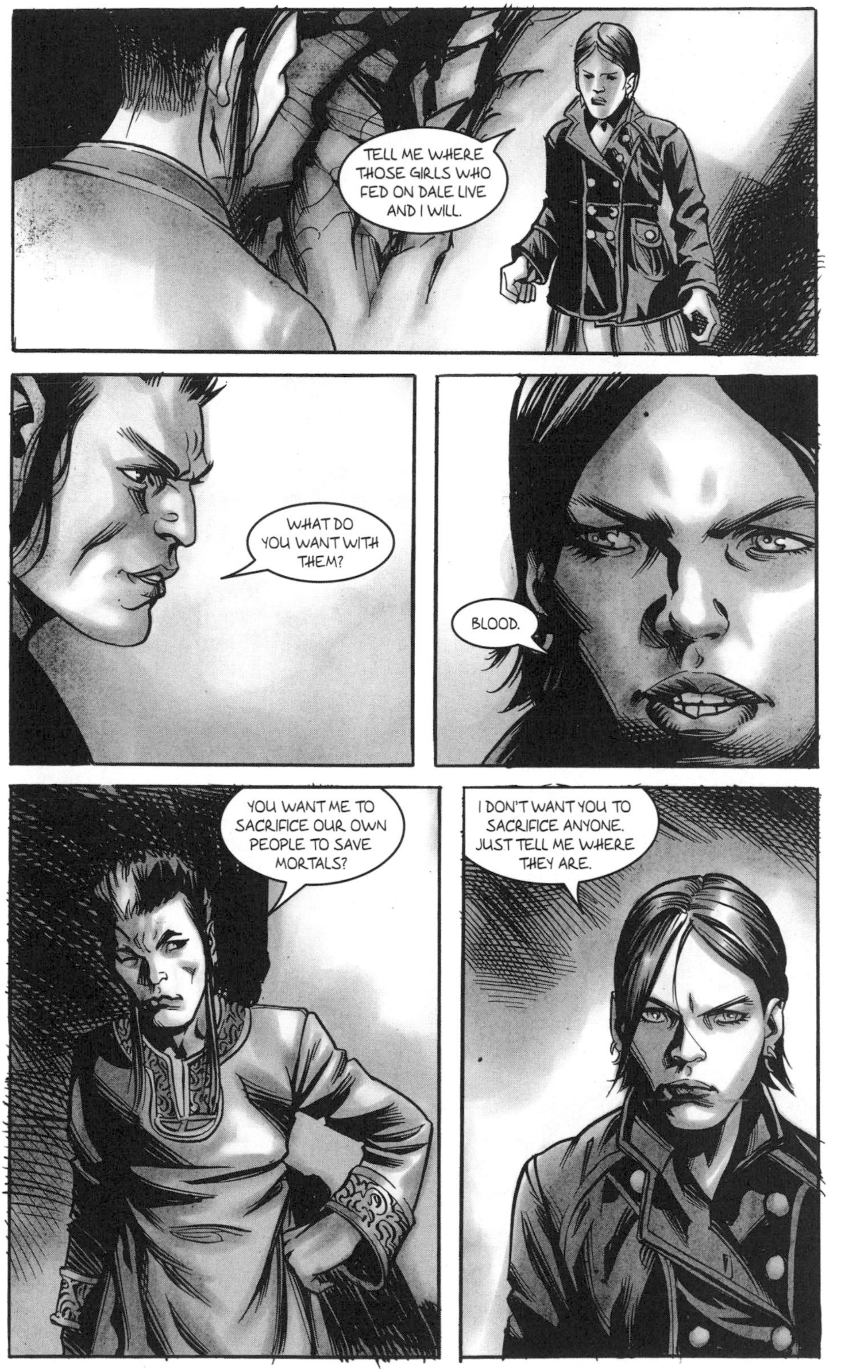
TELL ME WHERE THOSE GIRLS WHO FED ON DALE LIVE AND I WILL.
WHAT DO YOU WANT WITH THEM?
BLOOD.
YOU WANT ME TO SACRIFICE OUR OWN PEOPLE TO SAVE MORTALS?
I DON'T WANT YOU TO SACRIFICE ANYONE. JUST TELL ME WHERE THEY ARE.

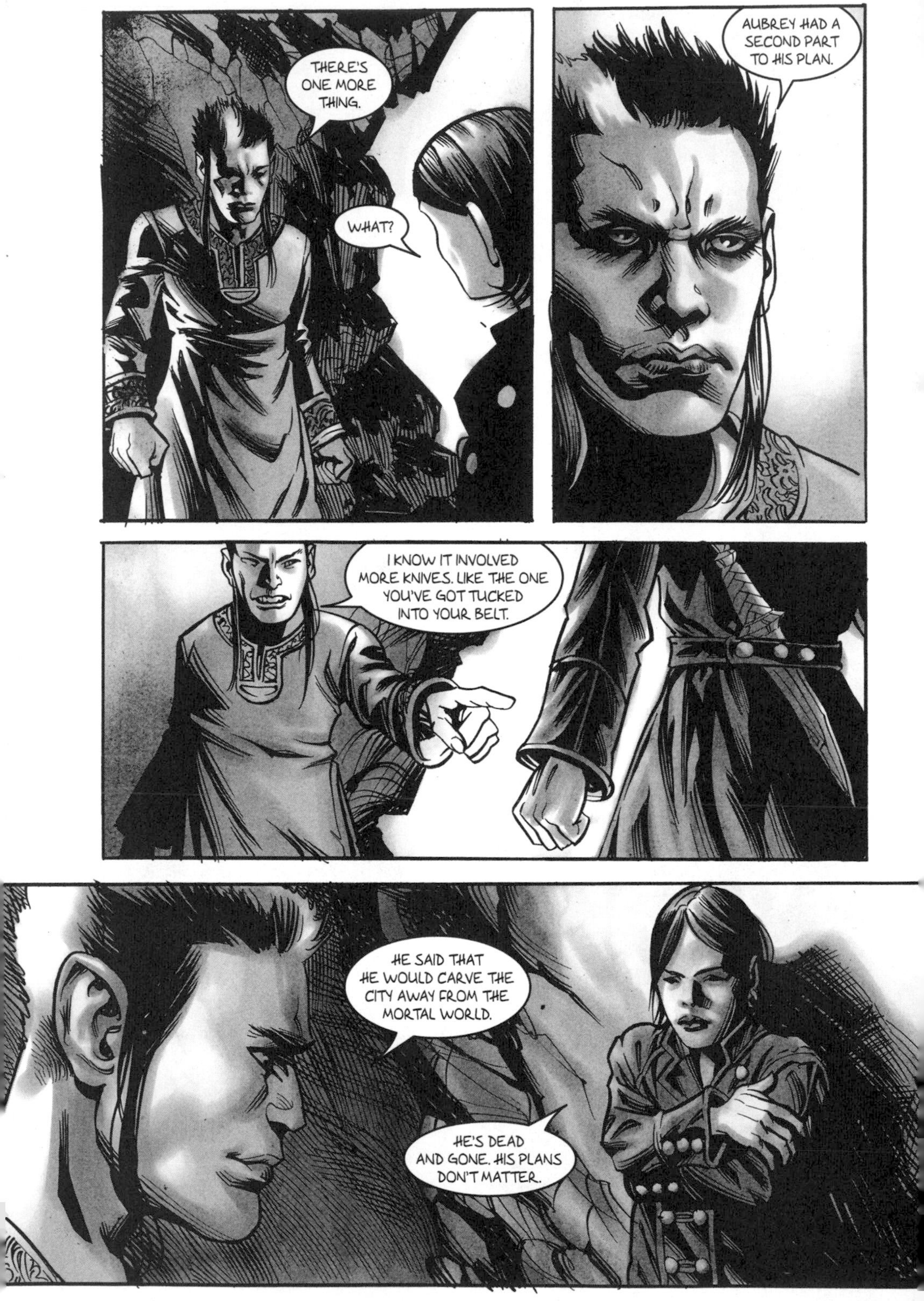
THERE'S ONE MORE THING.
WHAT?
AUBREY HAD A SECOND PART TO HIS PLAN.
I KNOW IT INVOLVED MORE KNIVES. LIKE THE ONE YOU'VE GOT TUCKED INTO YOUR BELT.
HE SAID THAT HE WOULD CARVE THE CITY AWAY FROM THE MORTAL WORLD.
HE'S DEAD AND GONE. HIS PLANS DON'T MATTER.

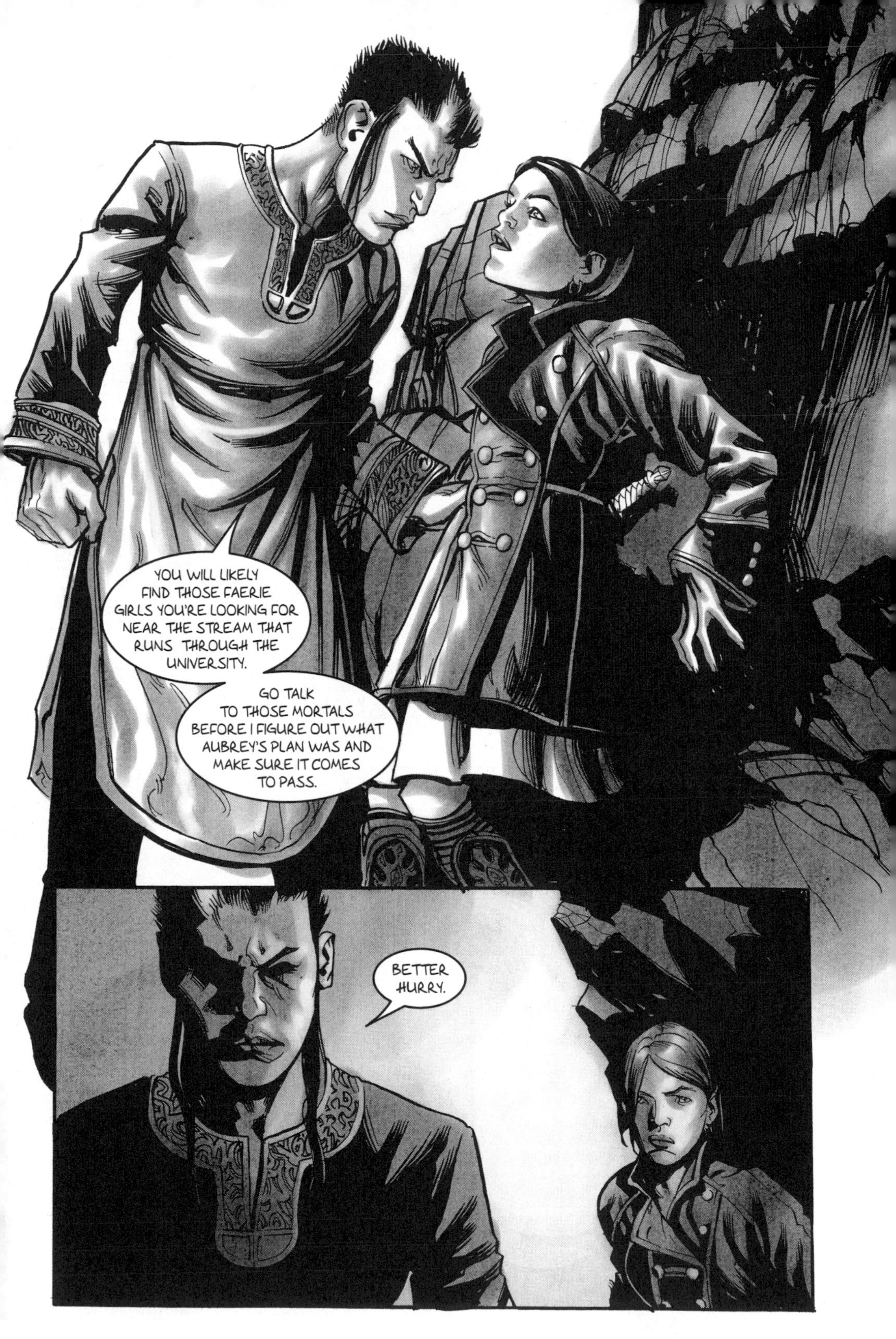
YOU WILL LIKELY FIND THOSE FAERIE GIRLS YOU'RE LOOKING FOR NEAR THE STREAM THAT RUNS THROUGH THE UNIVERSITY.
GO TALK TO THOSE MORTALS BEFORE I FIGURE OUT WHAT AUBREY'S PLAN WAS AND MAKE SURE IT COMES TO PASS.
BETTER HURRY.

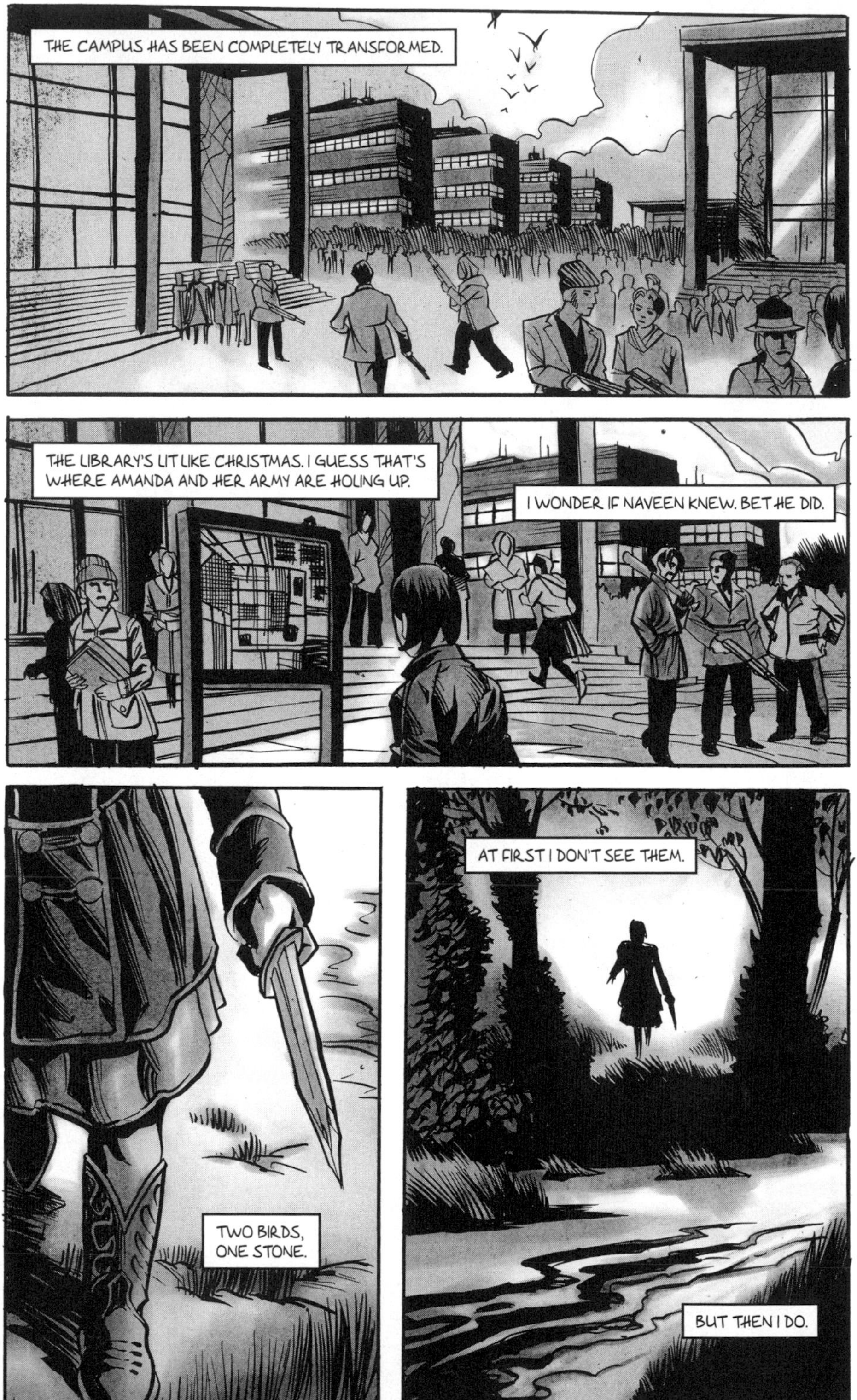
THE CAMPUS HAS BEEN COMPLETELY TRANSFORMED.
THE LIBRARY'S LIT LIKE CHRISTMAS. I GUESS THAT'S WHERE AMANDA AND HER ARMY ARE HOLING UP.
I WONDER IF NAVEEN KNEW. BET HE DID.
TWO BIRDS, ONE STONE.
AT FIRST I DON'T SEE THEM.
BUT THEN I DO.

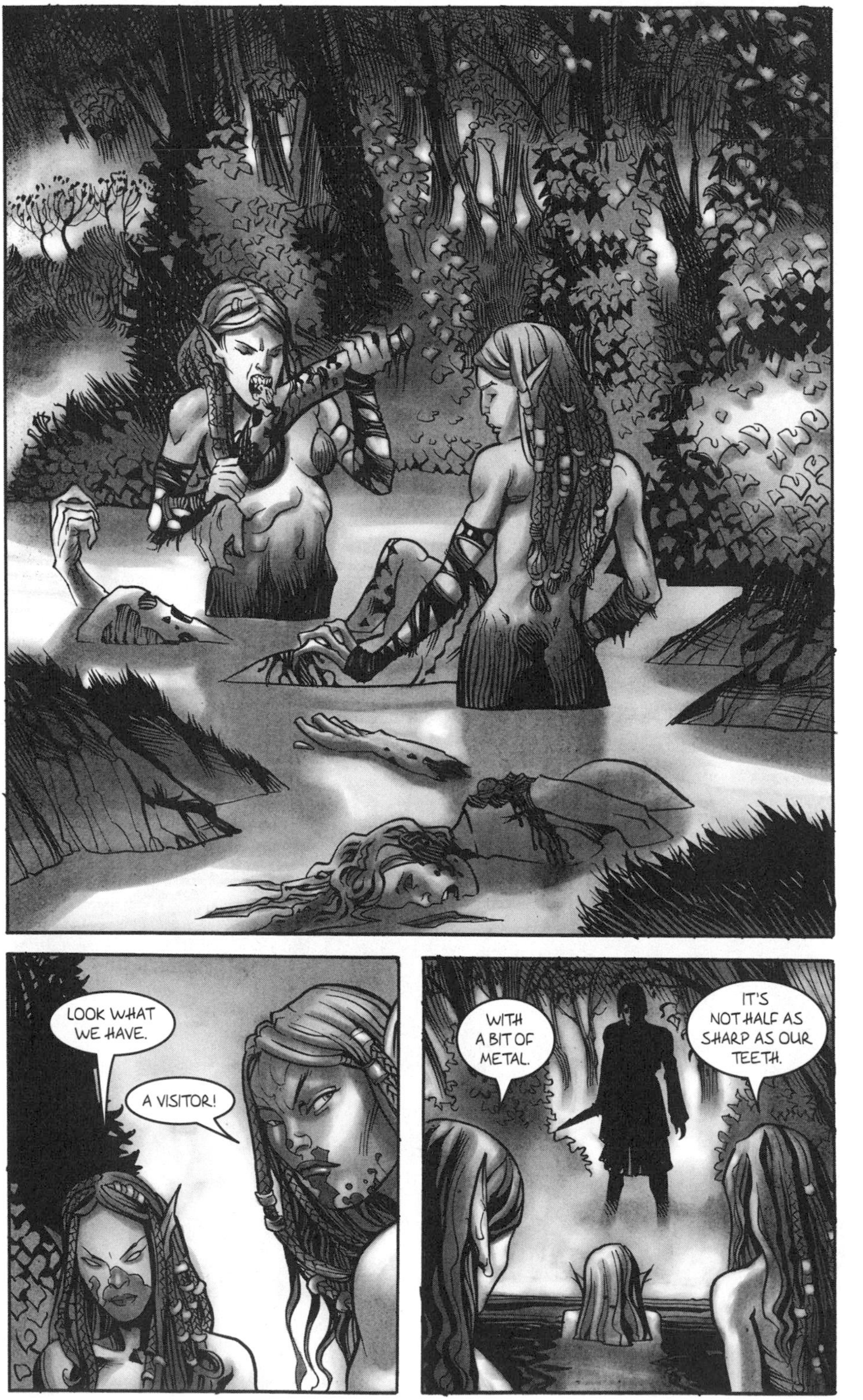
LOOK WHAT WE HAVE.
A VISITOR!
WITH A BIT OF METAL.
IT'S NOT HALF AS SHARP AS OUR TEETH.

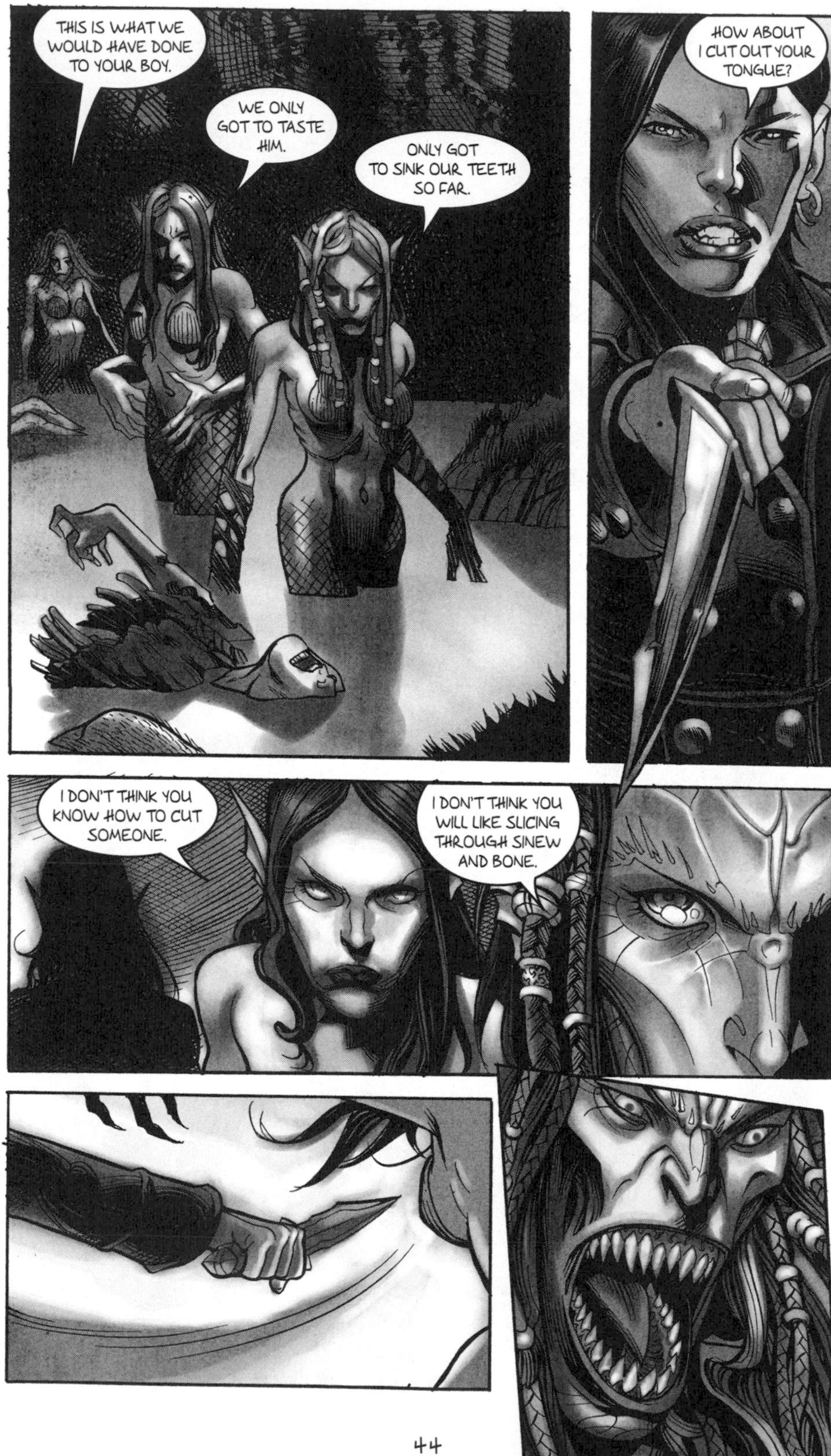
THIS IS WHAT WE WOULD HAVE DONE TO YOUR BOY.
WE ONLY GOT TO TASTE HIM.
ONLY GOT TO SINK OUR TEETH SO FAR.
HOW ABOUT I CUT OUT YOUR TONGUE?
I DON'T THINK YOU KNOW HOW TO CUT SOMEONE.
I DON'T THINK YOU WILL LIKE SLICING THROUGH SINEW AND BONE.

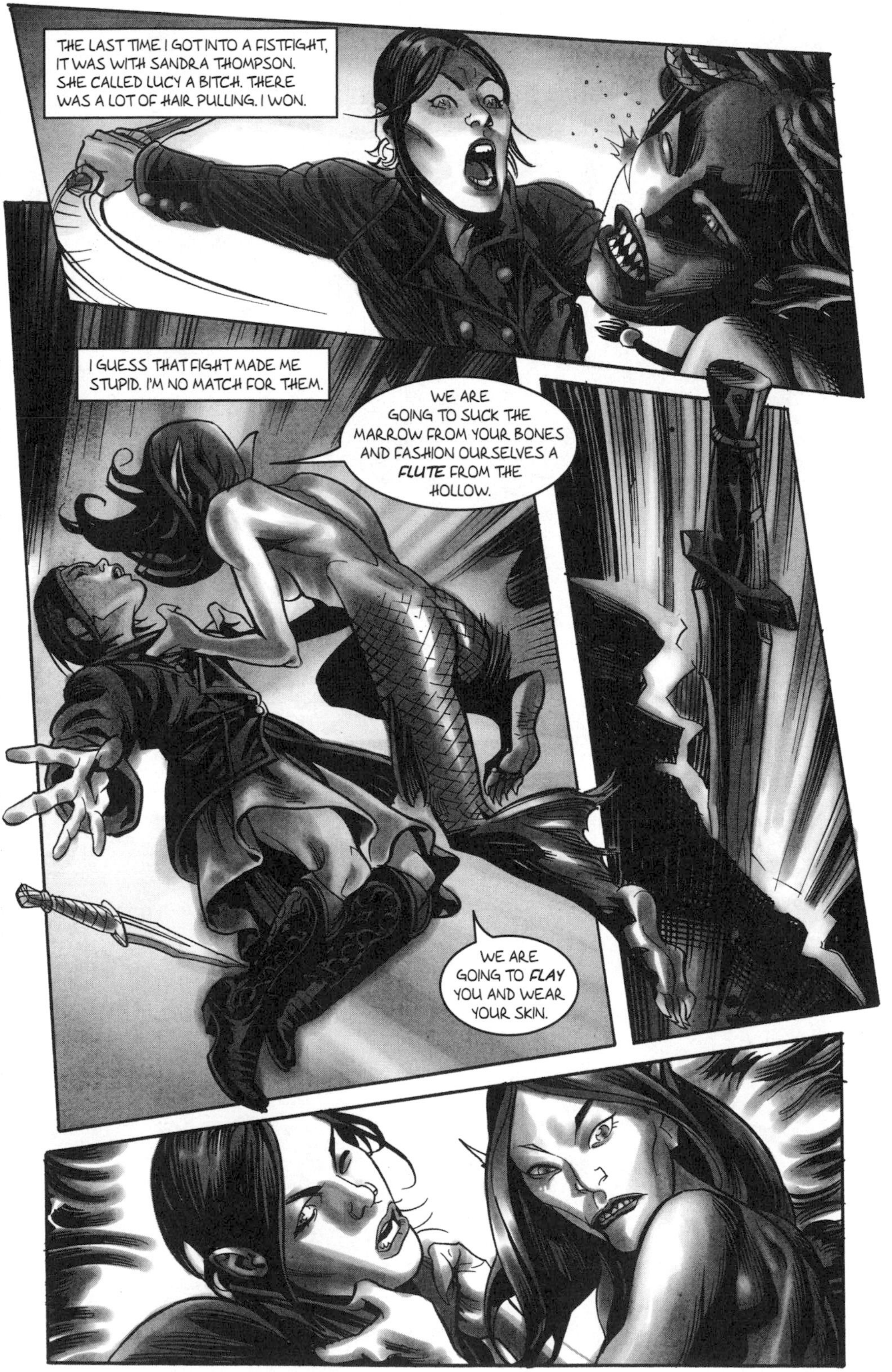
THE LAST TIME I GOT INTO A FISTFIGHT, IT WAS WITH SANDRA THOMPSON. SHE CALLED LUCY A BITCH. THERE WAS A LOT OF HAIR PULLING. I WON.
I GUESS THAT FIGHT MADE ME STUPID. I'M NO MATCH FOR THEM.
WE ARE GOING TO SUCK THE MARROW FROM YOUR BONES AND FASHION OURSELVES A *FLUTE* FROM THE HOLLOW.
WE ARE GOING TO *FLAY* YOU AND WEAR YOUR SKIN.

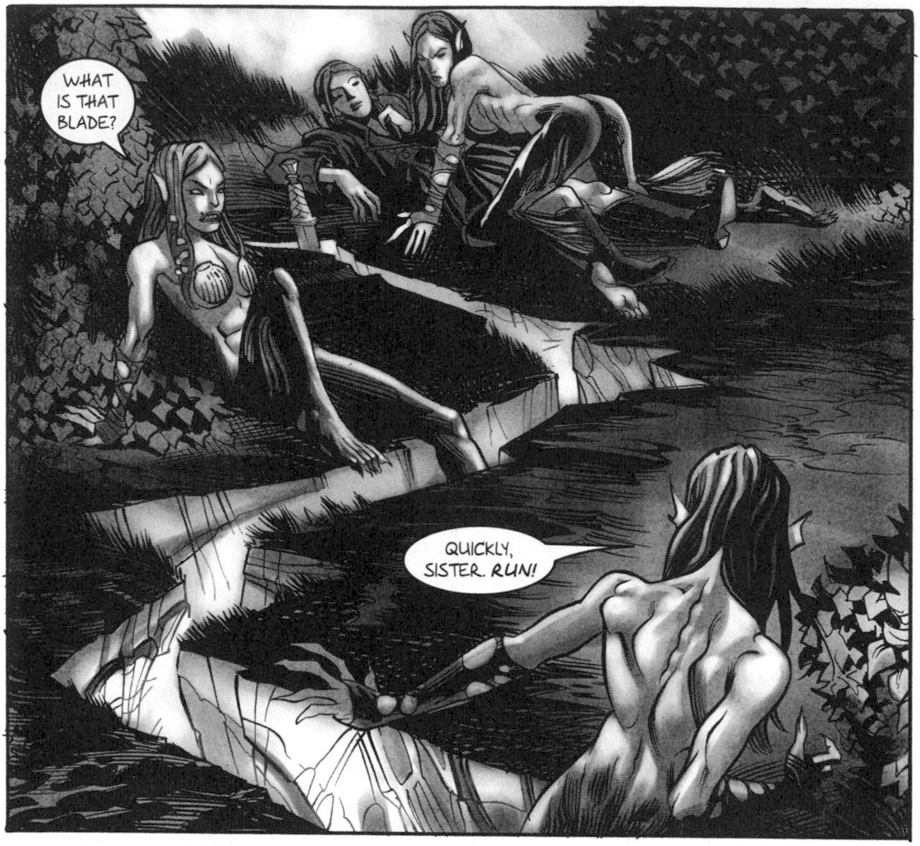
WHAT IS THAT BLADE?
QUICKLY, SISTER. RUN!

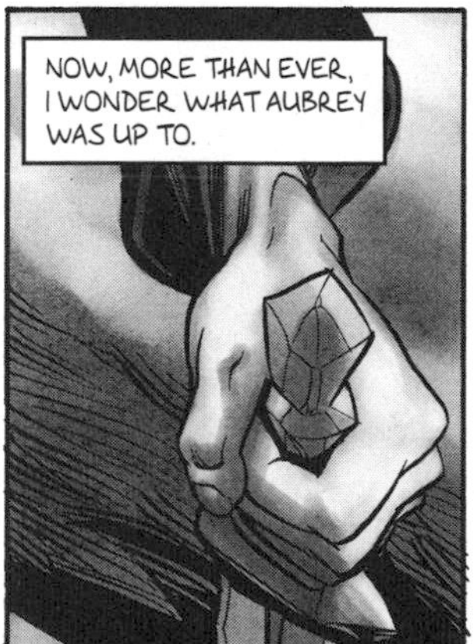
NOW, MORE THAN EVER, I WONDER WHAT AUBREY WAS UP TO.

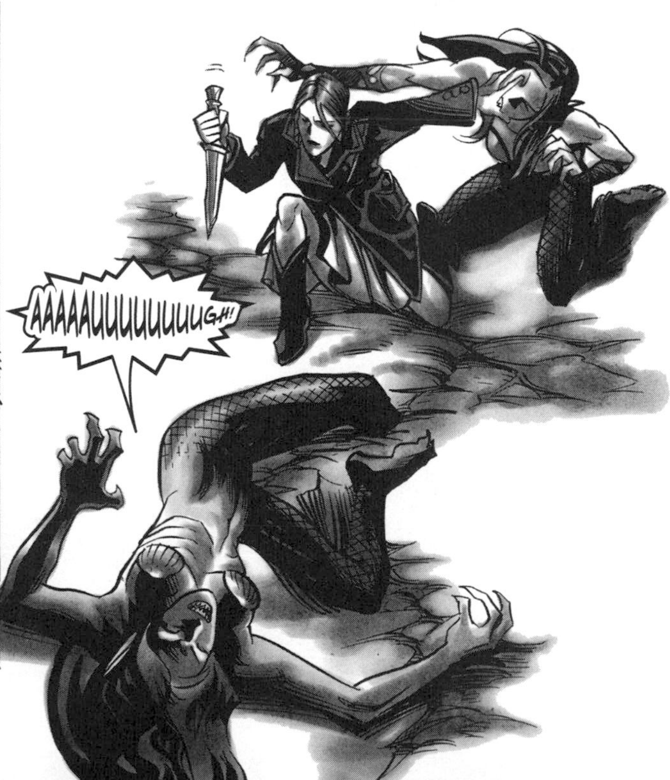
AAAAAUUUUUUUUGH!

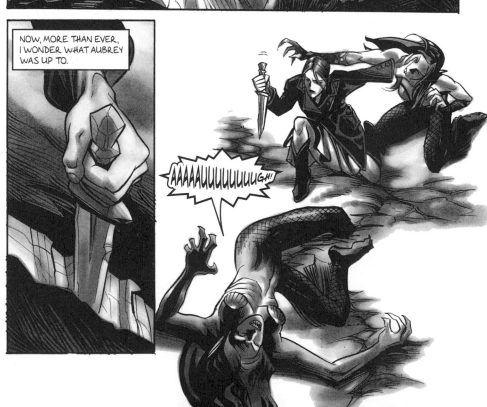

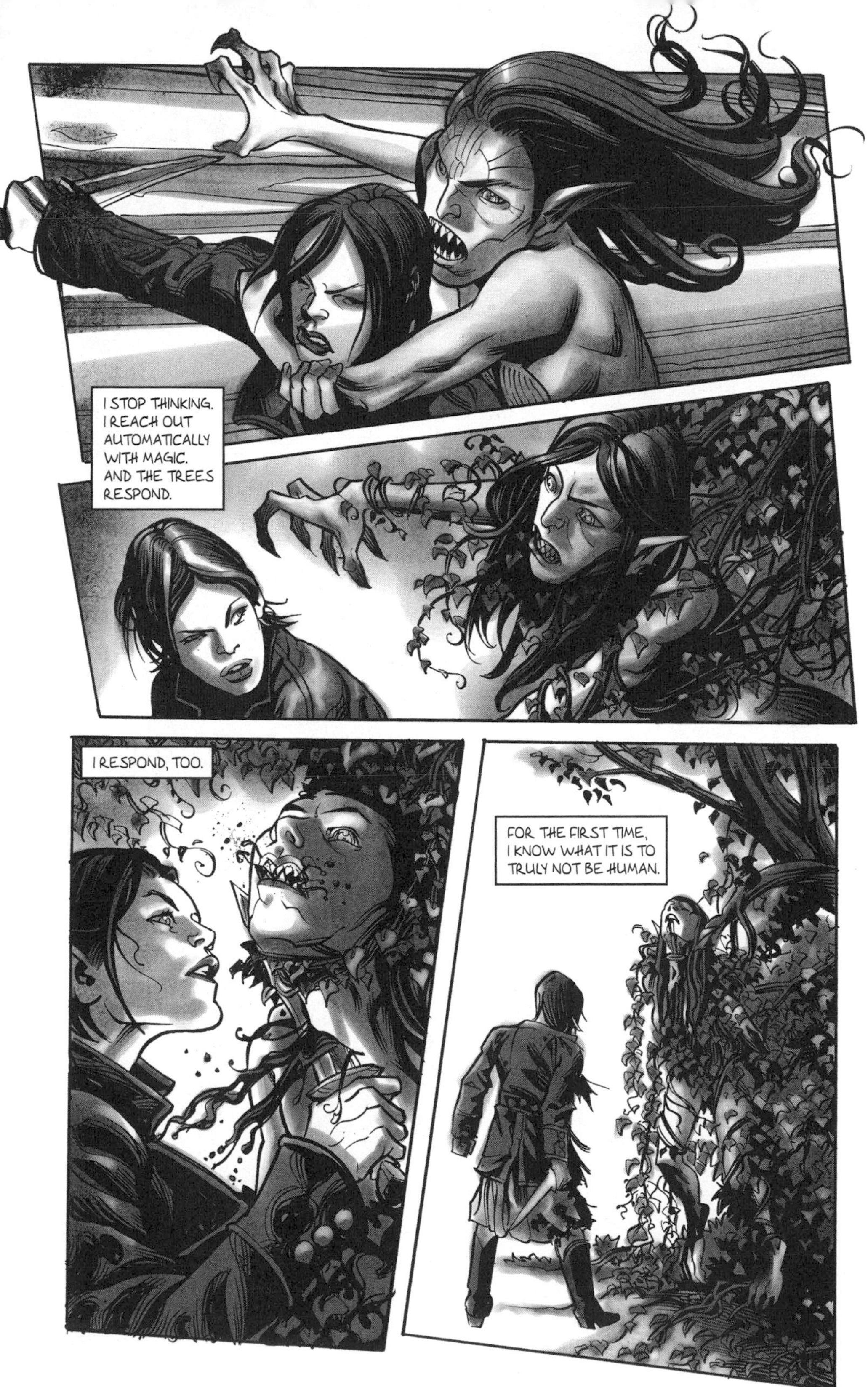
I STOP THINKING. I REACH OUT AUTOMATICALLY WITH MAGIC. AND THE TREES RESPOND.
I RESPOND, TOO.
FOR THE FIRST TIME, I KNOW WHAT IT IS TO TRULY NOT BE HUMAN.

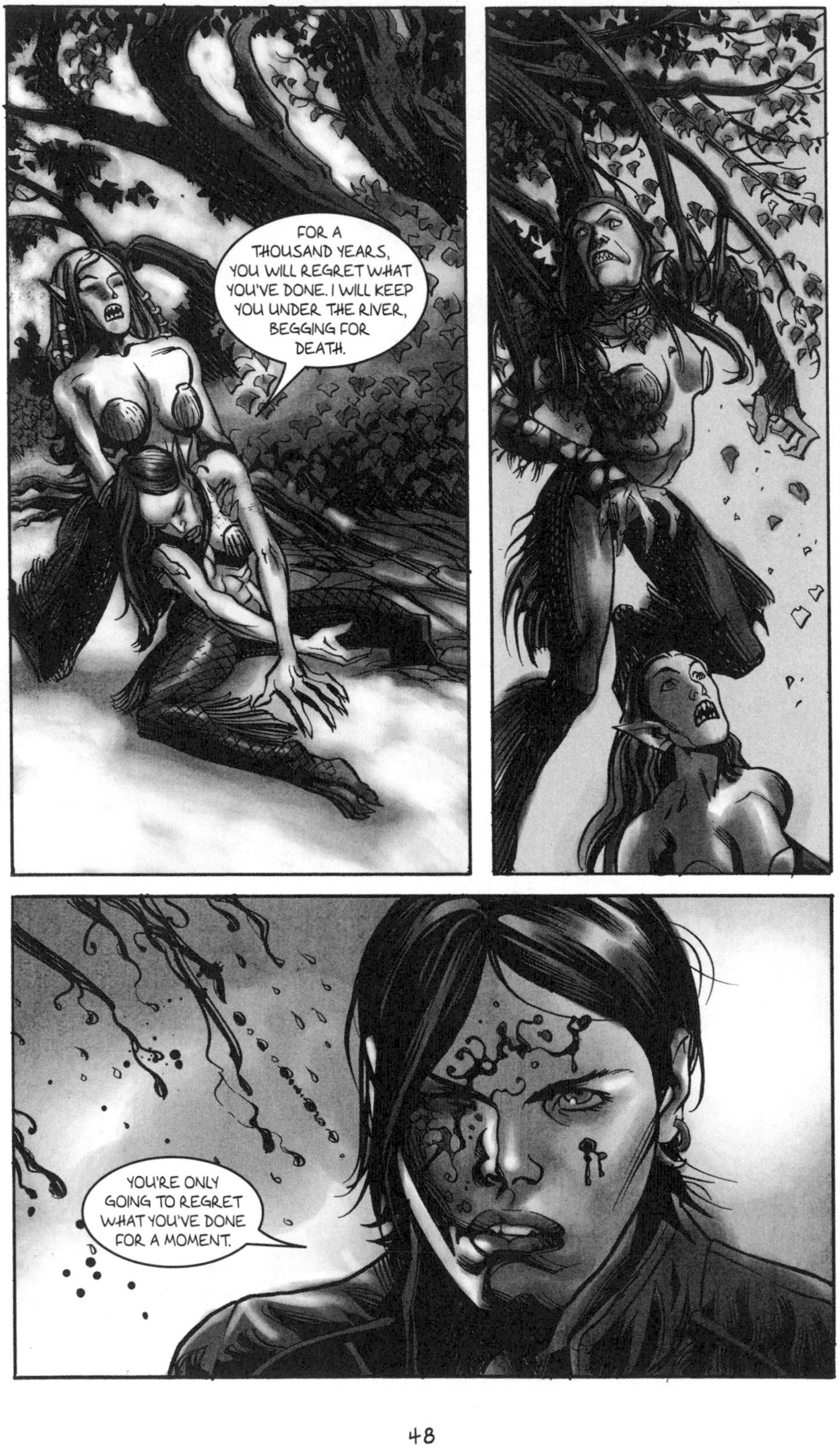
FOR A THOUSAND YEARS, YOU WILL REGRET WHAT YOU'VE DONE. I WILL KEEP YOU UNDER THE RIVER, BEGGING FOR DEATH.
YOU'RE ONLY GOING TO REGRET WHAT YOU'VE DONE FOR A MOMENT.

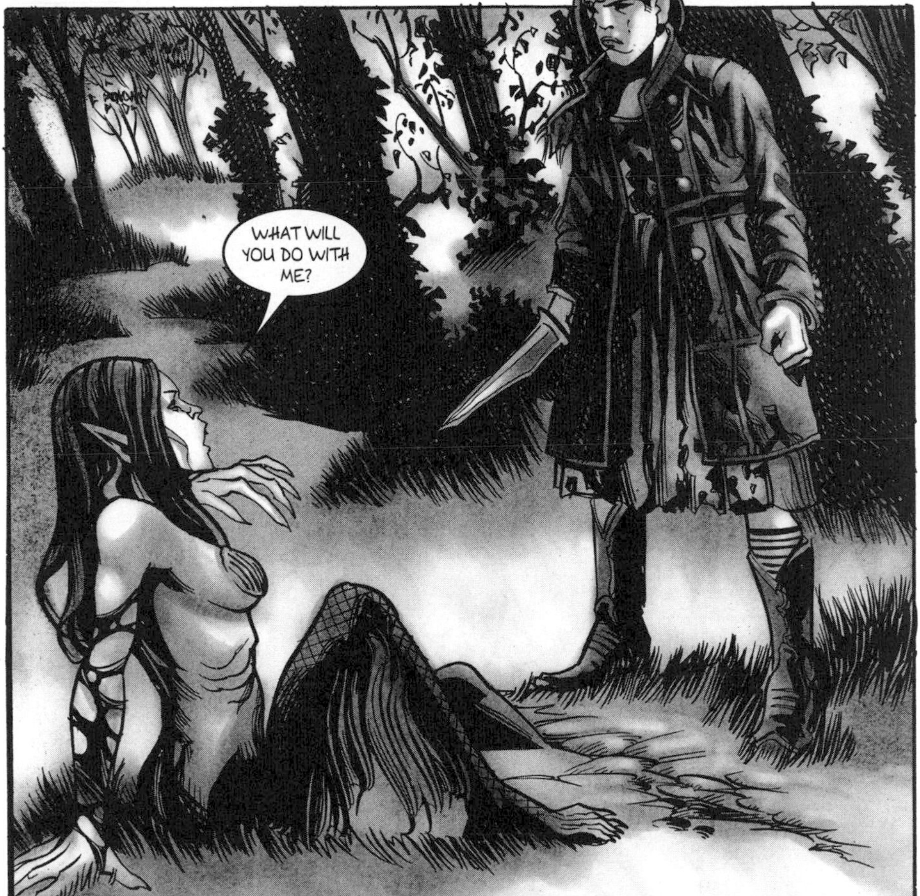
WHAT WILL YOU DO WITH ME?

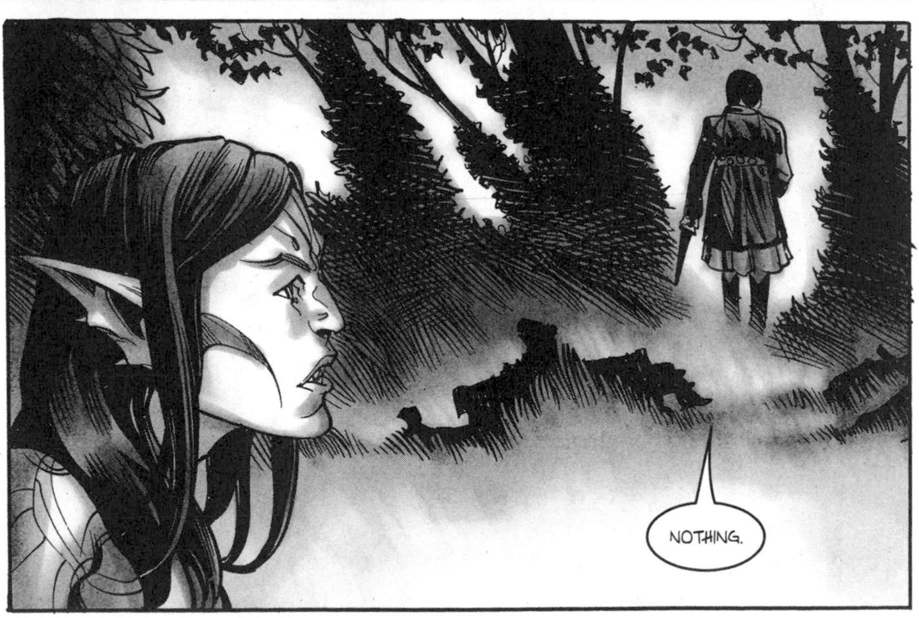
NOTHING.

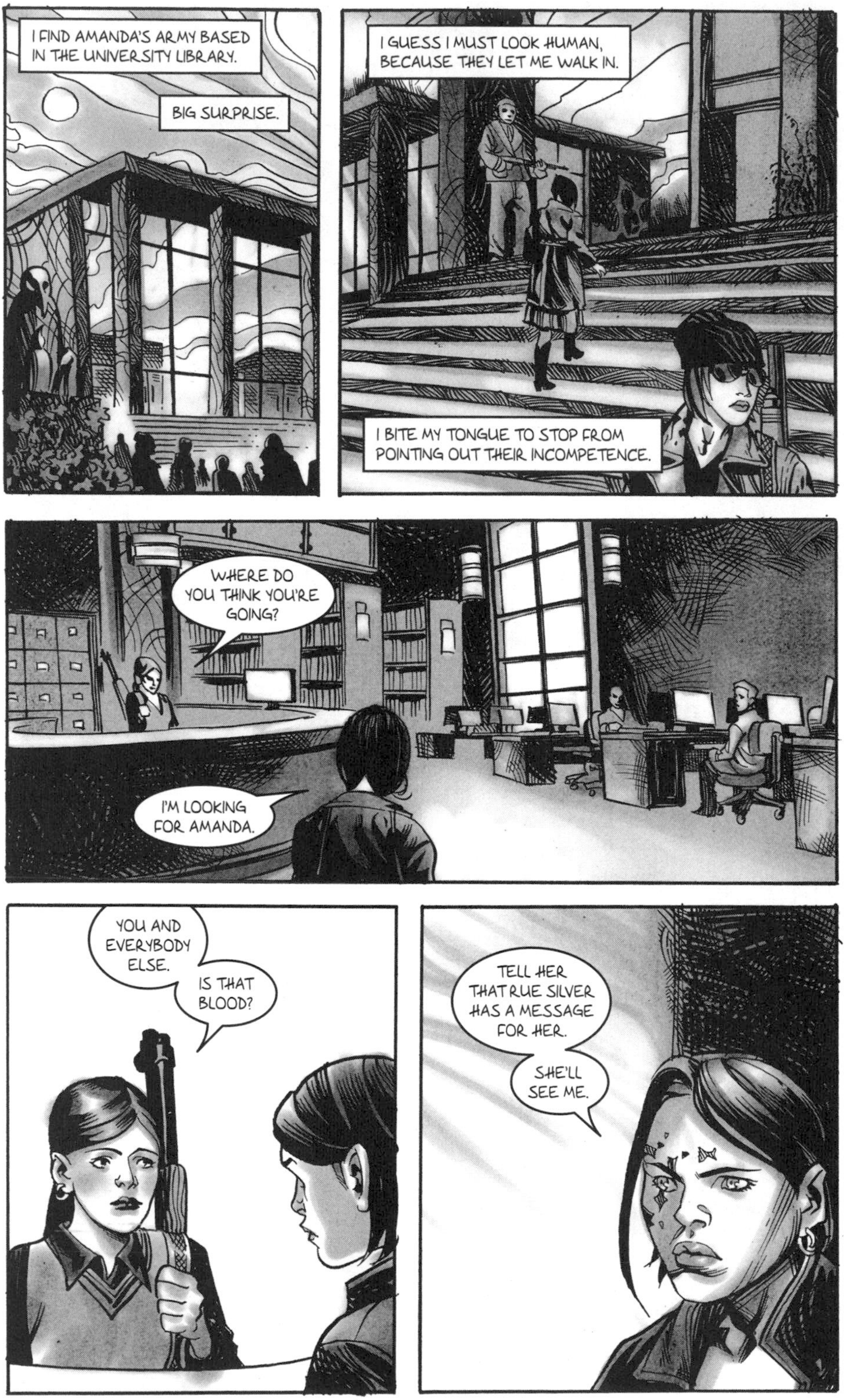
I FIND AMANDA'S ARMY BASED IN THE UNIVERSITY LIBRARY.
BIG SURPRISE.
I GUESS I MUST LOOK HUMAN, BECAUSE THEY LET ME WALK IN.
I BITE MY TONGUE TO STOP FROM POINTING OUT THEIR INCOMPETENCE.
WHERE DO YOU THINK YOU'RE GOING?
I'M LOOKING FOR AMANDA.
YOU AND EVERYBODY ELSE.
IS THAT BLOOD?
TELL HER THAT RUE SILVER HAS A MESSAGE FOR HER.
SHE'LL SEE ME.

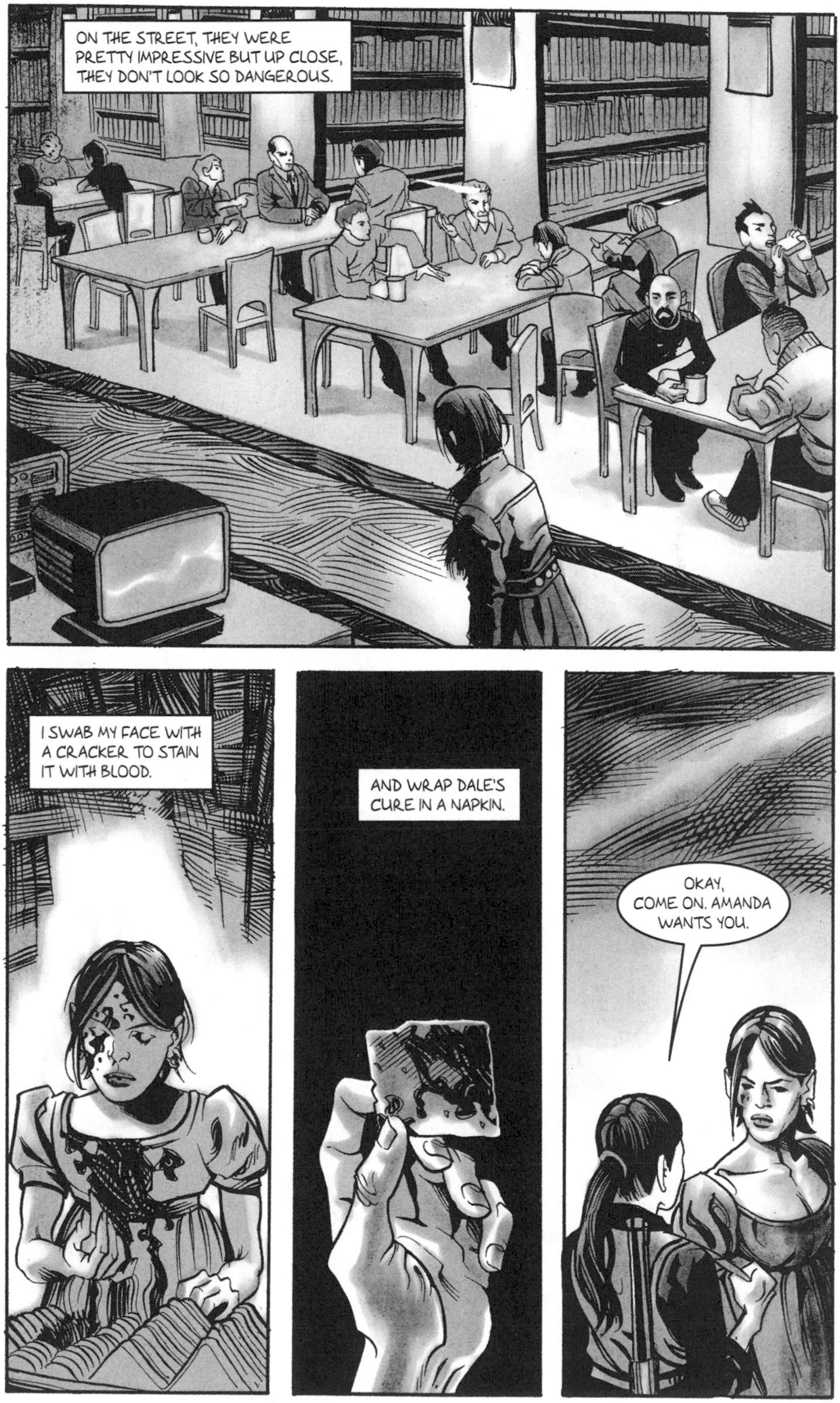
ON THE STREET, THEY WERE PRETTY IMPRESSIVE BUT UP CLOSE, THEY DON'T LOOK SO DANGEROUS.
I SWAB MY FACE WITH A CRACKER TO STAIN IT WITH BLOOD.
AND WRAP DALE'S CURE IN A NAPKIN.
OKAY, COME ON. AMANDA WANTS YOU.

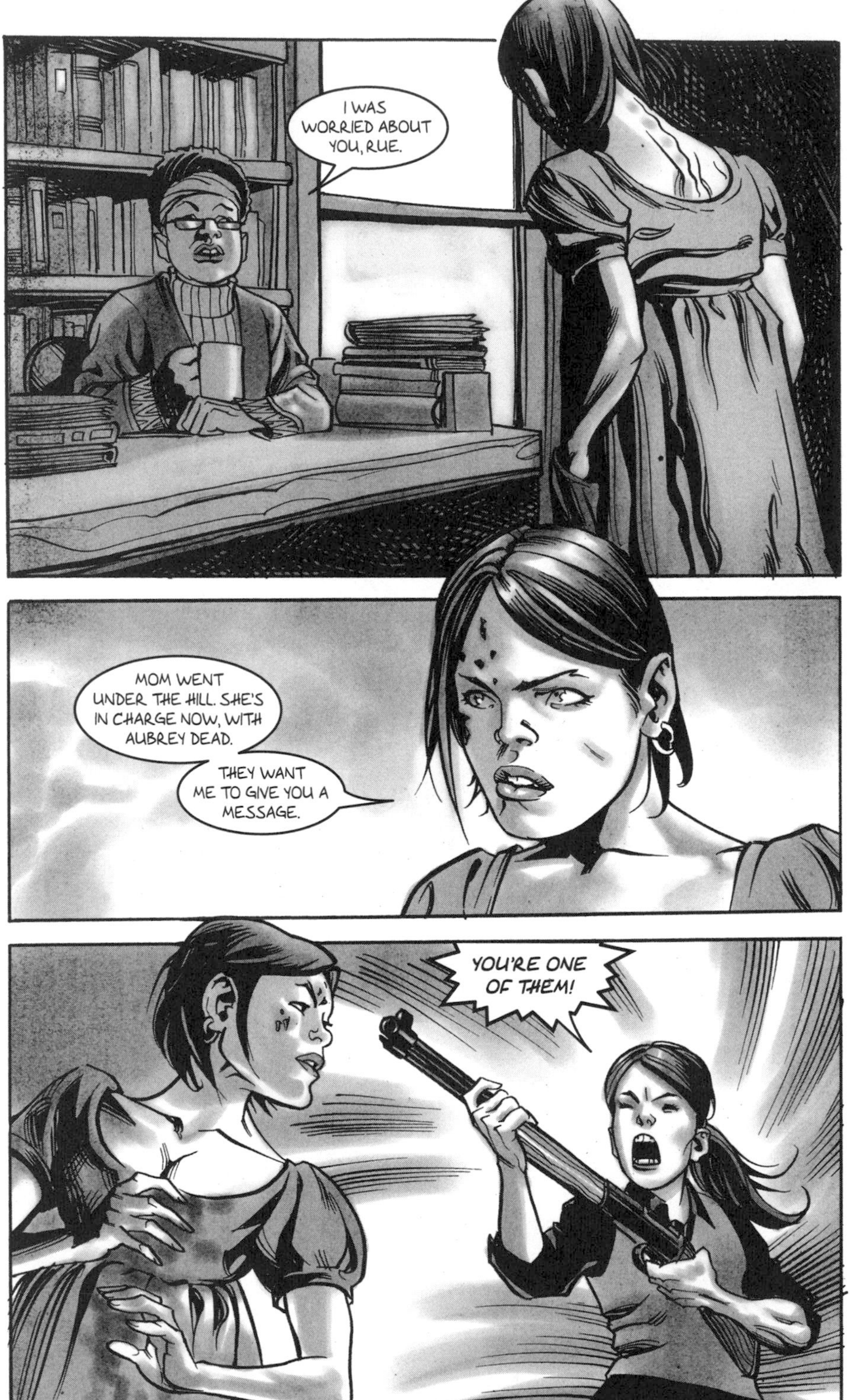
I WAS WORRIED ABOUT YOU, RUE.
MOM WENT UNDER THE HILL. SHE'S IN CHARGE NOW, WITH AUBREY DEAD.
THEY WANT ME TO GIVE YOU A MESSAGE.
YOU'RE ONE OF THEM!

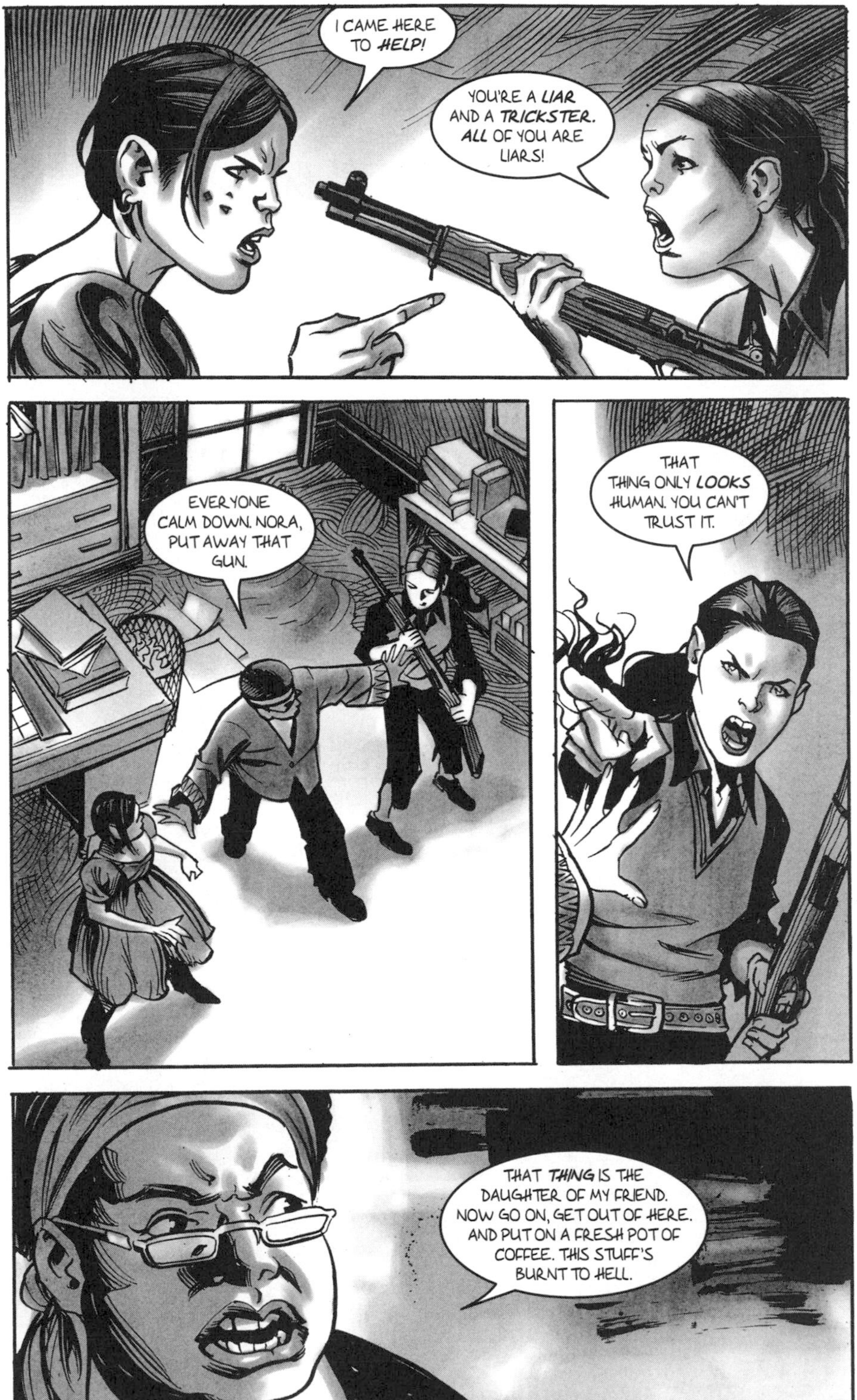
I CAME HERE TO HELP!
YOU'RE A LIAR AND A TRICKSTER. ALL OF YOU ARE LIARS!
EVERYONE CALM DOWN. NORA, PUT AWAY THAT GUN.
THAT THING ONLY LOOKS HUMAN. YOU CAN'T TRUST IT.
THAT THING IS THE DAUGHTER OF MY FRIEND. NOW GO ON, GET OUT OF HERE. AND PUT ON A FRESH POT OF COFFEE. THIS STUFF'S BURNT TO HELL.

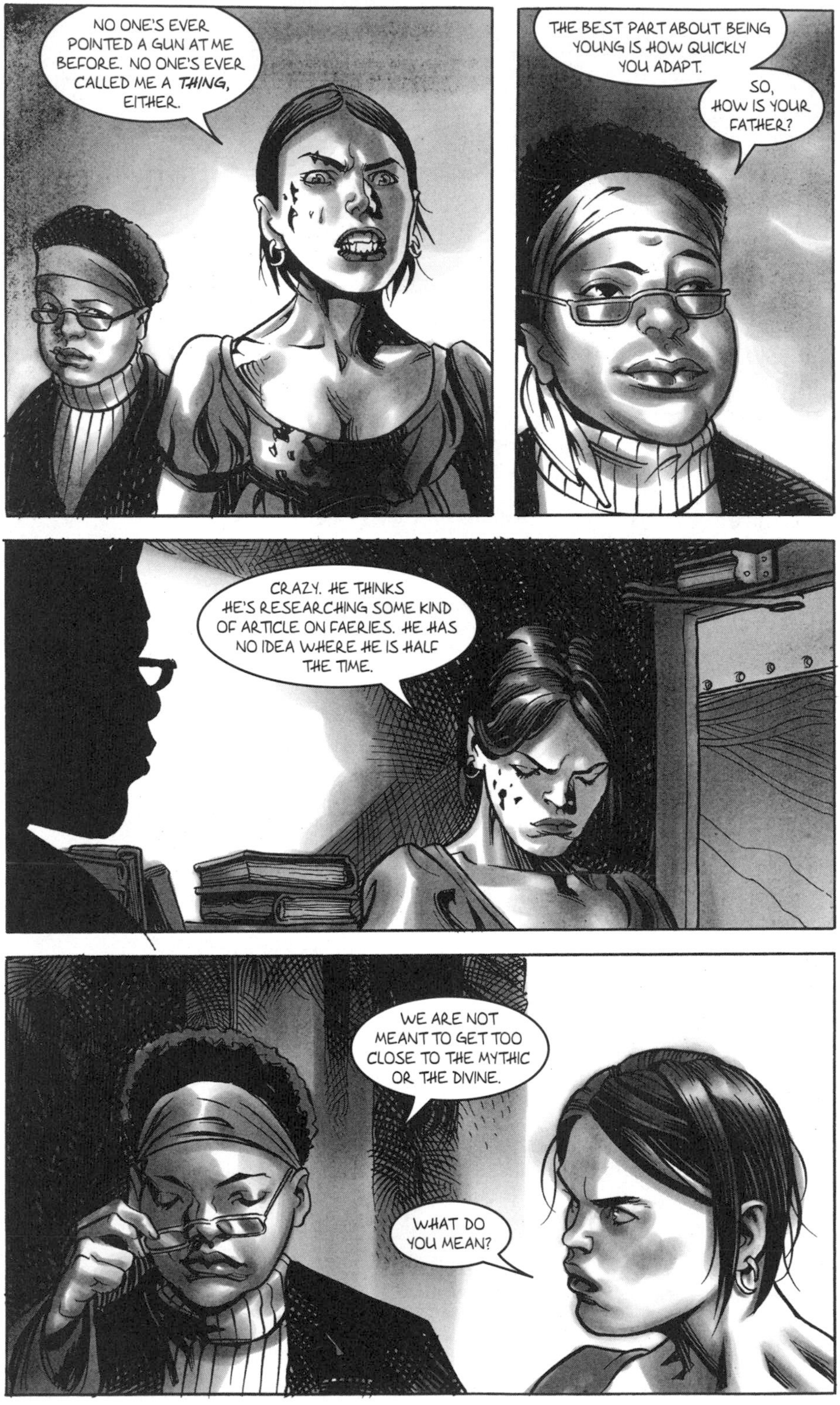
NO ONE'S EVER POINTED A GUN AT ME BEFORE. NO ONE'S EVER CALLED ME A *THING*, EITHER.
THE BEST PART ABOUT BEING YOUNG IS HOW QUICKLY YOU ADAPT.
SO, HOW IS YOUR FATHER?
CRAZY. HE THINKS HE'S RESEARCHING SOME KIND OF ARTICLE ON FAERIES. HE HAS NO IDEA WHERE HE IS HALF THE TIME.
WE ARE NOT MEANT TO GET TOO CLOSE TO THE MYTHIC OR THE DIVINE.
WHAT DO YOU MEAN?

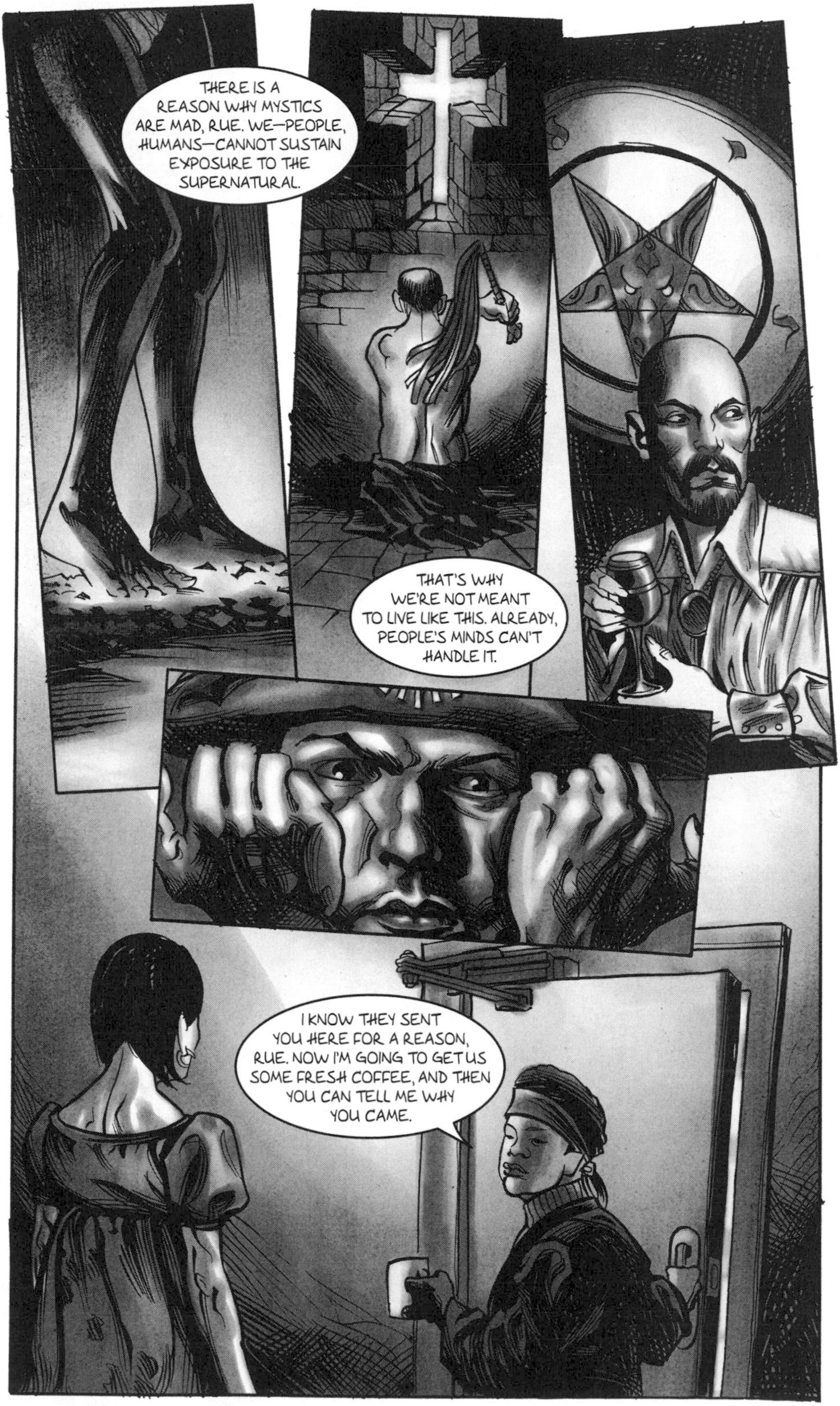
THERE IS A REASON WHY MYSTICS ARE MAD, RUE. WE—PEOPLE, HUMANS—CANNOT SUSTAIN EXPOSURE TO THE SUPERNATURAL.
THAT'S WHY WE'RE NOT MEANT TO LIVE LIKE THIS. ALREADY, PEOPLE'S MINDS CAN'T HANDLE IT.
I KNOW THEY SENT YOU HERE FOR A REASON, RUE. NOW I'M GOING TO GET US SOME FRESH COFFEE, AND THEN YOU CAN TELL ME WHY YOU CAME.

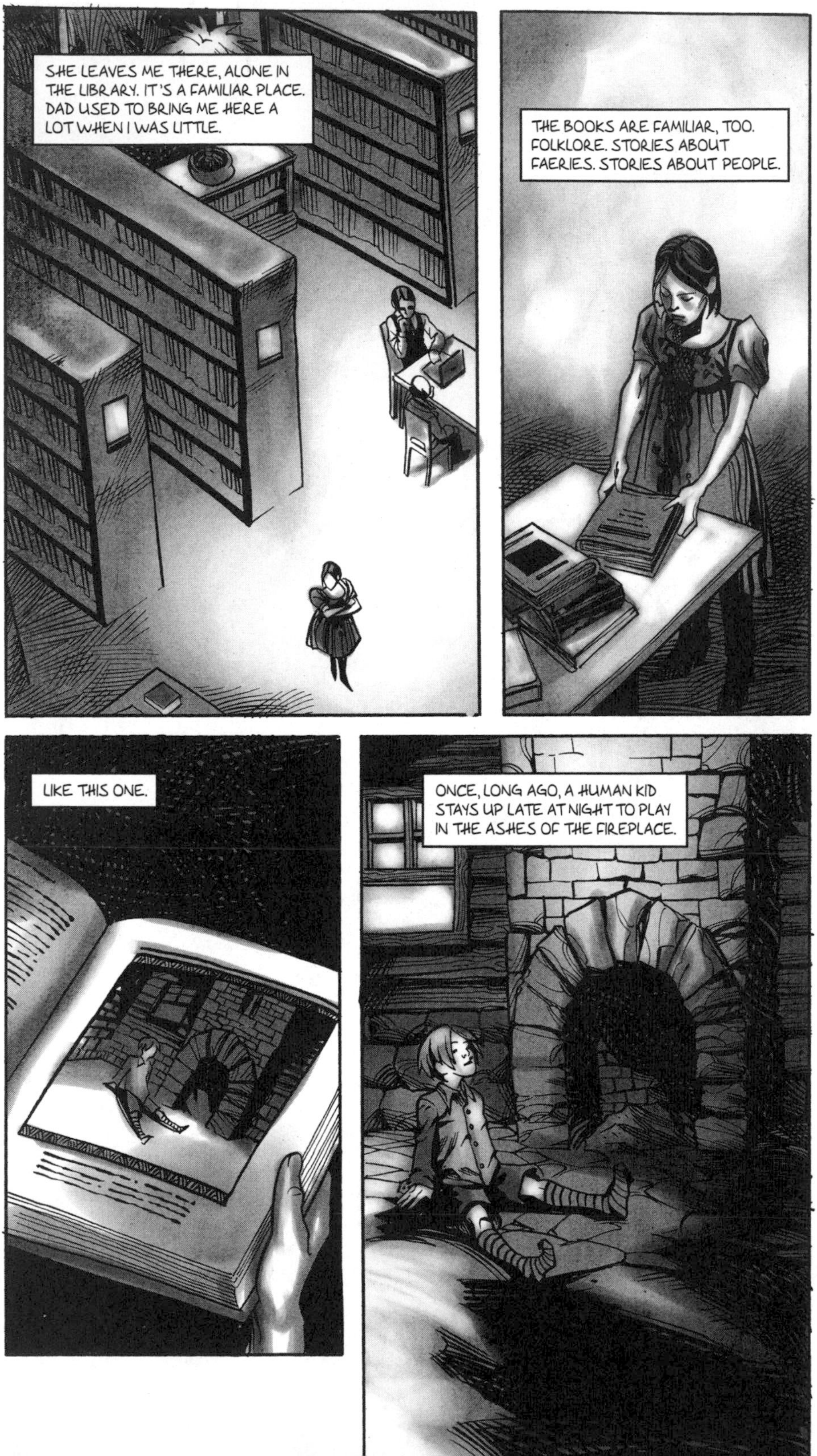
SHE LEAVES ME THERE, ALONE IN THE LIBRARY. IT'S A FAMILIAR PLACE. DAD USED TO BRING ME HERE A LOT WHEN I WAS LITTLE.
THE BOOKS ARE FAMILIAR, TOO. FOLKLORE. STORIES ABOUT FAERIES. STORIES ABOUT PEOPLE.
LIKE THIS ONE.
ONCE, LONG AGO, A HUMAN KID STAYS UP LATE AT NIGHT TO PLAY IN THE ASHES OF THE FIREPLACE.

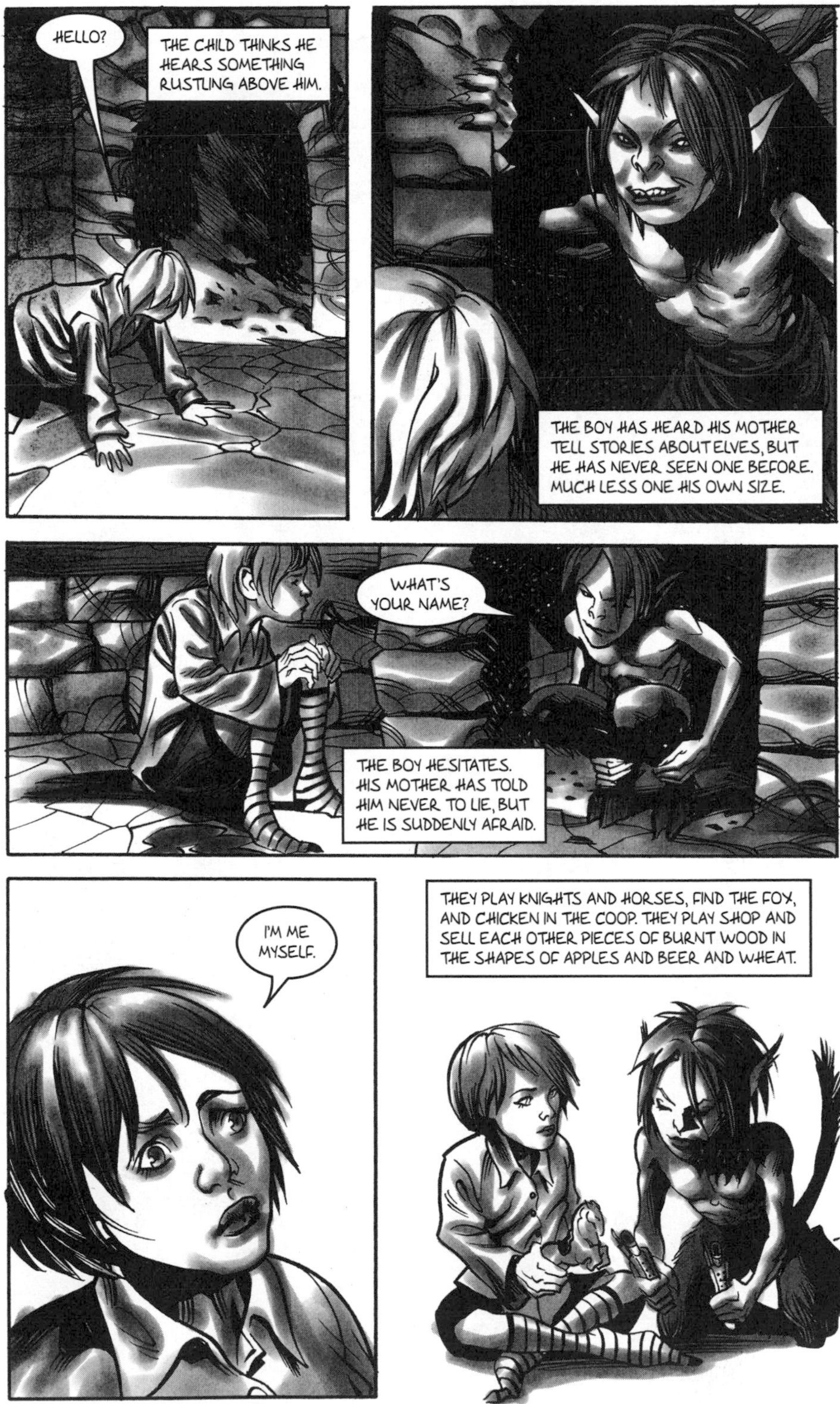
HELLO?
THE CHILD THINKS HE HEARS SOMETHING RUSTLING ABOVE HIM.
THE BOY HAS HEARD HIS MOTHER TELL STORIES ABOUT ELVES, BUT HE HAS NEVER SEEN ONE BEFORE. MUCH LESS ONE HIS OWN SIZE.
WHAT'S YOUR NAME?
THE BOY HESITATES. HIS MOTHER HAS TOLD HIM NEVER TO LIE, BUT HE IS SUDDENLY AFRAID.
I'M ME MYSELF.
THEY PLAY KNIGHTS AND HORSES, FIND THE FOX, AND CHICKEN IN THE COOP. THEY PLAY SHOP AND SELL EACH OTHER PIECES OF BURNT WOOD IN THE SHAPES OF APPLES AND BEER AND WHEAT.

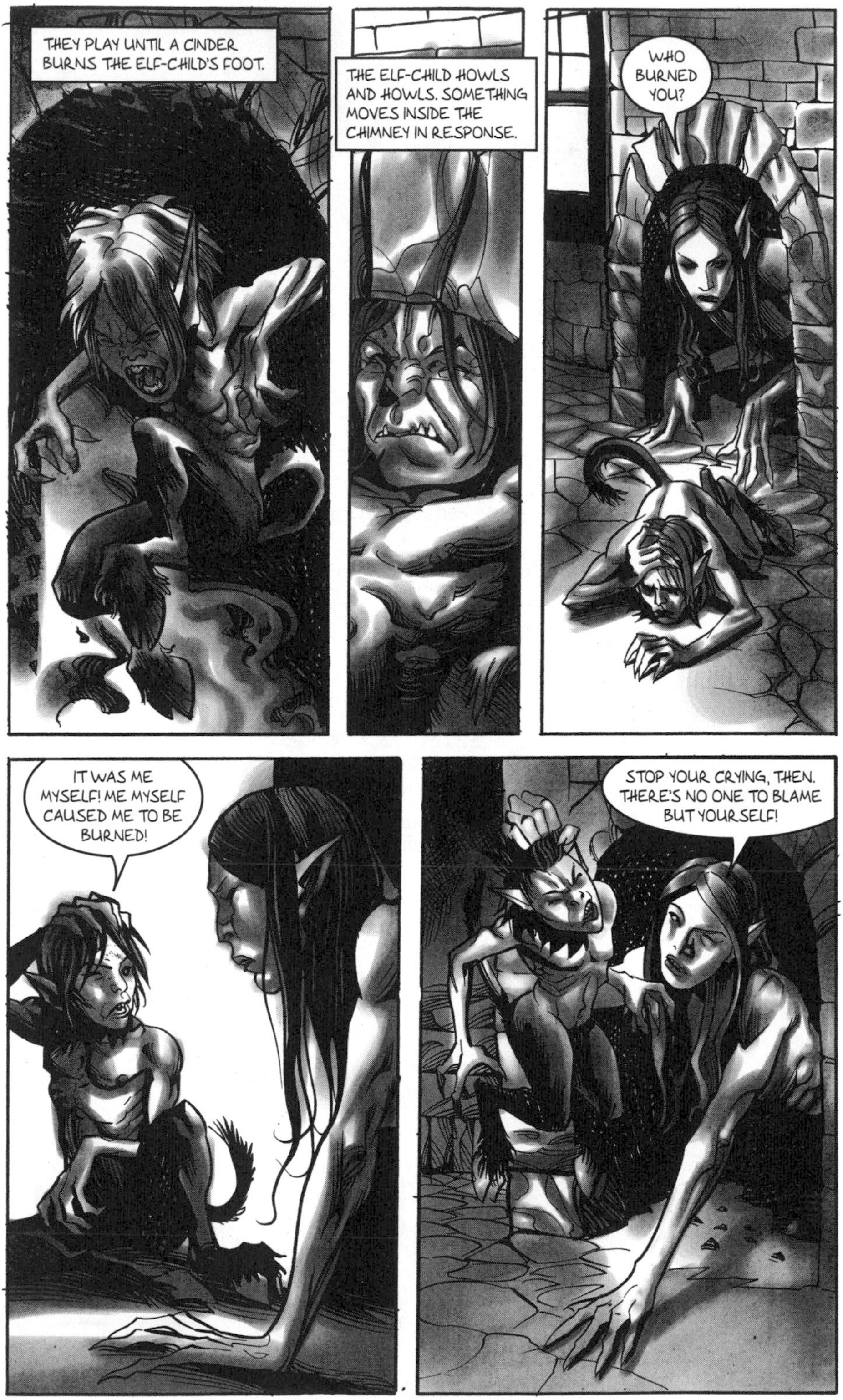
THEY PLAY UNTIL A CINDER BURNS THE ELF-CHILD'S FOOT.
THE ELF-CHILD HOWLS AND HOWLS. SOMETHING MOVES INSIDE THE CHIMNEY IN RESPONSE.
WHO BURNED YOU?
IT WAS ME MYSELF! ME MYSELF CAUSED ME TO BE BURNED!
STOP YOUR CRYING, THEN. THERE'S NO ONE TO BLAME BUT YOURSELF!

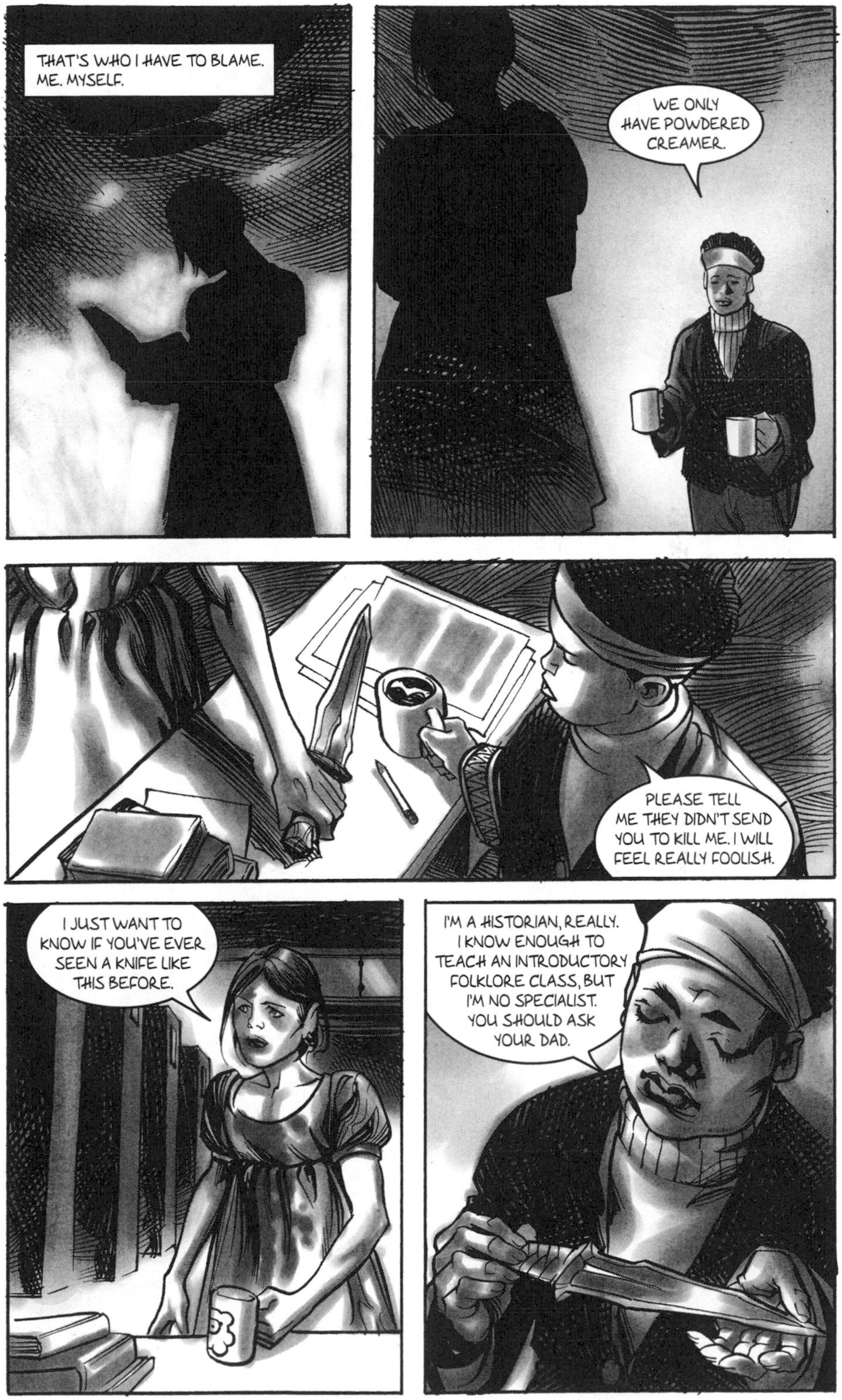
THAT'S WHO I HAVE TO BLAME. ME. MYSELF.
WE ONLY HAVE POWDERED CREAMER.
PLEASE TELL ME THEY DIDN'T SEND YOU TO KILL ME. I WILL FEEL REALLY FOOLISH.
I JUST WANT TO KNOW IF YOU'VE EVER SEEN A KNIFE LIKE THIS BEFORE.
I'M A HISTORIAN, REALLY. I KNOW ENOUGH TO TEACH AN INTRODUCTORY FOLKLORE CLASS, BUT I'M NO SPECIALIST. YOU SHOULD ASK YOUR DAD.

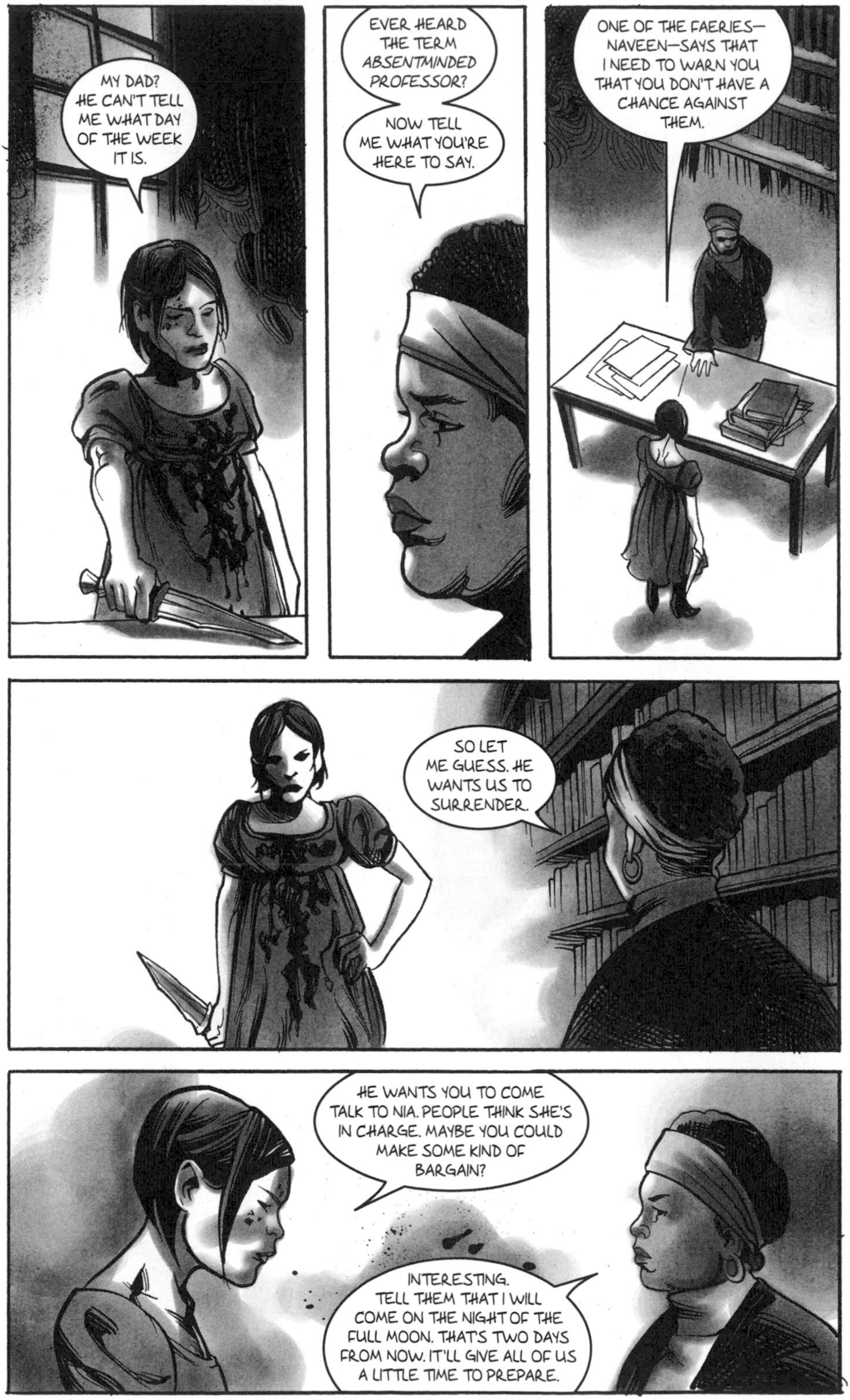
MY DAD? HE CAN'T TELL ME WHAT DAY OF THE WEEK IT IS.
EVER HEARD THE TERM *ABSENTMINDED PROFESSOR*?
NOW TELL ME WHAT YOU'RE HERE TO SAY.
ONE OF THE FAERIES—NAVEEN—SAYS THAT I NEED TO WARN YOU THAT YOU DON'T HAVE A CHANCE AGAINST THEM.
SO LET ME GUESS. HE WANTS US TO SURRENDER.
HE WANTS YOU TO COME TALK TO NIA. PEOPLE THINK SHE'S IN CHARGE. MAYBE YOU COULD MAKE SOME KIND OF BARGAIN?
INTERESTING. TELL THEM THAT I WILL COME ON THE NIGHT OF THE FULL MOON. THAT'S TWO DAYS FROM NOW. IT'LL GIVE ALL OF US A LITTLE TIME TO PREPARE.

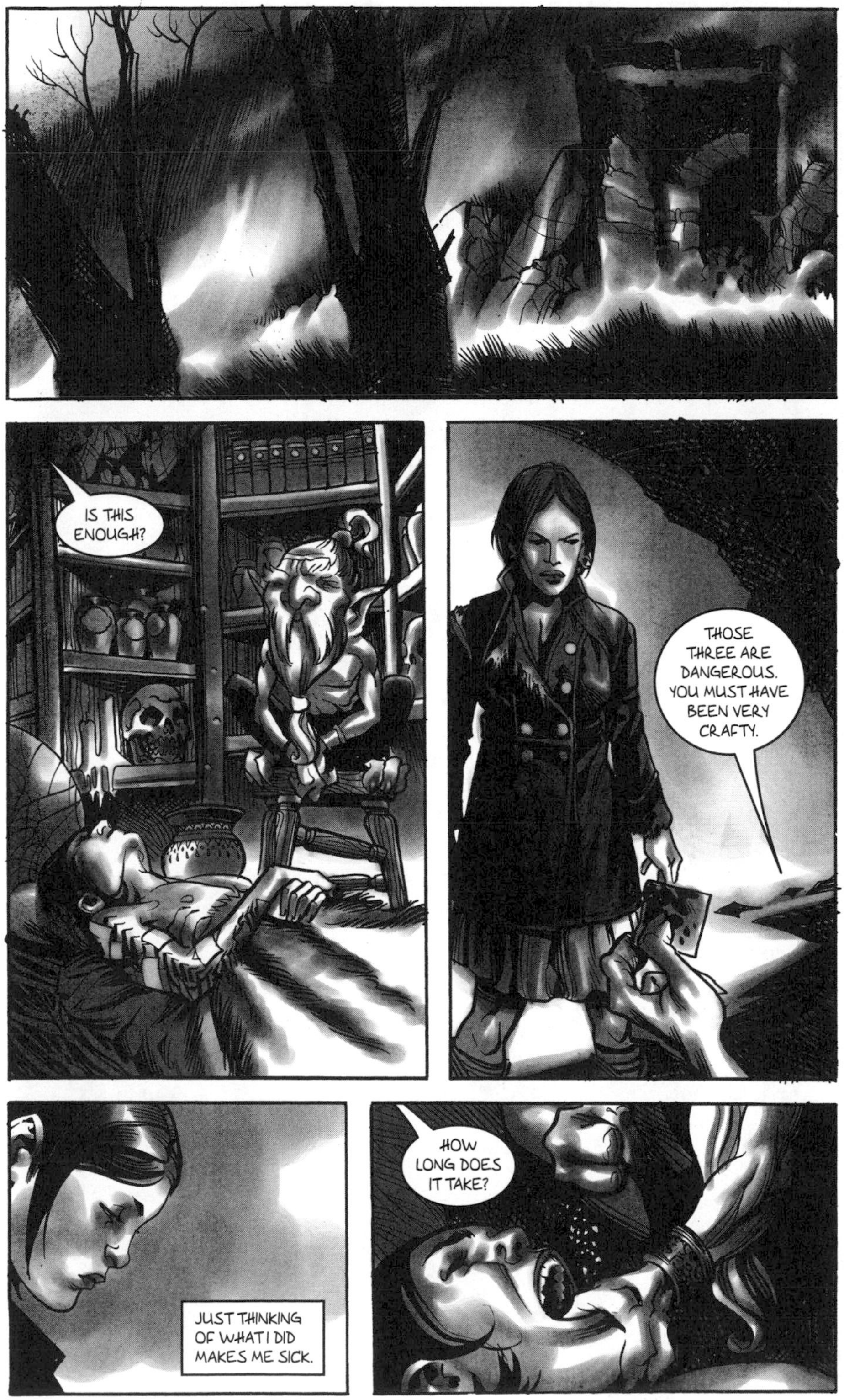
IS THIS ENOUGH?
THOSE THREE ARE DANGEROUS. YOU MUST HAVE BEEN VERY CRAFTY.
JUST THINKING OF WHAT I DID MAKES ME SICK.
HOW LONG DOES IT TAKE?

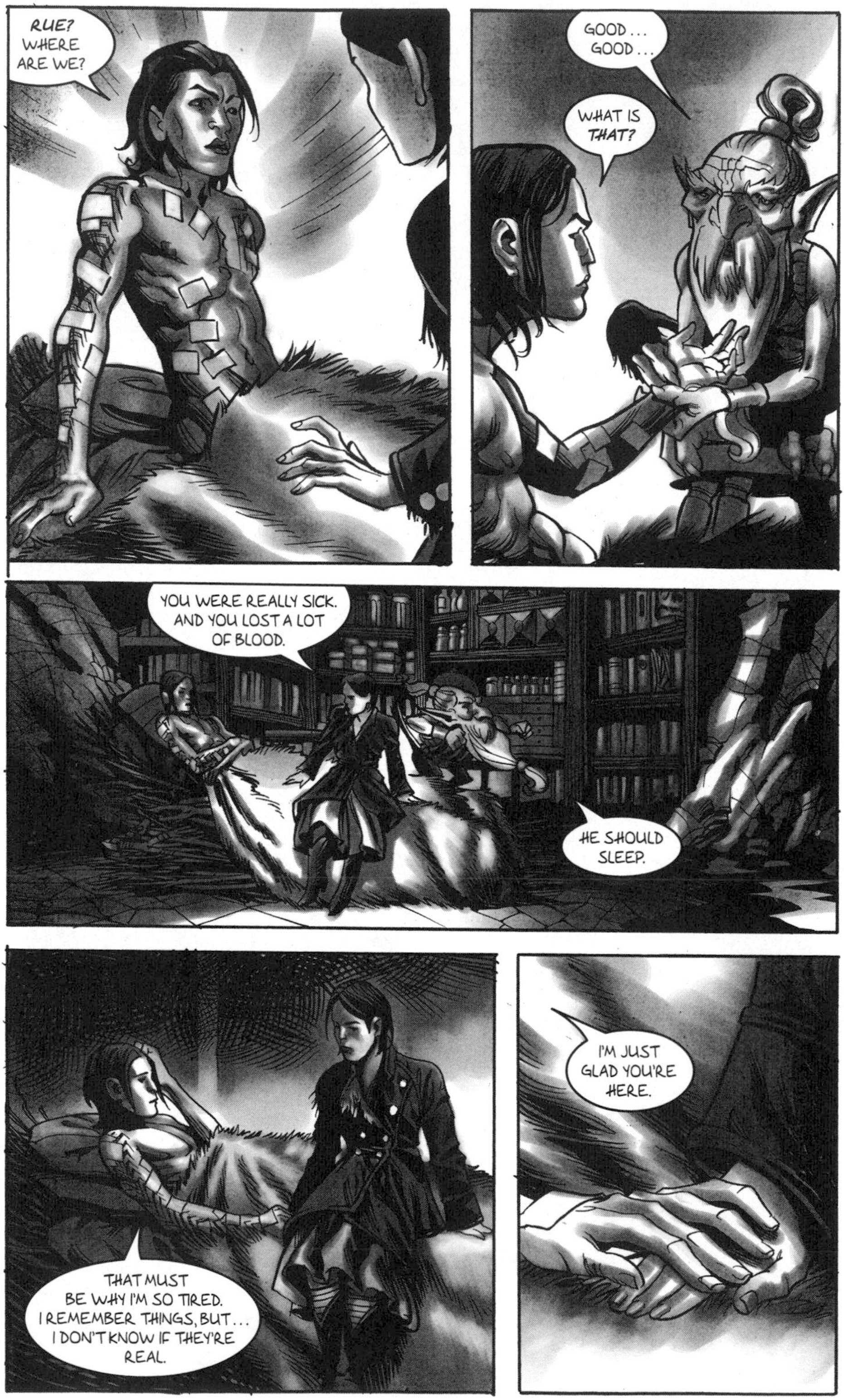
RUE? WHERE ARE WE?
GOOD... GOOD...
WHAT IS THAT?
YOU WERE REALLY SICK. AND YOU LOST A LOT OF BLOOD.
HE SHOULD SLEEP.
THAT MUST BE WHY I'M SO TIRED. I REMEMBER THINGS, BUT... I DON'T KNOW IF THEY'RE REAL.
I'M JUST GLAD YOU'RE HERE.

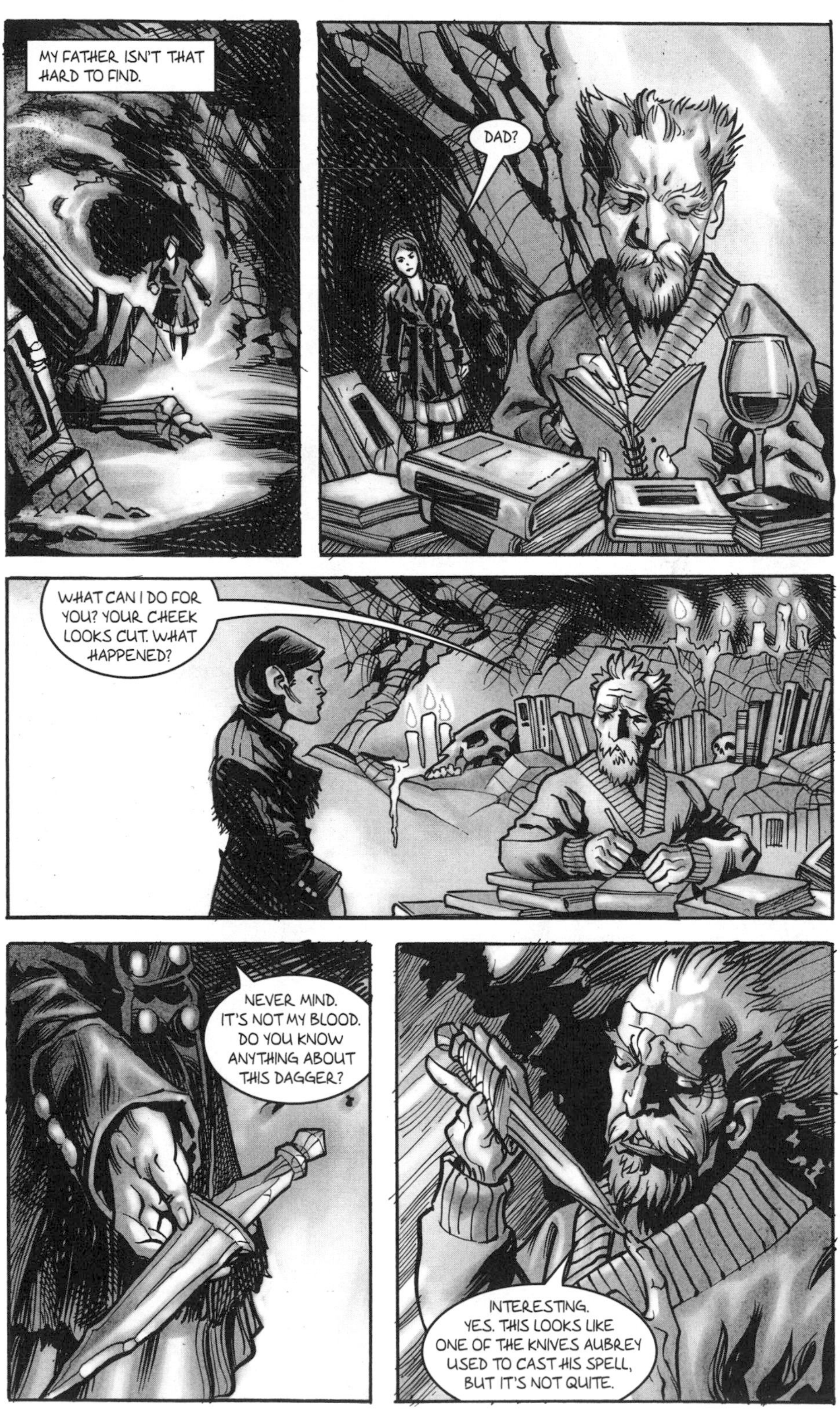
MY FATHER ISN'T THAT HARD TO FIND.
DAD?
WHAT CAN I DO FOR YOU? YOUR CHEEK LOOKS CUT. WHAT HAPPENED?
NEVER MIND. IT'S NOT MY BLOOD. DO YOU KNOW ANYTHING ABOUT THIS DAGGER?
INTERESTING. YES. THIS LOOKS LIKE ONE OF THE KNIVES AUBREY USED TO CAST HIS SPELL, BUT IT'S NOT QUITE.

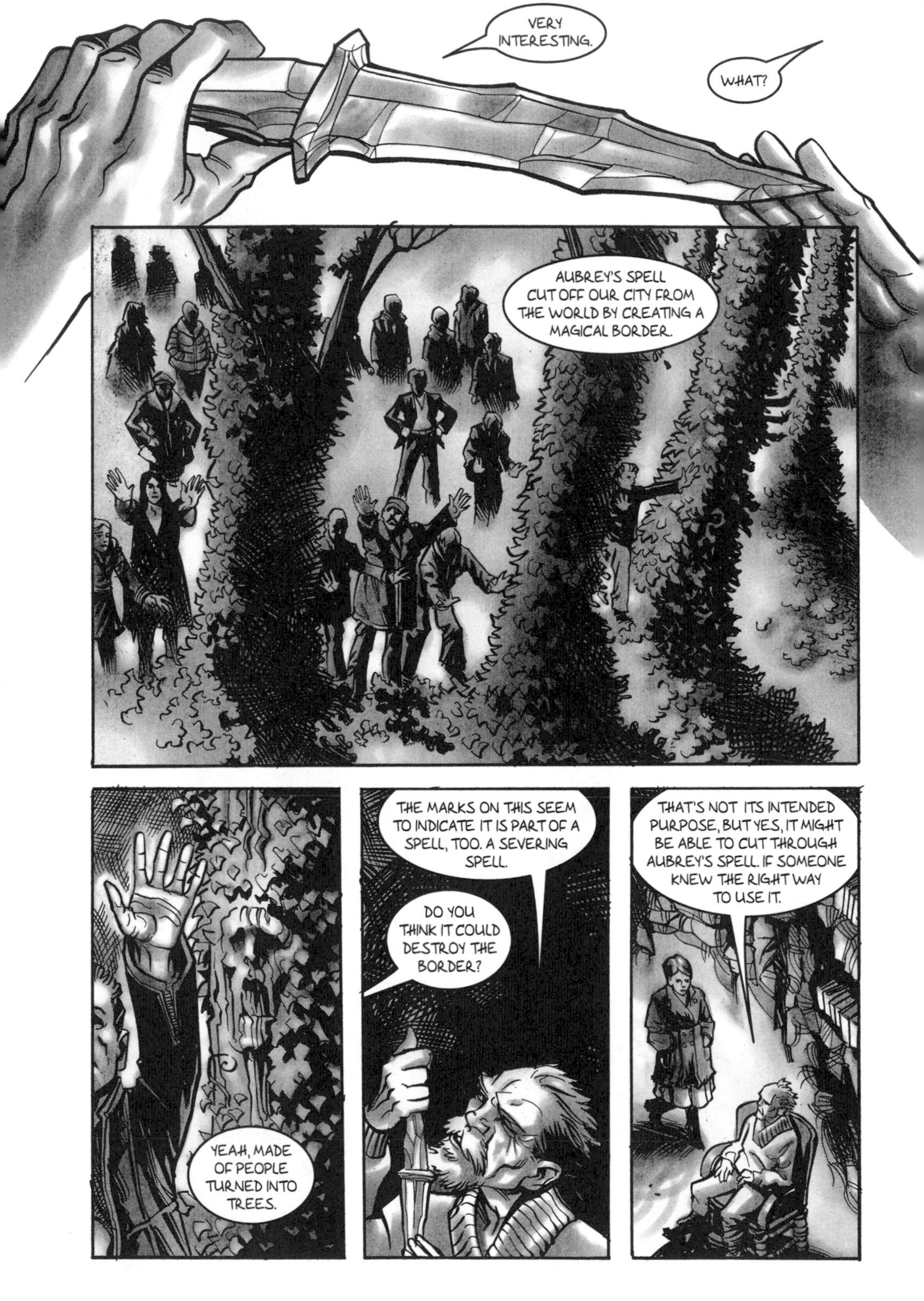
VERY INTERESTING.
WHAT?
AUBREY'S SPELL CUT OFF OUR CITY FROM THE WORLD BY CREATING A MAGICAL BORDER.
YEAH, MADE OF PEOPLE TURNED INTO TREES.
THE MARKS ON THIS SEEM TO INDICATE IT IS PART OF A SPELL, TOO. A SEVERING SPELL.
DO YOU THINK IT COULD DESTROY THE BORDER?
THAT'S NOT ITS INTENDED PURPOSE, BUT YES, IT MIGHT BE ABLE TO CUT THROUGH AUBREY'S SPELL. IF SOMEONE KNEW THE RIGHT WAY TO USE IT.

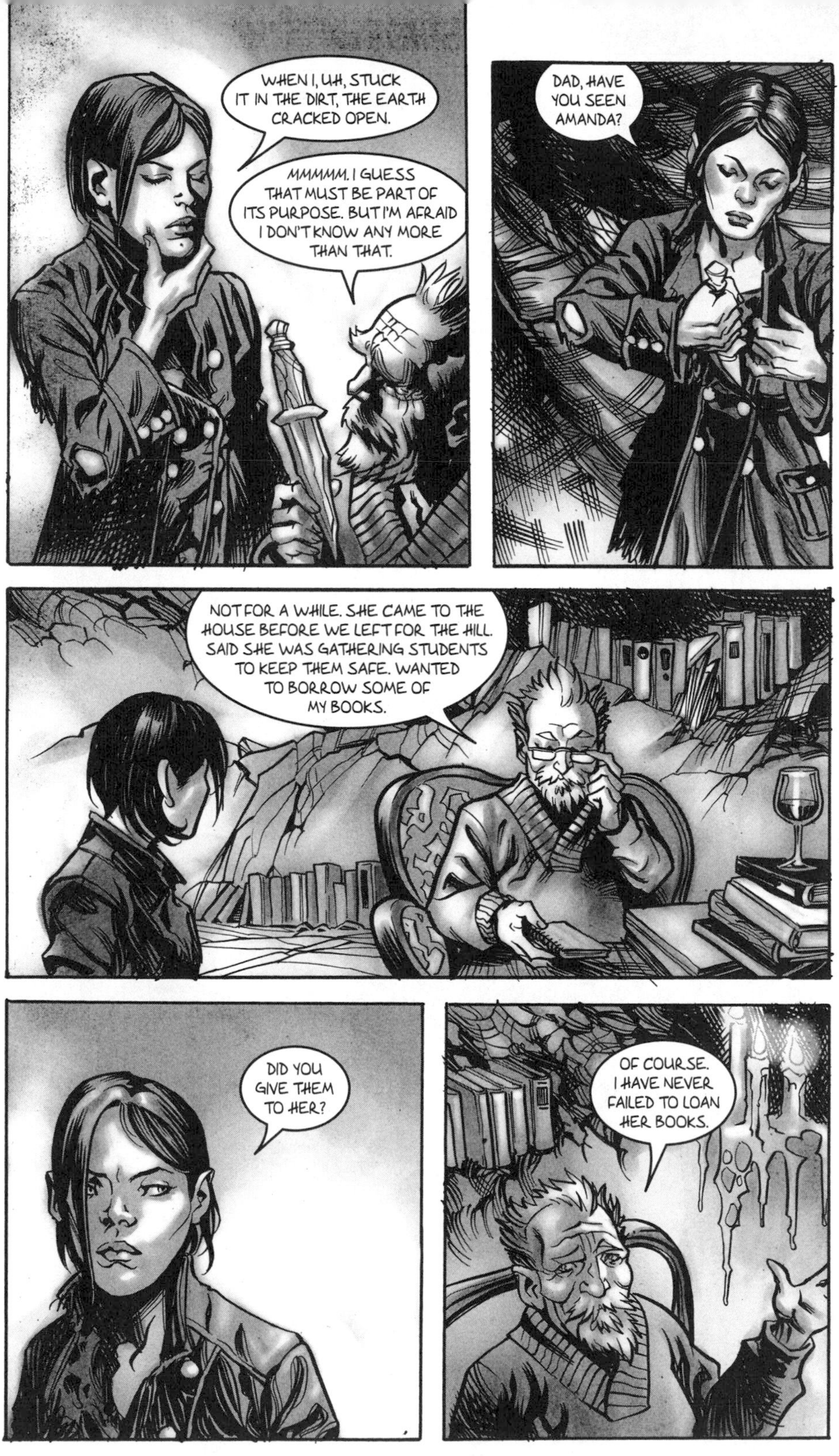
WHEN I, UH, STUCK IT IN THE DIRT, THE EARTH CRACKED OPEN.
MMMMM. I GUESS THAT MUST BE PART OF ITS PURPOSE. BUT I'M AFRAID I DON'T KNOW ANY MORE THAN THAT.
DAD, HAVE YOU SEEN AMANDA?
NOT FOR A WHILE. SHE CAME TO THE HOUSE BEFORE WE LEFT FOR THE HILL. SAID SHE WAS GATHERING STUDENTS TO KEEP THEM SAFE. WANTED TO BORROW SOME OF MY BOOKS.
DID YOU GIVE THEM TO HER?
OF COURSE. I HAVE NEVER FAILED TO LOAN HER BOOKS.

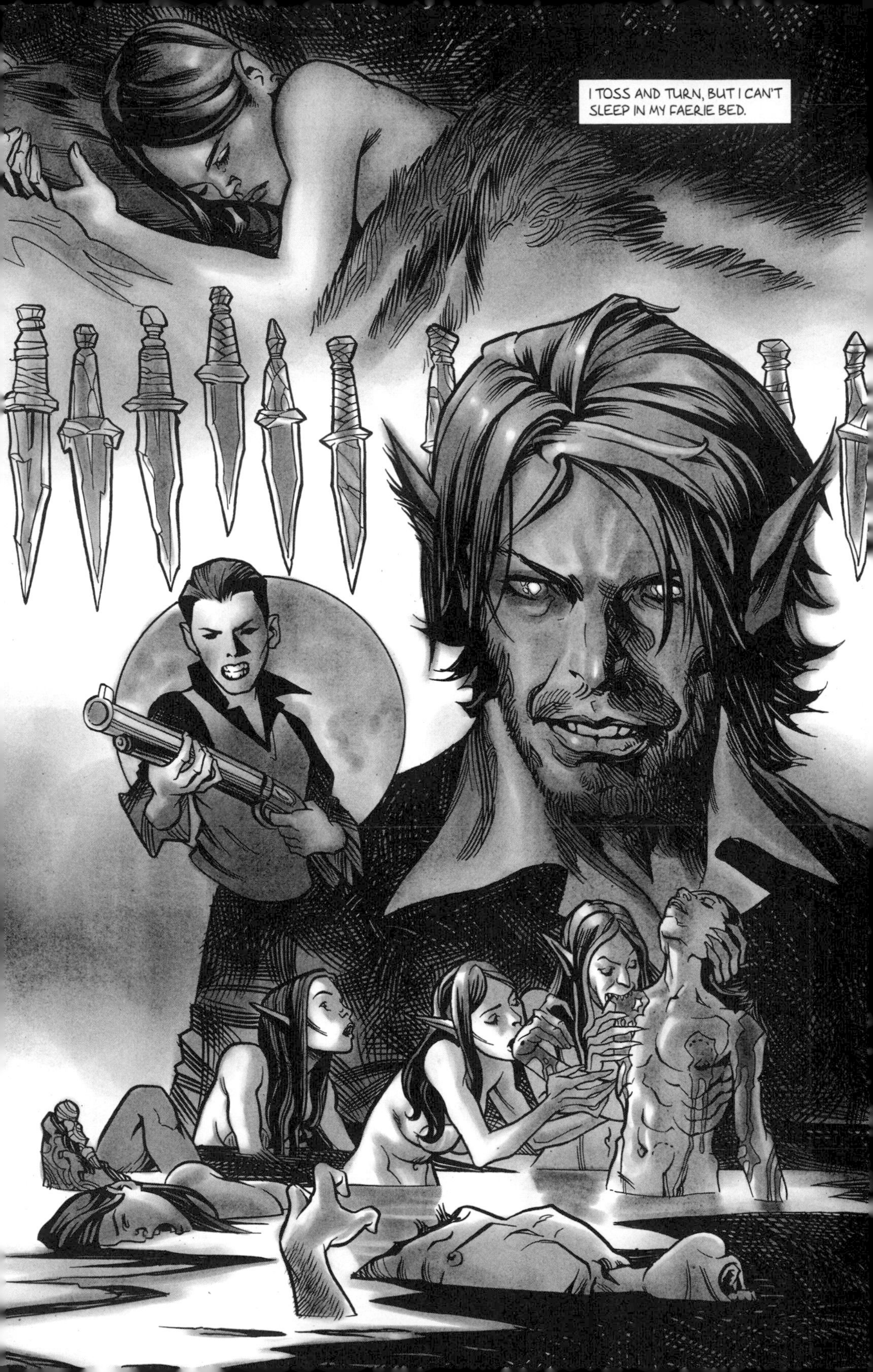
I TOSS AND TURN, BUT I CAN'T SLEEP IN MY FAERIE BED.

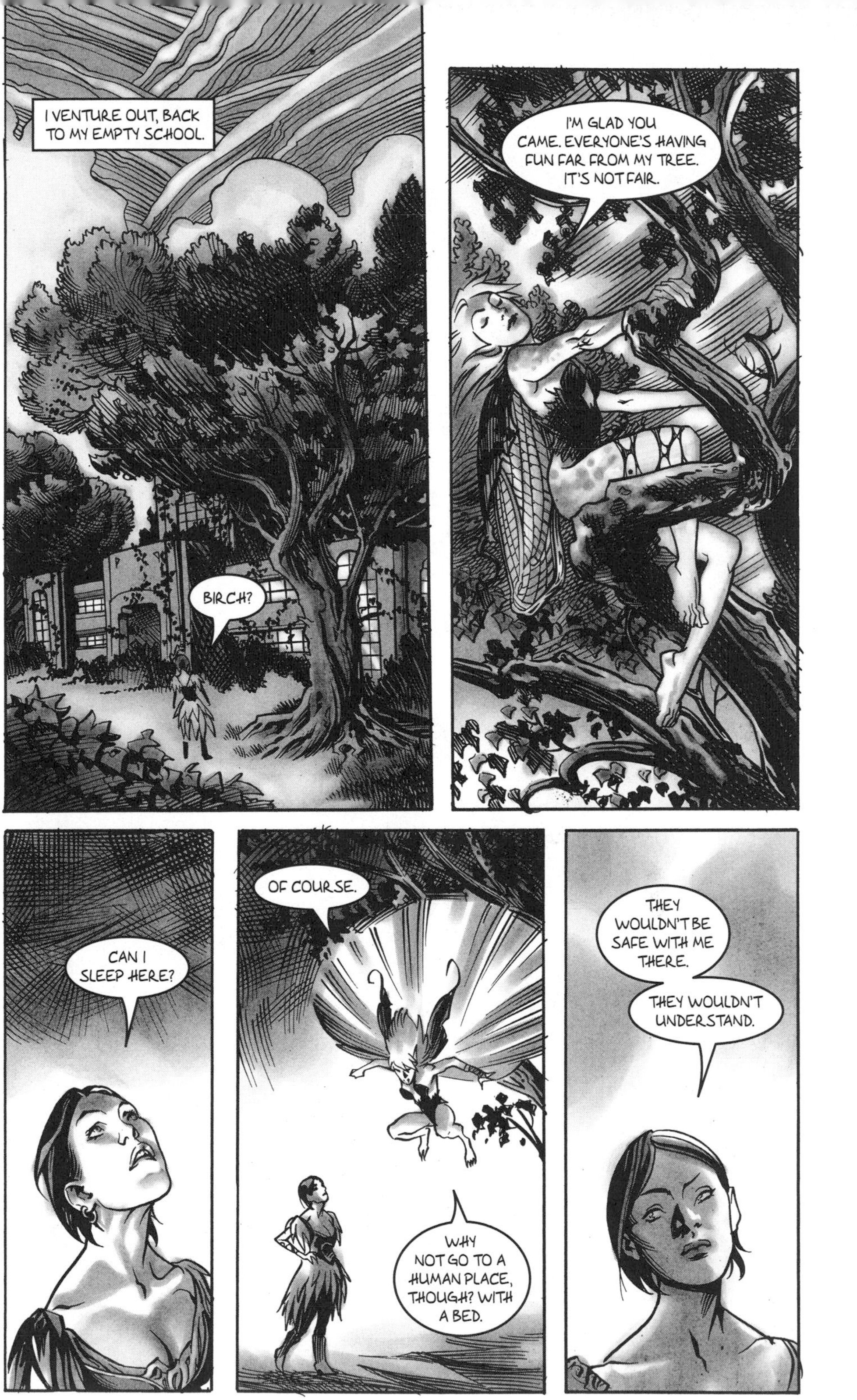
I VENTURE OUT, BACK TO MY EMPTY SCHOOL.
BIRCH?
I'M GLAD YOU CAME. EVERYONE'S HAVING FUN FAR FROM MY TREE. IT'S NOT FAIR.
CAN I SLEEP HERE?
OF COURSE.
WHY NOT GO TO A HUMAN PLACE, THOUGH? WITH A BED.
THEY WOULDN'T BE SAFE WITH ME THERE.
THEY WOULDN'T UNDERSTAND.

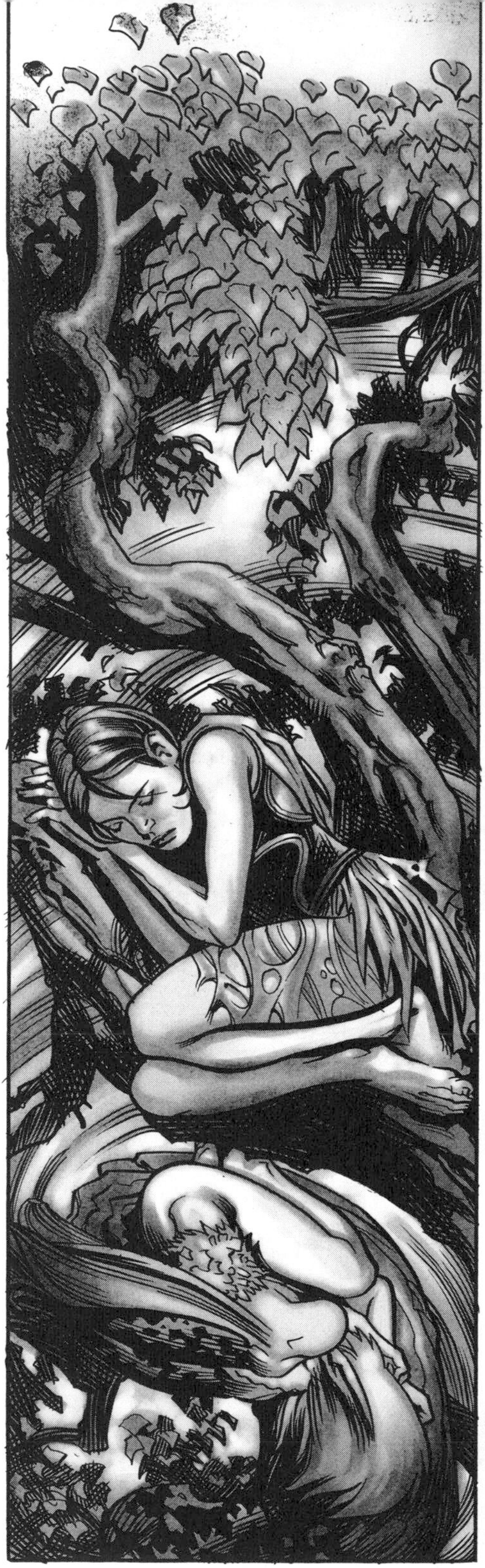

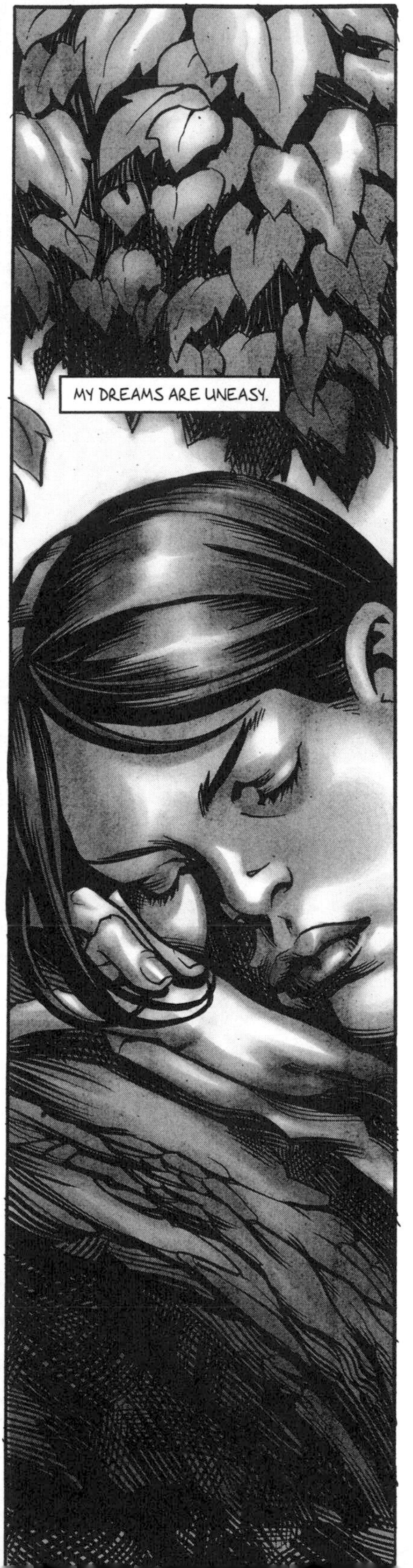
MY DREAMS ARE UNEASY.

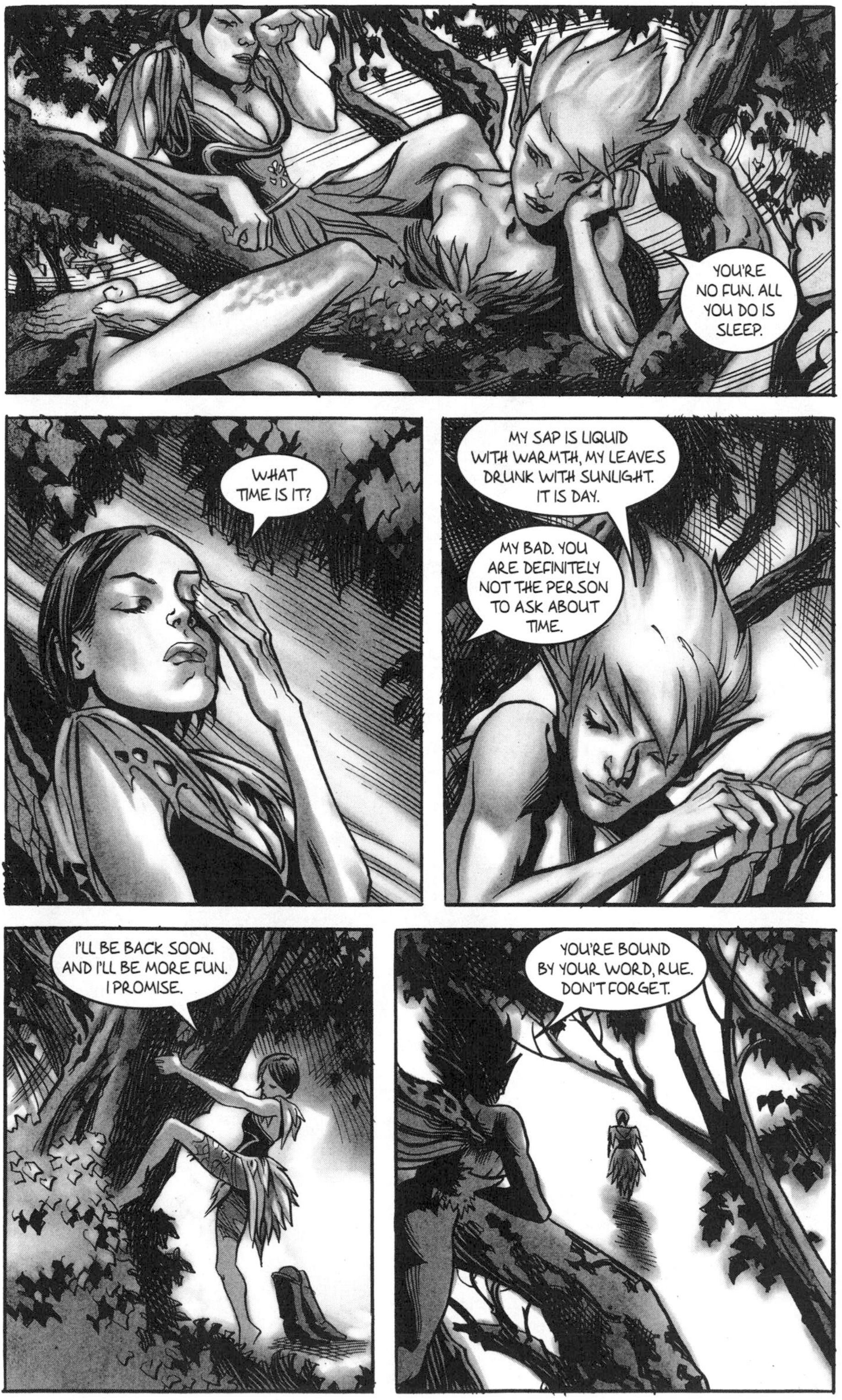
YOU'RE NO FUN. ALL YOU DO IS SLEEP.
WHAT TIME IS IT?
MY SAP IS LIQUID WITH WARMTH, MY LEAVES DRUNK WITH SUNLIGHT. IT IS DAY.
MY BAD. YOU ARE DEFINITELY NOT THE PERSON TO ASK ABOUT TIME.
I'LL BE BACK SOON. AND I'LL BE MORE FUN. I PROMISE.
YOU'RE BOUND BY YOUR WORD, RUE. DON'T FORGET.

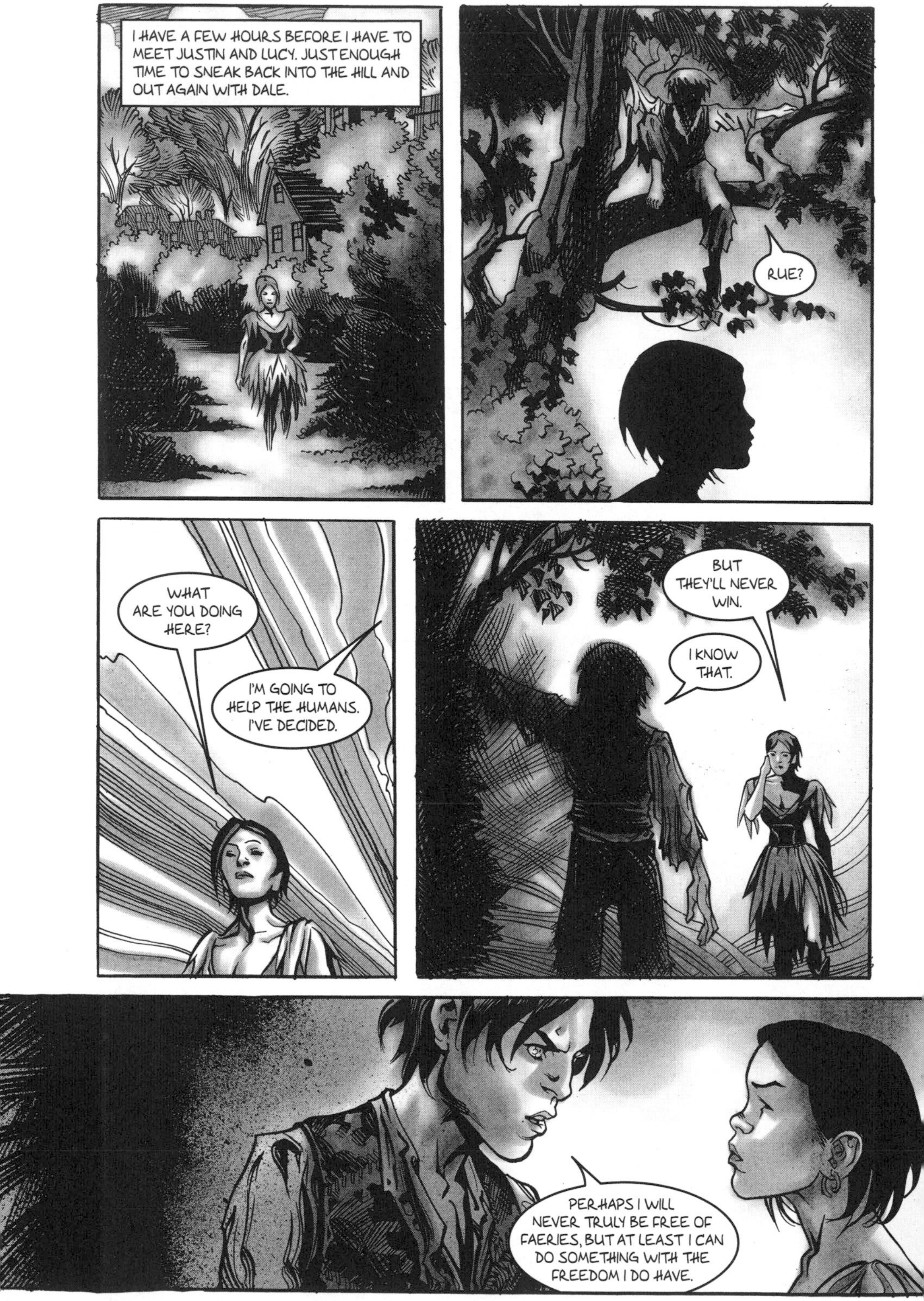
I HAVE A FEW HOURS BEFORE I HAVE TO MEET JUSTIN AND LUCY. JUST ENOUGH TIME TO SNEAK BACK INTO THE HILL AND OUT AGAIN WITH DALE.
RUE?
WHAT ARE YOU DOING HERE?
I'M GOING TO HELP THE HUMANS. I'VE DECIDED.
BUT THEY'LL NEVER WIN.
I KNOW THAT.
PERHAPS I WILL NEVER TRULY BE FREE OF FAERIES, BUT AT LEAST I CAN DO SOMETHING WITH THE FREEDOM I DO HAVE.

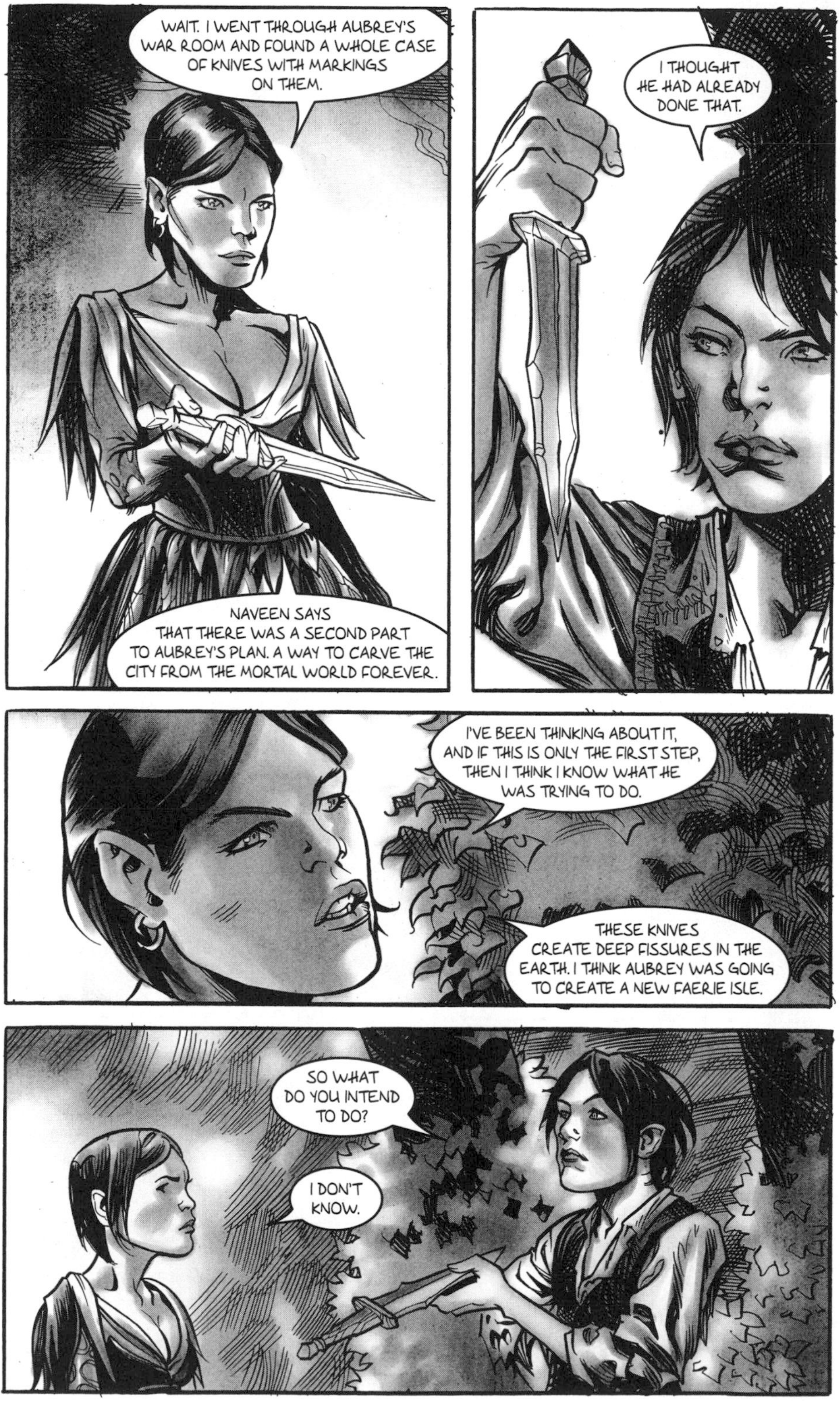
WAIT. I WENT THROUGH AUBREY'S WAR ROOM AND FOUND A WHOLE CASE OF KNIVES WITH MARKINGS ON THEM.
NAVEEN SAYS THAT THERE WAS A SECOND PART TO AUBREY'S PLAN. A WAY TO CARVE THE CITY FROM THE MORTAL WORLD FOREVER.
I THOUGHT HE HAD ALREADY DONE THAT.
I'VE BEEN THINKING ABOUT IT, AND IF THIS IS ONLY THE FIRST STEP, THEN I THINK I KNOW WHAT HE WAS TRYING TO DO.
THESE KNIVES CREATE DEEP FISSURES IN THE EARTH. I THINK AUBREY WAS GOING TO CREATE A NEW FAERIE ISLE.
SO WHAT DO YOU INTEND TO DO?
I DON'T KNOW.

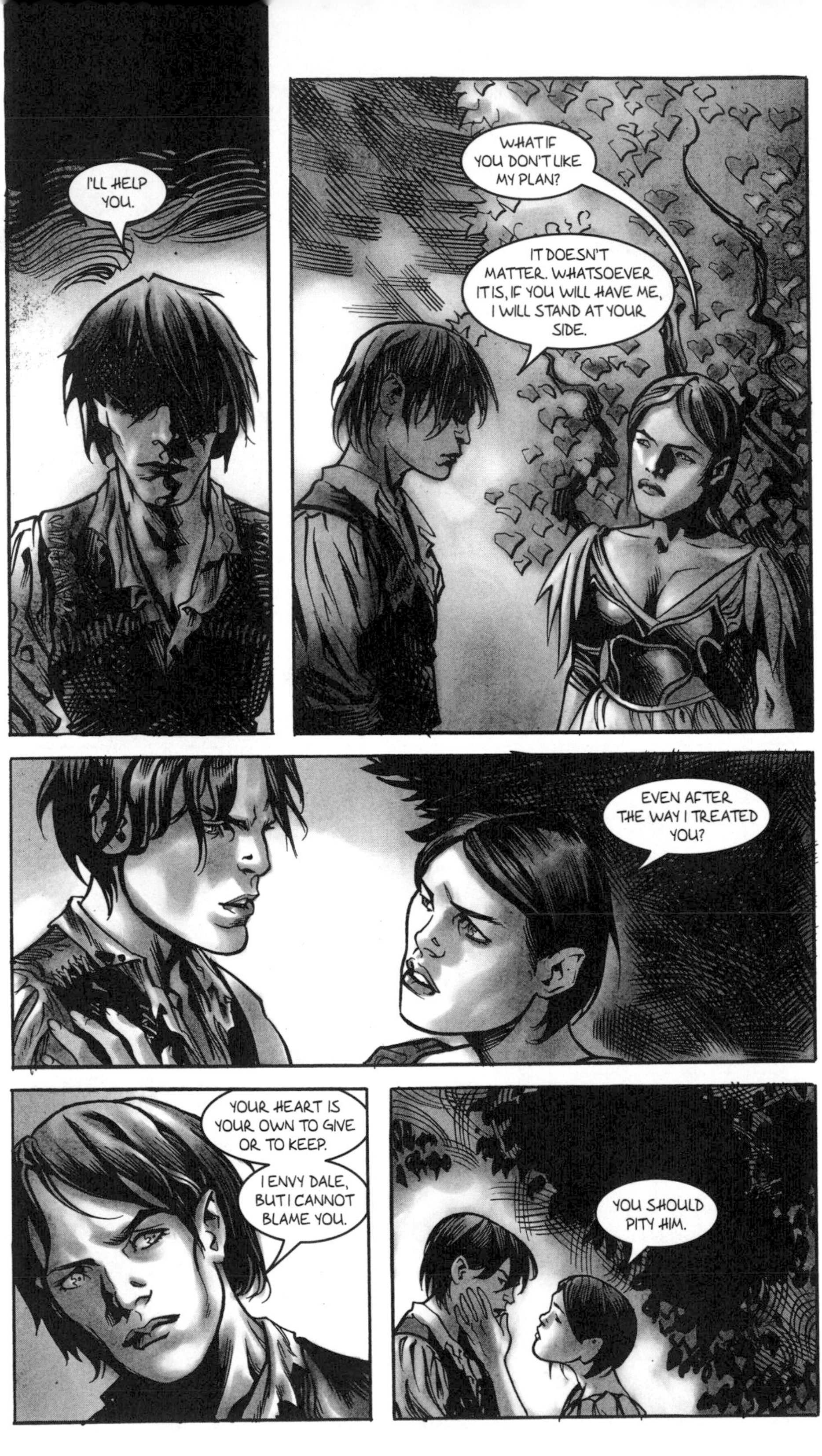
I'LL HELP YOU.
WHAT IF YOU DON'T LIKE MY PLAN?
IT DOESN'T MATTER. WHATSOEVER IT IS, IF YOU WILL HAVE ME, I WILL STAND AT YOUR SIDE.
EVEN AFTER THE WAY I TREATED YOU?
YOUR HEART IS YOUR OWN TO GIVE OR TO KEEP.
I ENVY DALE, BUT I CANNOT BLAME YOU.
YOU SHOULD PITY HIM.

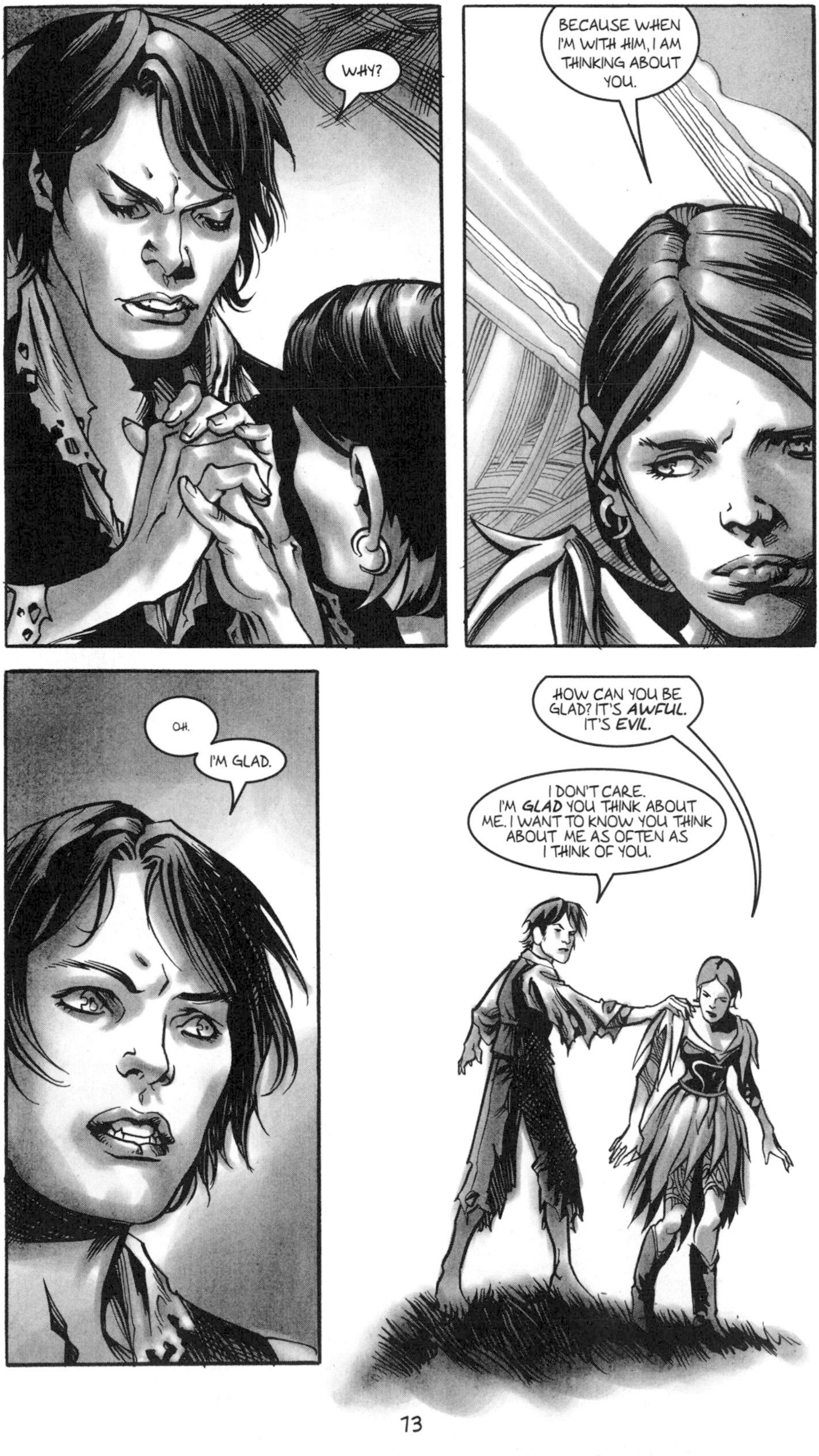
WHY?
BECAUSE WHEN I'M WITH HIM, I AM THINKING ABOUT YOU.
OH.
I'M GLAD.
HOW CAN YOU BE GLAD? IT'S AWFUL. IT'S EVIL.
I DON'T CARE. I'M GLAD YOU THINK ABOUT ME. I WANT TO KNOW YOU THINK ABOUT ME AS OFTEN AS I THINK OF YOU.

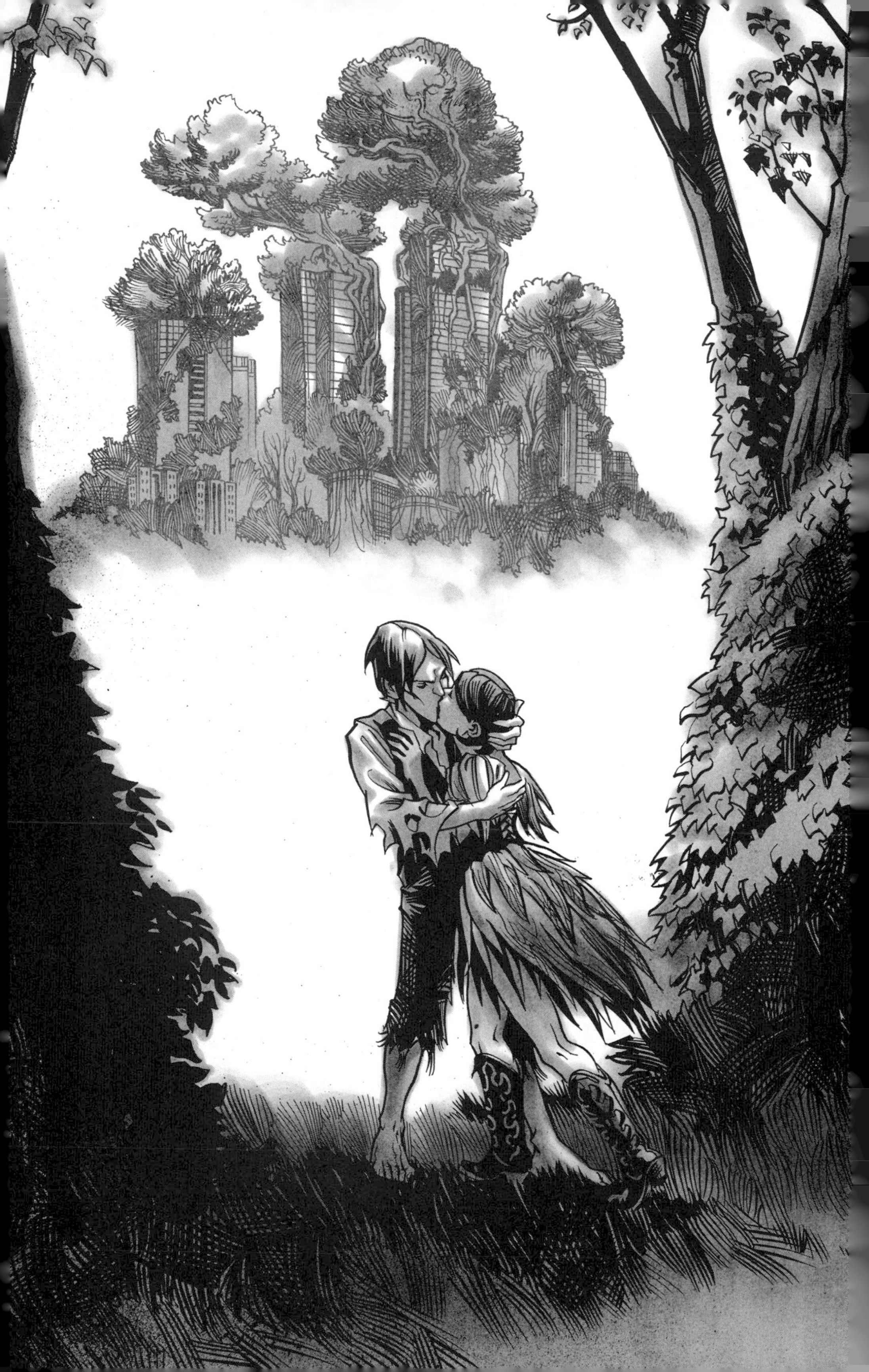

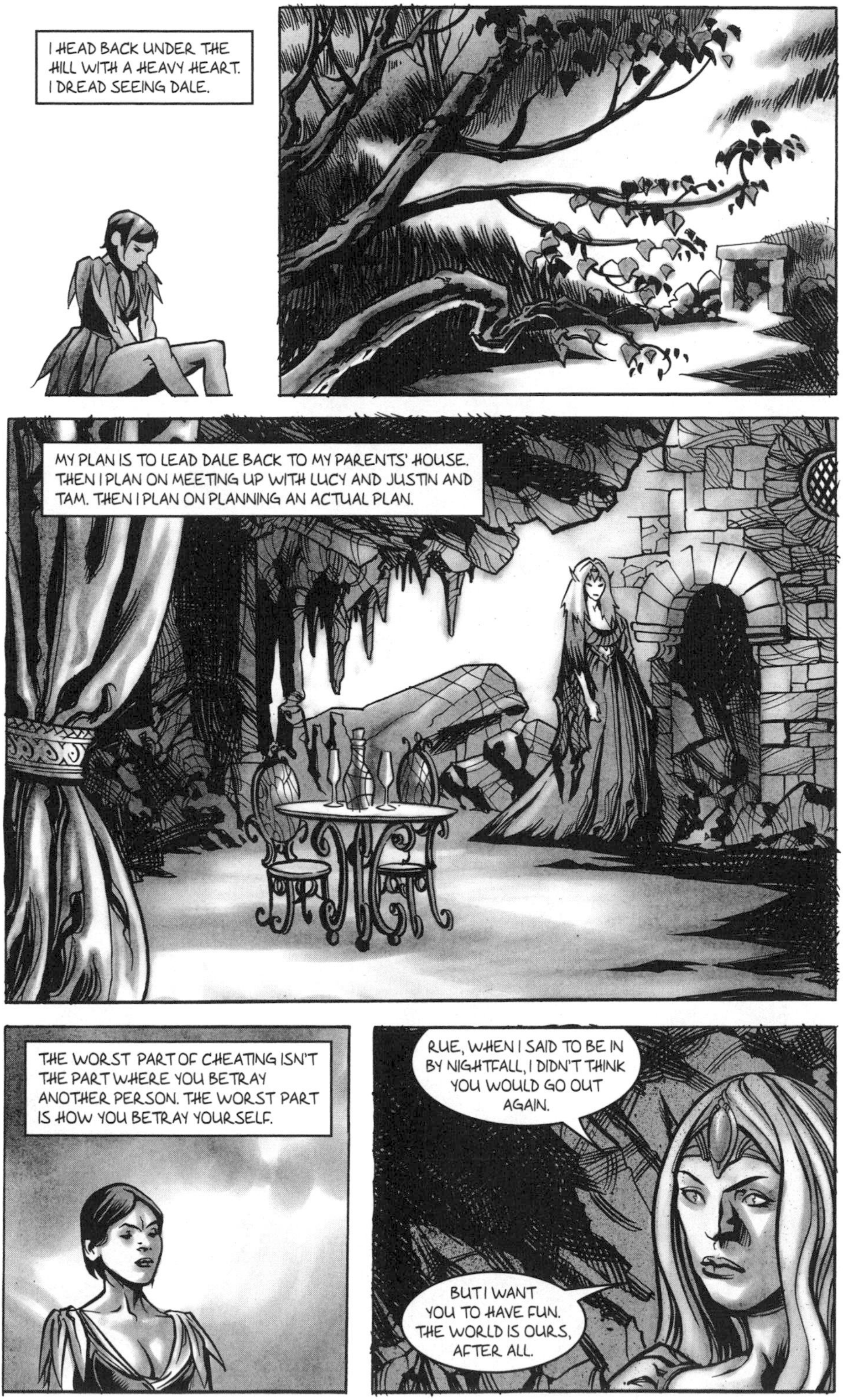
I HEAD BACK UNDER THE HILL WITH A HEAVY HEART. I DREAD SEEING DALE.
MY PLAN IS TO LEAD DALE BACK TO MY PARENTS' HOUSE. THEN I PLAN ON MEETING UP WITH LUCY AND JUSTIN AND TAM. THEN I PLAN ON PLANNING AN ACTUAL PLAN.
THE WORST PART OF CHEATING ISN'T THE PART WHERE YOU BETRAY ANOTHER PERSON. THE WORST PART IS HOW YOU BETRAY YOURSELF.
RUE, WHEN I SAID TO BE IN BY NIGHTFALL, I DIDN'T THINK YOU WOULD GO OUT AGAIN.
BUT I WANT YOU TO HAVE FUN. THE WORLD IS OURS, AFTER ALL.

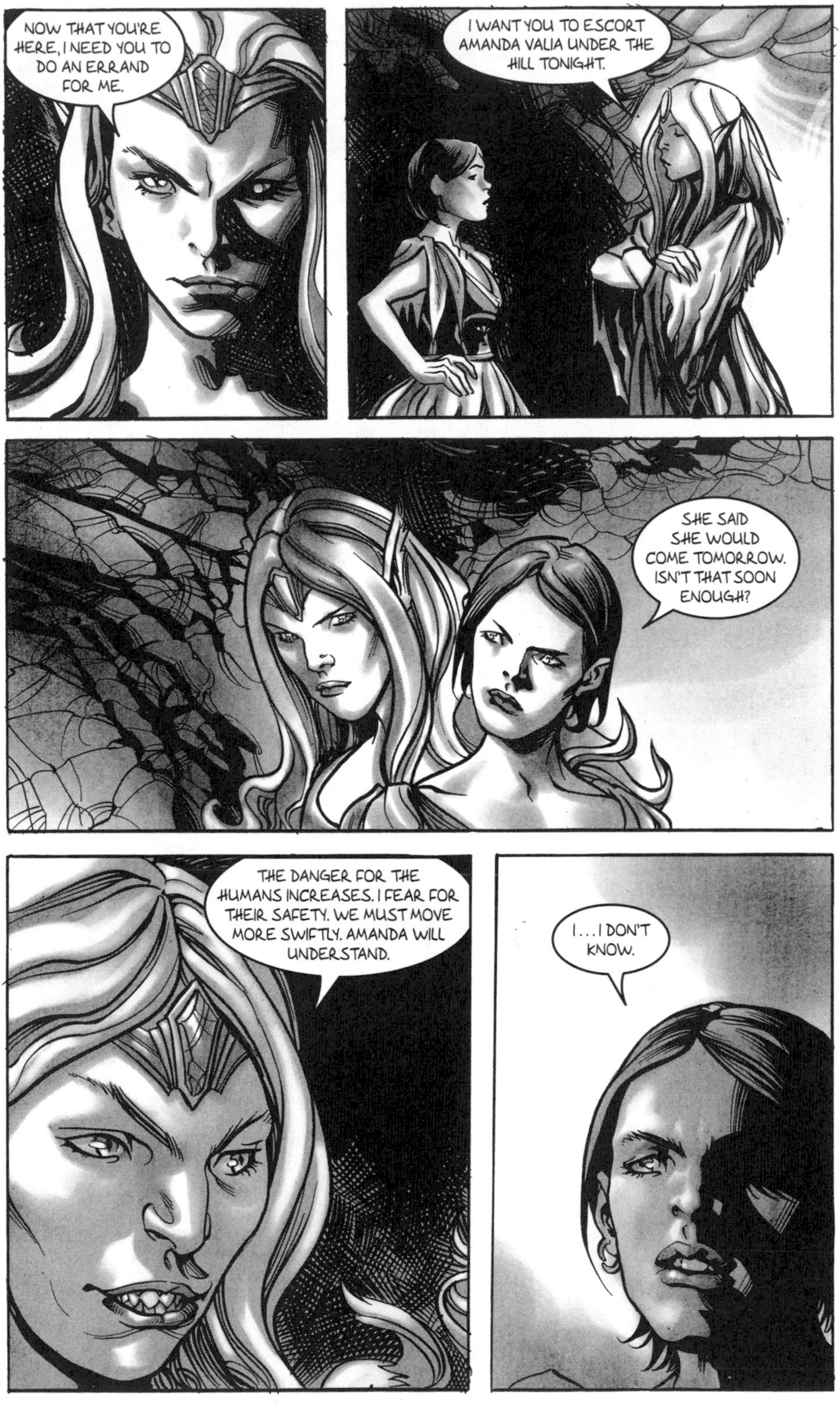
NOW THAT YOU'RE HERE, I NEED YOU TO DO AN ERRAND FOR ME.
I WANT YOU TO ESCORT AMANDA VALIA UNDER THE HILL TONIGHT.
SHE SAID SHE WOULD COME TOMORROW. ISN'T THAT SOON ENOUGH?
THE DANGER FOR THE HUMANS INCREASES. I FEAR FOR THEIR SAFETY. WE MUST MOVE MORE SWIFTLY. AMANDA WILL UNDERSTAND.
I... I DON'T KNOW.

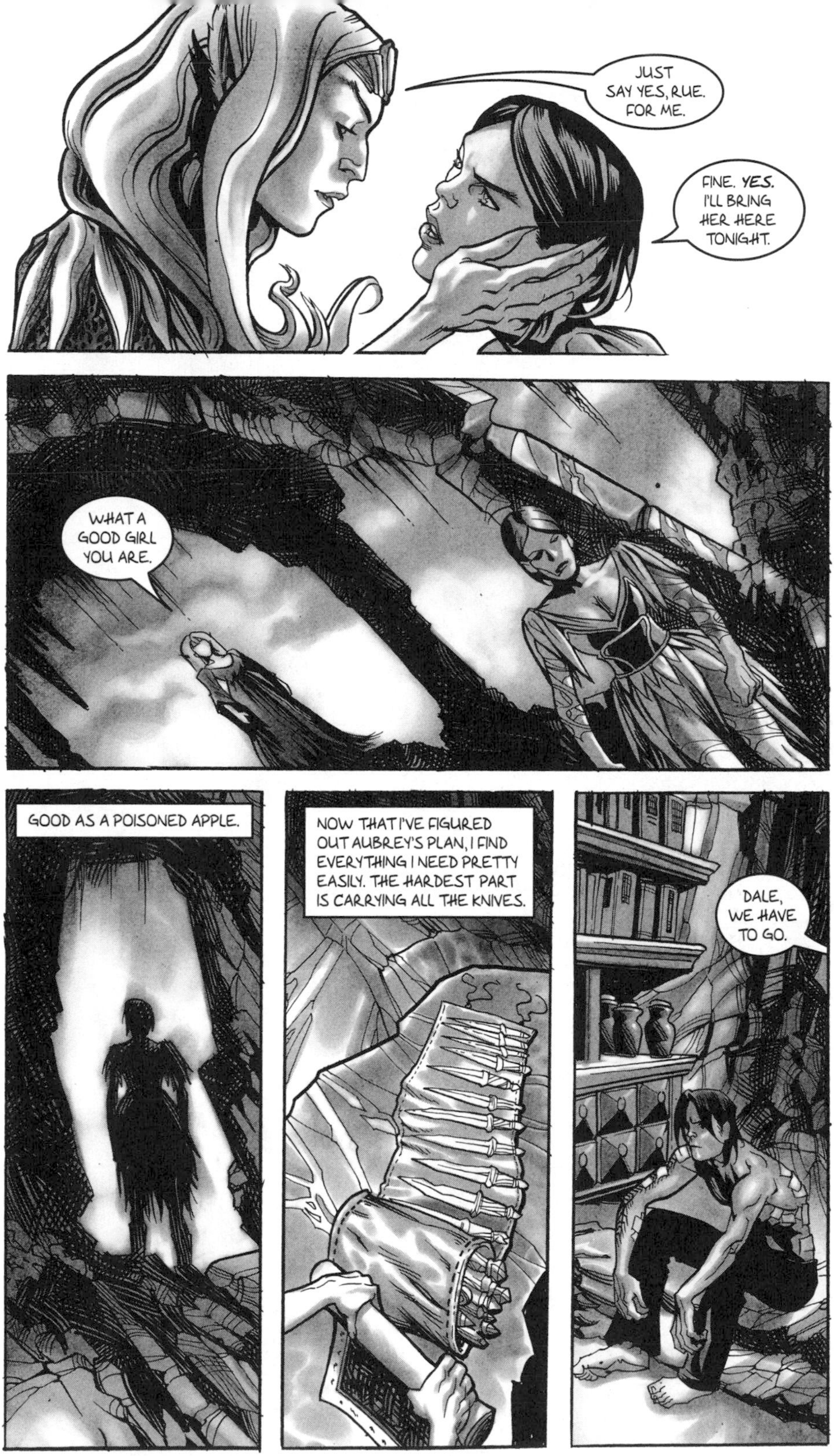
JUST SAY YES, RUE. FOR ME.
FINE. YES. I'LL BRING HER HERE TONIGHT.
WHAT A GOOD GIRL YOU ARE.
GOOD AS A POISONED APPLE.
NOW THAT I'VE FIGURED OUT AUBREY'S PLAN, I FIND EVERYTHING I NEED PRETTY EASILY. THE HARDEST PART IS CARRYING ALL THE KNIVES.
DALE, WE HAVE TO GO.

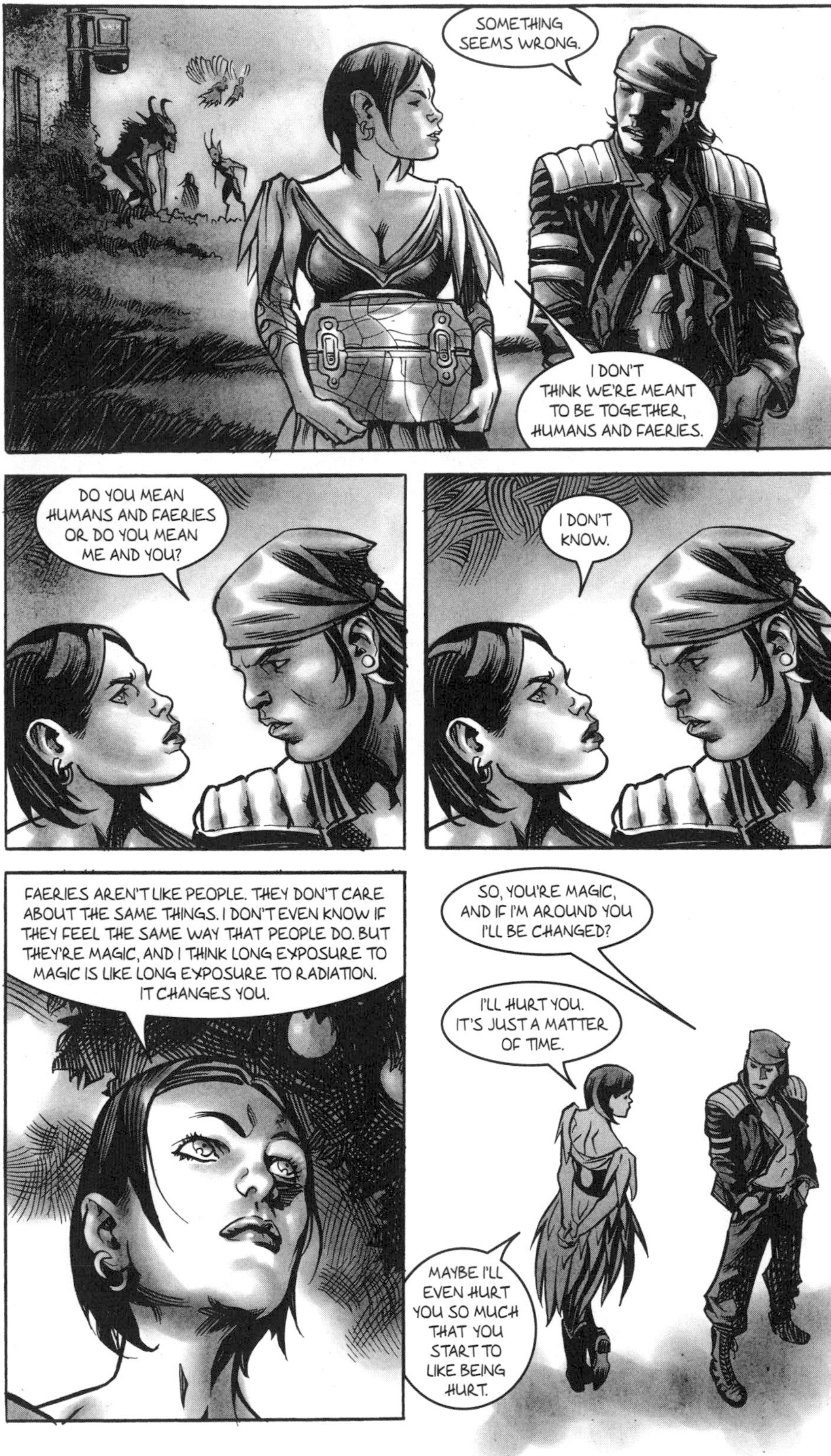
SOMETHING SEEMS WRONG.
I DON'T THINK WE'RE MEANT TO BE TOGETHER, HUMANS AND FAERIES.
DO YOU MEAN HUMANS AND FAERIES OR DO YOU MEAN ME AND YOU?
I DON'T KNOW.
FAERIES AREN'T LIKE PEOPLE. THEY DON'T CARE ABOUT THE SAME THINGS. I DON'T EVEN KNOW IF THEY FEEL THE SAME WAY THAT PEOPLE DO. BUT THEY'RE MAGIC, AND I THINK LONG EXPOSURE TO MAGIC IS LIKE LONG EXPOSURE TO RADIATION. IT CHANGES YOU.
SO, YOU'RE MAGIC, AND IF I'M AROUND YOU I'LL BE CHANGED?
I'LL HURT YOU. IT'S JUST A MATTER OF TIME.
MAYBE I'LL EVEN HURT YOU SO MUCH THAT YOU START TO LIKE BEING HURT.

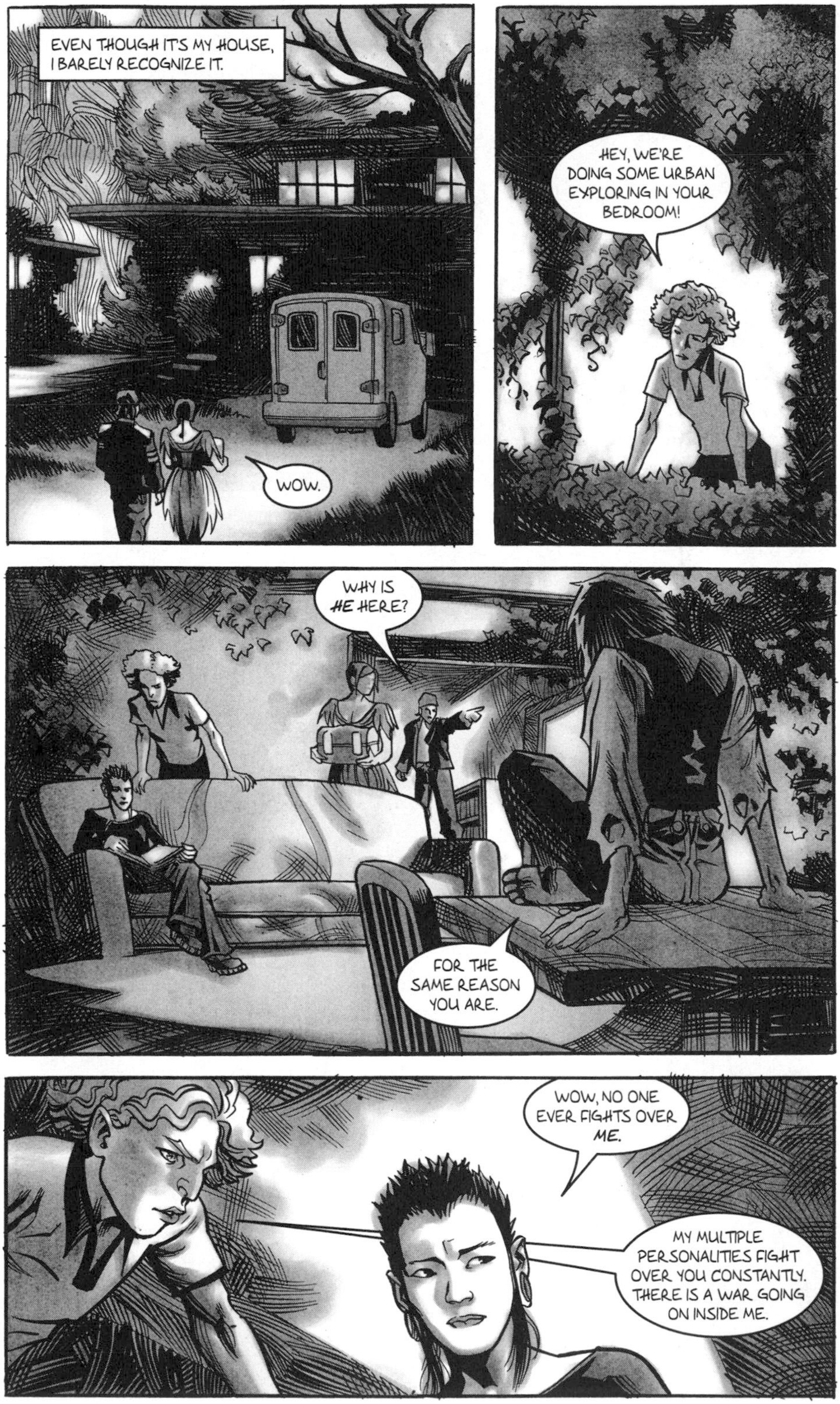
EVEN THOUGH IT'S MY HOUSE, I BARELY RECOGNIZE IT.
WOW.
HEY, WE'RE DOING SOME URBAN EXPLORING IN YOUR BEDROOM!
WHY IS HE HERE?
FOR THE SAME REASON YOU ARE.
WOW, NO ONE EVER FIGHTS OVER ME.
MY MULTIPLE PERSONALITIES FIGHT OVER YOU CONSTANTLY. THERE IS A WAR GOING ON INSIDE ME.

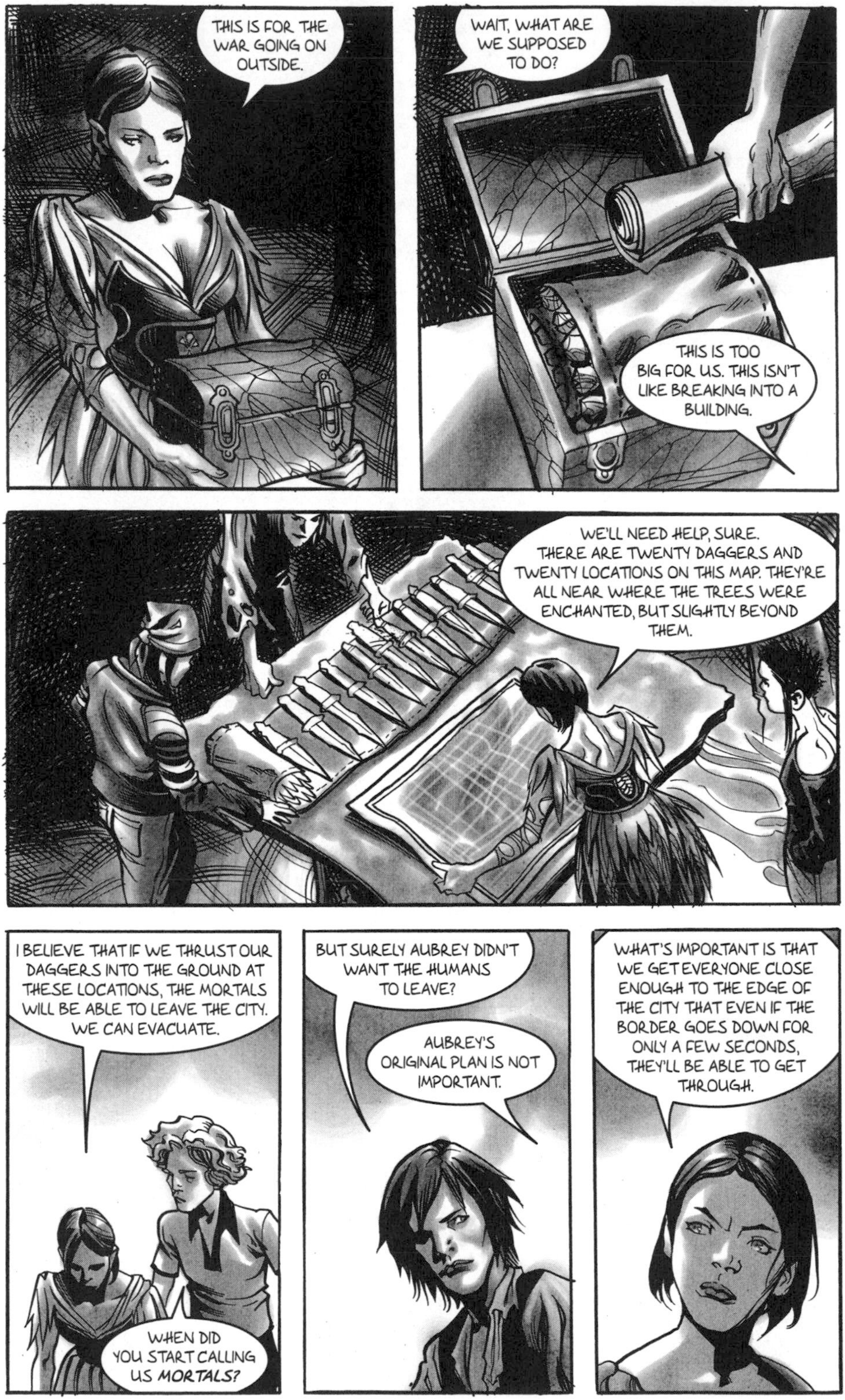
THIS IS FOR THE WAR GOING ON OUTSIDE.
WAIT, WHAT ARE WE SUPPOSED TO DO?
THIS IS TOO BIG FOR US. THIS ISN'T LIKE BREAKING INTO A BUILDING.
WE'LL NEED HELP, SURE. THERE ARE TWENTY DAGGERS AND TWENTY LOCATIONS ON THIS MAP. THEY'RE ALL NEAR WHERE THE TREES WERE ENCHANTED, BUT SLIGHTLY BEYOND THEM.
I BELIEVE THAT IF WE THRUST OUR DAGGERS INTO THE GROUND AT THESE LOCATIONS, THE MORTALS WILL BE ABLE TO LEAVE THE CITY. WE CAN EVACUATE.
WHEN DID YOU START CALLING US *MORTALS?*
BUT SURELY AUBREY DIDN'T WANT THE HUMANS TO LEAVE?
AUBREY'S ORIGINAL PLAN IS NOT IMPORTANT.
WHAT'S IMPORTANT IS THAT WE GET EVERYONE CLOSE ENOUGH TO THE EDGE OF THE CITY THAT EVEN IF THE BORDER GOES DOWN FOR ONLY A FEW SECONDS, THEY'LL BE ABLE TO GET THROUGH.

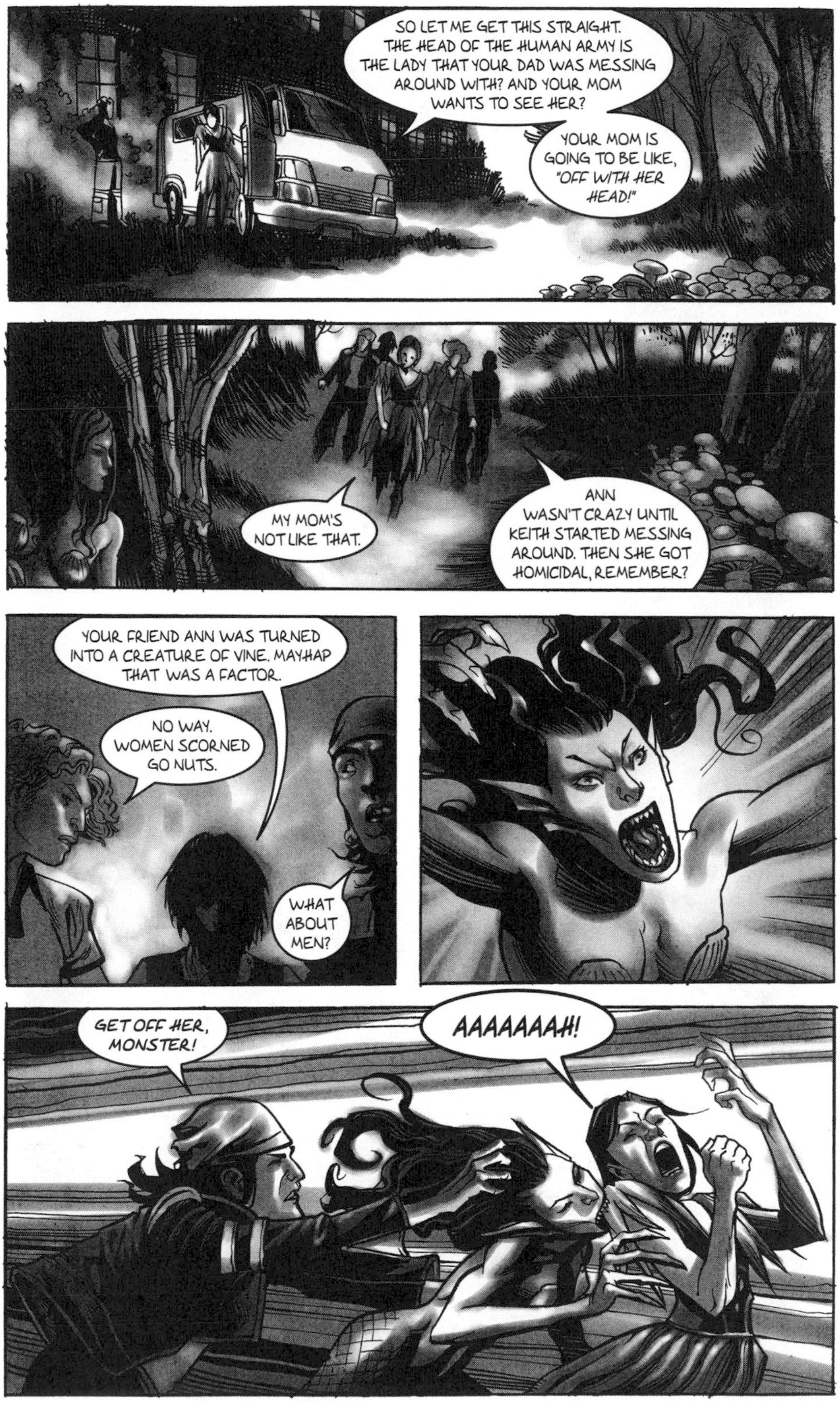
SO LET ME GET THIS STRAIGHT. THE HEAD OF THE HUMAN ARMY IS THE LADY THAT YOUR DAD WAS MESSING AROUND WITH? AND YOUR MOM WANTS TO SEE HER?
YOUR MOM IS GOING TO BE LIKE, "OFF WITH HER HEAD!"
MY MOM'S NOT LIKE THAT.
ANN WASN'T CRAZY UNTIL KEITH STARTED MESSING AROUND. THEN SHE GOT HOMICIDAL, REMEMBER?
YOUR FRIEND ANN WAS TURNED INTO A CREATURE OF VINE. MAYHAP THAT WAS A FACTOR.
NO WAY. WOMEN SCORNED GO NUTS.
WHAT ABOUT MEN?
GET OFF HER, MONSTER!
AAAAAAAH!

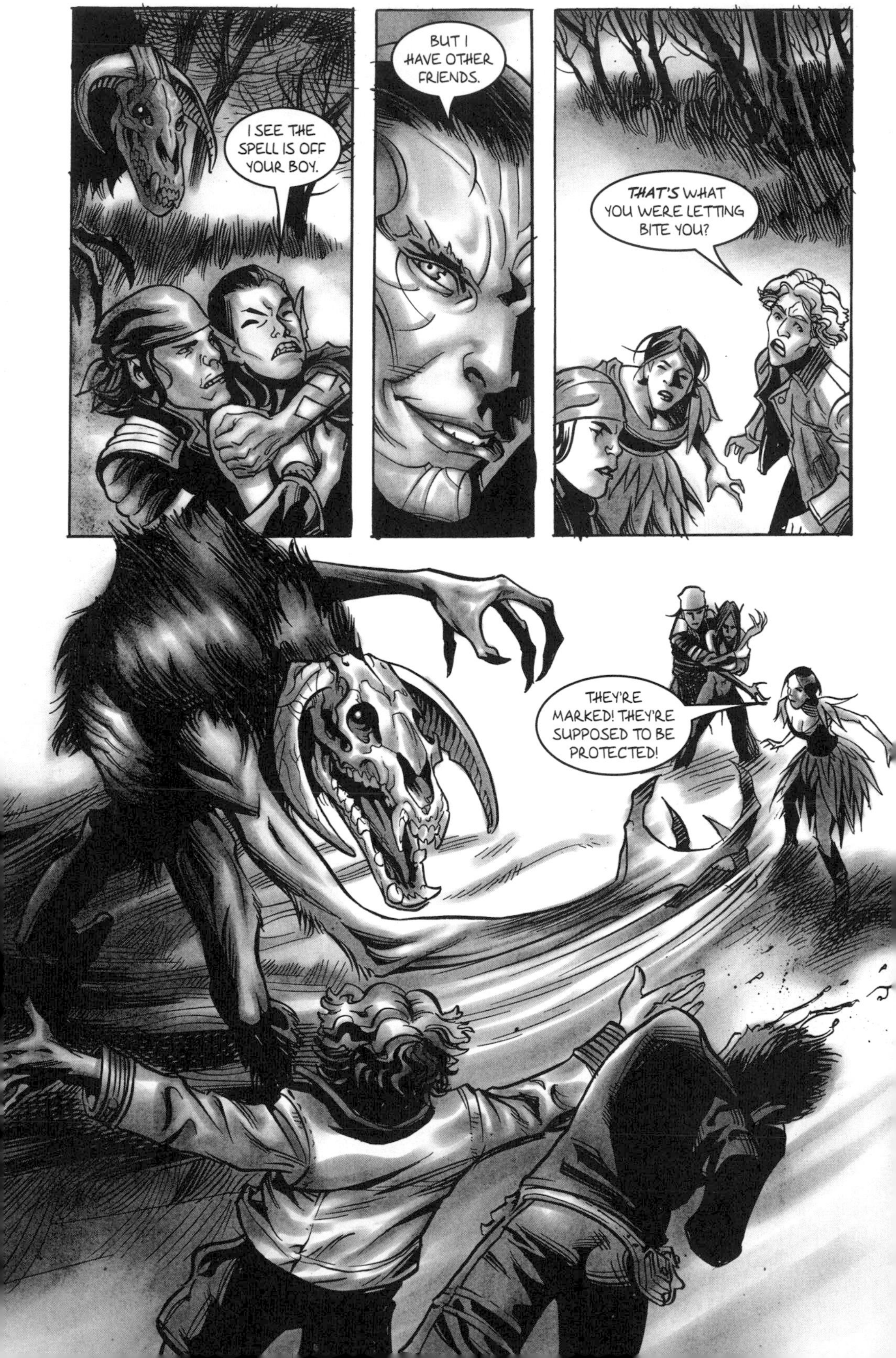
I SEE THE SPELL IS OFF YOUR BOY.
BUT I HAVE OTHER FRIENDS.
THAT'S WHAT YOU WERE LETTING BITE YOU?
THEY'RE MARKED! THEY'RE SUPPOSED TO BE PROTECTED!

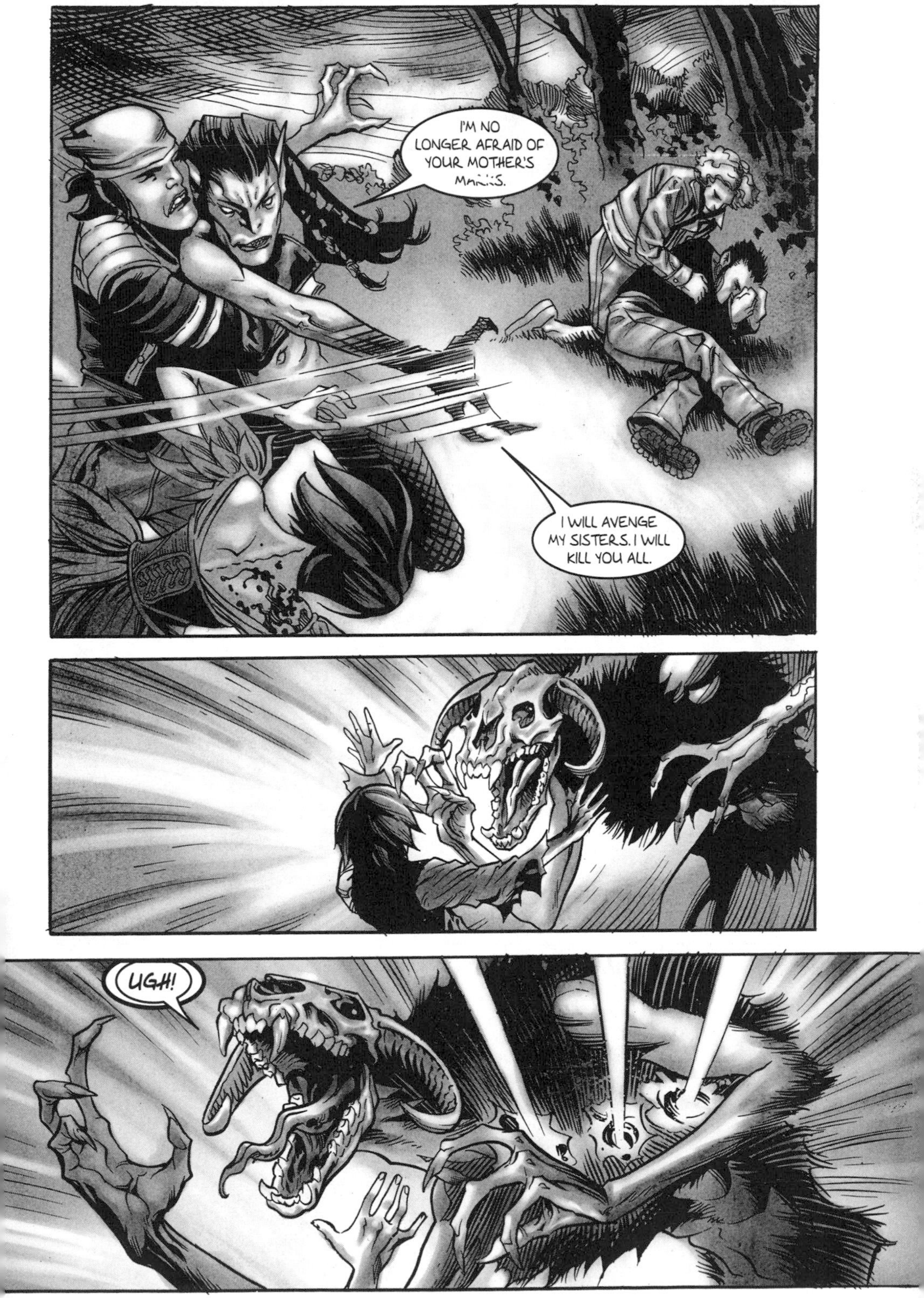
I'M NO LONGER AFRAID OF YOUR MOTHER'S
I WILL AVENGE MY SISTERS. I WILL KILL YOU ALL.
UGH!

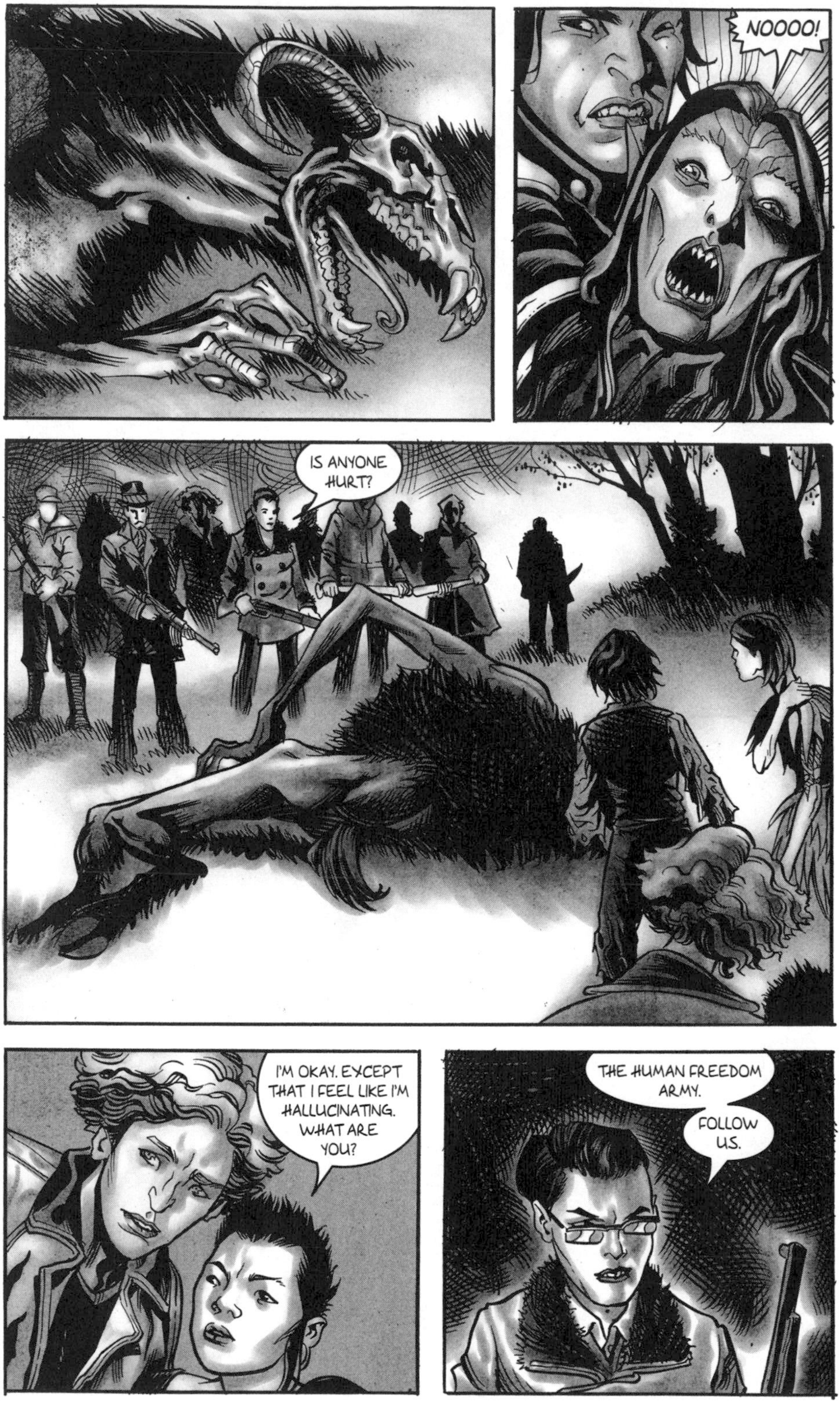

NOOOO!
IS ANYONE HURT?
I'M OKAY. EXCEPT THAT I FEEL LIKE I'M HALLUCINATING. WHAT ARE YOU?
THE HUMAN FREEDOM ARMY.
FOLLOW US.

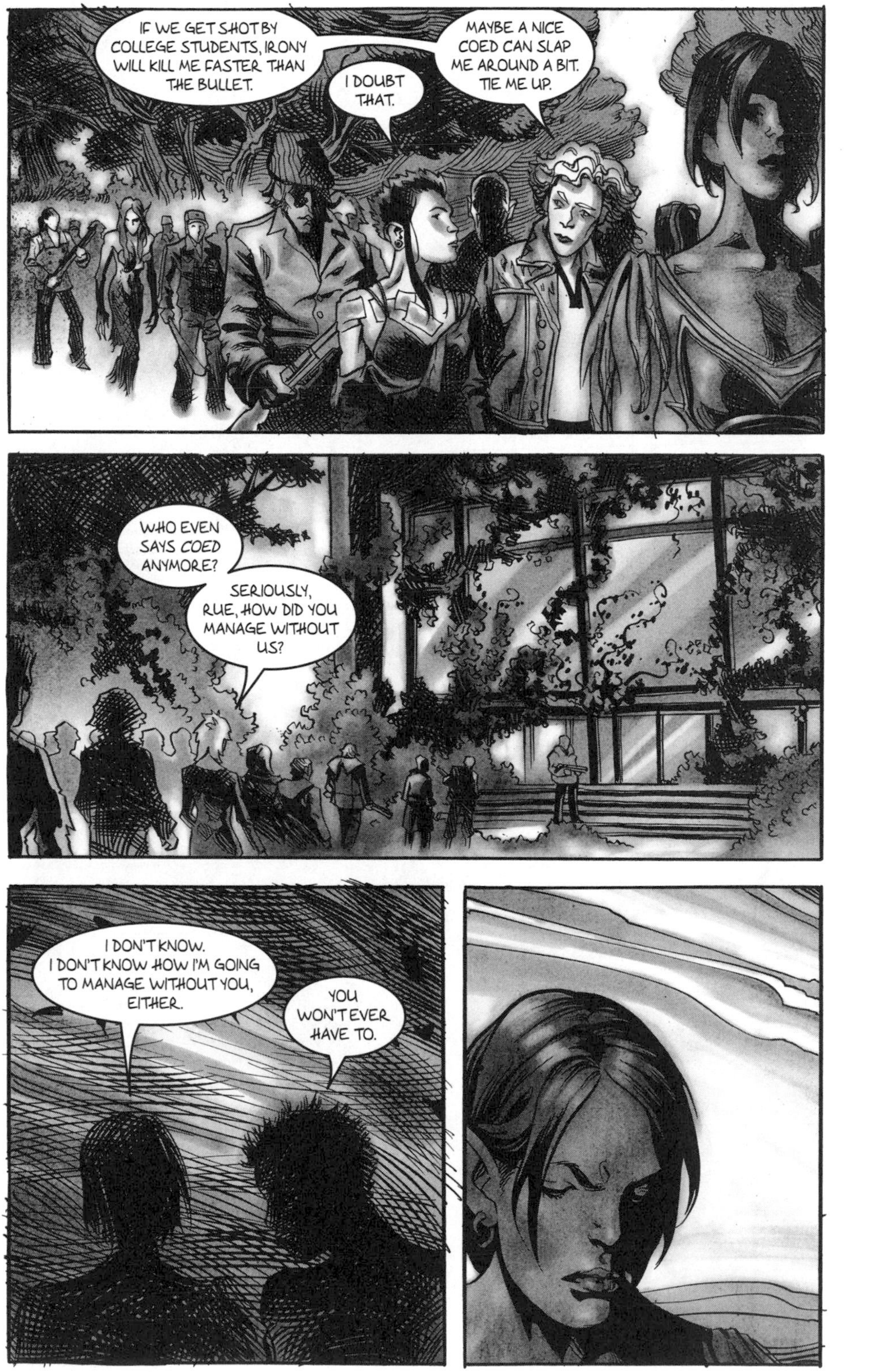
IF WE GET SHOT BY COLLEGE STUDENTS, IRONY WILL KILL ME FASTER THAN THE BULLET.
I DOUBT THAT.
MAYBE A NICE COED CAN SLAP ME AROUND A BIT. TIE ME UP.
WHO EVEN SAYS *COED* ANYMORE?
SERIOUSLY, RUE, HOW DID YOU MANAGE WITHOUT US?
I DON'T KNOW. I DON'T KNOW HOW I'M GOING TO MANAGE WITHOUT YOU, EITHER.
YOU WON'T EVER HAVE TO.

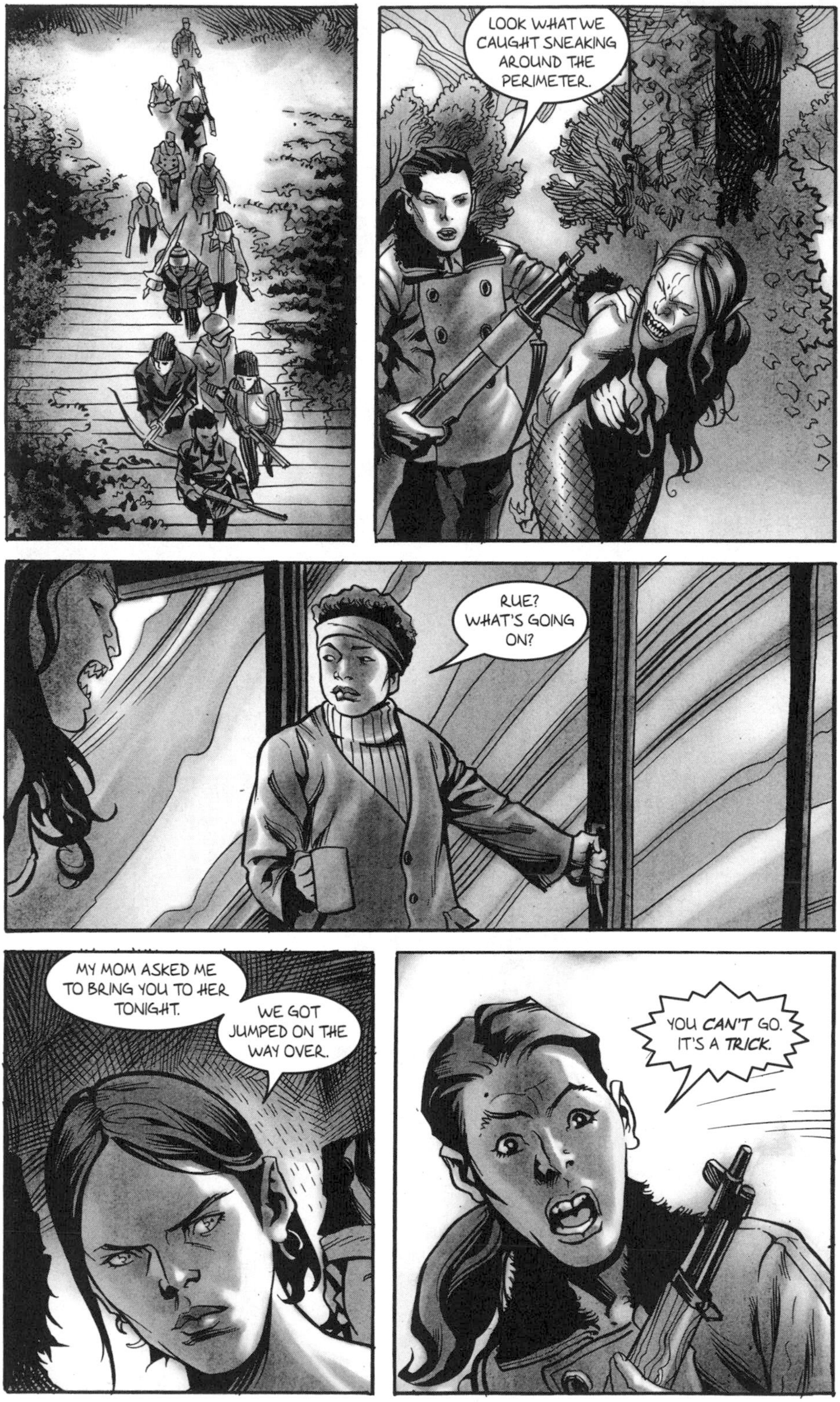
LOOK WHAT WE CAUGHT SNEAKING AROUND THE PERIMETER.
RUE? WHAT'S GOING ON?
MY MOM ASKED ME TO BRING YOU TO HER TONIGHT.
WE GOT JUMPED ON THE WAY OVER.
YOU **CAN'T** GO. IT'S A **TRICK**.

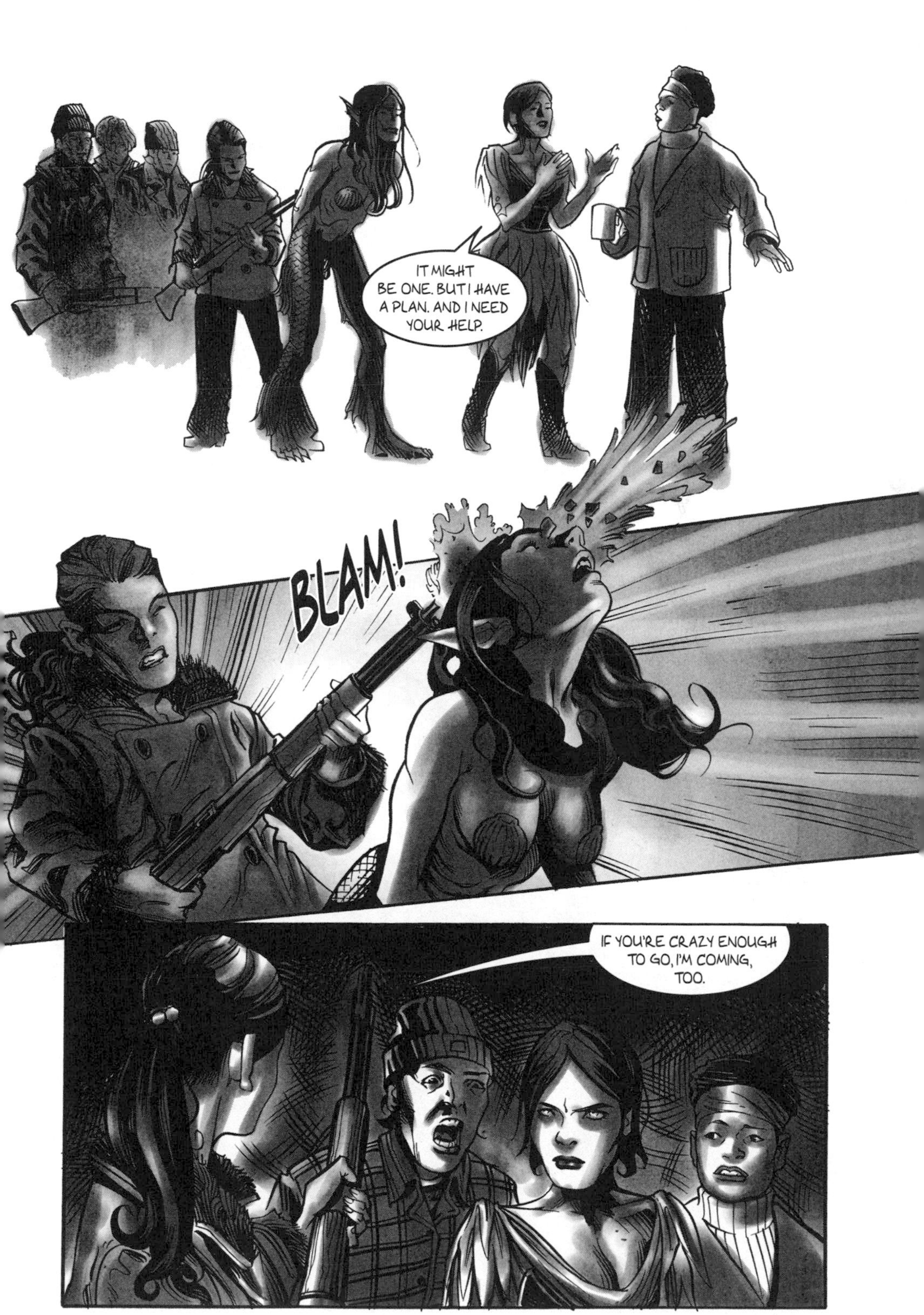
IT MIGHT BE ONE. BUT I HAVE A PLAN. AND I NEED YOUR HELP.
BLAM!
IF YOU'RE CRAZY ENOUGH TO GO, I'M COMING, TOO.

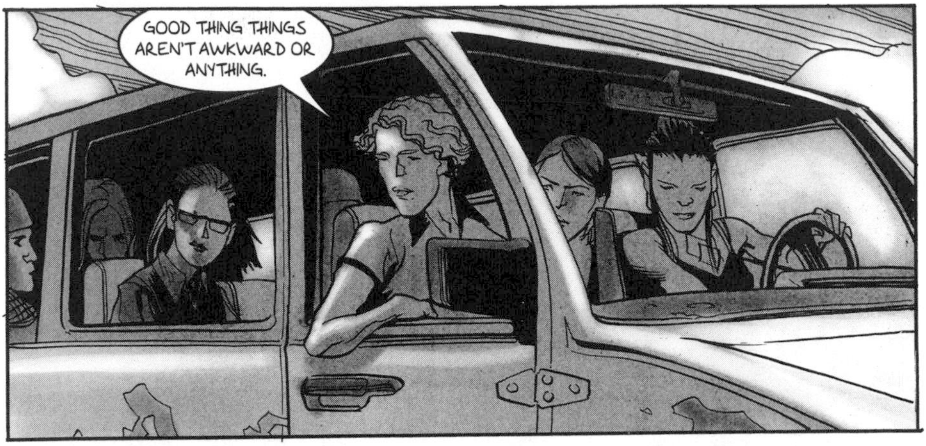
GOOD THING THINGS AREN'T AWKWARD OR ANYTHING.

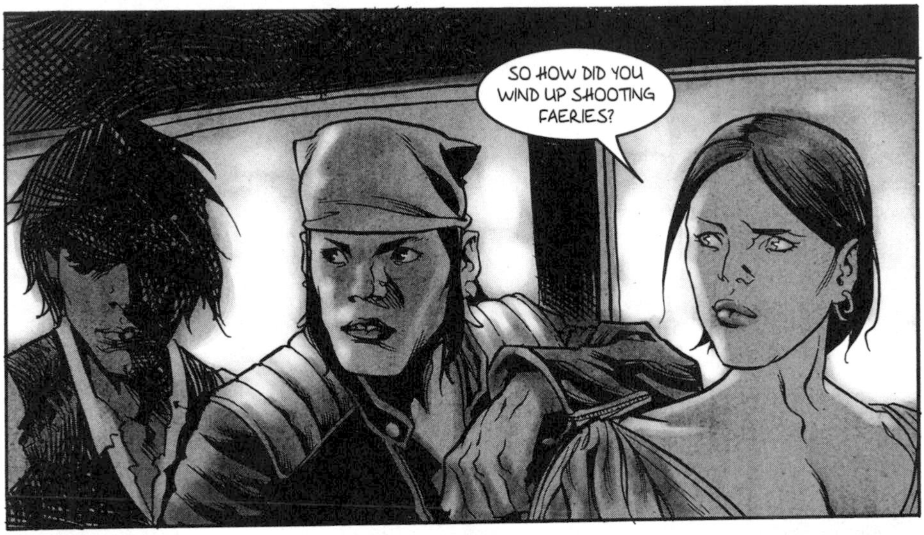
SO HOW DID YOU WIND UP SHOOTING FAERIES?

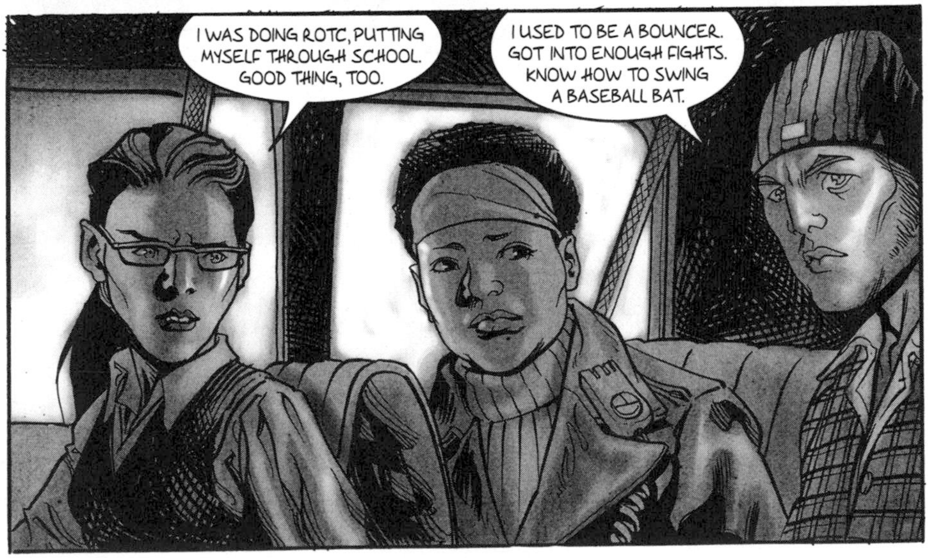
I WAS DOING ROTC, PUTTING MYSELF THROUGH SCHOOL. GOOD THING, TOO.
I USED TO BE A BOUNCER. GOT INTO ENOUGH FIGHTS. KNOW HOW TO SWING A BASEBALL BAT.

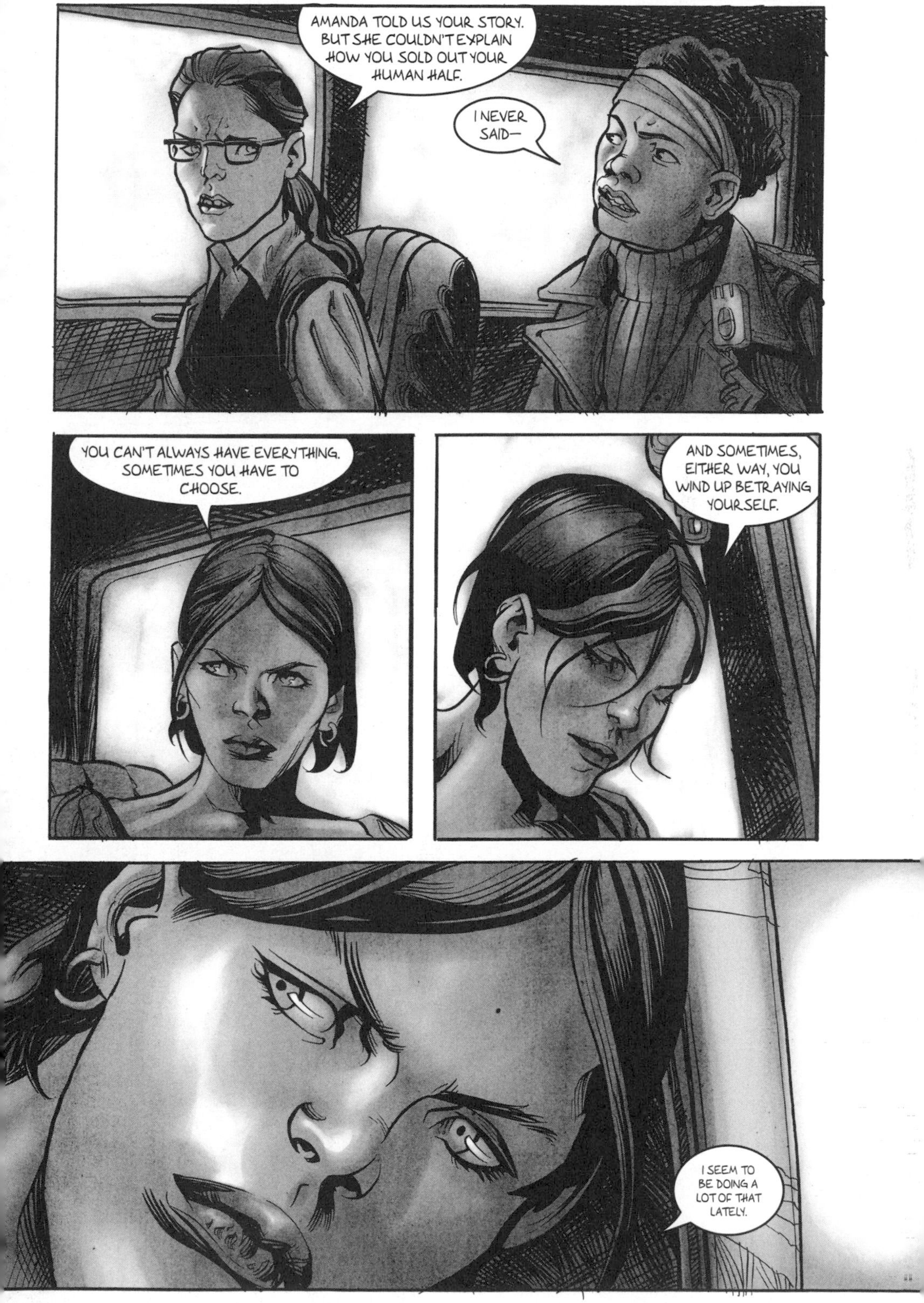
AMANDA TOLD US YOUR STORY. BUT SHE COULDN'T EXPLAIN HOW YOU SOLD OUT YOUR HUMAN HALF.
I NEVER SAID—
YOU CAN'T ALWAYS HAVE EVERYTHING. SOMETIMES YOU HAVE TO CHOOSE.
AND SOMETIMES, EITHER WAY, YOU WIND UP BETRAYING YOURSELF.
I SEEM TO BE DOING A LOT OF THAT LATELY.

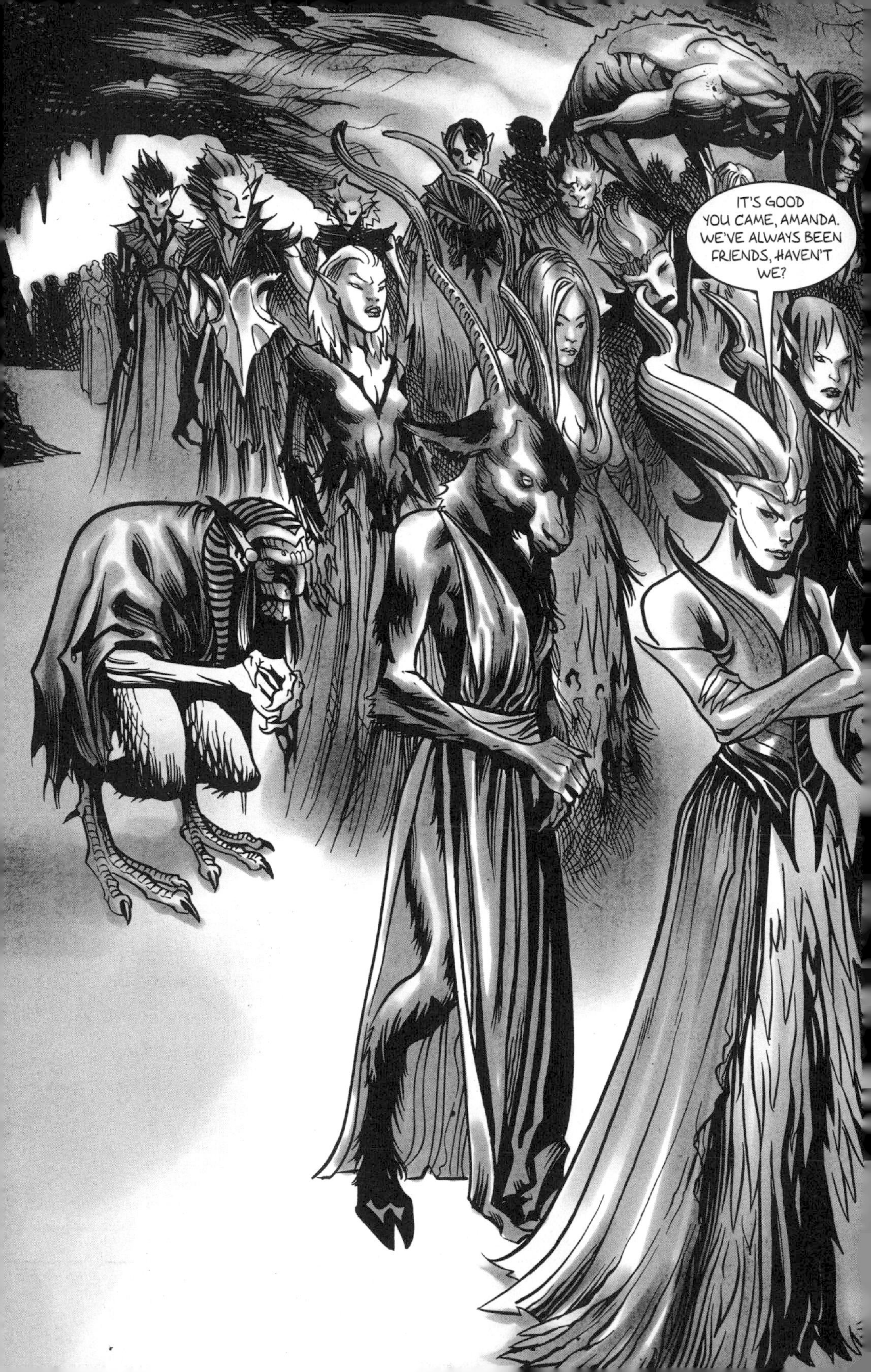
IT'S GOOD YOU CAME, AMANDA. WE'VE ALWAYS BEEN FRIENDS, HAVEN'T WE?

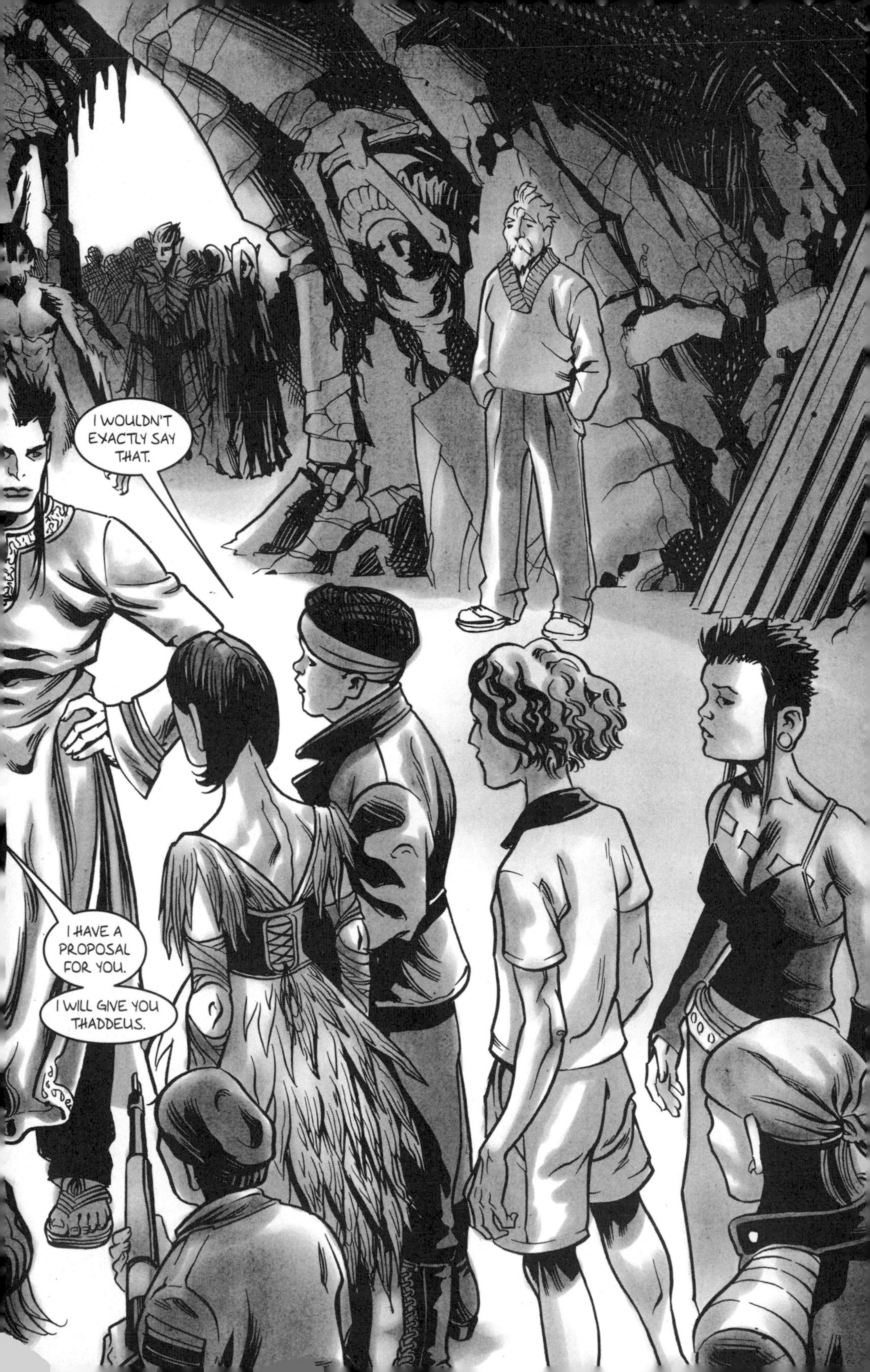
I WOULDN'T EXACTLY SAY THAT.
I HAVE A PROPOSAL FOR YOU.
I WILL GIVE YOU THADDEUS.

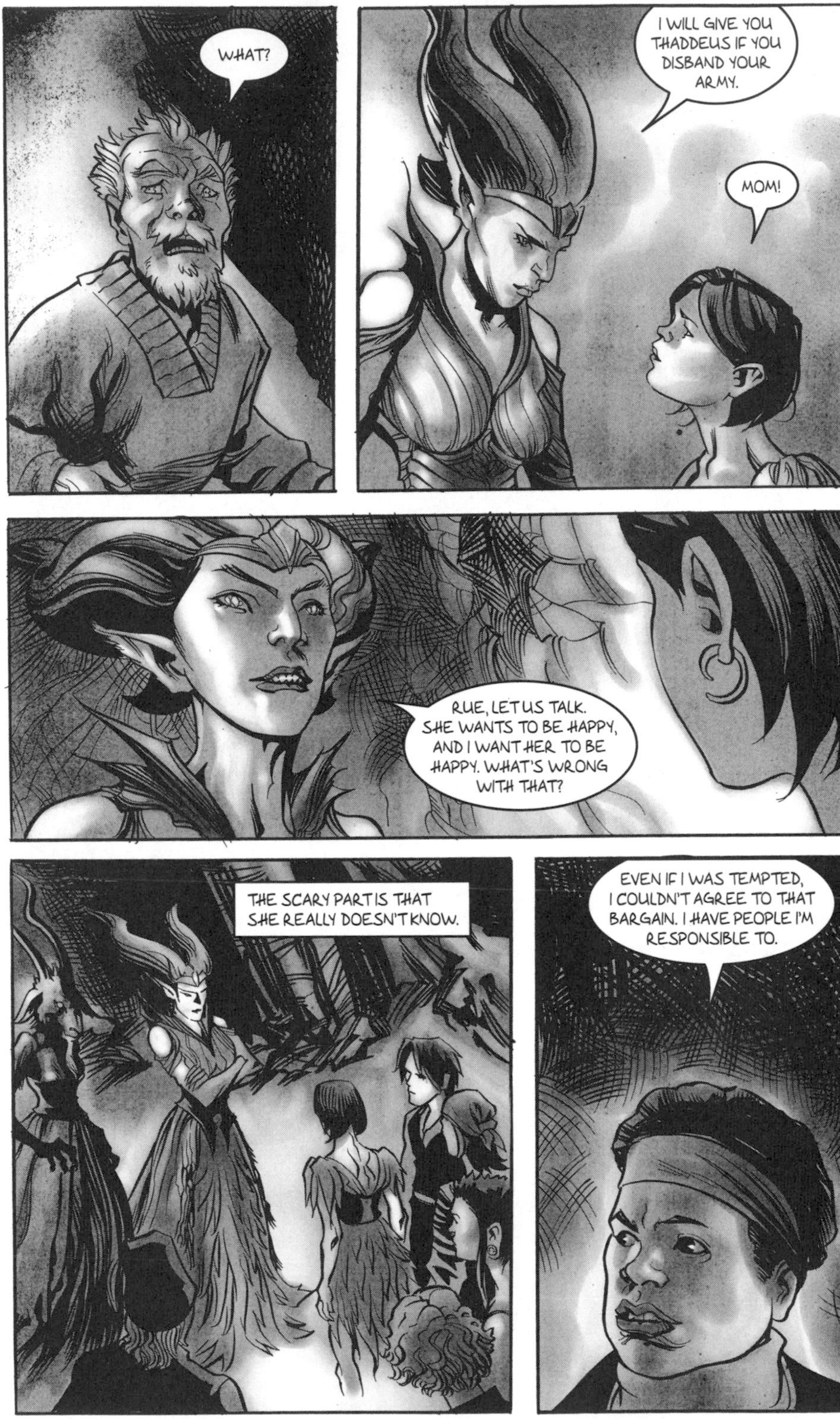
WHAT?
I WILL GIVE YOU THADDEUS IF YOU DISBAND YOUR ARMY.
MOM!
RUE, LET US TALK. SHE WANTS TO BE HAPPY, AND I WANT HER TO BE HAPPY. WHAT'S WRONG WITH THAT?
THE SCARY PART IS THAT SHE REALLY DOESN'T KNOW.
EVEN IF I WAS TEMPTED, I COULDN'T AGREE TO THAT BARGAIN. I HAVE PEOPLE I'M RESPONSIBLE TO.

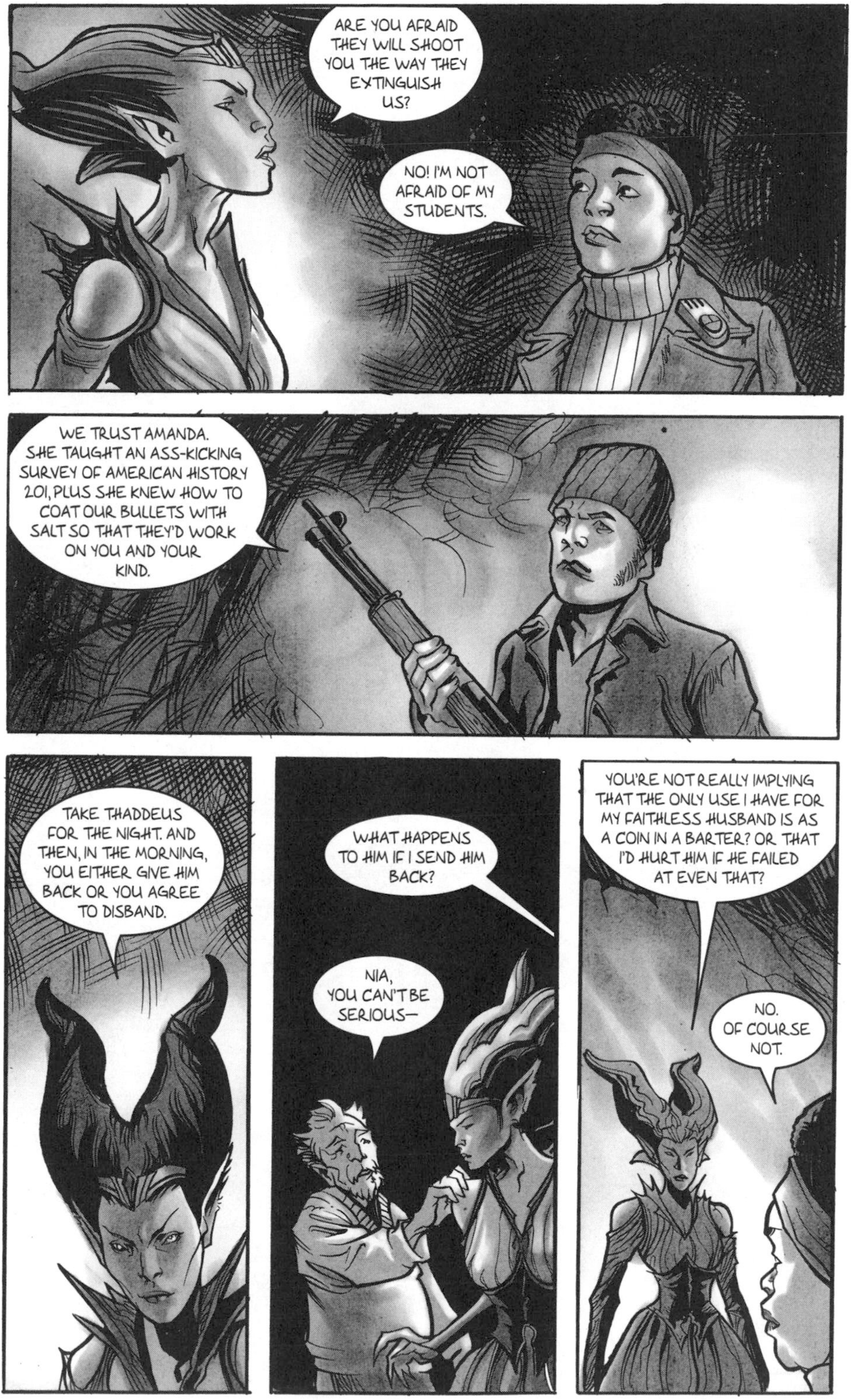
ARE YOU AFRAID THEY WILL SHOOT YOU THE WAY THEY EXTINGUISH US?
NO! I'M NOT AFRAID OF MY STUDENTS.
WE TRUST AMANDA. SHE TAUGHT AN ASS-KICKING SURVEY OF AMERICAN HISTORY 201, PLUS SHE KNEW HOW TO COAT OUR BULLETS WITH SALT SO THAT THEY'D WORK ON YOU AND YOUR KIND.
TAKE THADDEUS FOR THE NIGHT. AND THEN, IN THE MORNING, YOU EITHER GIVE HIM BACK OR YOU AGREE TO DISBAND.
WHAT HAPPENS TO HIM IF I SEND HIM BACK?
NIA, YOU CAN'T BE SERIOUS—
YOU'RE NOT REALLY IMPLYING THAT THE ONLY USE I HAVE FOR MY FAITHLESS HUSBAND IS AS A COIN IN A BARTER? OR THAT I'D HURT HIM IF HE FAILED AT EVEN THAT?
NO. OF COURSE NOT.

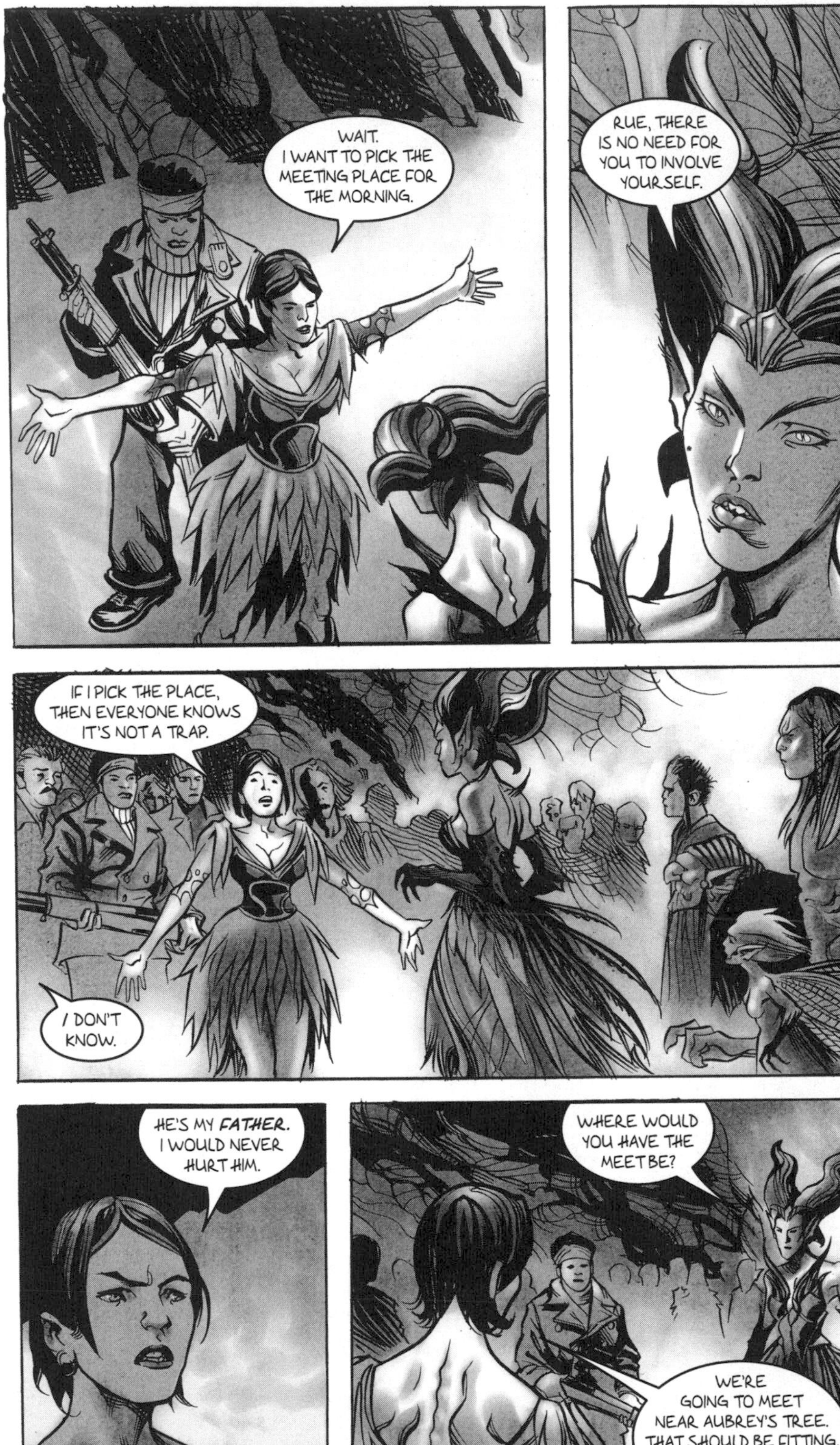
WAIT. I WANT TO PICK THE MEETING PLACE FOR THE MORNING.
RUE, THERE IS NO NEED FOR YOU TO INVOLVE YOURSELF.
IF I PICK THE PLACE, THEN EVERYONE KNOWS IT'S NOT A TRAP.
I DON'T KNOW.
HE'S MY **FATHER.** I WOULD NEVER HURT HIM.
WHERE WOULD YOU HAVE THE MEET BE?
WE'RE GOING TO MEET NEAR AUBREY'S TREE. THAT SHOULD BE FITTING.

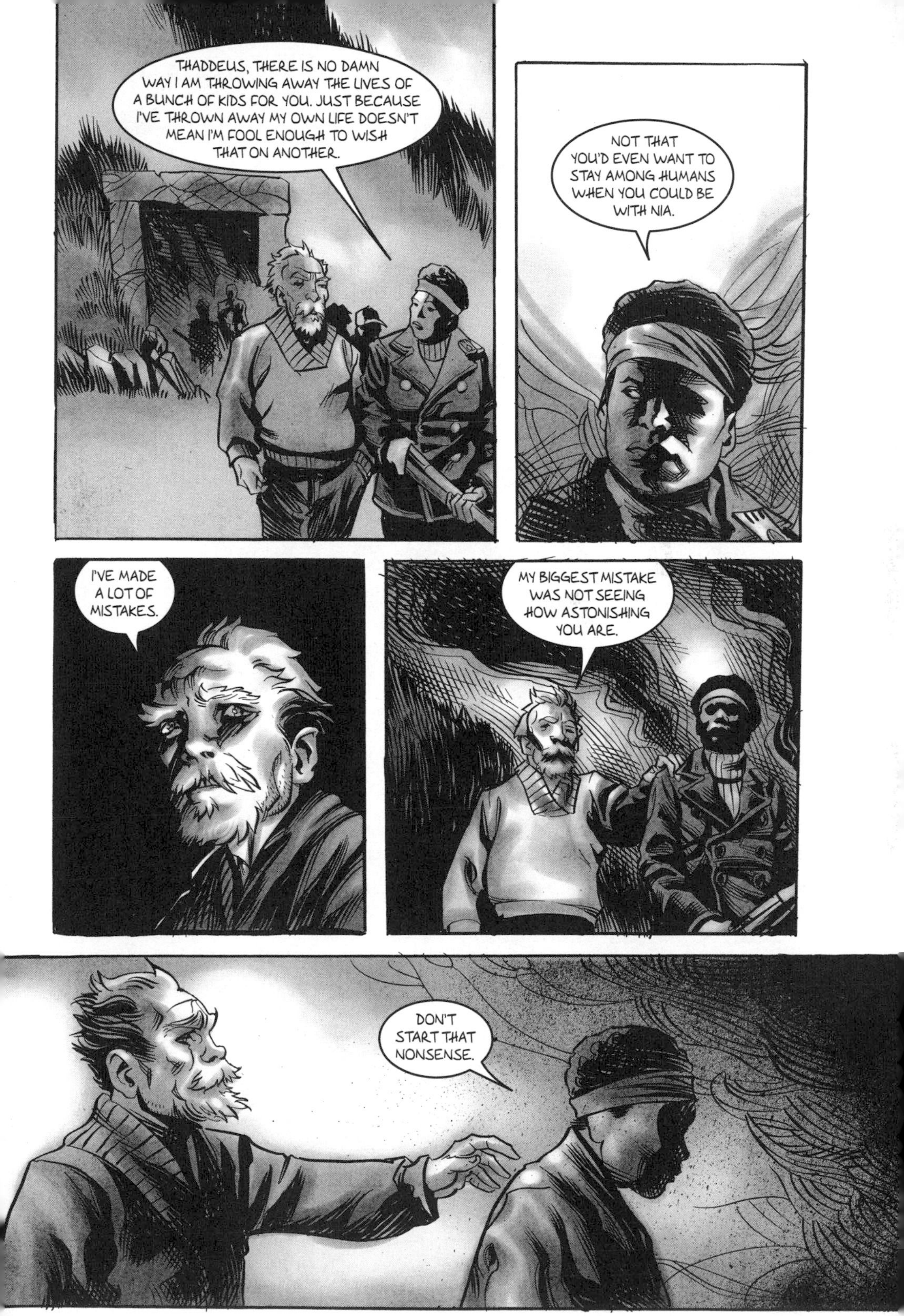
THADDEUS, THERE IS NO DAMN WAY I AM THROWING AWAY THE LIVES OF A BUNCH OF KIDS FOR YOU. JUST BECAUSE I'VE THROWN AWAY MY OWN LIFE DOESN'T MEAN I'M FOOL ENOUGH TO WISH THAT ON ANOTHER.
NOT THAT YOU'D EVEN WANT TO STAY AMONG HUMANS WHEN YOU COULD BE WITH NIA.
I'VE MADE A LOT OF MISTAKES.
MY BIGGEST MISTAKE WAS NOT SEEING HOW ASTONISHING YOU ARE.
DON'T START THAT NONSENSE.

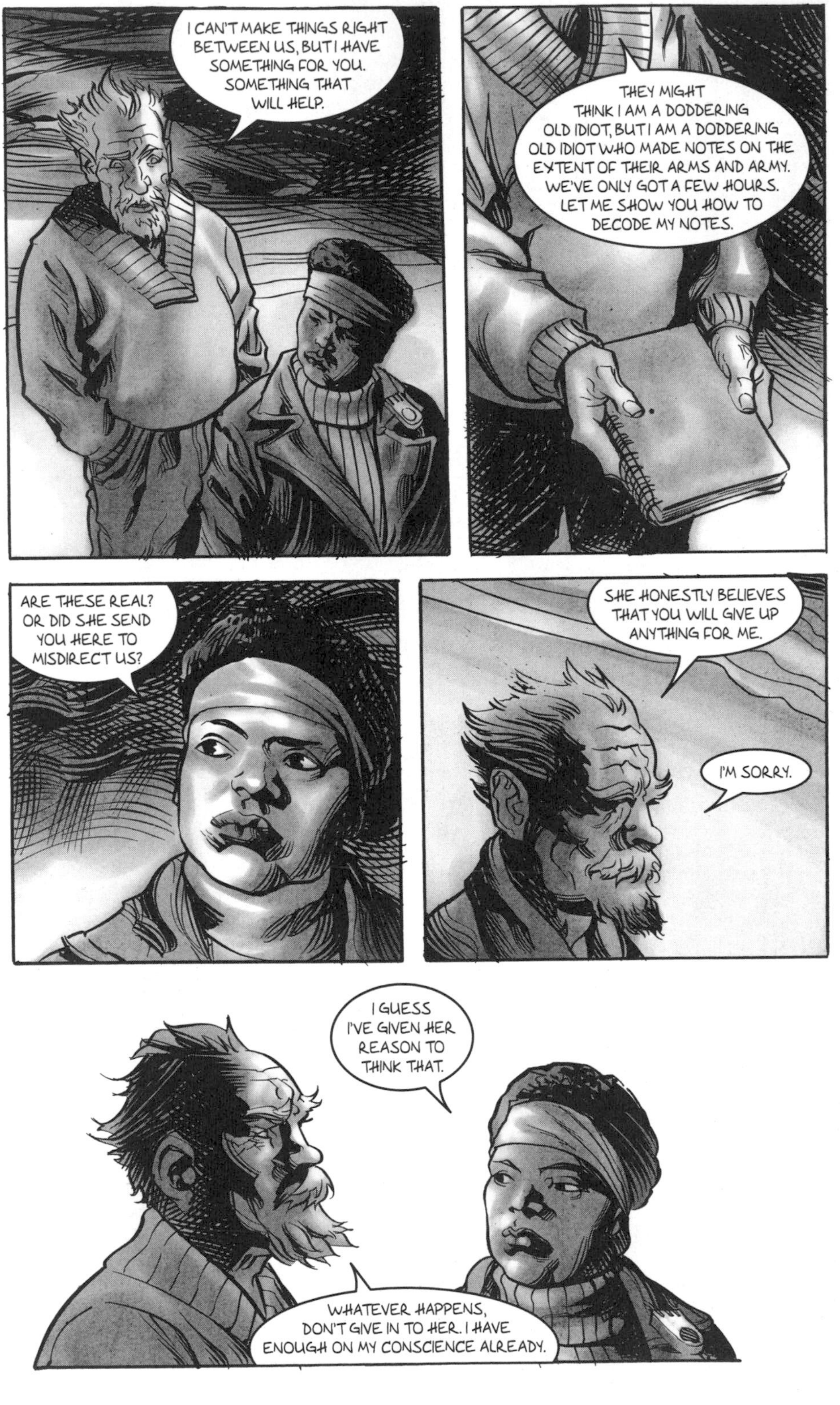
I CAN'T MAKE THINGS RIGHT BETWEEN US, BUT I HAVE SOMETHING FOR YOU. SOMETHING THAT WILL HELP.
THEY MIGHT THINK I AM A DODDERING OLD IDIOT, BUT I AM A DODDERING OLD IDIOT WHO MADE NOTES ON THE EXTENT OF THEIR ARMS AND ARMY. WE'VE ONLY GOT A FEW HOURS. LET ME SHOW YOU HOW TO DECODE MY NOTES.
ARE THESE REAL? OR DID SHE SEND YOU HERE TO MISDIRECT US?
SHE HONESTLY BELIEVES THAT YOU WILL GIVE UP ANYTHING FOR ME.
I'M SORRY.
I GUESS I'VE GIVEN HER REASON TO THINK THAT.
WHATEVER HAPPENS, DON'T GIVE IN TO HER. I HAVE ENOUGH ON MY CONSCIENCE ALREADY.

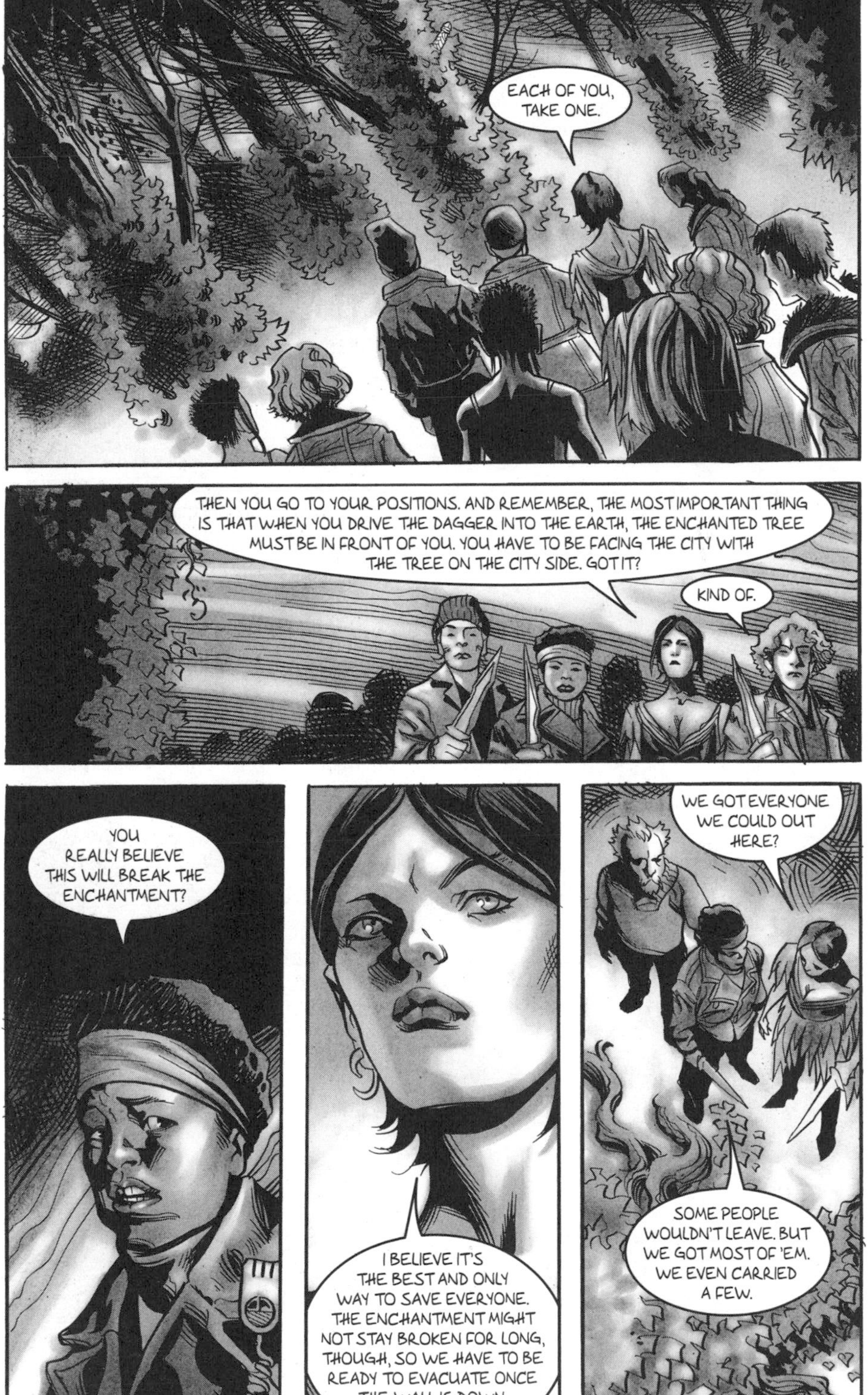
EACH OF YOU, TAKE ONE.
THEN YOU GO TO YOUR POSITIONS. AND REMEMBER, THE MOST IMPORTANT THING IS THAT WHEN YOU DRIVE THE DAGGER INTO THE EARTH, THE ENCHANTED TREE MUST BE IN FRONT OF YOU. YOU HAVE TO BE FACING THE CITY WITH THE TREE ON THE CITY SIDE. GOT IT?
KIND OF.
YOU REALLY BELIEVE THIS WILL BREAK THE ENCHANTMENT?
I BELIEVE IT'S THE BEST AND ONLY WAY TO SAVE EVERYONE. THE ENCHANTMENT MIGHT NOT STAY BROKEN FOR LONG, THOUGH, SO WE HAVE TO BE READY TO EVACUATE ONCE THE WALL IS DOWN.
WE GOT EVERYONE WE COULD OUT HERE?
SOME PEOPLE WOULDN'T LEAVE. BUT WE GOT MOST OF 'EM. WE EVEN CARRIED A FEW.

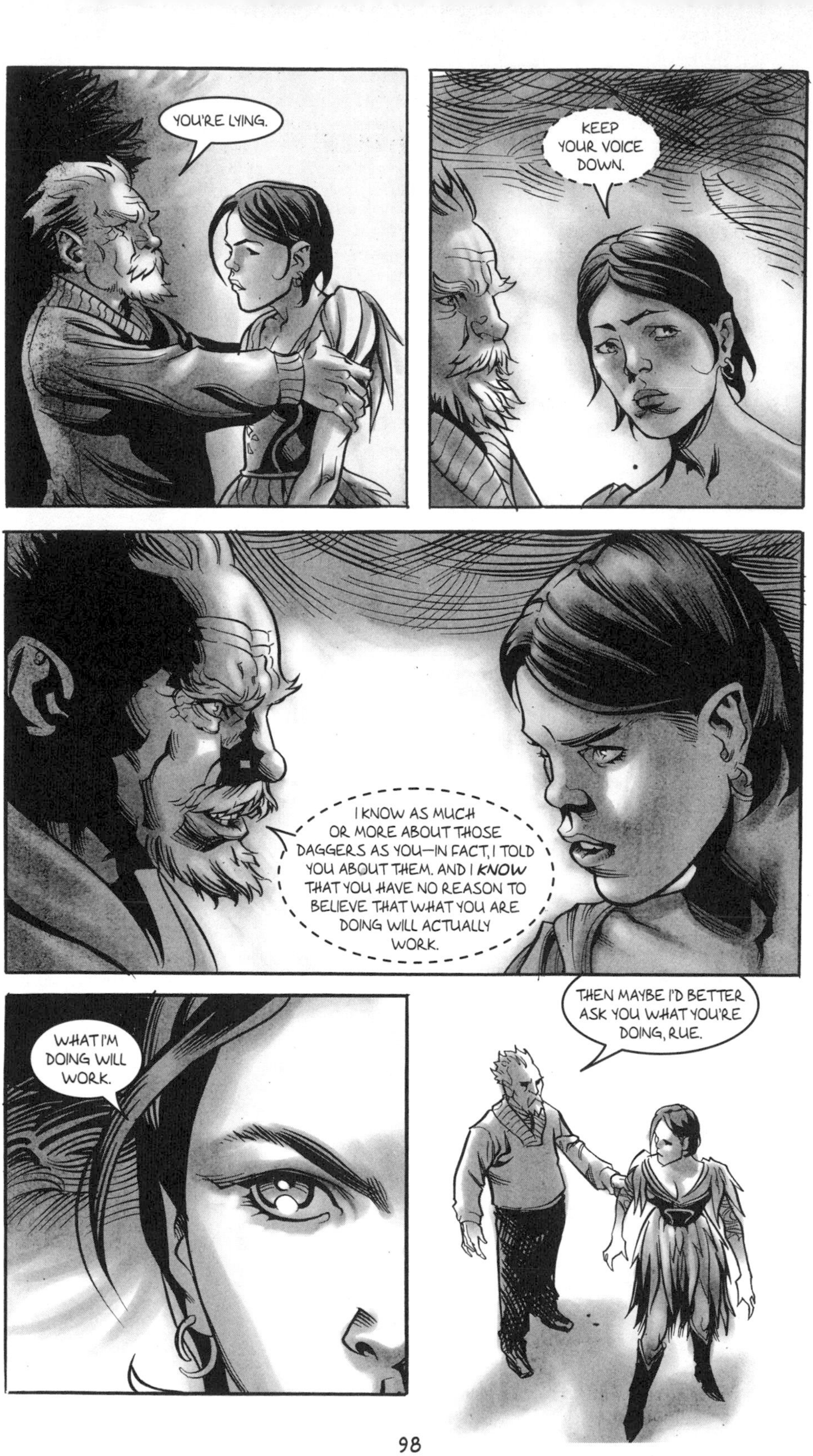
YOU'RE LYING.
KEEP YOUR VOICE DOWN.
I KNOW AS MUCH OR MORE ABOUT THOSE DAGGERS AS YOU—IN FACT, I TOLD YOU ABOUT THEM. AND I *KNOW* THAT YOU HAVE NO REASON TO BELIEVE THAT WHAT YOU ARE DOING WILL ACTUALLY WORK.
WHAT I'M DOING WILL WORK.
THEN MAYBE I'D BETTER ASK YOU WHAT YOU'RE DOING, RUE.

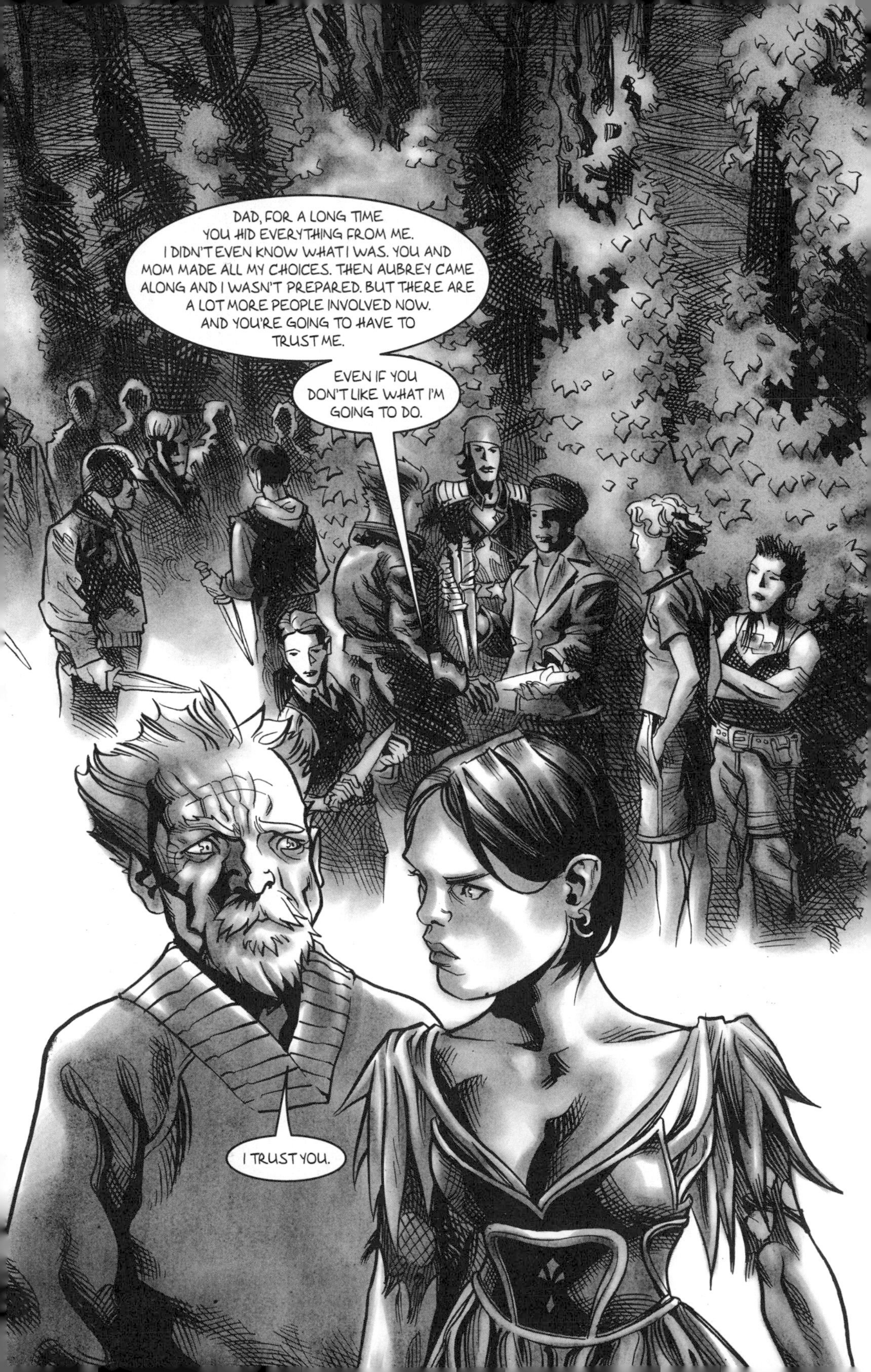
DAD, FOR A LONG TIME YOU HID EVERYTHING FROM ME. I DIDN'T EVEN KNOW WHAT I WAS. YOU AND MOM MADE ALL MY CHOICES. THEN AUBREY CAME ALONG AND I WASN'T PREPARED. BUT THERE ARE A LOT MORE PEOPLE INVOLVED NOW. AND YOU'RE GOING TO HAVE TO TRUST ME.
EVEN IF YOU DON'T LIKE WHAT I'M GOING TO DO.
I TRUST YOU.

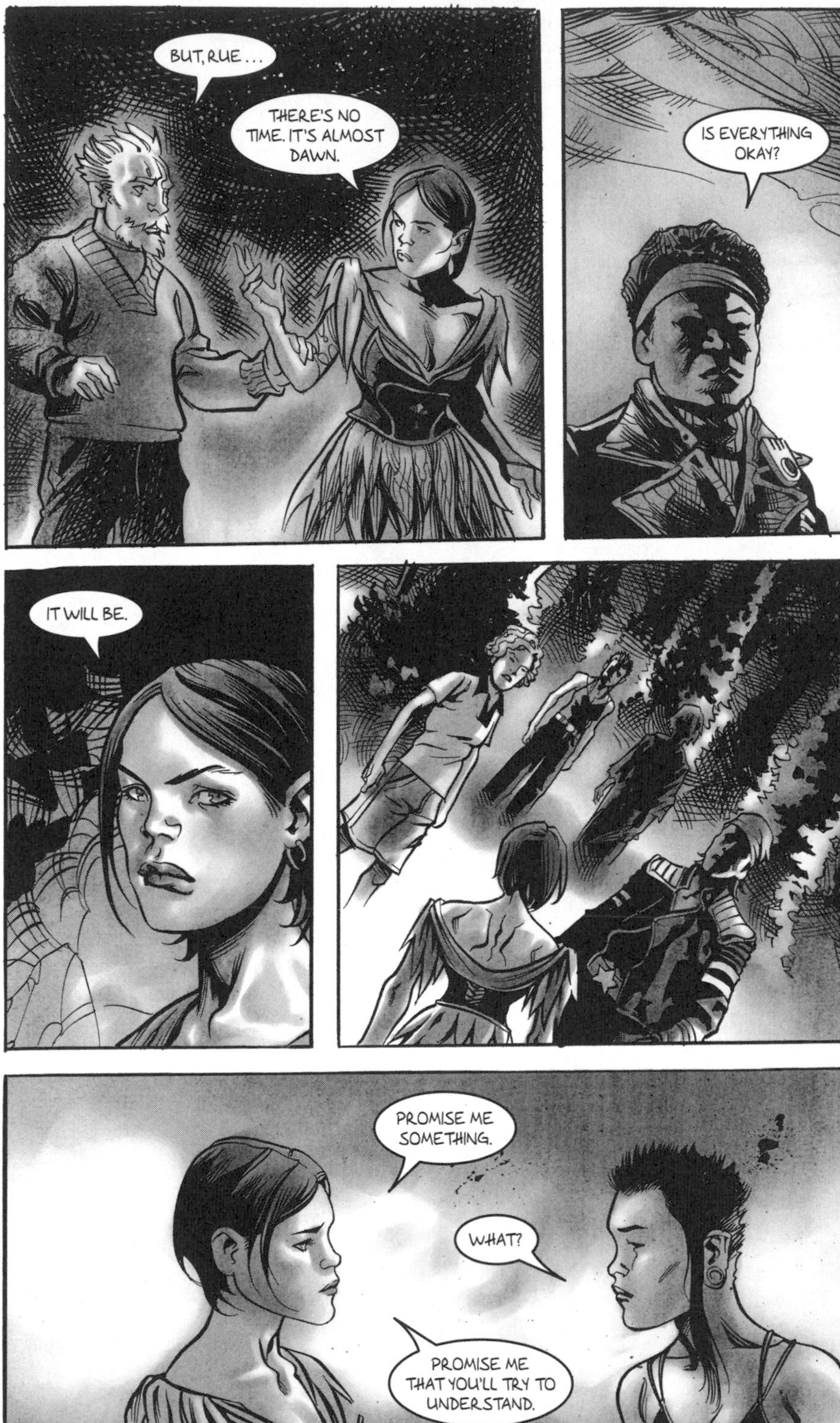
BUT, RUE...
THERE'S NO TIME. IT'S ALMOST DAWN.
IS EVERYTHING OKAY?
IT WILL BE.
PROMISE ME SOMETHING.
WHAT?
PROMISE ME THAT YOU'LL TRY TO UNDERSTAND.

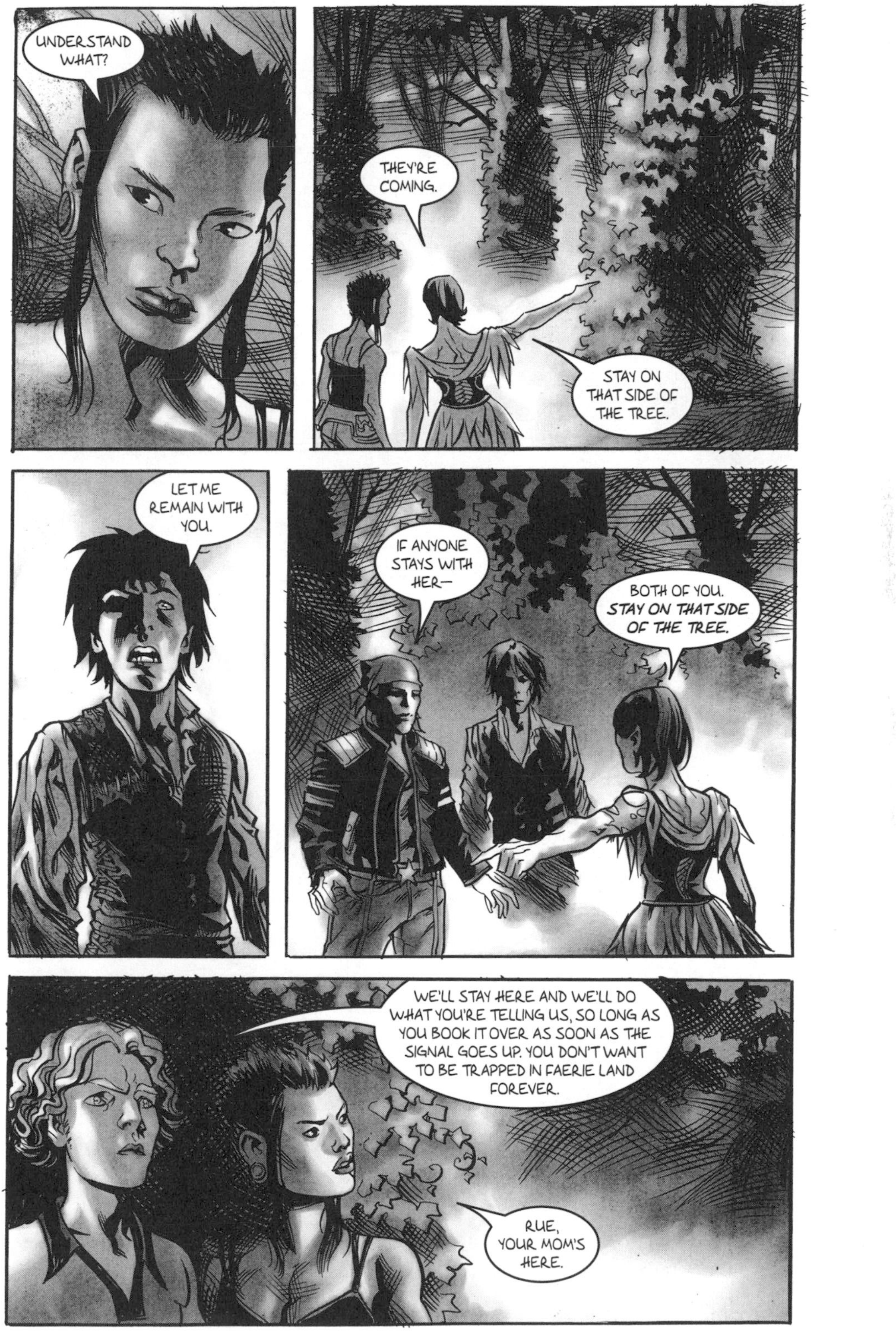
UNDERSTAND WHAT?
THEY'RE COMING.
STAY ON THAT SIDE OF THE TREE.
LET ME REMAIN WITH YOU.
IF ANYONE STAYS WITH HER—
BOTH OF YOU. *STAY ON THAT SIDE OF THE TREE.*
WE'LL STAY HERE AND WE'LL DO WHAT YOU'RE TELLING US, SO LONG AS YOU BOOK IT OVER AS SOON AS THE SIGNAL GOES UP. YOU DON'T WANT TO BE TRAPPED IN FAERIE LAND FOREVER.
RUE, YOUR MOM'S HERE.

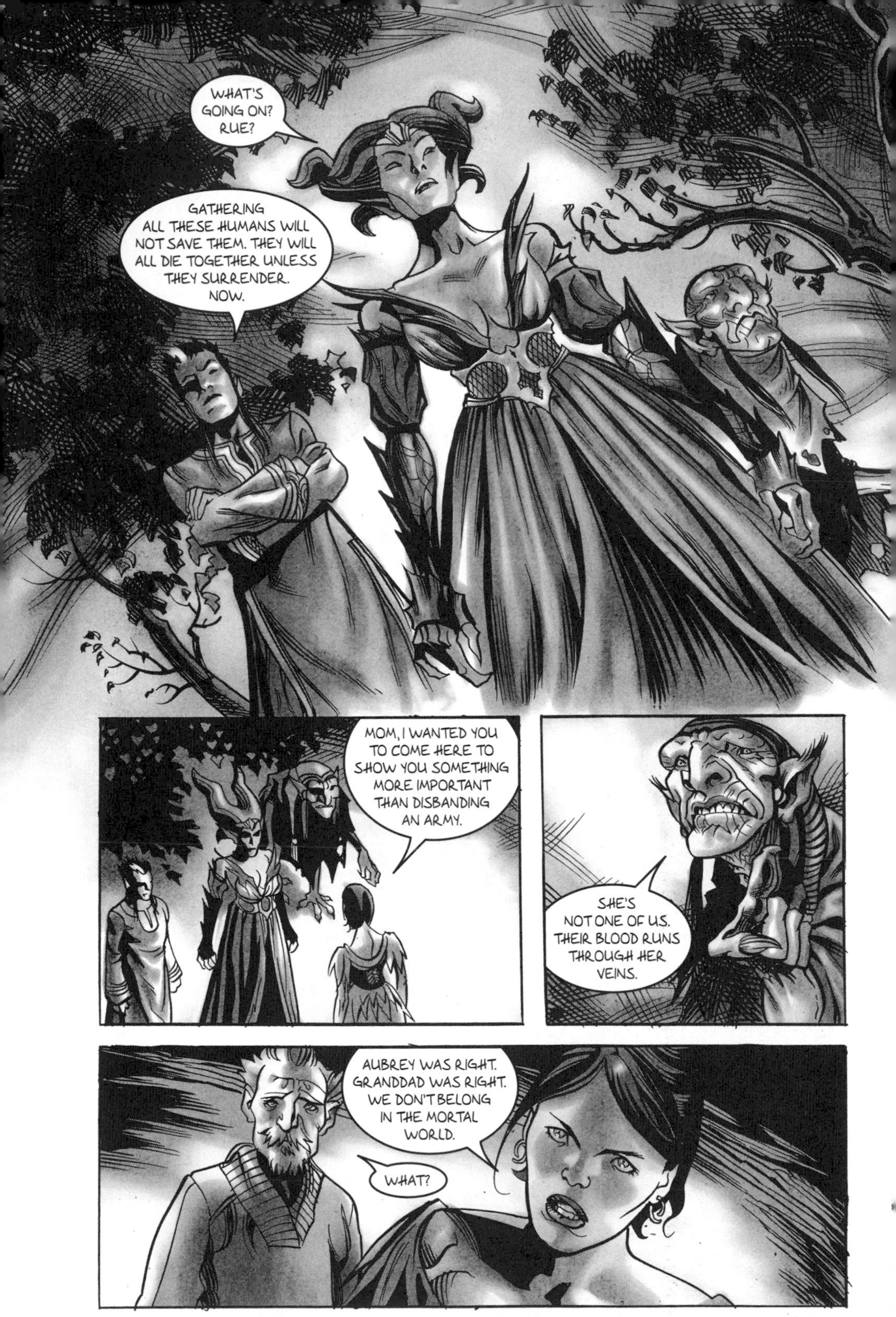
WHAT'S GOING ON? RUE?
GATHERING ALL THESE HUMANS WILL NOT SAVE THEM. THEY WILL ALL DIE TOGETHER UNLESS THEY SURRENDER. NOW.
MOM, I WANTED YOU TO COME HERE TO SHOW YOU SOMETHING MORE IMPORTANT THAN DISBANDING AN ARMY.
SHE'S NOT ONE OF US. THEIR BLOOD RUNS THROUGH HER VEINS.
AUBREY WAS RIGHT. GRANDDAD WAS RIGHT. WE DON'T BELONG IN THE MORTAL WORLD.
WHAT?

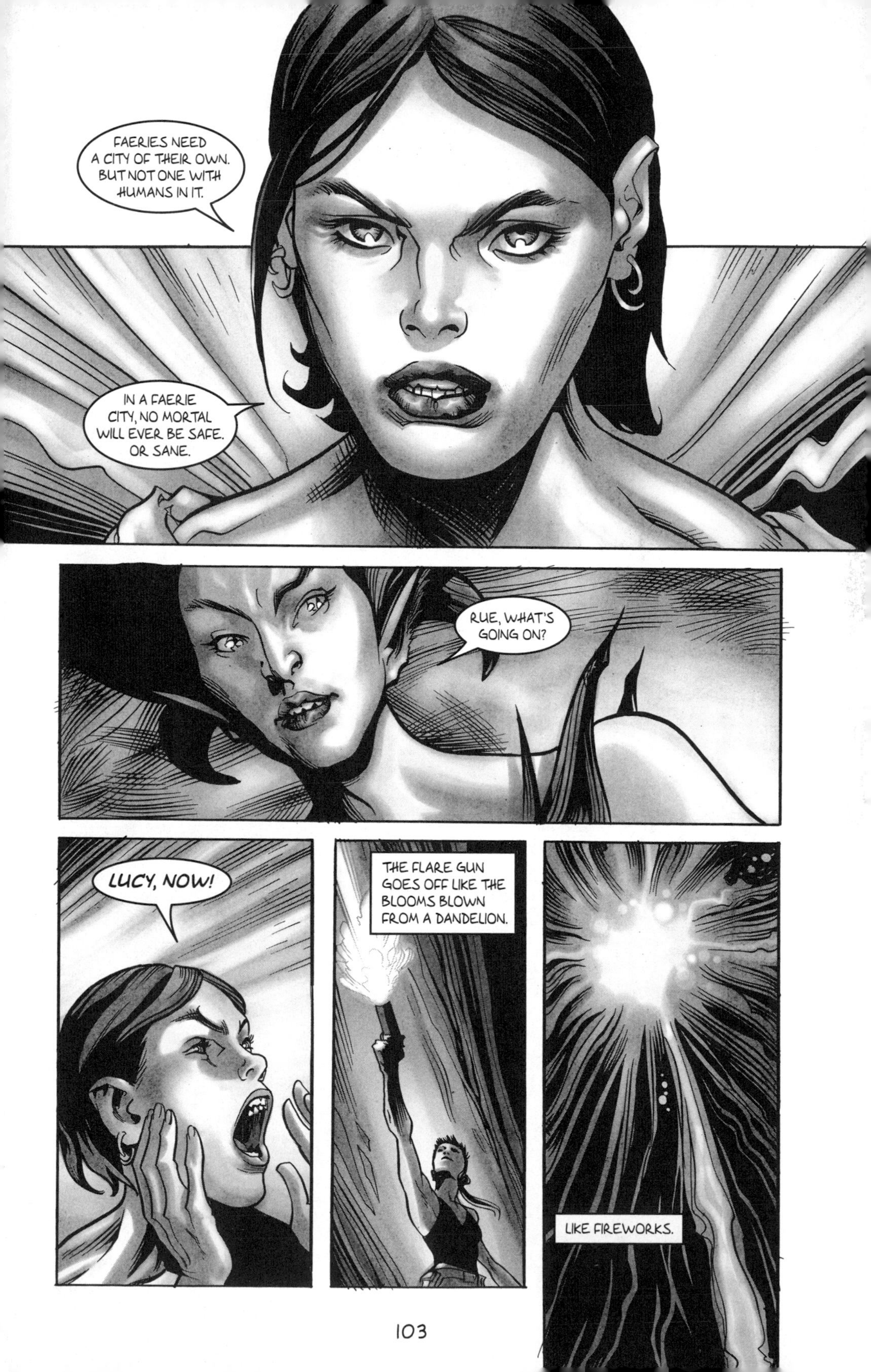
FAERIES NEED A CITY OF THEIR OWN. BUT NOT ONE WITH HUMANS IN IT.
IN A FAERIE CITY, NO MORTAL WILL EVER BE SAFE. OR SANE.
RUE, WHAT'S GOING ON?
LUCY, NOW!
THE FLARE GUN GOES OFF LIKE THE BLOOMS BLOWN FROM A DANDELION.
LIKE FIREWORKS.

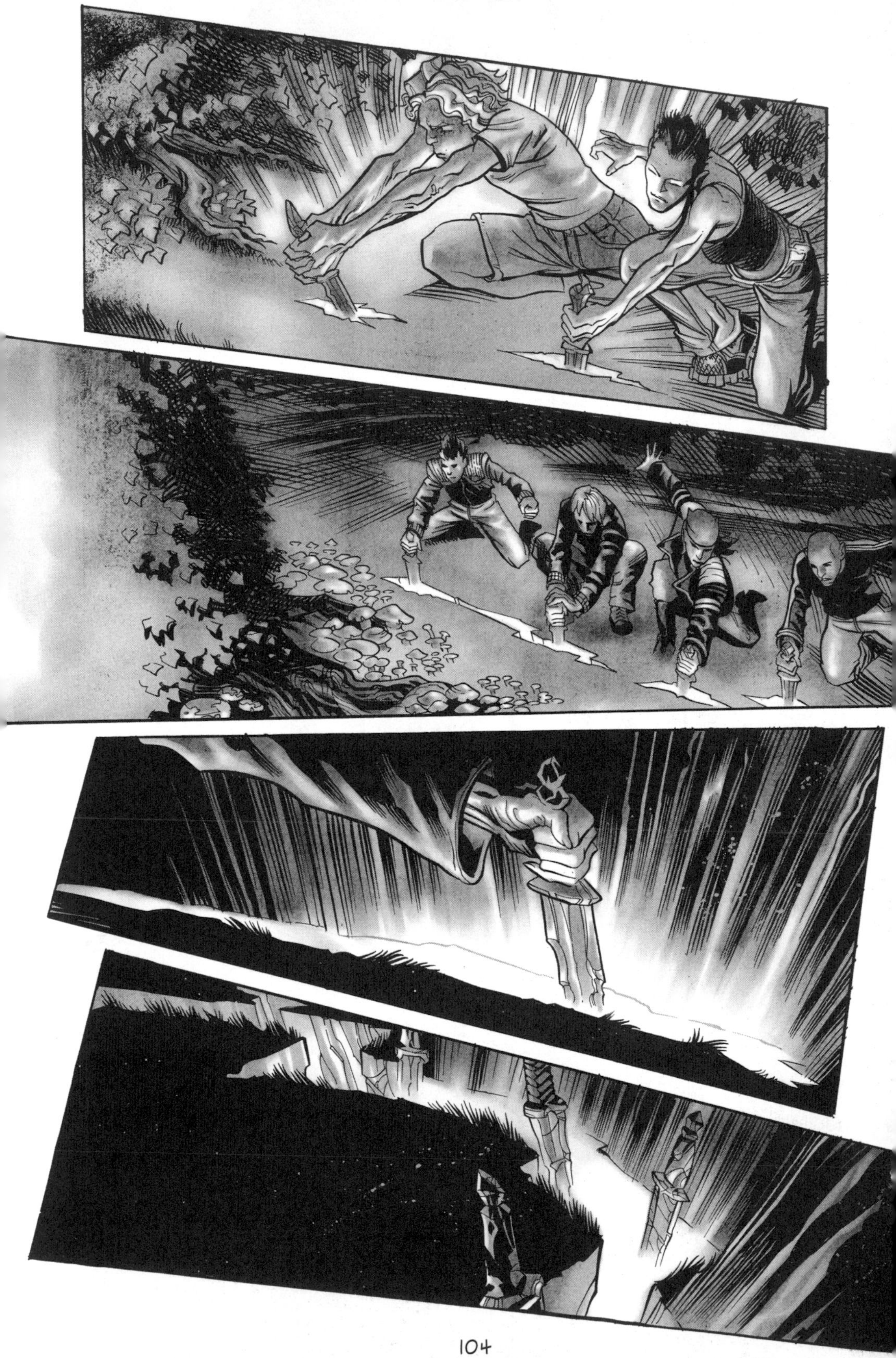

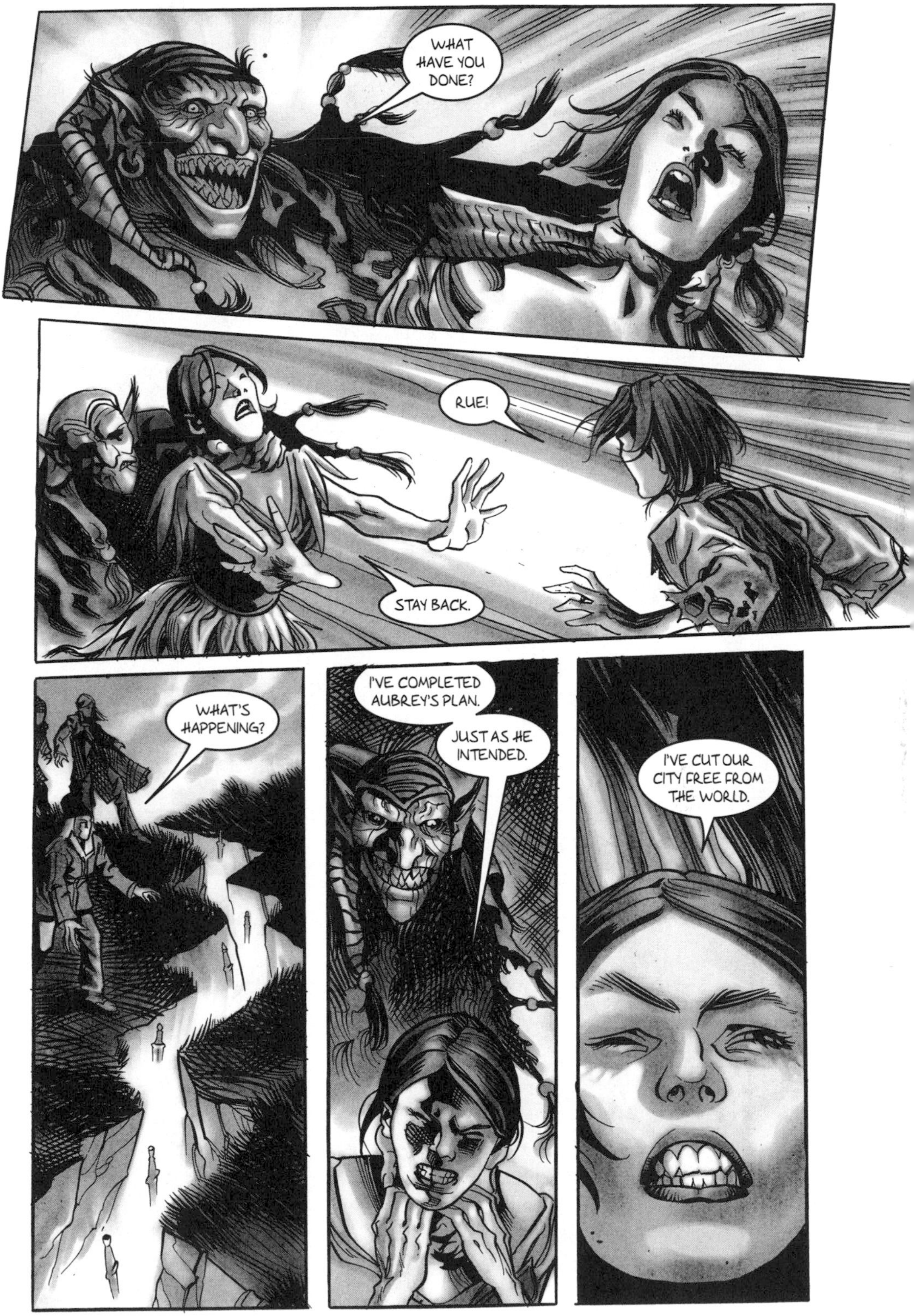
WHAT HAVE YOU DONE?
RUE!
STAY BACK.
WHAT'S HAPPENING?
I'VE COMPLETED AUBREY'S PLAN.
JUST AS HE INTENDED.
I'VE CUT OUR CITY FREE FROM THE WORLD.

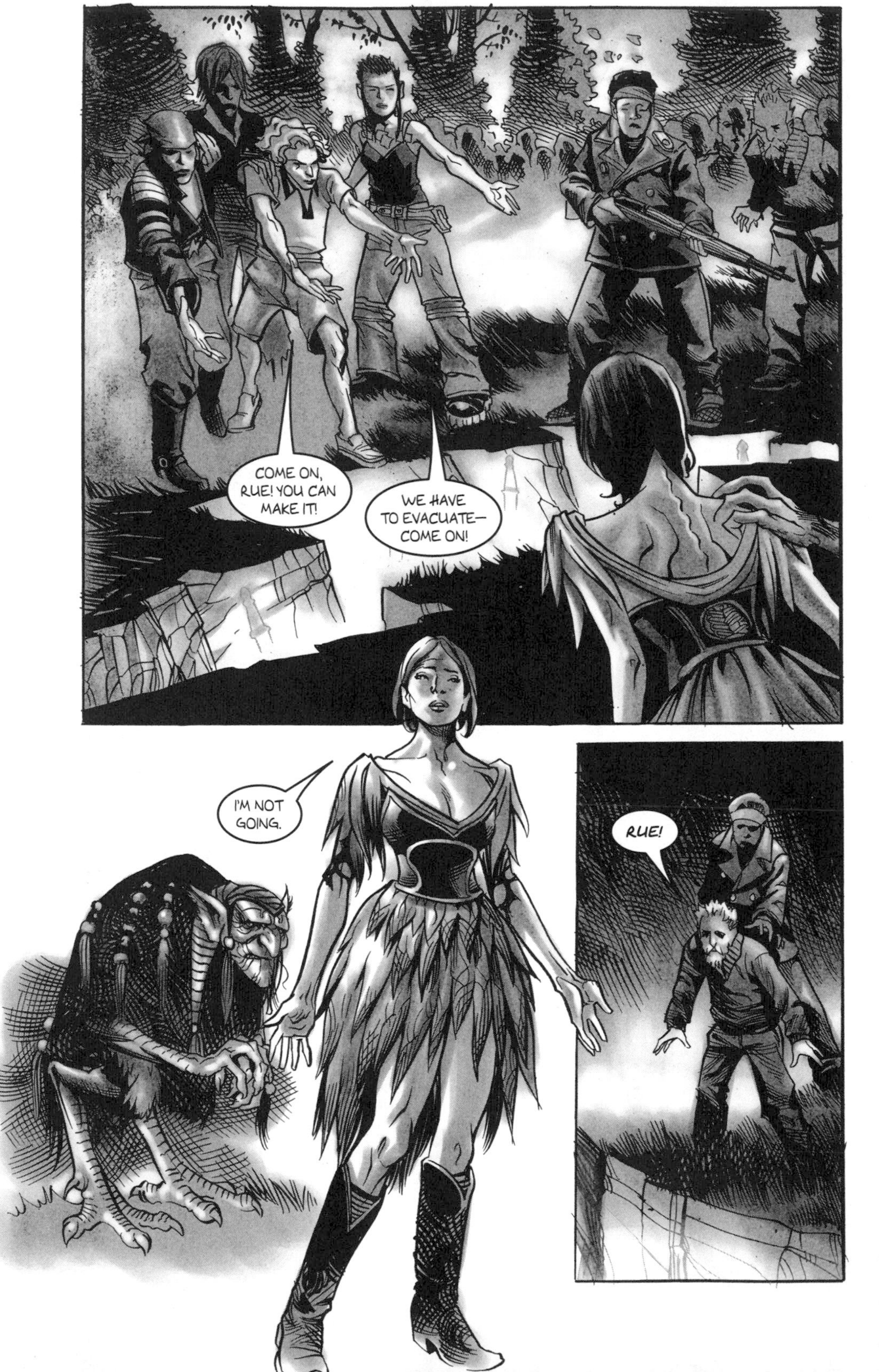
COME ON, RUE! YOU CAN MAKE IT!
WE HAVE TO EVACUATE— COME ON!
I'M NOT GOING.
RUE!

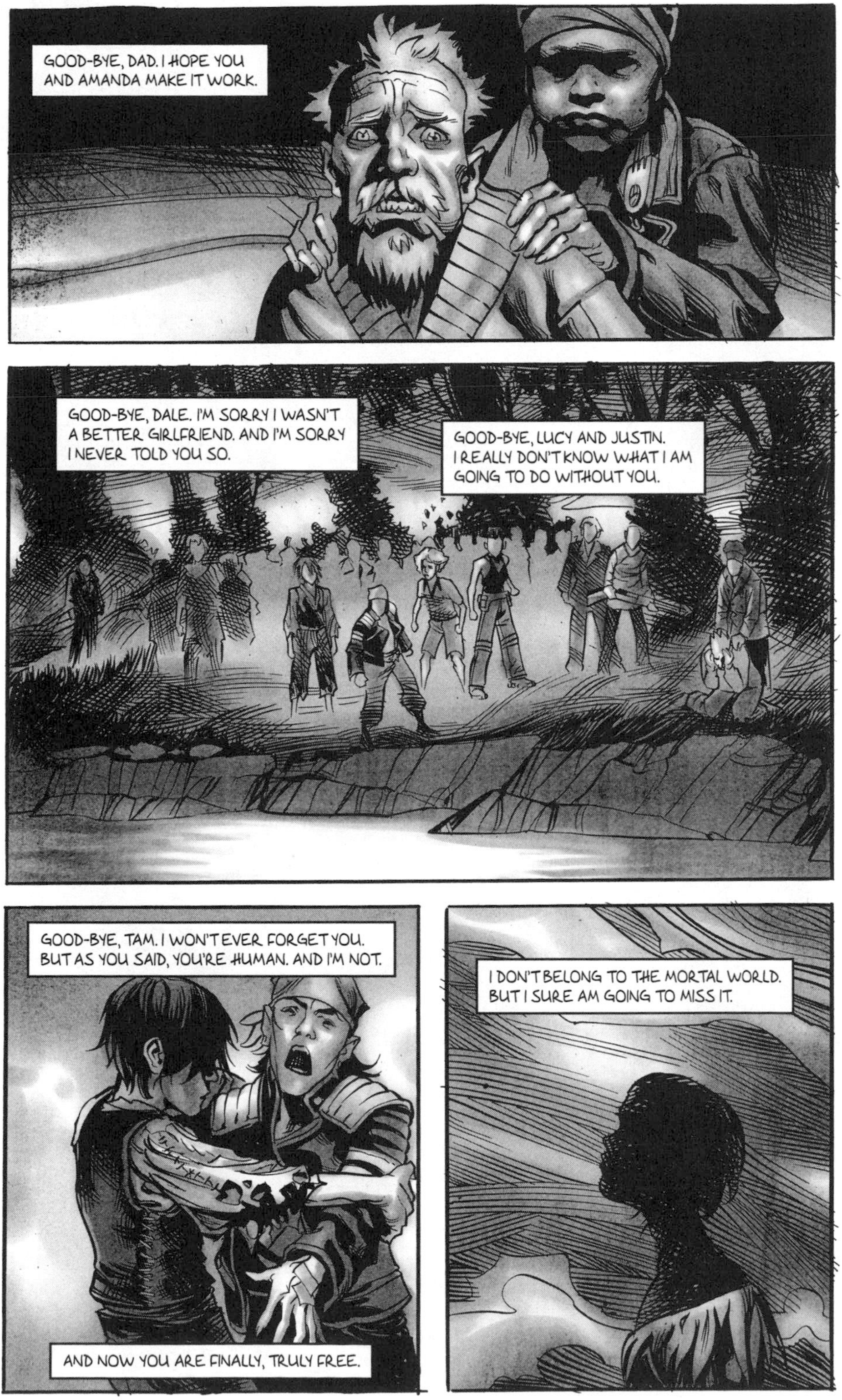
GOOD-BYE, DAD. I HOPE YOU AND AMANDA MAKE IT WORK.
GOOD-BYE, DALE. I'M SORRY I WASN'T A BETTER GIRLFRIEND. AND I'M SORRY I NEVER TOLD YOU SO.
GOOD-BYE, LUCY AND JUSTIN. I REALLY DON'T KNOW WHAT I AM GOING TO DO WITHOUT YOU.
GOOD-BYE, TAM. I WON'T EVER FORGET YOU. BUT AS YOU SAID, YOU'RE HUMAN. AND I'M NOT.
AND NOW YOU ARE FINALLY, TRULY FREE.
I DON'T BELONG TO THE MORTAL WORLD. BUT I SURE AM GOING TO MISS IT.

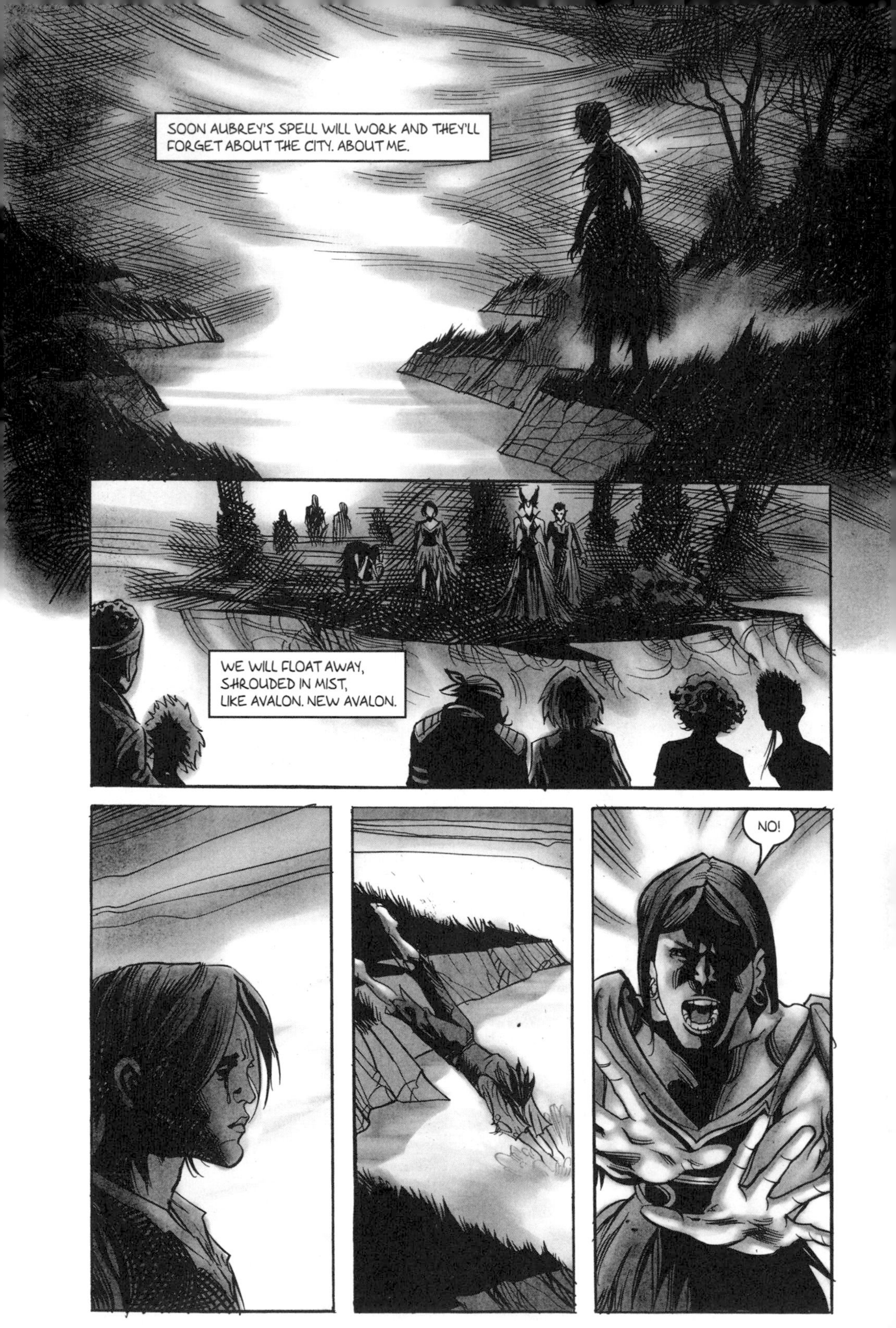
SOON AUBREY'S SPELL WILL WORK AND THEY'LL FORGET ABOUT THE CITY. ABOUT ME.
WE WILL FLOAT AWAY, SHROUDED IN MIST, LIKE AVALON. NEW AVALON.
NO!

WHY DID YOU COME BACK? YOU'LL BE TRAPPED HERE.

THERE IS NOTHING IN ANY WORLD I WANT MORE THAN YOU.

I LOVE YOU, RUE.

YOU'RE CRAZY, BUT I LOVE YOU, TOO.

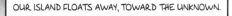

OUR ISLAND FLOATS AWAY, TOWARD THE UNKNOWN.

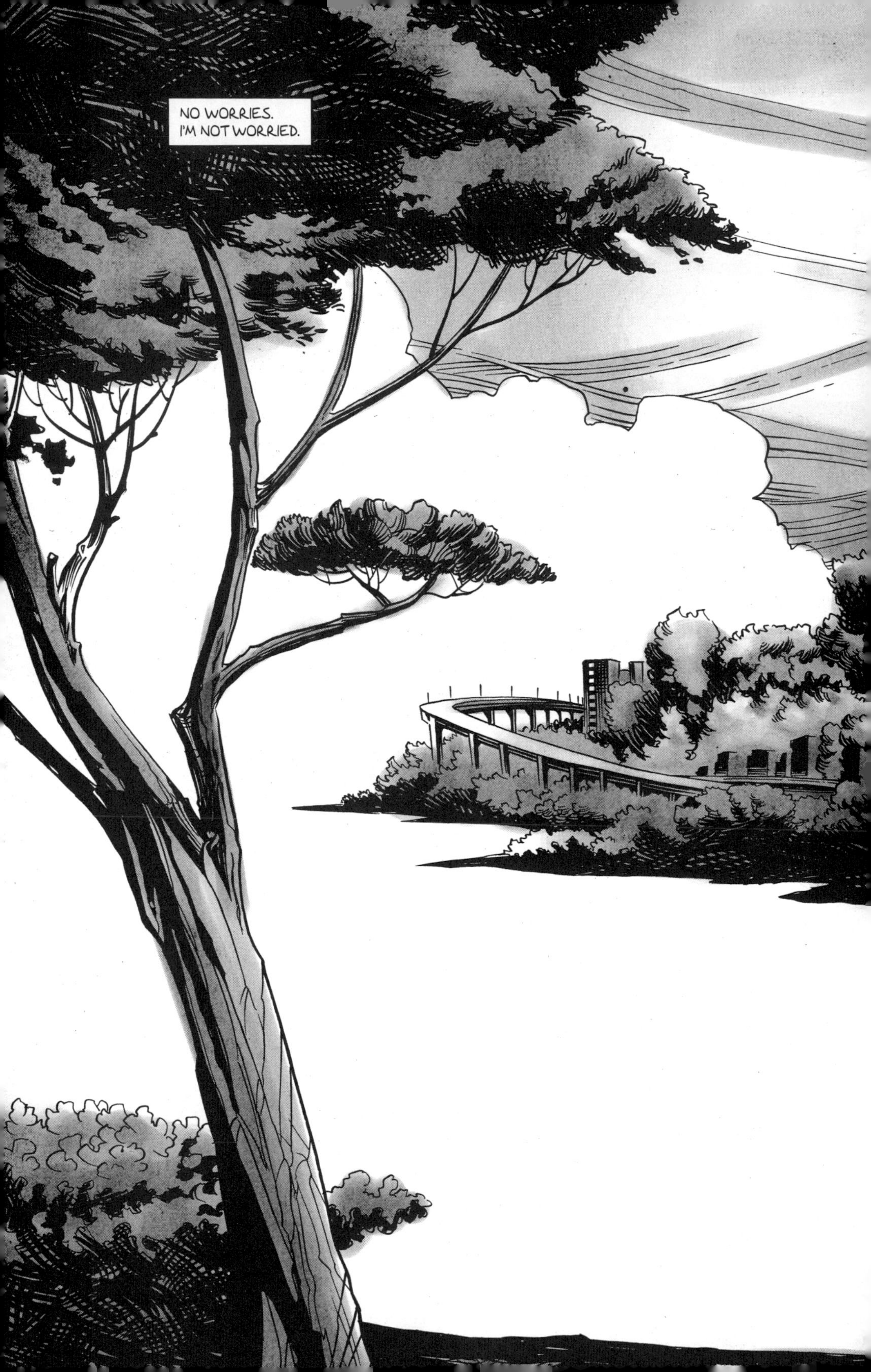
NO WORRIES.
I'M NOT WORRIED.

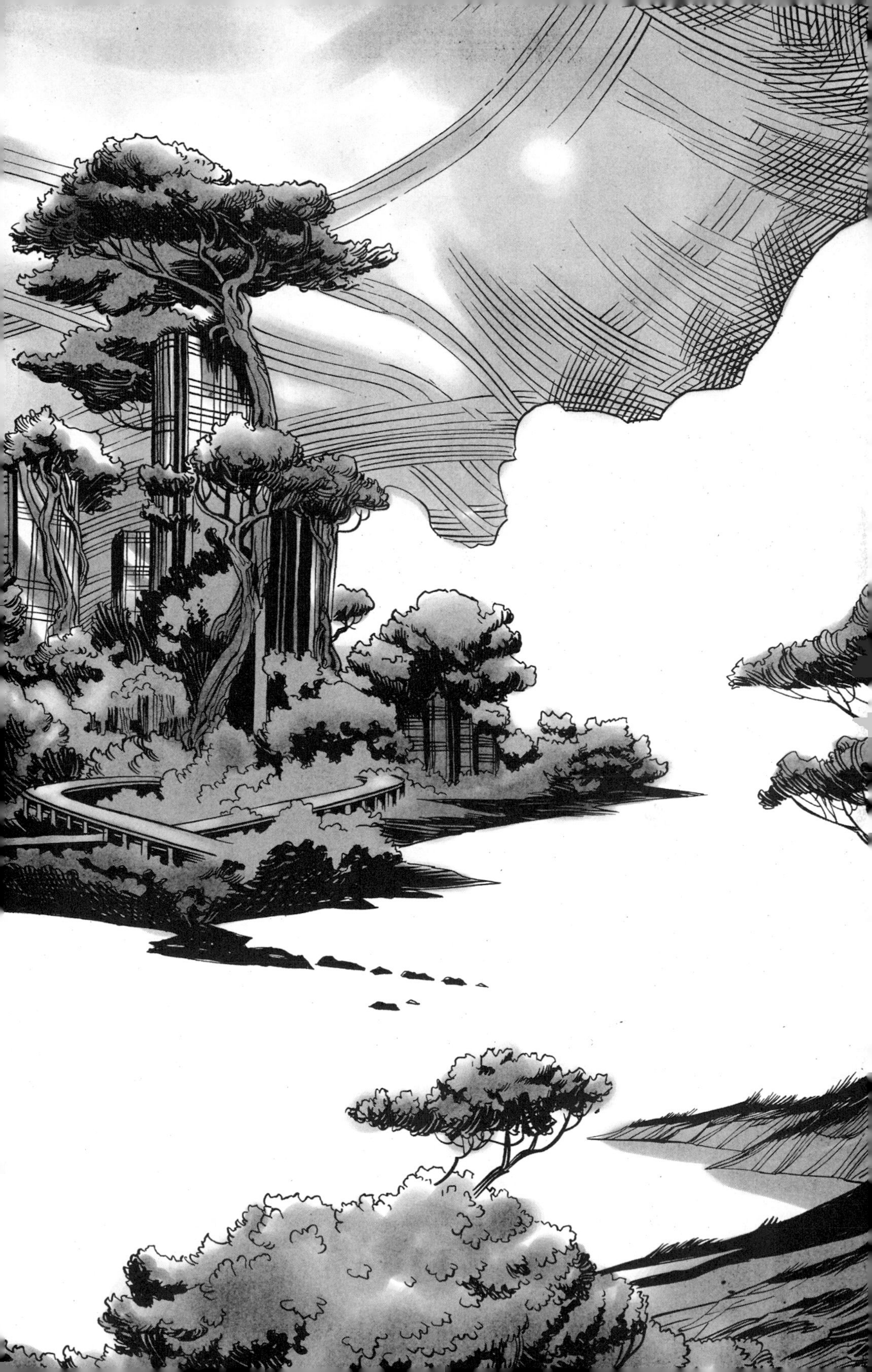

end

ABOUT THE AUTHOR

Holly Black is the author of contemporary fantasy novels for teens and children. Born in New Jersey, Holly grew up in a decrepit Victorian house piled with books and oddments. She never quite recovered.

Her first book, *Tithe: A Modern Faerie Tale*, was called "dark, edgy, beautifully written and compulsively readable" by *Booklist*, received starred reviews from *Publisher's Weekly* and *Kirkus*, and was included in the American Library Association's Best Books for Young Adults. Holly has since written two other books in the same universe: *Valiant*, a recipient of the Andre Norton Award for Excellence in Young Adult Literature, and *Ironside*.

Holly collaborated with her long-time friend, Caldecott Honor–winning artist Tony DiTerlizzi, to create the best-selling Spiderwick Chronicles. The serial has been called "vintage Victorian fantasy" by the *New York Post*, and *Time* reported that "the books wallow in their dusty Olde Worlde charm." The Spiderwick Chronicles were adapted into a film in 2008.

Holly's latest novel is a curse magic caper called *The White Cat*, the first in the Curse Workers series.

She lives in Massachusetts with her husband, Theo, and an ever-expanding collection of books. She spends a lot of her time in cafes, glaring at her laptop and drinking endless cups of coffee.

ABOUT THE ARTIST

Ted Naifeh swooped onto the comics and goth culture scene as the co-creator of *Gloomcookie* with Serena Valentino in 1998. Ted illustrated the first volume of the gothic romance hit before departing to pursue his own projects.

In 2002, he introduced us to the world of Courtney Crumrin, a young loner girl who learns magic from her mysterious and curmudgeonly Uncle Aloysius and uses it to navigate her world of school bullies and bloodthirsty goblins, adolescent peer pressure and deadly coven politics. Courtney's adventures have been published in five volumes: *Courtney Crumrin and the Night Things*, *Courtney Crumrin and the Coven of Mystics*, *Courtney Crumrin in the Twilight Kingdom*, *Courtney Crumrin and the Fire-Thief's Tale*, and *Courtney Crumrin and the Prince of Nowhere*.

Ted's next creation was *Polly and the Pirates*, also published through Oni Press, a swashbuckling tale of proper, rule-abiding young Polly Pringle, who is spirited away from her comfortable boarding school existence by pirates who insist that she is their rightful queen and captain. *Polly and the Pirates* was nominated for a Harvey Award.

Ted has also illustrated six volumes featuring video game character Death Jr. for Image Comics, and is the co-creator of *How Loathsome*, strictly for the 18-and-up crowd.

Ted lives in San Francisco, which influenced his aesthetic from a young age with its magnificently spooky Victorian houses, romantic foggy nights, and significant population of Night Things and other fantastic beings.

ACKNOWLEDGMENTS

A lot of people had a hand in pushing me to try writing a graphic novel and helping me along the way. Thanks to Jon Shestack and Ellen Goldsmith-Vein in particular, for asking me about another faery story and liking the one that I told them. Thanks to Steve Burkow for his calm counsel. I am indebted to my literary agent, Barry Goldblatt, and to my editor, the ever-encouraging and amazing David Levithan. And to Ted Naifeh, who brought these characters to life.

I am grateful to Cecil Castellucci, Kelly Link, Justine Larbalestier, Steve Berman, and Cassandra Clare for pushing me to write better and more cleverly. Thanks to Theo for letting me know when things made sense. And thanks to all of you for putting up with my whingeing.

I was greatly inspired by two books, *The Cooper's Wife Is Missing* by Joan Hoff and Marian Yeates and *The Burning of Bridget Cleary* by Angela Bourke. This book was written with the program Scrivener.

                                            – Holly Black

I'd like to thank my girlfriend, Kelly, for pestering Cassie Clare into friendship, and Cassie for suggesting me to Holly. Thanks to both Cassie and Holly for not freaking out at us weird San Francisco kids. I'd also like to thank Phil Falco for the gentle, cheerful nudging, and for being a friendly voice getting me out of bed before the day was completely wasted. Sorry it ran so late.

                                            – Ted Naifeh